Frontiers of Karma

The Counterstroke

Medha Deshmukh-Bhaskaran

First Impression in 2014

ALCHEMY PUBLISHERS

4767/23, Pratap Street, Darya Ganj,

New Delhi: 110 002

is a registered trademark of Mehras

and is licensed for use to Alchemy Publishers.

Distributed by

MEHRAS BOOKS PVT. LTD.

38 A, Akshoy Kumar Dutta Sarani,

Second Floor, Kolkata-700 006

4767/23 Pratap Street, Darya Ganj, Ansari Road, New Delhi: 110 002

This publication contains the opinions and ideas of its author and is designed to provide useful advice in regard to the subject matter covered. It is sold with the understanding that the author and publisher are not engaged in rendering legal, psychological, or professional services in this publication. Laws vary from state to state, country to country, and if the reader requires expert assistance or legal advice, a competent professional should be consulted. The author and publisher specifically disclaim any responsibility for any liability, loss or risk, personal or otherwise, which is incurred as a consequence, directly or indirectly, of the use and application of any of the contents of this book.

This book is a historical fiction and its events, though rooted in reality, also encompass the author's vision of incidents as they happened in the past.

ISBN: 978-81-927491-2-9

Cover design by Lara Jaydha

Layout by Nibedita Sen

To Vasant Deshmukh, my father who encouraged me to accomplish impossible things but is not here to see this book.

To Leela Deshmukh, my mother and my priceless worldly possession.

Foreword

17th century AD was indeed a turbulent period for the Indian subcontinent. Powerful Rajput kings had turned vassals of the Mughal Empire that was witnessing a meteoric rise in the north. The south, called the Deccan had its own despotic Hindu landlords working for the powerful Muslim kings whose ancestors had arrived from Central Asia and beyond. The coastal Deccan was full of the European sea-traders brimming with political aspirations, rising and imperial due to their technological might.

In the same century Shivaji Bhosale was born. He was a *jagirdar's* son and was expected to follow his forefathers, become a nobleman in the court of his Muslim king, live luxuriously, earn grand titles and occasionally fight wars to defend his king's kingdom. Instead, he chose to fight for his people's freedom, in a world that was riddled with slavery, religious conflicts, defeated attitudes of a fallen populace, exploitation, and mindless carnage. I believe that his greatness can only be explained in terms of his overarching vision. That's what made his challenge unstoppable; armies and cannons could not still such storms.

It was not long before Shivaji's aspirations had to rise up to the wrath of the Mughals. He faced Islam, a power that spanned half the globe and knocked on the doors of Europe. He faced Hinduism laden with inertia and resistance gathered over the millennia. He was called a guerrilla, a bandit, a rebel, a freedom fighter and even a mountain rat. In my state of Maharashtra he is akin to god. Who was he in reality? Did he present a different version of India? Was his war a clash of visions, clash of civilizations, battle for the very heart and soul of

India?

The answers lie in how he ignited the frozen hearts of his people with a feverish zeal, how he accumulated wealth to support his army, how he invented strategies like battle-ground creation away from home to reduce collateral damage, and how he dealt with his enemies, especially Emperor Aurangzeb. Thus Shivaji and Aurangzeb, men with decisive minds and enigmatic characters became the souls of my historical novel. It was significant for me to unfold the minds and the motives of my characters to understand their actions and the consequences. I have also tried to show the reader how they had drawn up their military strategies and how they had fought their battles.

Aurangzeb was and has remained the most inscrutable man in Indian history. Was he just a mindless murderer of his brothers or most worthy of being the Emperor? He declared war against the Shia kingdoms of the south. But again, we ask if he hated Shia Muslims then why did he dearly love his wife Dilras and his maternal uncle Shaista Khan who were Shia Muslims and why did he use famous Shia warriors like Mir Jumla to fight his wars? Why did he turn a jihadist to crush his own brother Dara Shikoh? Was it his piety or his stratagem or was it the beginning of his mission, where he would gain by hook or crook, by using all to his advantage, even religion?

Wars and battles of that era are written slightly differently in history books that I have used as references. Dr Ajit Joshi (the author of a famous history book on Shivaji written in Marathi, helped me to seek the most logical explanations. History books written by Sir Jadunath Sarkar, Mr Gajanan Mehendale, Colonel R.D. Palsokar, Mr Ravindra Godbole, Mr James Grant Duff and Mr G. S. Sardesai have explained how the battles unfolded. I have revisited history through their accounts and also taken my authorial liberties to express my creativity in such descriptions. Mr Ravindra Godbole made me understand how the men of power must have behaved and conversed while discussing wars. (Unfortunately Mr Godbole who was looking forward to my novel is no more). Mr Girish Jadhav, a private collector of medieval weapons enriched my knowledge regarding swords, daggers, bows and arrows.

When I started writing the first part of my novel, people were curious to know if I support a certain religion and am against another. The truth is that I was, am and will always be a supporter of the 'truth' and the eternal truth is that most of the wars were and are fought for land, freedom or power. Religions have been and are used as weapons to terrorize and kill, initiate wars and justify vile actions. I have been totally unbiased while writing the story, the story based on true history, yours and mine, as it happened, as it must have happened.

The *Frontiers of Karma* trilogy chronicles the life and times of Shivaji and Aurangzeb, it also opens up to the reader the scenario of seventeenth century India. *Frontiers of Karma – The Counterstroke* is the first book and will be followed by *Frontiers of Karma – The Stratagem* and *Frontiers of Karma – The Ultimatum.*

Our history has myriads of lessons that we can learn from. I believe that such a mission can only be accomplished by writing a novel, which gives the writer a poetic license to fill in details and personal interactions. However, I do not believe that I am the sole custodian of this monumental task. I feel small and terribly inadequate for my task but I have persevered sincerely as it has also been a journey of immense joy. It is actually the best journey that I have undertaken in my life.

In my journey, I also realised that the young and confident India does not know Shivaji the way I wish and want them to. India is changing and looking at its bright future but ancient chains still hold the nation. After years of working on this trilogy I believe that the life and times of Shivaji as well as Aurangzeb hold lessons that are relevant even today.

Medha Deshmukh-Bhaskaran

Note - The English translations of the Persian and Arabic poetry of Shah Jahan, Dara Shikoh and Aurangzeb have been taken from various books by Sir Jadunath Sarkar. I have tweaked some lines. The English translations of poetry written by Marathi saint poets are mine.

ACKNOWLEDGEMENTS

I must thank my family, my parents, my brother, Professor Ashutosh Deshmukh, his wife Hemangini, my husband Arun Bhaskaran, my sister-in-law Jayashree Jaipal, and my sons for tolerating a person who has flitted between the present and the past, spending more time in the seventeenth century. I also thank them for their encouragement and critical comments.

I would like to thank Alchemy Publishers and the young and inspiring team. I thank Anukta Ghosh for selecting my submissions, Sona Agarwal for trusting my work, Shivangi Mehra for always being there for me and overseeing the book cover design, my editor Rajrupa Das for months of hard work, guiding me professionally through the maze of words, paragraphs and pages, giving me frank advice without mincing words, and my second editor Deeptesh Sen for giving my manuscript a final touch.

I would also like to thank Lara Jaydha, the freelance visual artist and graphic designer based in Bangalore, who has designed a wonderful book cover. I will remain indebted to Mr Girish Jadhav for educating me in medieval weapons.

Finally, I deeply thank my family and friends who patiently read my manuscript even before it was edited or selected by the publisher, and gave me their valuable suggestions: Dr Ajit Joshi, Mr Ravindra Godbole, Dr G Vijayaraghavan, Rita Hemachandran, Shamala Balram, Ambika Sachin and Dr Ravindra Satalkar.

Contents

Where the story unfolds

• Bolan Pass

• Delhi
• Agra

• Gwalior

• Ujjain

• Burhanpur

• Aurangabad

Kalyan •
• Ahmednagar
• Pune
• Bidar
• Pratapgad
• Hyderabad

• Bijapur

Seventeenth century Hindustan

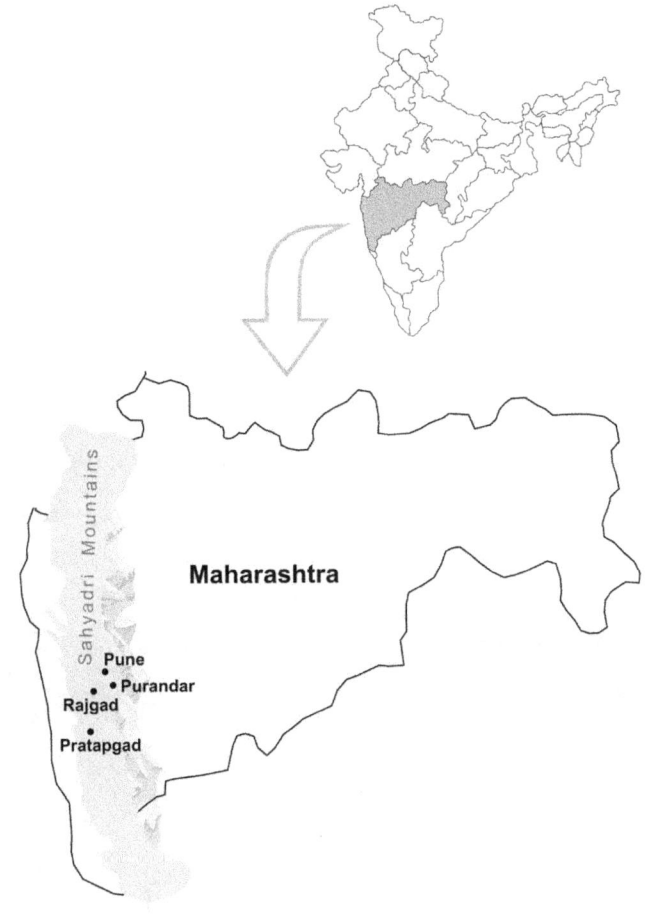

Maharashtra

Sahyadri Mountains

Pune
Purandar
Rajgad
Pratapgad

Prologue

Circa 1648

A chalky moon floats in the inky sky above the huge rock of Kandakada, flooding the slopes of Purandar hill with its pale light. Shivaji Bhosale narrows his eyes to peer down. The darkness at the base of the mountain is broken by the faint glow of torches. The Bijapur horsemen have arrived from the east. They must reach the northern side of the hill. Shivaji knows that their commander Fatte Khan is seething in rage. It is quite likely that the Khan will send his men – two thousand as per the scouts' estimate – up the hill. But Shivaji is not worried. Bijapur's cavalrymen are not trained to scale even small hillocks. And upon this hill, where even agile horses trained in hilly regions are rendered useless, the enemy will be forced to come up on foot.

The foothills are darker than the rest of the region as shadows of enormous trees fall on the forest floor, blocking the fragile moonlight. It is suicidal to climb, especially when the enemy is backed by a hill fort. But Musekhan has his orders from Fatte Khan and is determined to follow them. Shiva Bhosale is certainly up there and this is the chance to capture him or kill him.

'Move! Extinguish the torches, we are going up,' Musekhan shouts, as two thousand of his men leave their horses at the foothills and start climbing. It is worth the risk. The region belongs to his king, Mohammad Adil Shah, and the hill forts are his kingdom's military strongholds. He has come to reclaim their territory from a native rebel. Initially, the campaign was designed to teach Shiva a lesson and show him his place. When Musekhan was briefed by the king, he was told, 'Show the boy some muscle and he will kneel, he is barely eighteen.' Instead, the lad had bared his fangs. As they camped a few miles east of Purandar hill, Shiva's lightweight cavalry had started harassing them, first assaulting the detachments and then cutting off supplies. A week since, they had become more daring, and started attacking flanks of the main camp and then galloping away in the forests. Musekhan does not allow the odds to dampen his spirits. He is trained as a heavy-cavalry soldier and is protected by armour. But that darn life-saving chain-mail-armour suddenly feels heavy. His sandals, made for the flat plains, slip and make him fall on his knees, not once, not twice, but many times. The climb is riddled with steep slopes; at places they are simply vertical. Musekhan wonders about his soldiers, as he hears them grunt with fatigue. His heart stops with shock. The hill has started shuddering with drumbeats. He hears some of his men scream. He turns back at once. To his horror, he notices many of them fall to the ground, limp. An arrow whizzes past him, its shaft almost brushing his turban. Its whooshing noise makes him gasp and wince. The drumbeats stop suddenly, throwing the world in a strange abyss of silence around him. Stunned, he looks up and sees the faint outline of the fort's ramparts. The drums start beating again and Musekhan sees shadows leaping down from a cliff into the hill's shallow depression.

***

Shivaji has ordered his archers to stop shooting and start descending the hill to intercept the enemy. He watches as his ace infantrymen Sambhaji Kavji, Yesaji, Tanaji, and others leave the ramparts. Sixty-year-old Pasalkar is among them. From the ramparts Shivaji watches the shadows of his few hundred men glide through the Bini Gate in a file. They resemble a black snake swimming across dark waters, swift and silent. Most of them are peasants, goatherds, barbers, cobblers and blacksmiths, born to work with wooden sticks, nails, razors, and hammers. *The sword is a great leveller. Anyone is a warrior who learns to respect its power*, he thinks with pride, but his heart is also heavy with sorrow. The news from Bijapur is disturbing. They have arrested his father who serves them as a regent and thrown him into the dungeons so that he cowers down with terror and guilt, gives up his region and hill forts. He looks up at the rock of Kandakada which looms over him, warning him that his dream is above his guilt, fear, excuses or tragedies.

***

Yesaji leaps down as a strong wind hisses across his face. The enemy will soon reach the Bini gate and start climbing in the direction of the ramparts where his master stands with just a few men. He must stop the leader of the enemy's pack.

Before Musekhan can decide what to do, a shadow emerges from behind a tree, growing at an angle on the slope. He stops for just a moment to steady himself and waits for the shadow to come closer, in the range of his sword. But it does not move. Instead, he sees the outline of a spear flicker for a fraction in the air, and feels a colossal pain. The impact makes him lurch back and collapse. The straight blow of the spear, powered by speed, has broken the metal links of his armour and fractured his right ribs. He scrambles, keeping his shield and sword on the ground. Gritting his teeth to gather courage, he holds the shaft of the spear in both his hands and forces out its sharp iron head from his chest. Warm blood splutters out to bathe the lower half of his body. He grabs his sword and grapples to get up, trembling. It is difficult to breathe and he suspects that his lung is punctured. Cursing, he prepares to parry the enemy's blow.

Yesaji marvels at Musekhan's courage and knows that he has already lost a lot of blood. He holds the hilt of his sword with both hands. He is at a higher level of the slope and has the advantage of position. Musekhan, standing on the lower ridge and feebly brandishing his sword, looks utterly vulnerable, like a trapped bird. Yesaji's blade comes down with full force to pierce the enemy between his neck and his collarbone, the part that is not protected with armour. It travels effortlessly through Musekhan's body to reach his abdomen. His blade still stuck in the enemy, Yesaji sees the Bijapur men running away. He hears the familiar voice of Pasalkar screaming, "Har, Har, Mahadev!" hailing the might of God Shiva and sprinting down to hunt the enemy. The words of the sixty-year-old warrior infuse a fresh vigour for battle into his blood. Yesaji wrenches his sword out from the dead man, wields it in the air and runs down the hill to follow his men.

Abaji Ghadge and his hundred men do not want to escape. He has decided to fight Shiva Bhosale till death and has made such a promise to Fatte Khan. He watches as Shiva's men vanish down the slope. It is the right time to take the traitor by surprise. Shiva Bhosale is an ordinary native, a Maratha like him, but he wants to be a Sultan. It is a sin to challenge the ancient protocol. 'Follow,' he whispers to his men and starts climbing. Within moments, something makes Ghadge look up. He sees an enormous boulder rolling down towards him. Before he can move, it strikes him. He first buckles and then is flung into a ditch. The boulder crashes beside him. He feels the metallic taste of blood and a dislodged tooth in his mouth. An excruciating pain runs through Ghadge's body. He opens his eyes only to be engulfed by sheer darkness.

ONE | THE DECCAN OF 1656

The sun turns into a red orb and the waters of the Mutha River reflect the flaming colours to resemble a wildfire. It lasts only for a while and gradually the magic starts fading. The sun is swallowed by the hills of Maval, 'the sunset hills' in Marathi. The forest-clad mountains turn their colours shell-pink, indigo and peacock-green tinged with scarlet. Golden sunbeams quickly melt into a distant gloom making the hills look dull gray, like heaps of ash. The world around the town of Pune has merely become its own reflection in a dew drop trembling on a slender grass blade.

Standing on the parapet of the balcony of his palace, *Lal Mahal,* Shivaji says,' What you have just witnessed is the magic of Maya.' He does not glance at his *vakeel,* who has just arrived as per his summon.

Raghunath Ballal Korde, the fifty-year-old Brahmin, is Shivaji's *vakeel.* The political negotiator knows his master's habit of being cryptic. He says softly, 'Knowing that the world is an illusion, we still struggle, fight, and plan wars.'

'Because,' Shivaji snaps, 'many times the truth rips open its elusive cover and breaks free like a bee seeking to sting, especially when it comes from pangs of hunger and the pains of injustice. And this truth need not be seen but felt. Like the sting that brings tears to the eyes.'

'Raja, you called for me?' Raghunath asks hesitatingly, quickly trying to change the subject as he knows there is no point in arguing. The young Maratha has his own definitions of illusion, life, war and dreams that sometimes disorient him.

'*Puntoji*, you are aware that our *jagir* is small. It is barely a hundred miles east to west and fifty miles north to south with a few hill forts around the region of Pune, Chakan in the north, Maval in the west and Shirval, Supe, Indapur regions in the south east. We need to expand.'

How can Raja Shivaji expand his jagir? thinks Raghunath. The very ambition defies the laws of the land. For the last several centuries his country has been ruled by the Muslim invaders from Afghan, Turkistan and beyond. They have a system in place that suits them. A *jagir* is not expandable, unless the king grants more land to the *jagirdar*.

'Many of our *deshmukhs* have fallen in line though,' Shivaji smiles, taking the past into account as it may influence his future plans.

Raghunath raises his brows but does not comment.

'With our *deshmukhs* tamed and with no *subhedar* to watch over us, it is time to expand,' Shivaji insists.

Raghunath does not know what to say. Raja Shivaji's *jagir* is mainly hilly and secluded. It has never been rich enough to attract the prying eyes of the Bijapur's court officials and the king has not considered it important enough for a *subhedar*. There are other reasons for the neglect. The *jagir* was granted to Raja's father by the Nizam Shah of the Ahmednagar Kingdom. Nizamshahi was annexed twenty years ago. The region now belongs to Adilshahi. Ali Adil Shah is their new king. His mother, the recently widowed Badi or the big Begum, rules from behind the throne. The late king Mohammad Adil Shah was bedridden for ten long years, too sick to look after his kingdom's affairs and his son Ali, the present king, is too young to look after the far flung and remote regions of his kingdom.

'Our karma, our actions or what we do, defines us. Without freedom, we cannot do what we want to and what we aspire to. Without freedom we die not knowing the very purpose of our lives.'

Raghunath has heard it before. Raja's father is Adilshahi's regent and lives six hundred miles away. He has made Bangalore, his new *jagir* at the southern borders of Adilshahi, his home and has not visited his old *jagir* for years. Fate has provided enough liberty to Raja Shivaji since he was just eight, enough to cherish the freedom, enough to hate being under any authority and enough to dream of a sovereign kingdom, the Swaraj!

'We are not born with our destiny written on our foreheads, like some preordained script. It depends on two things, His divine wish and our karma, and we must do what we must. Javali is the key to our dream, our first step to Swaraj. If we cannot get the valley amicably then we shall take it by sword,' says Shivaji as his eyes shine with inexplicable optimism.

Raghunath smiles at the Raja's nonchalant defiance of the astrologers and the soothsayers of the land. The Brahmin wonders about which is more important in life: fate or karma. What is the true meaning of karma? Is it to blindly follow our forefathers or mutely do what men of power above us order us to do? Who decides our karma, is it God, or is it our mind, or our intellect, or our soul? What is the meaning of fate then?

Raghunath had met the *jagirdar* of Javali with a proposal for an alliance against the king and followed it with many warning letters. But the man had repeatedly and vehemently refused their offer and snubbed their threats. Raghunath is aware that for a *jagirdar* like Raja Shivaji, dealing with the defiant *deshmukhs* of his *paraganas* is an internal matter, but intimidating another *jagirdar* or seizing a *jagir* is treason. The Adilshahi rulers already hate Raja for grabbing and repairing the hill forts that lie in his *jagir*. Forts are the kingdom's military strongholds and are owned by the king but Raja Shivaji has claimed the abandoned forts of the region and manned them with his men. The new king calls him a traitor, a notorious rebel and a *namakharam*, who, after living on their salt, is not loyal to his masters.

Ten years ago, before falling ill, the late Mohammad Adil Shah had wanted to kill Raja Shivaji. Who can ever forget the battle of Purandar?

'You have seen the valley. Aren't the mountains of Javali far more hostile than the ones we have in Maval?' asks Shivaji, excited.

Raghunath nods in agreement. The Sahyadri range runs north-south along the western edge of the Deccan. These mountains separate the plateau called the Desh from the narrow coastal strip called the Konkan. At Maval, the hills are steep and rocky, girded towards the top by massive basaltic rocks. The lower slopes are riddled with deep snaking dells that look like enormous elephant trunks. Those hills are regarded as the war elephants of the region. Just fifty miles southwards, in Javali, the same mountains take on a more aggressive avatar. The valley turns the war elephants into rogue elephants. The hills become steeper, the valleys deeper and the forests at the foothills denser.

'To invade the valley one needs squadrons of hill men. Heavy, armoured cavalry is the main strength of our king. The valley will make it as redundant as a ship stuck in sand dunes. If Maval is our sword, Javali will be our shield. Remove Moray, the dictator *jagirdar* of the region,' Shivaji whispers, loud enough for the Brahmin's ears.

'That is the norm!' Raghunath muses with dismay. Many *jagirdars*, *deshmukhs* and *patils* turn ruthless and extract more than what is due from the ryots. If the peasants are unable to pay for some reason, their cattle is taken away, their wives and children are sold as slaves. If they protest, they are sent to gallows on the excuse of a charge of a revolt. Some run away to become homeless destitute. The king is least bothered since they, the *watandars*, can do what his Muslim officials cannot. The *watandars* are born with rustic cunning and collect as much revenue as they can to fill the king's treasury. It suits the king to ignore their deeds in their own regions, for his own good.

'We are trapped between the Mughal Empire in the north and

Adilshahi in the southeast. We live in the coils of two hungry pythons,' Shivaji sighs in resentment. 'The mightier one has already stirred. The Mughal prince Aurangzeb's army is on its way to Hyderabad. The eastern Deccan will soon turn bloody.'

Raghunath blinks, a revelation hits him. Moray may just be the first pawn to fall. It is Raja Shivaji's first step to prepare for a major, long drawn out war not just against his own king but against something far bigger and far more sinister. Perhaps even against the rich and mighty Mughals.

'They call me a *namakharam,* don't they? I am not loyal to those who feed me! If I am a *namakharam,* who are they? Their might is fed by the ryots, the peasants. Their coffers are filled with revenue collected from the sons of this soil,' Shivaji hits the nail deeper as he persists.

'Last year, the Mughal Empire has collected taxes worth two hundred and fifty thousand *ser* of gold. Adilshahi has collected one-fourth of that amount. And we, the so called native warriors, fight with each other for scraps of our own land thrown at us by them. They treat us as lesser humans and we prove them right by behaving like beasts.'

Raghunath feels his master's burning gaze and smiles bitterly. The king needs to keep the native warriors in control. He spins his own web by offering military ranks, new *watans* and titles to men of power, the men who have the means to challenge him. They get caught in feuds and remain trapped for generations. The *vakeel* remembers a famous bloodshed. Jedhe, the landlord of Kari region was getting too powerful to handle. The king had quickly sown the seeds of jealousy by offering him a *watan* and making him a *deshmukh.* The resentful Khopade, a rich farmer, trapped the new *watandar* in a narrow pass. Jedhe and his men were massacred. Then the avengers struck. During a wedding in Khopade's family, the Jedhe clansmen, on their horsebacks, entered the home that was adorned with colourful buntings. They rode over the crowd, and sent men, women and children, enjoying the occasion, spinning across the floor, dead or wounded. Some escaped only to be chased by the gallopers and slaughtered like sheep or goats.

'We cannot reason with men without vision. If this time the *jagirdar* of Javali does not yield, then you know what has to be done. If he smells danger, he will vanish; live someplace in exile and keep inciting his men against us. Make it happen during negotiations.' says Shivaji.

'I understand,' Raghunath says gravely, as he feels his heart pounding in his ribcage. It is a clear order, without any possibility of debate or justification. A *vakeel's* profession has unwritten rules – he will not kill and nobody kills him. Being a Brahmin, his verbal oath is also regarded as the pure truth. The diplomatic immunity allows him unhindered access into the homes of the landlords and the courts of Islamic rulers.

'Even laws are amended for a greater reason,' says Shivaji regarding his *vakeel,* who stands straight and looks younger than his years.

'How do you think our king will react?' asks Raghunath.

'The Muslim Sultans rule the cities and the Hindu Sultans like us rule the villages while the *ryots* continue to be the bondsmen, or *ghulams*, the slaves,' says Shivaji, ignoring the question.

Bells have started tolling for the evening worship at the Ganesha temple. Its echo burns holes into the shallow calm of the region, exposing the depth of its violent past. The peace that they enjoy now is so fragile, so brittle that it is almost a fantasy. He can already hear the gallops, the whooshing of blades, the cracking of bones, and the splatter of blood.

Raghunath maintains a solemn expression. Aurangzeb, the third son of Emperor Shah Jahan, is the *subhedar* of the Mughal-occupied parts of the Deccan. His military cavalcade of thirty thousand soldiers led by his first son Mohammad Sultan is moving towards the city of Hyderabad, the capital of Qutbshahi. Some say that Aurangzeb hates the Shia rulers of these kingdoms because they are Shia Muslims. Some say that he wants to remind the Deccan kingdoms that they are the tributary states of the Empire. Some say he wants to conquer the Deccan and expand his father's Empire. It is time to wait and watch. Instead of worrying about the obvious, Raja Shivaji has planned his own offensive.

'Our king Ali Adil Shah, the ruler of Adilshahi, seeks to eliminate us, and Aurangzeb, the Mughal prince, seeks to swallow the Deccan that includes Adilshahi. Someday we may come face to face with the mighty Mughal. It is time to search history to learn their weaknesses and our strengths,' Shivaji says softly.

Raghunath nods. The recent history is a quarry of lessons. The serious Mughal incursions had begun more than thirty years ago. Jahangir was the then Mughal Emperor. The Empire had already stretched from Bengal in the east to Sindh in the west and Kashmir in the north to Gujarat as well as Khandesh in the south. But further south, in the region of Deccan, it was another story. Unlike the north where the Mughal reigned supreme, the Deccan was ruled by three Muslim dynasties or Shahis. The Nizamshahi dynasty of Ahmednagar had ruled over Maharashtra, while Adilshahi of Bijapur had Karnataka and Qutbshahi of Golconda had Andhra under their control. The Mughal had turned thirsty for the Deccan. Physical proximity made Nizamshahi the first target of Emperor Jahangir's strategy of expansion. He had unleashed his army. Nizam Shah, the king of Nizamshahi, was a useless drunkard. His *wazir*, the African warrior Malik Ambar, had maintained order and forcefully defended the kingdom's northern borders from Dawlatabad fort. Raja Shivaji's father, then a regent of Nizam Shah, had shielded Ahmednagar, the capital that was seventy miles south of Dawlatabad. Time and again had Jahangir failed, his addiction to opium contributing to his defeats. And when his mind had been clear, he has busied himself in the bed of his voluptuous and scheming new wife, Nur Jahan. Meanwhile, his footloose generals had let the war languish. But times have changed, Aurangzeb is no Jahangir!

Raghunath glances at Raja who is now gazing in the direction of the hills of Maval. The Brahmin wonders if his Raja can see something that is not visible to him. The darkness sharpens his senses and kindles some old memories. Emperor Jahangir and Malik Ambar had eventually disappeared behind the curtains of time but Emperor Jahangir's passion for the Deccan had lived on like an immortal spirit, hovering in the Deccan skies, hungrier and meaner than before.

'Inaccessibility is the hallmark of military strongholds. Javali is one such place. Without such strongholds, we are exposed to the enemy and are destined to either serve them or die in their dungeons,' warns Raghunath.

'Our death is the least of the tragedies. If we fail, the region will be plagued by instability, fear, death and destruction,' Shivaji retorts.

That is so true, thinks Raghunath. After the death of Jahangir, his son Emperor Shah Jahan had marched in with more than a hundred thousand cavalrymen. The last king of Nizamshahi was captured and sent to the Gwalior prison to be killed by an opium overdose. But Raja's father had decided to guard the kingdom by guerrilla warfare, by using the hills and the hill forts of Maharashtra as his hideouts. He had also formed an alliance with Adilshahi against the Mughal. Shah Jahan had countered him intelligently by threatening the Deccan kingdoms. Abdullah Qutb Shah, the ruler of Qutbshahi had quickly turned the Empire's vassal. Mohammad Adil Shah, the king of Bijapur had decided to fight for his Adilshahi. Shah Jahan planned a bloody war. His army entered the kingdom from three different routes, destroying all traces of cultivation, burning down cities, towns and villages. They had driven off cattle and butchered the old people while capturing young men and women as slaves. It had continued till Adilshahi had become the tributary state of the Empire. The beaten Mohammad Adil Shah was forced to form an alliance with the triumphant Shah Jahan. Raja's father was alienated and captured. He was given an ultimatum to serve Adilshahi or die. The allied forces had even tried to flatten his *jagir*. Raghunath remembers vividly, how their cavalrymen had come to Pune, screaming 'Deen Deen, Deen!' hailing the way of their religion and the duties of Islam! Houses were set on fire, temples demolished, the stone gods wrenched out from their podiums and flung onto the streets. The land was ploughed with donkeys to make it ill-fated, so that no one dared to till it again and draw the wrath of the evil upon them. The ryots had fled into the nearby forests and regressed to being cavemen. Raja was a little boy of five then, living with his mother on the Fort Shivaneri near Junnar.

'Do not blame only the Muslim rulers, the men who fervently helped them flatten our *jagir* were Hindus. It was Jagdev who ploughed Pune with donkeys. And it was Rayarao who broke this earth with an iron axe, and the Bijapur rulers bestowed him with a lofty title, 'the Brave One,' Shivaji's words lance through the *vakeel's* conscience.

'*Puntoji*, it is a ruthless world out there, nobody spares anybody. Our history of past several centuries is a witness to bloody aggressions and mindless carnage. We need to evolve in the science of defence and be pragmatic while planning offensives.'

On his way home, Raghunath thinks about the vanished Hindu kingdoms. Those kings of the Deccan lived in their mythological world, where wars were fought on an assigned battleground. Even the time to begin the first battle was fixed by astrologers and the position of the planets influenced their moves and countermoves. Civilian lives were spared. Three centuries ago, Ala-ud-Din Khalji's army invaded the Deccan, breaking all the rules of war. At the end of the thirteenth century, he brought his armies into the bedrooms, slaying and slaughtering. Even the newborns were not spared. Soon the Hindu dynasties of the south, the Cholas, the Cheras, the Pandyas, the Hoysalas, and the Kakatyas were flattened under the hooves of Ala-ud-Din's cavalry. In the fourteenth century, Hassan Bahaman Shah from Turkistan had swiftly conquered northern parts of the Deccan. He, the descendent from the mythical Persian king Kai Bahaman, named his new kingdom as the *Bahamani* empire.

The sixteenth century saw Krishna Deva Raya, one of the greatest Hindu rulers of Vijayanagara. After his untimely death, the last of the Deccan's Hindu empires started shrinking. Even the Bahamani empire had broken into many fragments. History was changing in the north. The late sixteenth and early seventeenth century had witnessed the rise of the Mughal Empire as it flourished and grew under the rule of Emperor Akbar. In the years that followed, his son Jahangir and then Jahangir's son, Shah Jahan expanded the Empire in all directions except south where three Muslim Shahis and bits of Vijayanagar Empire had managed to survive. Nizamshahi was eventually swallowed by the joint armies of the Mughal Empire and Adilshahi, and the remnants of the Vijayanagara empire were devoured by Adilshahi and Qutbshahi.

And today, in the middle of the seventeenth century, his master, Raja Shivaji has asked him to break the unwritten law for a bigger purpose. Raghunath looks at the clear sky through the window of his palanquin. The stars flash and dim alternatively, charting his future etched on a palm leaf according to his birth-date and time. But Raghunath diverts his gaze to his hands; he needs to refresh his moves with daggers and swords. His destiny is his doing, his karma. He has been blind all along, now he longs to see the world hidden inside Raja Shivaji's vision.

***

Shivaji is back in the corridors of the *Lal Mahal,* the red palace. Not the usual palace with gardens, or domes, or cupolas, or carved parapets, or pillared courts. It is actually a large, two-storied building made with red brick and is near the southern boundary of Pune. It has a frontyard covered with neem and peepal trees. The backyard has sheds and stables for cattle and horses. The house has a central courtyard, used as a meeting place. A cold riverside breeze blows in from the north-west.

Shivaji walks towards the steps leading to the ground floor. A servant standing on a step-ladder struggles to light an oil lamp placed in a large glass urn hanging from the ceiling. Another has started shutting the doors. The house is unusually quiet and the prayer room where his mother chants mantras to evoke the powers of the family deity, Goddess Bhavani, is vacant. Gently rising smoke spiralling out from the incense sticks tries to fill the void. His mother, wives and daughters have left for the Purandar hill fort. It is becoming increasingly dangerous to live on the flat plateau of the Sahyadri Mountains. He removes his sandals, shoves them away using his feet, walks inside the prayer room and kneels before the family deity. She is the violent avatar of goddess Parvati - the giver of life. Her kohl-smeared, enormous eyes glare at him.

'Swaraj is God Shiva's wish,' he prays, 'and you are his energy. You have brought me here for a purpose.'

Twenty years ago, his father was forced to serve Adilshahi and was asked to move six hundred miles away to Bangalore, the kingdom's southern borders. Shivaji remembers how his father had taken his elder brother and left, while his mother and he stayed put on the hill fort of Shivaneri near the town of Junnar, for Junnar was a part of his father's *jagir.* The years that followed saw the Emperor Shah Jahan and the king of Adilshahi rip away portions of the Nizamshahi, like dogs fighting over a dead rabbit. The region to the north of the Bhima river that included prosperous cities of Ahmednagar, Junnar and Nasik were swallowed by the Mughals. The region to the south of Bhima like north Konkan, Pune, Vangi, Paranda and cities of Solapur and Pandharpur were devoured by Adilshahi. The Bhosale *jagir* was axed into two.

The Mughal armies had galloped across Junnar and Ahmednagar to find and slaughter families who had served the Nizamshahi. His mother and he had to flee to the southern part of their *jagir* that had come under Adilshahi. His first journey to this terrain was etched on his heart by sharp, cutting memories. Even now, after twenty years, when he recalls them, they bring along the heartbreaking sorrow of those times. He can even hear the sound of pebbles rolling under the hooves of the horses when they cross the stone-covered riverbeds of the Bhima and Mutha rivers.

He was a little boy, eight years old, living with his mother on the hill fort of Shivaneri near Junnar. One night he was woken up by anxious cries and screams and saw people scampering around him. He could hear them whisper words like 'Mughal', 'armies' and 'marching'. 'No torches,' he remembers his mother yelling. 'We must cross the River Bhima as soon as possible, for all the region north of the Bhima has been claimed by the Mughal,' he heard someone shout. They were twenty of them and had started to climb down even before the morning star shone in the eastern sky. The slopes of Shivaneri were dark, but they knew the trail so well that they could have climbed down blindfolded. He enjoyed it, he always did when he trekked the hills with his mother. At the foothills, the horses waited for them.

He wanted to ride his pony but mother had refused, and forced him to sit behind her. After a few miles they had heard hoof-beats. They had stopped to hide behind bushes as bats from nearby caves fluttered above them. 'The Mughal gallopers,' his mother had whispered to him. He was more afraid of the bats. They had finally reached the River Bhima at dawn.

It was almost dry and its bed was a perfect place to play 'battle-battle' using boulders as forts, and pebbles as cannonballs. A ditch filled with brownish water was enough to water his war-horses. Shallow dry drains would have made perfect trenches in case of an enemy attack. But to his dismay, his mother and the others did not wait. He was told that the region south of Bhima was his father's jagir *as well, it was his kingdom. They stopped only once to eat near a well. A servant had struggled to draw water for them and the horses. Words like 'destruction', 'famine' floated in the air. A maid riding with them had carried* jawar *roti and some vegetable seasoned with groundnut oil and spices. He ate with relish, and wiped his mouth on his mother's sari pallu. They had soon moved on. It was almost evening when they crossed another riverbed, it was dry too. 'River Mutha,' someone had said, 'we are almost there'.*

To his left, he had noticed a huge, meandering wall, its fortifications falling apart and yellowing reeds jutting out of its gaps, as if someone had left the wall to its fate, to die a slow death. His eyes had wandered with hope. Mother had said that they would be living somewhere here, but he could see no houses. There were no streets. He held his mother in a tight grip from behind as she steered her horse through narrow paths. The paths were covered with sallow grass blades. The earth had looked broken and caked, as if the soil had not seen a drop of water for years. He spotted ruins of temples, with crumpled mortar, and broken pillars. And the dead animals, cows and goats swollen like billows, with all four legs stiff and stretched. Some had turned into bone, pale and broken to shards. Columns of dust-devils swirled above the remains.

The dust had made him cough and his eyes teary. He rubbed them against his mother's sari so that he could see. The air stank with smells that he could not recognise. He noticed strange people staring at them. They looked different, large eyed, faces covered with dust, tangled hair looking like bird's nests. He had thought that they were enemies and would suddenly attack him. His wooden sword was gritted to his belt. But mother had told him that to face a real enemy he needed a real sword made of steel. He wanted to ask her when he could have such a sword. It was getting dark. He tried to see as far as he could to search for his kingdom. To see temple spires going high in the air, with saffron flags fluttering above them and pillared palaces behind their walled courtyards. For streets busy with trundling elephants and galloping horsemen.

His kingdom was not waiting for him. Someone had lied to him.

***

Hyderabad, the capital of Qutbshahi, also called the Golconda kingdom, is surrounded by the imperial army. A waxing moon throws pale light on the surroundings. Winter is almost over but the cold cuts through his bones. Despite wearing a woollen sweater below his armour, Mohammad Sultan, the first son of Aurangzeb, shivers as chilly winds sweep across the flat highlands of the eastern Deccan. His war elephant sways like a ship in rough seas. But he is busy admiring Hyderabad, its countless minarets, domes and spires that shimmer in the moonlight like artefacts of polished silver. He has heard of the wealth hidden beneath the veneer of the city's splendour.

Looking at the capital of Qutbshahi, Aurangzeb's first son thinks about his father, the *subhedar* of the Deccan regions under imperial rule and the third among the four sons of Emperor Shah Jahan. In recent times, his father seems to be possessed with just one thought – to swallow the Shia kingdoms of the south. He does not want the southern kingdoms as the tributary states of the Empire; he wants them to be a part or a *subha* of the Empire!

'Sunni in Arabic comes from a word meaning the one who follows the traditions of the Prophet, Peace Be Upon Him. Sunnis are born to rule,' Mohammad Sultan has heard his father declare with pride. The

Prophet's death (Peace Be Upon Him) has axed Islam that meant peace and submission, into two worlds filled with intolerance and anger. Shias hated the Prophet's friend who was declared as the first caliph of the Islamic nation and thought that the leadership should have gone to Ali Bin Abu Talib, the cousin of the Prophet. The Sunnis loathed the very idea and called the Shias, Shia-tu-Ali, the gang of Ali. Sultan's father, Aurangzeb, always called them *ghul-i-bayabani*, the corpse-eating demons and regarded them as *rafizi*, the heretics and even *batil mazhaban*, the misbelievers. 'We will destroy the Shia kingdoms for they do not follow the traditions of the Prophet, Peace Be Upon Him,' Sultan's father had said in open courts before some of their finest Shia and Rajput Military Officers, who had stood with downcast eyes and faces red with embarrassment. Sultan has much to enquire on this issue. But who is he to question? Sultan's own mother is a Hindu, now a mere convert, a secondary wife to his staunch Sunni father. And what does that make him? It is too disturbing to think. For the time being Sultan is happy to be a part of his father's battles of expansions. The first area in their agenda is the Qutbshahi ruled by Abdullah Qutb Shah. The plan of this battle was hatched at Navkhanda Palace in Aurangabad, their Deccan capital with the help of Mir Jumla, a Shia and the recently-ousted grand *wazir* of the Golconda Kingdom.

'A desperate man like Mir Jumla, whose family has been thrown in the dungeons by the Golconda king, and who thinks we are the ablest to help him, will give us all he can offer,' Father had told Sultan before the meeting.

The first gift Mir Jumla had given to Sultan's father was indeed priceless. It was a seven hundred and fifty six carat uncut diamond, that was bigger than the fist of a man. While falling to his knees, Mir had announced, 'If this stone is finely cut, it will be a Kohinoor, a mountain of light.'

Mohammad Sultan would never forget the evening when Mir

Jumla had arrived on a caparisoned elephant at the high pillared patio of their palace. The howdah was made of silver and glittered with precious stones. More than a hundred horsemen in silk robes and colourful turbans strutted behind the trundling elephant. All the palace servants had gathered in the patio. The trumpeters walking ahead blew their instruments. And the fair Persian sat in the howdah, wearing a kimoush turban fixed with a crown band. It was like a king coming home.

Sultan had stood in the midst of his people who stared awestruck at their glamorous guest. The man wearing a long black robe with a sash dazzling with diamonds had climbed down from his elephant. 'Mir Jumla always wears black, it is his style statement,' someone had whispered. Mir Jumla was his title, and the world knew him just by his title that meant the grand *wazir*! Sultan was briefed about Mir's status as the wealthiest *jagirdar* of Qutbshahi, his land yielding four million rupees of yearly revenue. He had done some quick calculations keeping the most frequently used imperial coins in mind. One could mint two hundred and fifty thousand *Ashrafi muhurs* with that money, each made with a tola of pure gold.

And that was not all. Mir Jumla was also the owner of several diamond mines. He was famous too, and was known the world over as a renowned diamond merchant. His wealth that overshadowed the grandeur of his kings' court, his scholarly knowledge of artillery, his capacity to demand loyalty from the kingdom's top military officials, his private, well equipped cavalry and his networking abilities had soulfully affected the king of Golconda, making him jealous and sleepless. The king's minions further fanned his insomnia. Mir Jumla's arrogant son Amin had added fuel to the already explosive situation. He had arrived drunk in the king's court and pissed shamelessly on the floor. In a fit of rage, the king had thrown his grand minister's family in the dungeons of Golconda fort. At that time, Mir Jumla had been away in Bengal. For a year, the man, famous for his black, diamond studded robes had roamed the world, visiting men of might from the Empire, Shahis and even the smaller kingdoms for help.

Mohammad Sultan's father had warned everyone against saying anything derogatory against Shia Muslims. Sultan had sensed that Mir Jumla indeed needed them but they needed him more. The courtroom was spruced up for the meeting, with a large new gilded chandelier and new silk curtains. Unlike other times, Father had been waiting on his guest.

Mir Jumla had entered with a swagger and then bowed slightly.

'*Shahzade*,' Mir had called Mohammad Sultan's father 'prince' in chaste Farsi and continued, 'I have served the kingdom of Golconda for the past twenty years, joining them as a military officer and have risen to become the grand *wazir*. You need not worry about Golconda's military commanders. They consider me as their leader. I have led them to victory in battles of expansion and have annexed countless temple cities of the south. The king, Abdullah Qutb Shah, never leaves the luxury of his palaces in Hyderabad. Only when he smells danger does he hide behind the walls of the Golconda fort. He has been rather busy with wine and women, perceiving himself to be a connoisseur of art. My king is a romantic man and lives in a fantasy world. He will hope for truce and is likely to be in Hyderabad waiting for us. He is not worthy of being the Shah of the state that yields several million rupees a year only in land revenue. Taxes collected on the diamond and tobacco trades fetch him a few more millions. We cannot lose this war. We will surround his palace and bar his flight to Golconda fort that is a few miles west of Hyderabad.' Saying thus, the ousted and angry Mir Jumla had put forth his strategy.

Sultan had known what his father was thinking. The Shia kingdoms of the Deccan had become the Empire's vassals twenty years ago, but they had stopped paying the tribute money.

'If Abdullah Qutb Shah is a fool as you say he is, call him for a meeting and slaughter him. Lighten the burden of his head on his neck,' Sultan's father had eagerly suggested.

'That may anger his followers as well as my followers. Instead, we will march into Hyderabad. If he is in the city, and offers resistance, we will kill him. If he runs away to the fort, we will besiege the fort later. Once the fort falls, the kingdom is ours. This land is a gold mine. The villages to the north of Hyderabad are famous for high quality iron ore that is greatly valued by blacksmiths all over the world. The weavers of the port city of Masulipatanam export chintz to Mecca. The carpet makers of Ellore are renowned for their skill for centuries.' Mir Jumla had rolled his eyes and and then, spreading his arms in the air announced, 'It is not just the diamond mines, consider the forests teeming with herds of elephant, keenly sought by cavalry commanders and also the trade of tobacco and toddy that brings in enormous funds in taxes for the ruler.'

Sultan had glanced at his father and noticed, just for the flicker of a moment, a glint of greed creeping into his eyes. He suspected that even Mir Jumla had noticed it.

The Persian had not come alone. He had his own, well mounted cavalry of six thousand horses, a fully armed infantry of fifteen thousand, a hundred and fifty war elephants and regiments of modern light artillery of easy mobility that could fire modern explosives that Mir Jumla had himself invented.

'I will be with your son like a shield, my precious *Shahzade*,' Mir Jumla had promised Father.

With the help of Qutbshahi's ousted grand *wazir*, Sultan's journey to the banks of the River Musi has been hassle-free. He is fascinated by what he has seen. Even in winter, the rambling meadows have retained a part of their post-monsoon lushness. At places they were broken by huge rocks and boulders piled on one another. Sometimes they appeared like unstable hillocks, ready to tumble on any intruders. Sultan has encountered man-made lakes, sweeping across the land, till they vanished into the horizon. The villages were surrounded by patches of cultivated earth covered with saplings swaying in the wind. They had camped on the banks of the Hussein Sagar Lake on the northern borders of the city. The kingdom has offered no resistance. Even when he had moved in with his large military into the suburbs, he was greeted only by terrified residents, wealthy and vulnerable, with much to lose. After they set the Karwan neighbourhood on fire, not a single Golconda soldier appeared to stop them.

The fires still rage behind him, as the rising clouds of black smoke make the northern sky pitch dark. Sultan can still hear faint cries of the fame and fortune seekers, the artists, merchants and the scholars who had come from far and stayed back in Hyderabad. Mohammad Sultan is least bothered. They have now reached the boundaries of the inner, walled city. To his left, on the western horizon, he can see a faint outline of the Golconda Fort. But that is not his target, the city of Hyderabad is. Now, between him and the destination lies only the Musi, and its dark waters do not seem daunting.

'The inner, walled city and the fort are separated by the Musi River. The city is on its southern banks and the fort on its northern banks, eight miles upstream. It is protected by a mile-long outer wall, six to twelve *guz* thick, twenty *guz* high and fortified with eighty-seven bastions overlooking a deep, water-filled and crocodile-infested moat. Unlike the fort, the city is not protected,' Mir Jumla has said.

Feeling safe with the Persian warrior hovering around, Sultan asks his *ankush*-wielding mahout to goad the animal further towards the river. The high-arched bridge above the waters of the river is deserted and the massive gate studded with steel spikes at the other end of the bridge is closed shut. The ramparts of the fortified wall do seem hostile, yet ripe for the invasion. He has been duly warned that above the bastions near the bridge are archers waiting for his men to come over. His ears pick up the sound of splashing from the river. His scouts have slipped into the water to swim across. He narrows his eyes to a slit to focus. The river seems calm even with a few hundred men under her belly. Scouts must be like vapour, difficult to spot, difficult to catch, and yet, able to reach odd places, if need be. He looks down from the howdah and can see a sea of horsemen. For the first time in his twenty years of life, his father has entrusted him with ten thousand of the finest horsemen, and also given him a high calibre warrior like Mir Jumla and his army.

***

For a while, Mir Jumla moves around Sultan's elephant, covered with iron panels and chainmail. But, within moments, he steers his horse between the scaffolding, holding numbers of enormous cannons. His artillerymen, hanging like spiders on the scaffolding, are mostly fugitives from the Portuguese army. They are far more skilled than the imperial experts and far quicker at loading the muzzle with explosives. He makes sure that they are aiming in the right direction and that the spiked gate flanked by bastions and surrounding ramparts fall in the range of their fire. He has chosen the latest bombards, European Granados, iron shells filled with explosive material fitted with a slow-burning fuse. His gunners have already inserted the right amount of propellant-explosives in the cannons that will soon start exploding one after another. The men are almost through with shoving the shells in. His men are the best but only he knows how to design the fuse, so that it burns at the right time and the shells explode at the right place. It is his trade secret. He has also added extra saltpetre to the gunpowder to make the explosions stronger and noisier. For him it is not just about damaging the enemy's property or killing them; the blast must coax their minds to yield to thoughts of surrender.

'Take position,' he barks as artillerymen minding the cannons prepare themselves to open fire. The fire has to hit the gate before the scouts emerge from the waters.

'Fire!' he shouts as his men spring into action.

The earth shudders several times as the spiked wooden gate catches fire. More shells fired by the cannons explode. The horses squeal in panic and the elephants trumpet with fear. The explosions continue and the sky is covered with burning specks. Sultan can see a small part of the wall, adjacent to the gate, blow up. The flames fly high and the sky is lit in a riot of reds and yellows. He notices tiny shadows of archers scurrying over the ramparts, running away from the flames rising from the bastions. In the midst of the fire and noise, the imperial scouts jump out of the river. Soaked, shivering in their clothes that have become heavier, they scuttle and run zigzag to avoid arrows shot by the enemies. The Golconda cannons mounted on the other, yet intact bastions, start flinging fire too from across the river. It does little damage, as Mir Jumla knows exactly where the fire will strike, and has asked everyone to keep away from those areas. He has ordered his henchmen to cease fire.

A scout manages to reach a gap in the wall made by the explosion, his soaked clothes protecting him from the still-smouldering slivers of explosives. After entering the city, he first stumbles over the fallen mortar. In the trembling light of flames still rising over the charred gate, he can see the tree-lined avenue going towards a mosque. It is a famous one, called the Charminar. He has heard about the monument, four soaring minarets and enormous arches built at the intersection of city's four major streets. The king's palace is at its west. He is aware that the grounds hidden behind the trees are teeming with enemy men. Within moments they will come marching out. Time is of great essence. He turns to his left and realises that some of his men are following him. He is told about the secret staircases leading to the ramparts. The guards at the entry points have run away. Armed with daggers, he and his followers climb the narrow, poorly lit, spiralling staircase tunnels. Once on the ramparts still intact, they first hide in the shadows of the turrets with daggers, waiting for the archers to pass by. The enemy men fall silently, their quivers still full of unused arrows. He runs further east to look for archers but finds to his surprise that the ramparts are empty. Jumping near the parapet looking north, he pulls out a small trumpet from his belt and blows it hard, emptying his lungs till he gasps for breath.

The gate has stopped burning. The inferno has vanished.

'Move in!' Sultan orders as his ears pick up the trumpet calls. A few horsemen around him take flight to pass on his message to his commanders, Kartalab, Rai Simha and Abdul Munim, who are sitting on their armed elephants a little distance away. Soon they march over the bridge that is built over many arches.

'We will be safe on the bridge. They will not fire explosives there,' Mir Jumla has assured. 'The bridge is their pride, a reminder of their past glory, built seventy years ago so that the then prince could visit his Hindu beloved who lived on the other side of the Musi River. He later married her and made her his queen.'

Thousands of imperial soldiers cross the bridge and enter the city. Some take the avenue leading to Charminar. Some steer their horses to streets lined with mansions of the ministers and nobles, yelling 'Deen! Deen! Deen!' hailing the ways of Islam. They toss torches randomly onto balconies encased in wooden parapets, starting fires that flush out panicked residents. Thousands of Mughals and Mir Jumla's soldiers have entered the city. The Golconda soldiers, their hair tied tightly in buns over their heads, seem overwhelmed by the waves of the Mughal's men. The war-hardened Mughal soldiers cut through their shocked regiments like a blade through enemy flesh. And Hyderabad, 'the-city-of-the-brave' watches silently with mute rage. The city's soldiers are startled to see a fully armoured Mir Jumla, wearing his famous black tunic and golden sash riding towards the palace. There is no mistaking him – he is their Mir Jumla, who has led them to success in battles of expansion. He is surrounded by several horsemen holding torches, throwing a bright glow over him. He is the ousted one, and has come back for his family. Even the Golconda archers gaze at him, forgetting to shoot. It is a risk Jumla has taken. And it has paid off. By the time some come to their senses and stretch their bows, he is gone. After seeing him, the commanders of Golconda are no longer sure whether to fight or not. The squadrons are left without proper orders. However, the Mughal men know what they want and what they must do.

The ousted grand *wazir* of Qutbshahi first makes sure that he is noticed by the maximum number of Golconda soldiers. Then he kicks his horse and brings it before Sultan's elephant. He is tired of waiting and has started worrying about his family. The king is hiding somewhere in the city, waiting with some hope to negotiate with them. But Jumla has other plans. Now he is eager to see a shackled Qutb Shah standing amidst the ruins of Hyderabad.

'Follow me, young *shahzade*,' he waves his hand to signal the eldest son of Aurangzeb, the only man who has offered him help. Sultan Mohammad's tusker thumps behind Mir Jumla's mount. A hundred horsemen have encircled the fully armoured war mammoth, to watch over their master who is a mere boy of twenty. Sultan decides that the city is even more glorious than Agra, never mind its streets that are littered with limbs, torsos and heads. As they move through a street lined with shopping arcades, he stares ahead in amazement. Four sky piercing minarets with rings of balconies gleaming in pale moonlight, they rise above the enormous arches and appear to be the city's everlasting guardians. When his procession crosses the major intersection through its archway, he glances up. In the light of torches held by horsemen riding around him he notices a massive dome shaped ceiling with a large lotus engraved at its center. The vault-like dome is bordered with a stone balcony. It is empty; his men have slaughtered everyone praying in the mosque built above the archway. After crossing the massive arches, he notices enormous flames rising above the residential areas.

The sky has turned pale with smoke. He hears the faint screams of people when his elephant turns to the left and enters a wide road lined with columns of cypress trees leading to the king's palace. With numerous torches around, the pillared corridors of the king's palace amplify the darkness lurking across its arches. Its cupolas and domes are shrouded in smoke drifting from the burning city. The courtyard is littered with the dead. Crimson streams roll randomly across the marbled floor. Once they reach, he climbs down with the help of a ropeladder. He has to jump over the bodies and avoid blood streams to enter the palace. It is more like a museum with its chandeliers from Europe, carpets from Persia, ceramic from China and many such priceless artefacts. Behind the court, where the king holds meetings, is an enormous foyer with marble shelves. Sultan's jaw drops as he stares at the ancient leather bound manuscripts, some written on paper and some etched on palm leaves in languages he does not know. The walls are covered with brass murals of parts of the world he has not even heard of. The windows are painted with printed fabric that he has never seen.

'What must be done, young *shahzade*?' Mir Jumla asks, with a smirk on his face. His men have marched through the maze of courts and corridors, apartments and underground vaults. The king is nowhere to be seen. He has fled.

Sultan manages a blasé expression and looks at Mir Jumla. The treasure is too huge to carry. 'Lock the palace and guard it,' he orders, not knowing what else to do.

Outside, the plaza covered with polished marble is being thronged by the quivering brides-of-the-town. The Deccani, Turkish, Persian and Armenian courtesans have never seen a battle. The glimpse of women makes the lice-ridden imperial soldiers, who stink of sweat and grime, abruptly stop their mounts, leaving behind clouds of dust. A large number of them start encircling these women with oiled hair and smooth skins, each trying to hide behind the other. The rustle of their silk skirts and jingle of their anklets make the men laugh as if tickled. Some start whistling and some make lewd comments. Their whistles and words are quickly drowned in a nerve-shattering sound. A hundred imperial war elephants have moved in, crashing into the enemy lines guarding the market, the last stronghold of Golconda soldiers. They move, trampling whoever comes in their way and swing their trunks to knock down the enemy pikemen or toss them in the air. The Golconda soldiers meant to protect the market become rooted to the ground in terror. The iron gates leading to the market places crumble and fall like a pack of cards when the armoured tuskers run through them. The broken pieces of the gate hit the ground with a crushing sound. Plunder rages in the city unchecked. A vast amount of cash and kind is seized by the sword-wielding Mughal men expert in breaking locks and window bars.

Two | The Undercurrents

A slightly podgy Abdullah Qutb Shah has escaped the palace from a secret tunnel. He curses himself for not having fled earlier. Deep in his foolishly naive heart, he had hoped that Sultan Mohammed would offer an alliance. After all, his kingdom is already a tributary state of the Empire. There would not be a battle if his commanding officers welcomed the imperialists. But that was not to be. Aurangzeb's army forged ahead, dashing his hopes to dust. His heart thumps hard as he wipes his forehead, damp with sweat. The tunnel is cool and smells musky. Though dark in there, he has refrained from lighting a torch.

The stony ridges of the tunnel graze his skin, and he starts bleeding. After half an hour of walking and stumbling in the dark, he reaches a narrow lane where the city's poor live. He emerges from the shadows and enters an area crowded with people in grubby clothes. He walks through the multitude unnoticed. As he is about to enter a bigger road, his ears are deafened by a blast. A few yards away he sees people turning into balls of fire. The air has turned heavy with the sulphurous fumes of gunpowder. The soot has swept at him, smudging his face, stinging and watering his eyes.

It is difficult for him to see. He rubs his eyes with his wrists and glances at the skyline that is blazing red with arson. His eyes search for the minarets. He has to reach them if he intends to live. Half a mile away, Charminar, built to bring peace and prosperity to the city, stands helplessly as the imperial horsemen gallop away through its archway.

The minarets glare down on armoured elephants and their javelin-wielding raiders searching for targets to break in. Its granite, mortar, limestone and marble shakes with each resounding explosion.

The man on the run moves cautiously towards Charminar, avoiding imperial horsemen who are busy hunting down his men. Behind him, his palace, where he was born and grew up, is invaded by the enemy. The streets of his city are littered with corpses. The torches, in iron baskets on pavements, have been deliberately lit by the imperialists. In their dim yellow light, he is forced to see that which he had never wanted to. The bodies have turned crimson, some with throats slit and others with their viscera pulled out. A strong smell of freshly spilled blood churns his innards. He can see horsemen dragging women by their hair to some quiet place. At one dark corner, he notices a soldier ripping off a girl's clothes, as another frenzied man thrusts himself against her. Her screams seem as futile as his life. He closes his eyes in shame.

The monument built by his ancestors lies deserted. He swiftly moves into its shadow. The vault built below one of the minarets opens into a long tunnel. It was dug by special engineers to join the city on the southern banks of the Musi to Golconda Fort that lies on the northern banks of the river. The mile-long tunnel, after crossing the river, turns westward to reach the fort protected by eighty-seven bastions. Even Mir Jumla is unaware of this escape route. He quickly searches the hidden pockets of his cloak and pulls out a single large key.

Two days later Abdullah Qutb Shah, sitting in his private theatre on the third floor of his many-arched Balahisaar Baradari, wants to forget what had happened to his beloved Hyderabad. He wants to wake up and discover that he has had a nightmare. He does not want to remember how he had escaped to the safety of his fort, leaving his subjects in the hands of those cold-hearted, lice-ridden, libidinous and uncouth men of Aurangzeb. He reads Aurangzeb's letter again and again till his eyes ache. The Mughal prince has written in chaste Persian.

The war against you is ordained by Allah, not just as a leader of the Sunnis but also as the destroyer of those who do not conform to His idea of Islam. Twenty years ago, my father, the Emperor Shah Jahan, had warned you - you, a Shia Muslim ruler who has gladly agreed to be the vassal of the Empire and pay yearly tribute of a million rupees. Let me remind you of the arrears. You owe us two million rupees that is one thousand five hundred ser *of pure gold. And it is not just about the money. With great distress, we consider you a* rafizi, *and* ghul-i-biyabani, *a corpse-eating demon. We have pledged to protect your subjects from following your perceptions of our faith. We want to save them from hell. If we allow you to rule, we will do injustice to the soil of Hindustan. You have left us with no alternative but to destroy you.*

The letter has Aurangzeb's palm impression.

Slightly tipsy after a few goblets of wine, he wanders unsteadily towards the eastern windows and narrows his eyes to stare at his beloved city of Hyderabad. It was captured two months ago and torn apart by the savage soldiers of Aurangzeb, the extremist Sunni, backed by his own grand *wazir*, Mir Jumla, a Shia.

And what had he done, the king of Qutbshahi? He had run away from the city to hide behind the fortified walls of Golconda fort. The city has fallen and once the imperial army is successful in capturing this fort, his kingdom will only be a distant memory. His eyes scan the battlefield between the city and the fort. The earth looks wounded with freshly dug trenches. The uprooted trees have fallen on the ground with their branches sprawling around them like limbs of dead soldiers. The northern side of the Musi has become a burial ground.

He has lost thousands of his swordsmen, archers and musketeers. The air is heavy with the stench of dead flesh and the odour of spent gunpowder. Beyond the battlefield, he can see the siege. Now the Mughals are trying to take over his fort. Hundreds of carts carrying cannon stand in a circular line covering a few miles. Aurangzeb has arrived personally from Aurangabad with fresh reinforcements. His personal squadron has the most brutal, remorseless beasts. Aurangzeb's favourite commander, and maternal uncle, Shaista Khan, has also joined him to fight the war against Golconda.

'It is all over,' he says to himself and nothing else matters to him anymore, not even his most favourite courtesan. The shortage of cannonballs and explosives has rendered his long range high calibre cannon, mounted on the fort's ramparts, useless.

Behind him, his most beloved courtesan, Taramati, sings a song devoted to God Krishna. Her body sways as she personifies Carnatic music in her mystic dance of bharatanatyam. A sole musician seems lost in the *tha-tdhi-thom* rhythms of his mrudangam. Suddenly a messenger walks in gingerly and whispers something in his ears. Qutb Shah does what he has never done before - he waves his hand to stop the music. He leaves the venue with unusual agility in spite of his overweight body stuffed in a brocaded robe, laden with pearls and diamonds and woven in gold. After descending the stairs of his Baradari and crossing the gardens, he climbs down another three hundred and eighty steps. Finally he arrives at the alabaster buildings, adorned with decorative niches, delicate embellishments, arches, alcoves and frames that house his harem. He runs towards a lone palace that stands at the edge of the hill. Shah is in a hurry to consult his mother, Hayat Baksh Begum, who has always insisted on doing away with Mir Jumla.

The old lady sits alone in her chamber, wearing a white ankle length skirt and a loose, pearl studded jacket. Her matronly figure is slumped in her gilded chair, her blue eyes distant.

'Ya, Allah,' she cries raising her hands and says, 'I had warned you that Mir is not like what we had initially perceived.'

The tall and sharp-featured Mohammad Saeed who was later given the title of Mir Jumla, had arrived from her home town, the city of Isfahan in Persia, famous for its mosques, carpets and the intelligence of its traders. He had remained meek and obedient in the beginning and had addressed her as 'reverend mother'. As the years had gone by, the Persian seemed to be in a hurry to grab the loyalty of Golconda's army officials. He had taken over all the diamond mining and trading activity and had amassed enough wealth to maintain a private cavalry and infantry. His mastery over Persian, Arabic and Urdu, had earned the trust of the diamond traders from all over the world. She could then feel the shift in power and had started warning her son, who remained immersed in his art and artisans.

'Son, you never listened. We were nurturing a venomous snake, and now he is striking back, emptying his venom to destroy us,' she says sadly. 'I do not want to live to see our kingdom in flames, our cities crushed under the hooves of these marauders, and our lakes crimson with the blood of our people.'

There is a long silence. She shudders and frantically searches for a quick solution.

'There is but one hope,' she hesitates.

'Tell me, Mother,' Abdullah is anxious to know.

'Start paying the tribute money. And offer our princess Fatima to Aurangzeb's son Sultan in marriage,' hisses the elderly woman.

***

Seventy miles south of Pune, the village called Javali seems oblivious to the outside world of battles and wars. But its ruler, Chandrarao Moray is angry and feels his temper rise. Fuming, he looks out of the window of his den on the second storey of his walled fortress. Beyond the small village, cramped between vertical hills, more hills rise to unbelievable heights thus forming a natural wall around his valley. He does not need to bother about thugs like Shivaji. Still, when he looks at the crumpled paper in his hand, he has an urge to read it again and again.

Ten years ago, we had helped the barren widow of the then legitimate Javali ruler to adopt you; you, the then thirty-five-year-old man without any worthy achievements. Our word, we being the jagirdars *of this region for years, carried weight. All the worthy landlords voted for you. In turn you had promised your unflinching loyalty to us. The sudden rush of power has given you amnesia that afflicts people who want to forget their promises. You have ignored our hand of friendship. We are aware of your deeds. You call yourself a king and send your revenue collectors into our jurisdiction, our* jagir *to fleece our ryots. Merchants from Konkan are forced to use the mountain tracks passing through your valley. You demand unreasonable taxes. If they refuse, your goons kill them. You are also trying to thwart our policy of bringing the* watandars *of the region together. We hear that you have gone ahead and made an anti-Bhosale coalition in the king's court. Remember, your duty is to serve us in our struggle to establish a Swaraj, a state not ruled by external powers. Decide today, else, tomorrow, we will annex your valley and haul you out in shackles.*

The letter has Shiva Bhosale's seal and the message therein is provocation beyond all fairness.

The *jagirdar* of Javali jerks his head in disgust and something makes him glance back. His brother stands near the door, his hands resting on his large waist.

'*Vakeel* Raghunath Ballal Korde is coming with armed men,' he hears his brother announce.

'Not in large numbers though,' he frowns and continues, 'Let us see how far they go with their verbal threats.'

'Do you think they can really march in and cut right though the heart of this valley in large numbers?' asks his brother.

He does not nod. The ruffian son of Shahji Bhosale has been trying to bully them for years. In the beginning his letters were polite, but later turned threatening and then outright mean. Initially he had ignored the scoundrel who had forced many big landlords to join him to form a united sovereign Maratha state, a Maratha kingdom!

'I doubt it,' barks Chandrarao suddenly.

The brother nods pensively and asks, 'Shall we ask Murarbaji to stay till the *vakeel* and his men are here?'

'No, let him guard his post. Our usual security is enough. Allow only the *vakeel* and one more man to enter the fortress,' he waves his hand and dismisses his brother's idea.

Chandrarao Moray drops his gaze to his feet. A hundred years ago Javali belonged to the Wai province of Adilshahi kingdom. It was granted to the then head of the Moray family, as *jagir*. The then king, Ibrahim Adil Shah had bestowed a title of Chandrarao, meaning the ruler of the moon, upon the original Moray. The first Chandrarao and his men had slaughtered the tribal and flattened their habitats, cleared part of the forests and tilled the land. The valley is also close to the port city of Dabhol in coastal Konkan, a rich trading centre under Adilshahi. Essentials like salt, spices, textiles and wood come to Dabhol from other ports. The goods are then trasported to Bijapur through the mountains. In the region there are several ghats, the tracks skirting the mountains. Only two are wide enough for the merchants and both pass through Javali. Thousands of oxen enter his valley carrying goods. The money from toll taxes has made him rich, very rich. The valley is like a treasure locked and forgotten. Today, he, the new Chandrarao of Javali has a few thousand soldiers. His treasury is filled with a thousand *ser* of pure gold and five thousand *ser* of pure silver.

All this has not come to him easy and free. Born in a poor family remotely related to the Morays, he had burrowed his way into the heart of a woman branded as barren, the widow of the last Chandrarao. He had run errands, dealt with young men from her family who were vying to be her adopted son. But he had outwitted all of them and had become the adoptee, making sure that the adoption was done with all the rituals and official paperwork. Documents filled with his new mother's palm thumbprints were locked up in his vaults.

'This is the last time I will entertain Shiva's *vakeel*,' he looks up and says. The aroma of freshly-cooked chicken curry wafts in the air. He likes to eat his lunch a little early in the afternoon. But he has to finish a job. He goes near the window and glances down; the men still wait in the courtyard for his order. They need to know how to tackle the peasant who has failed to pay revenue.

'Beat the life out of him and drag his blessed cow to our shed,' he barks at them before moving away from the window and taking the steps down to the dining hall near the kitchen. His brother follows him. His wives hover in the kitchen. The cooks are busy stirring the curries and roasting *rotis* on firewood stoves. Two silver platters stuffed with food appear on a low desk surrounded by rangoli designs and incense sticks that stick out from silver stands with tiny holes. His brother has already sat down to eat. Steaming bowls brimming with curries, vegetables and soups are kept around the plate.

Midway through the meal, Chandrarao looks at his brother. He has bent forward over his food, his hand shoving lumps of rice mixed with curry into the mouth with slurping sounds.

'Have the escorts left to bring Shiva's *vakeel?*' he asks irritably, holding the succulent bird leg in his hand as ginger curry spiced with pepper, dribbles down his fingers.

His brother belches, stops eating reluctantly and mutters, 'Long before dusk...'

Chandrarao tries to nibble on the meat but his mind goes back to Shiva Bhosale. His valley is not so easy to march in. Perhaps the son of Shahji Bhosale is considering his valley as a safe retreat if and when Aurangzeb comes marching to Pune.

***

At the western end of the village, near the huddled mud houses, a lonely peasant stands and watches his reed-thin daughter. Her dark face is flush with happiness. She swings and claps, jumps and whirls as her ankle length skirt, darned at several places, balloons and spins arround her. She abruptly stops, pulls her pleated hair up in the air like two horns and asks her father, 'Ba, shall we get new cow bells for Kapila?'

The peasant's heart aches as he searches the pockets of his grubby *angirkha* for a *damdi*. He knows they are empty. He has not seen even a copper coin for several weeks and he has nothing to barter, neither does he have grains nor fodder. A spasm of regret tears through his body as he thinks about the herd of elephants that had rampaged through his small patch of tilled land, allotted to him by the rulers. Fear lances through him. He thinks about the revenue collectors who had come for their share of his produce. He had begged to be pardoned and showed them the trampled cobs. He had fallen prostrate at their feet but they had whisked away his oxen as penalty. Bile surges in his mouth when he remembers their latest demand – they want his cow and even the calf. The girl senses that she won't get what she wishes for. Men had come from the big house and had taken their oxen away. The men had come again and shouted at her father. She is suddenly afraid for him, but is soon distracted by Kapila's calf sprinting across the shed, kicking its hind legs in the air. It gambols away as if chasing a butterfly and vanishes. The girl runs behind it leaving trails of her laughter that engulfs the shafts supporting the frayed wickers of his shed with spurts of joy.

Outside, the air has filled the narrow lanes of the village with the strangely soothing smell of cow dung. Flimsily thatched roofs of cow sheds rear their heads from behind the huddled mud houses. Facing those hovels are some carts that lie at an angle as a few oxen languidly chew the cud under the shade of a tamarind tree. A group of women wearing tattered saris squat near a huge mound of dung mixed with husk. Their oiled hair is tied in buns of various sizes. Most have horizontal lines drawn with vermillion on their foreheads. They mutter ceaselessly in a rustic dialect of Marathi while removing handfuls of the cow dung from the mound. A few women raise their eyebrows on seeing the girl sprint behind the calf to match its movements.

'Dhondiba's daughter, she has recently broken into blood,' a woman who has lost her teeth whispers, as if letting out a secret of utter importance.

Other women look at her sunken face and ponder for a while. A widow, who has tattoos of suns and moons on her forehead, instead of vermillion lines, pitches in, 'Who will marry her, her father has nothing left to give her in dowry.'

'She is ill-fated. She devoured her mother within weeks of her birth,' whispers a newly-married one, dipping her voice, darting her eyes in the direction of the calf and its pursuer.

'Leave the wretched child alone,' admonishes a shrivelled woman of several monsoons in a quivering voice, 'her mother died when the great plague swept the mountains'.

The women glance at each other.

'Now our *jagirdar* is after her father,' someone comments as they glance at the massive gates of Moray fortress with its spiked doors and round bastions.

In their living memory, all the villages in the valley were and are always at the *jagirdar's* mercy. Their fathers, husbands, brothers and sons are his bondsmen. They plough, harvest, gather the produce in the barns, thresh and winnow the grains, mow and store the hay, cut and collect the wood, for their master. Even though peasants maintain their own farm animals, the land belongs to the ruler. If they fail to give the expected produce to the ruler, they bear punishment. But nobody speaks about this, other than glancing in the direction of the fortress.

Without halting their chatter, the women continue making fuel cakes, grabbing the mix and throwing the portions in the air and then spreading the lumps like pancakes on the earth to dry. The village is otherwise quiet, with most menfolk labouring away in nearby fields. Between the women and their mud dwellings, a few scantily-clad children bend, twist and shake their wiry bodies to knock their opponent's clay skittles from a dirt circle etched on earth. Their occasional shrieks of victory force the sparrows, hopping on the ground in search of scraps of food, to take flight. A bell from the temple of Kal Bhairava chimes repeatedly from behind the cow sheds. Its high-pitched sound resonates with the chilling reminders of life's frailty. A lone goat starts bleating away as if to announce its loneliness. Water in a nearby pond quivers, trying hard to ripple through the grimy layers of moss. An enormously spread banyan tree with roots hanging from its branches stands with deaf ears on the edge of the slimy pond, wrapped in its own world.

Dhondiba's cow, his only worldly possession, sits in the corner of his shed with peaceful passivity, occasionally jerking its tail to ward off flies. The bells in its neck clink amidst the buzzing of a large bee that seems to be leisurely fleeting across the shed. He needs to prepare something to eat. With the pain of hunger churning in his stomach, he mulls over whether to guard the cow or head home that is just a few yards away. They have not eaten anything since yesterday. The village women have loaned him some sorghum flour. Just as he is about to decide in favour of going home and lighting the firewood to roast *rotis*, he hears his cow's fierce snorting. The sudden change in Kapila's behaviour makes the peasant nervous. 'It is weary of the bee,' he tries to smother his anxiety but when it jerks its body and staggers on its feet, he feels his palms getting cold and sweaty. There is something unusual in the noise that the animal makes. It is then that the peasant hears the footsteps pounding his small courtyard.

Just a day before, he had begged, bending his head on the ground, but his master's men had turned a deaf ear to his words. They had left, leaving behind the ominous silence loaded with violent hints. Now they seem to have returned. Dhondiba dashes out and sees a group of armed men wearing short leggings march towards him. The muscles of their arms bulging through their sleeveless vests makes the peasant feel weak. The stout men with bushy whiskers do not bother to look at him. They brutally strike the shrubs with iron bars in a way that the air swishes about with a sharp sound.

'You, *randichya*, get the cow,' screams one of the men spitting obscenities and wielding a bar as if it is a sword.

Dhondiba watches helplessly as two men leap inside the shed; one holding a rope knotted to make it into a noose. He is paralysed as weakness overwhelms every part of his body. He collapses on his feet holding his head in his hands. The men shout and curse inside the shed that shudders with the cow's bellowing and stomping. A cloud of dust emerges from the shed. It is a long struggle, but the men are successful in heaving his Kapila out, its neck almost twisted with the leash they have thrown. The animal baulks as they drag it while its hooves root with refusal. Once it is out, the others circle around the helpless beast. Its brown coat dotted with white patches shimmer in dismal grief in the warm rays of the afternoon sun.

He feels tears stream down his face. He must do something and instinctively falls flat before one of the men.

'I touch your feet, please don't,' he yells till his throat aches. The men ignore his screams. They are busy shouting at each other and hauling the cow on the uneven earth, across the hamlet towards the heavily guarded residence of the Morays, the owner of the region.

The women have stopped their work and their gossip. They stand abruptly, letting the dung slip from their hands. Unmindful of their thickly smeared fingers, they cover their mouths with their sari *pallus*, lest a provocative sound of fear or shame escape from their throats. They have seen a lot. This is just a cow and its calf. At times, even young women are taken by force, and are never seen again. They watch in horror as one of the men return with an iron rod. Dhondiba is still lying flat on the ground, weeping. The women hear him scream in agony. Everything else remains as before, including the pond that is covered with moss and the solitary, half closed white lotus that floats on its stagnant waters.

A stranger to the village hides behind a cart. He has witnessed the incident. He leaps and darts in the direction in which the girl has gone.

THREE | BATTLE OF JAVALI

Circa 1656

This is Raghunath's second visit. The house of Morays, surrounded by high walls and strengthened with bastions, stands tall. Countless men brandishing swords, axes and spears wait in its huge courtyard. The entrance of the house is lit by a number of torches kept in iron brackets that are nailed into the walls. The assembly chamber is enormous, with *baithaks* covered in *jajums* and carpets spread over floor. Carved silver chandeliers and glass urns holding oil lamps hang with the help of gilded chains. A few men, about twenty in number, rest at the other end, idly lounging on the bolsters and listening to their master, occasionally breaking into a collective laugh.

Fat and overbearing Chandrarao Moray, wearing a large yellow turban, gestures animatedly. He seems comfortable on a high platform with his legs tucked under him. Two men with vacant faces fan him with fluffy feathers fixed to silver sterns. Raghunath, standing at the entrance of the chamber, is surprised by the unhealthy pallor of Moray's skin, usually noted in heavy drinkers. On Moray's right a wiry scribe sits behind a writing desk and fiddles with his feather nib. On his left, near but not on the platform, a man rests his back on a bolster and sniffs tobacco. Raghunath has seen him before: Hanumanth, the administrator of the *jagir*. Fortunately the captain of Moray's army, the man called Murarbaji, who Raghunath should be wary of, is not in the room.

'Come come, sit,' he hears Chandrarao Moray. The ruler of Javali has finally noticed his guests.

Raghunath and his aide bow deep while their host accepts their greetings by nodding lightly and waving his stubby fingers. They choose to be away from the Moray clansmen and sit near the exit. From here Raghunath can see the trident-holding sentries who guard the entrance to the house.

'You are back,' Moray says and swings his face sideways to show his disgust for the *vakeel*.

'It is my fortune,' mumbles Raghunath.

'And who is the man accompanying you?'

'He is Sambahaji. Sambahaji Kavji, captain of the horsemen has accompanied us,' replies Raghunath, glancing at his aide, a dark skinned man wearing a fine jacket.

Moray keeps mum, letting the silence grow between them. Raghunath too does not bother to reply. After a while, an obviously irritated Moray asks, 'What happened to Shiva Bhosale's plan to annex Javali? Or you have come back for the bangles?'

Raghunath remembers his last visit. After reading Raja's message, Moray, in a fitful rage had asked his scribe to write an immediate reply. While dictating the letter, the words had frothed in his mouth as he had changed them repeatedly to make them more edgy, and more demeaning.

You are just an ignorant kid of a jagirdar. *What do you know? 'We' are the hereditary 'owners' of this region, and not just mere* jagirdars. *Hundred years ago Bijapur rulers had honoured us with a throne and given us the title of "Chandrarao". I am the undisputed 'king' of Javali. You are welcome to annex it but you will die like a hunted beast on the very soil of my valley. I am not one of your* deshmukhs *whom you can tame. Why are you waiting till tomorrow? Come today if you are a real man. If not, please wear bangles, I will send you some as a gift.*

That was a month ago.

At this very moment Raghunath needs to take stock of things. Last night, after they arrived, they had not been allowed to enter the courtyard. They had spent the night in the barracks built in the midst of animal stables and sheds behind the fortress. The smell of the dung and the mosquitoes had kept him awake. The day had dawned without cheer as the shadows of enormous mountains made the valley look bleak. No one from Moray's side had come to meet them. The people tending to the animals had given them food and water. In the late evening, a servant, looking grim, had suddenly appeared and rudely announced, 'Only two may come with me, the third will be kept waiting outside the gate.' As Raghunath and Sambhaji Kavji had followed him, darkness had settled in. Outside the barracks, men who had come with him, were relaxing around small fires, bantering loudly.

Raghunath feels uneasy now as all depends on those Mavali men. They are supposed to get rid of Moray's men minding the stables and the sheds. Get rid of the guards at the main gate. Gain entry into the fortress and eliminate armed guards minding the courtyard. But if they fail, he will face a certain death. Escape is impossible; the valley is a death trap.

Despite the escorts sent by the Morays, reaching this place had been an ordeal. The Ghats had, at places, narrowed down to slim trails with escarpments on one side and steep drops on the other. Above, the mountains hovered, blocking the sun. Twice he had spotted leopards, sitting on the edges of the cliffs looming over him. Countless times their horses had panicked when snakes slithered in their paths. The only thing that had made the place less sinister was the calls of parakeets, bulbuls and slurred whistles of orioles. The air had smelt sharp and pungent, perhaps a mix of wild berries and tulasi herbs. At places, brooding bamboo forests had replaced the trees. Here only tiny babblers hopped around making 'churr churr' sound. What Raja had said was right. Heavy cavalries would be like ships stuck in sand dunes in this valley.

Raghunath gathers himself and softly says, 'I have another letter for you from Raja Shivaji Bhosale.'

'Before I read the letter, do explain, why a Maratha kingdom?' Chandrarao Moray snaps. He thumps his wrists on the wooden platform that he sits on to show his temper. 'I had not asked you last time and you had never bothered to explain. You owe me an answer.'

Raghunath takes a few deep breaths as he knows that the answer needs to be diplomatic, the vaguer the better. He responds monotonously, 'At the end of the thirteenth century Muslim invaders set foot in the Deccan. The mighty Hindu dynasties, the Yadavas of Devagiri, Kakatiyas of Warangal, Pandyas of Madurai and Hoysalas of Dwarakamudra vanished. The invaders turned into rulers. Now it is time to fight them. And I suppose, to fight them, we need to unite.'

There is a long silence in the chamber. Moray regards the overtly intelligent *vakeel* for a while. Then suddenly he throws his hands excitedly in the air and says, 'Brilliant rhetoric! But you have still not answered my question. All these lofty explanations are good to impress a child with milk teeth still hanging on his gums. You tell me, why is your Shiva interested in my valley?'

Raghunath thinks hard. Moray might be a drunkard but he is cunning. It is better to give the right answer. Or at least an answer that sounds right.

'Raja Shivaji is interested in strong Marathas like you. Also, we believe that the mountains in your valley are the best in the region to build hill forts, they can be the sentinels of the Maratha kingdom.'

'Do you think of us as brainless *vakeel sahibji*? Now let me tell you your Shiva's ulterior motive. The Mughal prince Aurangzeb has already sent his armies to Hyderabad. I see the entire Deccan being swallowed by him in the near future. Even your master's *jagir* will soon be *khalisa*.' Moray speaks slowly, so that the *vakeel* deciphers his dialect of Marathi.

'Your Shiva Bhosale needs this valley to hide when their armies come. Just to buy some more time and keep himself alive. He is nothing more than a rodent searching for a safe hole. If he had a little dignity, he would come marching to the valley with his army and claim it like a warrior,' Moray announces, winking at his manager. He further mutters, 'What say Hanumanth?'

'I have a letter for you from Raja Shivaji,' Raghunath does not want to waste time. He gets up holding an epistle. Even before he steps forward, a servant comes running from somewhere, seizes it from him and hands it over to his master.

Moray holds the epistle between two fingers as if holding a dead scorpion and shouts, his voice gruff. 'Look at the audacity of the man! His lofty seal reads, "Like a crescent moon, grows the Kingdom of Shivaji, son of Shahji, always seeking the welfare of the people."'

Moray stops for a moment to breathe.

'Read, brother, read it,' a man who resembles Moray walks in chewing a betel leaf and declares scornfully. The *vakeel* guesses the man is Pratap, the younger of the Moray brothers.

Moray throws the epistle on the desk of his scribe, who picks it up, opens it carefully and starts reading loudly.

We have given you enough time and warnings. This is the last one. Remove all your titles, abandon the throne, stop calling yourself a king, tie your hands and come to me as a servant. We leave you with no option, join us in our struggle for Swaraj or die.

The words fall like granadoes from a cannon. A deathly silence fills the air for a few moments before the brothers, red in the face, explode in verbal infernos. Moray again thumps his wrists on the platform while Pratap grits his teeth and dredges his brain for the right words to express his fury. He turns ill-temperedly towards the *vakeel*, jerks his head in disgust and explodes. '*Harami*! The son of Shahji! Shahji, the servant of Adilshahi! Who does Shiva think he is, 'the leader of the Marathas' or 'the Emperor of Hindustan'?'

His words become faint under the robust protests of the Moray clansmen who wave their hands in the air, almost trying to punch some invisible objects with their fists, each one shouting in his own strain, none understanding the other.

Raghunath avoids looking at Kavji, for the rage in his own eyes may ignite his captain's fury. It takes a while before the din melts into a silence. Sambhaji Kavji can barely control his temper but he tries to keep a dumb face. This is his second important assignment after the battle of Purandar and he wants success. With its sheer position, the valley has barred the expansion of his Raja's Swaraj in the south and south-west. And with years of power without struggle, Chandrarao has turned into a proud, good-for-nothing drunkard.

A sound filled with scorn rattles the air. Pratap has started laughing, but he stops abruptly as if blessed with a divine vision and barks, 'The leaves of Shiva Bhosale's dream will soon be swept away by the gales of kingdoms and empires.' The Moray clansmen take cue, and debate among themselves, their whispers growing louder and louder.

'In uncertain times like these Shiva Bhosale must scramble to help our esteemed king, Ali Adil Shah of Adilshahi. Shiva's father is the king's regent. That makes serving Adilshahi Shiva Bhosale's duty, his karma. And as you Brahmins say, it is his opportunity to attain moksha if he is killed defending his true masters.' Pratap shouts, loud enough to be heard.

Raghunath smiles bitterly. The four ways that lead to moksha, the cosmic freedom from the circle of life, have become ways to either divide or fool others. *Dharma* the religion, *karma* the duty, *bhakti* the devotion and *vairagya* the detachment. Especially the word karma is used like a whip, to make weak men do what powerful men want them to do, even if it means dying in the battlefields of the invaders. To die for them is the easiest way to live. At least the servants of the invaders die with titles and their children remain alive and wealthy. The rebels of the land are hunted down as though they are dogs with rabies, thrashed and slaughtered, their heads displayed as trophies, their families captured, wives molested and children sold as slaves.

Moray claps loudly, trying to draw attention to something important that he is about to say. His eyes shine with malice.

'Tell him, if he is a warrior, he must stop sending us *vakeels*. And tell him what I think of the piece of paper on which he has written his letter.'

The scribe takes clue, jumps out from behind the desk and hands his master the letter. The master, his face wincing in disgust, crushes the paper into a ball and throws it in the *vakeel's* direction. Raghunath has not expected this kind of a flinging match. He misses the catch and turns to pick up the paper. His eyes fall on the wall that is painted with pictures of Lord Shiva performing his deathly rudra tandava dance – the raging divinity crushes the demons under his thundering feet, some severed and bleeding heads of evil men rolling over to the adjacent walls.

'I am just a humble *vakeel*; pardon me if we have hurt your sentiments,' he says after moments of silence, and fingers the hilt of his knife under his clothes.

'You are a Brahmin. You wear your huge red *pagari* turbans, silk robes, fat gold earrings and those horizontal sandalwood paste streaks on your forehead to show your supremacy. But you could have done something more – put some sense in your master's head,' Chandrarao Moray shouts.

'Let me ask you a question. If Shiva Bhosale is oozing with patriotism then he should first ask his very own father who licks the feet of the Bijapur king to join him, what say brother, Uh?'

The Brahmin keeps cool, and secretly prays that his men are at their job and doing just the right thing. And the timing needs to be perfect. Even if the fortress looks formidable, there are no archers on the ramparts. The watchtowers rising over the bastions are empty. The main gate is guarded by only a few but the courtyard is full of armed men. Raghunath tries to concentrate on his Mavali men to draw some comfort and feels safe just knowing how confident they had looked during their journey through the forest.

The armed men who have come with him are mostly Balutes, some are even the untouchables, but he has felt safe having them around. These men and their captain Sambhaji look like a squadron with their uniforms, a pair of tight breeches and pleated *angirkhas* of quilted cotton. During the journey, they had covered their heads with Turkish turbans with one fold passing tightly under their chins. Their *dhop* swords, gritted to their belts, were not ordinary. Raghunath was told that the blades of these *dhops* are more than one and half guz long. They are pointed to pierce, and are lengthy enough to cut a footman even from horseback. The lower edge of the blade is sharp all through its length, making the sword an extraordinary chopping machine. The upper edge, pipala, is the most lethal, jagged to tear the flesh with ease. If the enemy ducks and avoids the swordsman's forward blow, he gets chopped by its backward blow. All this happens at the blink of an eye. The bottom end of the hilt has tang rods tapering to make its lower end pointed enough to kill. If the enemy is too close to use the long blade, hilts can be held vertically above the enemy to hit the head and crack the skull or used horizontally as a dagger to tear through the enemy's viscera.

'Have you lost your voice?' shouts Pratap.

'It is complicated,' Raghunath says reluctantly. 'Raja Shahji had no choice.'

'But we have a choice! Do you have anything more to say?' Pratap sounds as if he has reached the edge of his patience.

Raghunath glances at his captain for a brief moment before he turns to Chandrarao Moray and says, 'We, Sambhaji Kavji and I, think you deserve to know the truth.'

'What truth?' Moray asks casually and glances at his estate manager who shrugs and moves his head helplessly.

'Say it,' Pratap throws a challenge.

'I need privacy. Some truths are not meant to be revealed in public.' Raghunath is resolute. The *vakeels* frequently asked for a private talk.

Chandrarao takes a deep breath and thinks rapidly. It is the first time that the *vakeel* has been assertive. Years of wealth and authority have made Moray presumptuous, like, one is assertive only when one is being honest. And the *vakeels* have always been good sources of information. Sometimes they seek better prospects in terms of pay or even bring marriage proposals. He nods while the others seem shocked by his affirmation. He ignores them.

'It is important for you to know what we know. Also, we must maintain its confidentiality. Raja Shivaji must never know that we have shared this information with you.' Raghunath says softly.

'Do not play tricks!' yells Pratap.

'Why would we? What do we gain?' And if you do not want to

know, so be it,' the *vakeel* says, retaining his cool.

'What would you get by telling us the truth?' snaps Hanumanth.

'Now stop it. Let's go to my den. I want to know what this 'truth' is.' Chandrarao staggers to his feet, saying, 'You must have patience and good ears brother, come with me if you please.'

Four men exit the chamber and head for the staircase. It is well lit with tiny earthen lamps kept in alcoves carved in the wall. Pratap keeps his right hand on the hilt of his sword gritted to his belt and hovers behind Raghunath. And Raghunath walks behind the ruler who struggles and pants while climbing. The Brahmin realises how obese Chandrarao Moray has become. Sambhaji Kavji remains at the end of the file, his face solemn, his eyes watching Pratap's hand on the hilt.

Chandrarao's den is a small room with arched windows. Pale outlines of hills are seen as an inky blue sky is illuminated with sparkling stars. There are no chandeliers here, only a few tall brass lamps that burn in the corners of the room. Their flames quiver as the the gentle breeze blows from the windows.

'My apologies for the trouble,' says Raghunath, trying to be polite.

'No pretences, out with your truth,' Chandrarao clamours at him, his eyes show fleeting shades of anxiety. From somewhere inside the house, children squeal and women talk noisily. Strong aromas of food, meat and spices ride on the wind.

'The truth is that my master has formed an alliance with Bijapur rulers. He has promised them Javali if they offer him protection when and if the forces of Aurangzeb come marching towards his *jagir*,' says Raghunath, without any fuss.

'I will kill you if you are lying, and feed you to the jackals roaming in the valley,' Pratap says menacingly.

There is silence for a while as this brother of Moray caresses his beard and regards Raghunath for a long time. But the hush soon subsides. Something has happened in the courtyard. Sound of men crying hoarse fills the room. There is a faint sound of swords hitting on swords.

'I knew it!' Pratap screams and moves towards the window to inspect. Chandrarao is left alone for a moment. He notices something sinister floating in the eyes of Shiva Bhosale's *vakeel*. The Brahmin's narrow face has become mean. His jaw is tight and the veins on his forehead look swollen under the horizontal lines of sandalwood paste.

Raghunath glares at Chandrarao and pulls out a bichwa dagger hidden in his sash, its long blade shaped like a scorpion's stinger. He has to go for the jugular, as the cut needs to be mortal for a quick and noiseless death. Kavji has slunk behind Moray and is holding the fat man in a tight grip. Raghunath darts forward and slits Chandrarao's throat with the sharp and recurved blade of his bichwa. The cut is clean and precise. The dying man's eyes fill with astonishment. He tries to say something but his voice is lost to him. Only a guttural sound leaks through his bloody throat. Kavji lets go of his grip allowing the Javali ruler to fall on the floor, limp, like a rag doll. Blood splutters out from the gash onto the carpet. Pratap turns back. He has opened his mouth to tell his brother that something is terribly wrong. Something sinister is taking place in the courtyard. Instead he starts screaming like an animal. However, before Kavji can catch him, he is gone.

Raghunath looks at his hand that still holds the dagger – it is bloody right up to the hilt. Kavji has pulled out the dead man's sword from the scabbard. They rush down to the chamber. Moray's clansmen run around like hares. Hanumanth and Pratap are missing. Chaos reigns supreme, commotion fills their ears. They rush out. The chamber entrance is littered with twisted bodies of the guards who have been beheaded, and the place is messy with blood. The main gate is wide open. The courtyard echoes the sounds of clashing blades and the screams of those dying. In the light of the torches fixed on the outside wall, the *vakeel* can see shadows of men, some fleeing, and some charging. They remain near the entrance till calmness dawns on the scene and only then they enter the courtyard. Their men stand in small groups, victorious. The Brahmin quickly unties the strings of his *angirkha*, pulls out a small trumpet and starts blowing; Kavji does the same. The valley around vibrates with the calls of their trumpets.

***

The forest between the banks of Koyana and the foothills of the western hills is raven dark. Shivaji strains his eyes to see as one horseman after the other appears from the forest around him. It is impossible for any army to march into this valley. One has to make way through too many narrow passes. It is impractical to form multiple columns as a maze of passes open up in different directions. For a month each of his two thousand soldiers have roamed Javali, as goatherds, cattleherds or farm hands. Each one of them had learnt the hideouts of Moray's garrisons. Each one had figured his own way to come to this place, a few miles north of Javali village. Five smaller squadrons comprising two hundred men each have stationed themselves at various locations in the valley.

Under the canopies of the rain trees, dirt tracks fill up with his horsemen. The forest ahead swarms with the tribals and the outcastes who work for him as scouts. He is aware that they, at this very moment, are hacking the wooden vines of liana to clear the way, and also scanning the hills to spot human movements. He notes their signals as they hoot like owls and snarl throatily like tigers, their animalistic sounds rising above the never-ending drone of cicadas. The time has come to move on. He signals and the shadows of his horsemen start moving, southwards. His horse trots like a mountain goat under him, stretching its front legs to climb up and raising its haunches to climb down. Somewhere in the distance, a tiger growls, its call echoing through the valley. Then there is another sound that is carried on the wind, a call of the trumpet that has travelled through the woods and the hills. It is time to go towards the village of Javali. Chandrarao Moray is dead.

'Raghunathpunt and Kavji have done it,' Shivaji hears Tanaji Malusare scream in sheer excitement. As per the plan, Tanaji has kicked his horse to a canter and has gone ahead. Another has followed him, he is Yesaji Kank.

Their vanishing shadows bring the memories of how he had met his best swordsman and his best wrestler after a night of utter disappointment. A time at the end of his first voyage when he had just discovered that there was no kingdom waiting for him.

Shivaji was eight and had already learnt his lesson: 'the kingdom was not waiting for him to come and rule.' Their long journey from Shivaneri fort had ended. They had reached a village. There were no pillared palaces, hiding in the dark lanes or vanishing between the rows of huddled houses. He remembered how at nightfall their horses had slowed down; his mother's horse has started snorting with hunger. Icy winds had started blowing, wafting in the smell of wood smoke. A few torch bearers had joined them on foot, lighting their way. A Brahmin with a stern face had come on a horse to greet them. 'He is Sonopunt Dabir, he used to be your Pitajisahib's advisor,' mother had informed him. The man had smiled and said, 'This is a part of your jagir, *your kingdom.'*

He had seen Bijapur and had thought that that kind of city would await him. There were no streets teeming with trundling elephants, scurrying palanquins or galloping horsemen, instead there were gangs of muscular wild dogs, their reddish coats gleaming in the dim light of torches. Their eyes had shone like embers as they had looked for food, waiting for their chance. Their bold grunts of disapproval had made him hold his mother tighter, till his hands ached. But the torch bearers had not been perturbed. They had finally arrived at a small stone house with red tiles for its sloping roof. It had been enclosed in a short fence made of flat stones piled on each other.

Someone had lifted him from the horse and carried him inside the compound. He had not protested. There had been something more urgent. His bladder had been full. As he had emptied himself with utter relief behind the house, he had noticed a large hole in the fence wall. Looking through, he had caught glimpses of dense shadows of tree trunks at the edge of the skyline that was covered with hills. The moon had been unusually large and hung over a lone boulder like an orb of silver. When about to turn, he had noticed something moving beyond the wall, a large animal. A wild dog again? Narrowing his eyes, he had realised that there were many out there. One beast had climbed the boulder, and raised its jaw as if to look at the sky. The beast had then started howling, a deep reverberating sound. It had certainly been a wolf, its shadow against the moon undoubtedly terrifying. He had run to the frontyard, his heart beating louder than the howls. He had stayed put in the front of the house for a while to quieten his fear, watched men tie their horses to the nearby trees, and even draw water from a well, throwing a large vessel tied to a rope.

A little while later, he had gone inside the house to investigate. His mother's maids had lit the firewood to make roti. *The rooms were clean. The floor was covered with soft quilts. He had just wanted to sleep. It was only in the morning, when he had gone out rubbing his eyes and had noticed the mass of leafless trees around their house that the thought that his new home was in the midst of mean, leafless trees while packs of predators roamed around had left him shuddering in fright. He had to live here.*

Instinctively, he had gone to the backyard to see if the wolves were still there. The darkness, the looming moon, the shadow of the wolf, the howling, had all vanished. Instead, golden sunrays swept across the parched earth. Even the large boulder had gleamed in its light as two boys ran around its girth laughing and jumping. One of them was Tana and the other Yesa, both older and taller than him.

***

The morning star appears in the east. A few miles south of Javali village, sitting on the charpoy, Murarbaji sniffs tobacco. He is suddenly jolted by the sound which he recognises as that of trumpet calls from the direction of his master's fortress. Initially, he links it with the previous day's incident of Dhondiba. But the villagers are incapable of even raising their eyes, leave alone blowing trumpets in protest or anger. He remains confused for a few moments but then he knows. There can only be one reason.

'*Tuzya maila,*' he swears under his breath. Someone is at mischief. He jumps out of his bed and strides out of his barrack built on the banks of Koyana River. His men, sitting and chatting around small fires, look startled; they too have heard the calls. Never before has anyone blown trumpets in the valley. And tonight, at this late hour, someone blows persistently, as if giving out a signal to someone else, perhaps calling a squadron hiding in the forest. He thinks about their garrisons scattered among the dense growth and wonders if these calls would rouse the men from their drunken trance. Or else, it would be only him and his men to face whatever lay ahead. He remembers that Shivaji Bhosale's *vakeel* was to meet his master tonight. But he had come only with a few horsemen. The trumpets are surely a signal, but to whom? Murarbaji has heard about Shivaji Bhosale from the merchants who used to come from Bijapur. The mongers loved to gossip and talked more after a few pegs of wine. Shivaji, his appearance, his clothes, his training camps where villagers from Maval region are taught horse riding and sword fighting. Dutifully Murarbaji had told his master about the latest news that he had learnt but Chandrarao Sahib had brushed him off, saying Shiva Bhosale was too insignificant to worry about. They must watch Afzal Khan, the *subhedar* of Wai province of Adilshahi at the eastern borders of the valley.

'Move!' he shouts at his men, picks up his *shela*, a long cloth he also uses as pillow, and ties it around his waist. He bends to pull out an unusually long scabbard from under his charpoy. The time has come to use the sword. He quickly straightens up and runs towards a wooden shelf fixed to the wall to pick up his weapon, gifted to him by his master. A *pata* sword, kept on a soft cotton cloth, shimmers and smells of clove oil that is used regularly to polish it. It is more than one and half guz long. Its straight blade has ridges that taper to sharp, lethal edges on either side, thus, making it difficult to break or bend. Its metal arm-guard is long enough to protect his arm till the elbow. It also allows the sword to be a part of him, an extension of his hand. Once fixed, he can use the muscles of his arm in full force. And, unlike other swords, its handle bar is not in line with its blade, but perpendicular to it, making it a horizontally striking weapon. He gently picks up the sword, and lets it glide into the scabbard. Before exiting, he fetches a leather shield hung on the wall.

Guilt overpowers him. He should have stayed behind for the meeting with Shiva's *vakeel*. It was the question of his master's life. His men are ready to follow him. As they jump over the nettles and sprint through the dirt tracks towards the village, time, for him, keeps stretching like the path before him.

A raucous sound travels on the wind. It is the jackals on their edgy hunt for food. The sound pervades the hanging darkness of the forest. It lingers, dies away only to come alive to a crescendo and then to die again. Murarbaji's ears pick up faint sounds of hooves from the direction of the village. He tries to calm his mind; whoever is waiting for them near the village can be handled by his five hundred men. He has been through such circumstances countless times. Gangs of moneylenders roaming with swords have been made to crumple down in red heaps. Villages failing to give required revenue have disappeared in the columns of smoke rising from their blazing homes. Landlords who have not sold their produce to the merchants of his master's choice have vanished in the forests.

He looks back and sees flames of torches carried by his men. In the dim yellow light, their faces look grim, as their hurriedly worn *angirkhas* balloon behind them. He wishes he had wings to fly while his hands long to kill. The narrow trail has finally ended. Scaling a small hillock to scout the northern expanse, he peers down. The enormous spiked gate of the fortress is ajar. From inside the courtyard, a dim light filters out to form a long yellow patch on the dark earth. The surrounding forest is a mass of moving shadows with moonlight falling over the swaying canopies. The faint sounds of hooves have stopped; still he feels an unusual movement in the forest. Something tells him that some of them have barged into the fortress. He must rush before they shut the gate. And he must take his men through the narrow lanes of the village, because he is not sure what's hiding in the woods. Even if there is a wee bit chance to save his master, he will grab it.

'To the fortress,' he says in a hushed voice to his men and leaps across the slope to reach the main gate through the village. The gate is closing on them. His heart starts pounding. He grits his teeth and leads his men to punch their way through the closing gate, like water through the falling wall of a dam. The courtyard is well lit by torches hanging in iron baskets near the main house. He spots long shadows of horsemen on the floor, not one, not two, but countless.

'These are the notorious Mavali men of Shiva,' he shouts to warn his men but his words dissolve into the sounds of hooves. He knows the truth at once. The trumpet calls were from the *vakeel* meant for Shiva Bhosale to advance towards the fortress. This means something terrible has happened to Chandrarao Sahib.

Murarbaji watches helplessly as his men run blindly into the arms of a powerful enemy. The enemy horsemen move ahead swiftly, striking slashing blows of their *dhops* on Murarbaji's men who have arrived on foot, carrying shorter and curved swords. The courtyard is filled with sounds of whooshing of blades and the splatter of blood. Shivaji's Mavali men seem to know how to hit footmen from horseback. Their strikes are so powerful that their blades run deep into his men. The swords are easily wrenched out by holding the hilts with all their might as their horses keep sweeping past.

A little away from Murarbaji, Shivaji Bhosale's captain Tanaji Malusare rides through the carnage, brandishing his *pata* and occasionally slaughtering an enemy who has dared to wander in his path. 'Har, Har, Mahadev!' he screams a battle cry hailing the might of God Shiva, his dark face flushed with a burst of vigour gushing through his veins, his muscles bulging behind the tight sleeves of his short *angirakha*, his cries sparking valour in the hearts of his men. Soon the ground is covered with bodies and swords. Yesaji hovers around his master, scanning the fortress and its open windows for archers.

Shivaji watches with interest as his Mavali men wipe out enemies, striking the forward and backward blows with equal ease, chopping off the limbs and torsos. This battle is their military test. Then he notices a man with a *pata* sword, his right hand fixed into a gauntlet and his left, holding a large leather shield. The blade of the *pata* is long and moves in slightly elliptical movement as he swirls, leaping over the dead and avoiding the ground that is sodden with blood. The blade moves like a tongue of flame, gleaming and fading. The man spins in the midst of the horsemen like a wasp. His movements are rhythmic, creating an unbeatable fence with his ridged, killer blade. Soon he starts reaching the enemy horsemen, who in turn, struggle to reach him with their swords. But they are confused and are unable to use their *dhops*. Instead some are hit by the *pata* blade of the enemy and collapse, dead or writhing in pain.

Shivaji stares at the man and for a moment his movements reminds him of his own favourite stances. The man moves in perfect circles. His movements are too swift for others to judge his next attack. Handling the *pata* sword is an art and only the outstanding can master it. Shivaji wrenches at his reins as his horse jerks into a trot. Tanaji Malusare too has kicked his horse and has moved towards the man.

'Retreat,' Shivaji screams. He directs his horse in a circle around the man who continus to swirl and dance. It is a dangerous to handle a *pata* swordsman. One thing that he is sure of is that after a while, the *pata* swordsman loses the fear of death. This man might take risks and become vulnerable. But in the depth of his heart Shivaji does not want him to die.

'Halt and that's an order, I know who you are. You are Murarbaji!' Shivaji screams.

Murarbaji seems deaf to the outside world. Shivaji wishes he too had a *pata* sword. It may have been easier to stop the man. He is planning to move closer but before he nudges his mount, like a flash, Tanaji jumps down from his horse and moves between him and the *pata* swordsman.

Tanaji's hand moves in several directions, as if he knows the orbit of the enemy's *pata* well in advance. Tanaji knows that one wrong move and the enemy's blade can dislodge a chunk of his body. Shivaji brings his horse to a halt, not believing the drama of *pata* swords unfolding before his very eyes.

Murarbaji is furious but senses that his opponent is not an ordinary swordsman. Both spin wildly. Even before the enemy can grasp his moves, Tanaji suddenly stops and steps forward, spreads his hand and glides his *pata* blade to strike a horizontal forward blow. The unexpected shift startles Murarbaji and he skips back, swaying his hand that holds the shield. Within a flash Tanaji moves his hand backwards in an anti circular motion. The tip of his blade brushes against Murarbaji, tearing his *angirkha* over his chest. He loses his balance and tries hard not to trip. In a flash, Tanaji strikes a forward blow. It lances through the shoulder of Murarbaji's right hand that holds the sword. Blood splutters out. Murarbaji keeps spinning, but feels his power waning. Tanaji moves closer still. One strike and it will all be over.

'No, Tanaji don't,' Shivaji weilds his fists in the air. Tanaji leaps back, away from the reach of enemy's *pata*.

Murarbaji slouches in fatigue. He realises that someone wants him to live, but he is still filled with a heady feeling that comes after killing a number of men. Despite the shooting pain that almost makes him clutch his hand and roll on the ground, his eyes rove. The man firing instructions looks like a leader. His face is familiar, someone he has heard of. He is fair, and wears a saffron turban that looks like the spire of a temple. The *angirkha* is of a pale colour, finely cut. His silvery sash shimmers in the yellow light of the torches. Murarbaji instantly knows who the man is.

Shivaji dismounts and stands in front of Murarbaji, whose eyes shine with hatred. 'Where is my master?' Murarbaji screams. 'Your *vakeel* has killed my master, hasn't he? I knew of your plan the moment

I heard the trumpets.'

'Chandrarao Sahib had welcomed your *vakeel* but he had an agenda. *Randichya!*' Moray's man calls the Brahmin a son of a prostitute. Something snaps inside Shivaji.

'Murarabaji, you are so clever,' Shivaji says mockingly, gritting his teeth. 'You are either blind or choose to be so. Don't you see that the people of your valley have become *ghulams*, bonded slaves? He used them, stole from them, tortured them and murdered them at his whim. The people of the valley live like helpless goats in your pens, meek and ready to be slaughtered.' Shivaji then stops for a moment before saying, 'And what did you do all your life? You made a show of your valour by terrorising the helpless peasants, sucking them dry in the seasons of harvest, so that your master could reap benefits. Kindly do not consider yourself a warrior. You are a petty bully, working for a depraved despot.'

Murarbaji looks to the ground, nobody has talked to him like this before. He breathes heavily in rage. Blood oozes from his shoulder, drenching his clothes.

Shivaji removes his hand from the hilt and starts pacing. This is a man he can use. He suddenly stops and says, 'You have another duty, a very noble one. You and your goons tax the merchants coming from Konkan as per your whim. If they protest, you slaughter them and feed them to the wolves. You do not even spare the lamani gypsies and their oxen. The ridges of the cart tracks going down to the coast are covered with the shards of their bones. Is that not true?'

Murarbaji does not reply in defence or otherwise.

'There is another world beyond the hill to your east, the world of Adilshahi. And there is another world far away from the northern boundaries of this valley, the world of the Mughal Empire. These Emperors and Shahs have built forts, palaces, gardens, mausoleums and baths from the wealth produced by our ryots. Their armies are fed by this soil. And they don't care if these peasants live a distressed, disdainful life of a *ghulam*, under men like Chandrarao Sahib Moray. And men like Moray don't even care if they live at all.' Shivaji stops for a while, then asks, 'And do you?'

Murarbaji avoids looking up.

'No, you don't care either. Your men have beaten and robbed a peasant just yesterday. His field, swaying with samplings, had been crushed by wild elephants, and hence he had failed to pay his share of the revenue. But your men turned a deaf ear to his pleas. First they took his oxen and then demanded his cow. When he begged them to spare the animal they attacked him. And how does your master dare to perform such vile acts? It is only because he has people like you, you, a noble soul of Javali!'

The night is almost over. Dawn sets in. The main gate is shut. The watchtowers over the ramparts of the wall teem with Shivaji's archers. The leader of the Marathas looks at Murarbaji who sways with fatigue, his hand fixed into the *pata* sword that now dangles loose. As the sun throws its first rays over the sky, Murarbaji faints and collapses in a heap.

'Get him out of here. I want him alive,' Shivaji swings around and says, his voice loud and clear. Something else happens near the house entrance. Raghunath and Kavji shove an abusive man out from the house. The captive has turned violent; his abuses can be heard from a distance. He is finally dumped in front of Shivaji.

'The ruler's brother Pratap has fled. Even this man was running away. He is Hanumanth, the ruler's estate administrator,' informs the *vakeel*, wiping the sweat from his forehead.

'Where will Pratap run?' Shivaji asks.

Hanumanth slowly lifts his head and spits.

'Kill him,' Shivaji orders Kavji who quickly pulls his sword out and leaps forward.

'Wait,' Hanumanth raises his hand to parry the attack. He breathes rapidly. His face has turned sallow. He knows that he is losing blood from the gash on waist at an alarming rate. 'Spare my life, will you?' he asks, staring at the Mavali rescuers. He has started panting and frothing at the mouth.

'We might, we just might,' announces Shivaji blithely.

'Prataprao Sahib has fled through a tunnel going northwest, and will probably head for Rairi,' says Hanumanth rapidly.

'How do we know you are speaking the truth?'

'That is his favourite hideout,' blurts the estate manager.

'Kill him,' Shivaji orders, waving his hand in the air.

A blade shines for a split of a moment in the first rays of the sun, while the ground turns crimson with blood.

Shivaji turns to look at Tanaji and says, 'Let the womenfolk and the children of the house go wherever they want to. Send escorts with them. And remember, the valley is swarming with Moray's men. Clear the nearby forest and hack the branches of large trees that block our view. Keep our best archers at the ramparts day and night. Our squadrons gone deeper in the valley must have attacked the enemy garrisons in the night. Inform all those who surrender that Murarbaji has already joined our military.'

The last sentence brings a smile to everyone's lips.

But Shivaji is not joking, he is serious. He wants to be powerful and needs men like Murarbaji who are ready to die for their masters. There is one last thing Shivaji must do before he goes into the house to see Moray's treasury.

***

A mile away, morning sunrays sneak in through the gaps of the hut's rickety door and reluctantly permeate the loneliness hovering around Dhondiba. Alone in his barren hut, he squirms in pain, his skin raw and bloody, his clothes torn, dusty rags. It is been two days since the men have beaten him with rods. All he wants is to give up and pass out, go to sleep and never wake up. Dying is far lesser painful and better than wallowing in one's own filth with broken limbs. Though it is agonising to think about his daughter's fate, it is also the root of his endurance and his will to live. She had run after the calf and that was the last time he had seen her. After the incidence not a single person has come to see him. Or tell him what had happened to his daughter, his Kapila and her calf. But there is solace. Without food and water he will not last long; his pain and worry will also die with him.

He thinks he hears a faint sound of footsteps. Outside, the dogs have started yelping with excitement. A wave of weakness strikes him. Someone has opened the door of his hut. He can see a few men peering in. 'Are they back to beat or kill?' He recoils in horror. The men have entered his room. He wriggles helplessly with fear as two men start tending to him, dabbing his wound with cloth drenched in warm water. He groans but feels happy too.

Then he sees them, two brown eyes looking at him. He wants to cry, for no one has looked at him with so much kindness, so much love. The man looking at him is smiling, patting his head.

'Your daughter is safe,' the man whispers to him. Dhondiba stares into those eyes and to his astonishment they well up with tears. The very thought that someone sheds tears for him stirs his soul. A wish to live overwhelms him, and it is not just the survival instinct of his flesh, it is his heart, yearning for life.

FOUR | HIS KARMA'S FRONTIERS

Circa 1656

It is just a week since Aurangzeb has come to Hyderabad. He has travelled three hundred and fifty miles southeast from Aurangabad to reach this place. But a *firman* has already arrived for him, as if the Emperor has been keeping a watch on his third son. The third prince waits on the banks of Musi River for the ceremonial camel to arrive. His memories churn. The first one is of when his father, Shah Jahan, then known only as Prince Khurram, had been a mere fugitive.

Aurangzeb was ten. His family had been camping in the northern parts of the Deccan. They had everything – diamonds and rubies the size of beetles and private servants and elephants for each of his brothers and sisters. They had emerald studded chalices to drink water from and all the comforts in the world, but they had been under constant observation. His father, the oldest of the Emperor Jahangir's sons had been accused of rebelling against the Emperor. It was a night to remember. The forest around had turned pitch dark. They had been waiting for the imperial soldiers to arrive. Father had been holding Darabhai who was thirteen, in his arms while mother had looked worn-out after sobbing for several hours. Her face was all puffed up and her stole covering her bosom was wet with tears. Aurangzeb was old enough to know that it was something serious - a matter of life and death. His mother's aunt, Nur Jahan, had married his grandfather, Emperor Jahangir who, casting aside all his other wives, had declared her as his Empress. It was rumoured that Nur Jahan secretly ground opium and added it into the Emperor's food, poisoning his mind against her stepson, prince Khurram. Her daughter from previous marriage was wedded to prince Sariyar, the Emperor Jahangir's youngest son. She had planned to make him the next emperor. She had demanded Shah Jahan's two sons as hostages, so that their father, her stepson, could be kept in leash. Aurangzeb was not afraid of being a hostage, because he was not quite sure what it meant to be one. But something else had nagged him incessantly. While he had been sitting near the entrance, waiting for people to come and fetch Darabhai and him, he had noticed something strange. Father had been fussing over Darabhai. It had been funny to see father tousle Bhai's hair, kiss his head over and over again, and gaze at his face as if to etch its outline on his heart. Aurangzeb's other siblings, Jahanara Didi who was fourteen, Suja Bhai who was twelve, Roshanara who was eleven and Murad who was just three had been sitting around their mother, silently gazing at their mother's face. Some had tried to bury their faces in her clothes. But she had looked distant, almost indifferent to them.

It was the first time he had felt jealous of his brother Dara. A question had haunted him too. Why had step-grandmother chosen Darabhai and him as hostages? Why not the others? What was so special about them? Much later, when Darabhai and he were put under house arrest in Nur Jahan's palace at Lahore, had he known the truth. It was not quite simple. Even if their step-grandmother had plans to kill them, they were protected by the grand wazir of the Emperor. He was their mother's grandfather, and the new Empress's father. Their mother's brother, uncle Abu Talib alias Shaista Khan was in Lahore too. And he had always loved his sister's sons. He had watched over them, had inspected the food given to them and had kept his personal guards to keep vigil at nights. Once when they were chatting, Uncle Abu Talib had unwittingly told them that the Empress had demanded Dara and any other child of the family. Uncle had said that the Empress had known that Dara was the fragment of his father's heart. The words had shattered little Aurangzeb. The truth had hit him like an arrow. He was regarded by his father as an expendable commodity.

He was the one his father would throw to the wolves to save the others in the family. But Aurangzeb had decided to keep it a secret, like boys keep skittles and bird feathers hidden in their closet. He had hoped that Father might change. At the age of ten any emotion could be turned into hope. Even the dark secrets turn darker only with time.

Old memories bring a bitter smile to Aurangzeb's lips. All his life he has sought his father's love, at least his approval. Mother had died when he was fourteen and his sister, Jahanara who could have showered affection on him, loved Darabhai dearly. Perhaps things may change once the Golconda fort is captured. The forty-year-old Aurangzeb suddenly feels a bit faint. The strong stench of burning human flesh and sandalwood churns his stomach. The northern banks of Musi have turned into a cremation ground for his dead Rajput soldiers. Under the morning sun, flames of countless pyres look pale and lifeless while the dark columns of smoke rise above them, robust and conspicuous. He might have lost three thousand men but his soldiers have slaughtered seventeen thousand Hyderabadi soldiers. A harsh rattling sound makes him glance to his left. Countless cannon carts are dragged by his men to be placed behind the trenches dug around the Golconda fort. Dust from under the cart wheels floats above his battlefield like a fog rising over a body of water, slowly yet assertively. Beyond the shroud of dust, he sees the fort over the western horizon, above a hill. Terraces above terraces of domes, minarets, spires, pillared corridors and arched balconies seem to be locked up inside the miles long, several guz thick, meandering stone walls. According to rumours, the fort is unbreakable, as is a diamond, but Aurangzeb has seen even flawless diamonds shatter when struck heavily with a hammer. This invincible fort is defended by eighty-seven bastions, with massive cannons mounted on each of them. But, according to his informers, the fort's storehouse of explosives is almost empty.

'My prince, the Emperor's farman has arrived,' Aurangzeb hears a slave announce.

He looks northwards as the sound of drum beats echo above the din of the carts. Narrowing his eyes, he sees a camel, surrounded by drummers, appear on the horizon. Soon the procession stops at a distance, waiting for him to make his next move as per the imperial protocol. Taking cue, Aurangzeb strides towards the camel, alone. The cremation ground, burning pyres, trenches, cannon carts, the fort, its bastions, nothing matters anymore. Like a little boy seeking parental approval, he is eager to read what his father has written. It is crucial now, more than ever before as father is getting old and weak. And that is where its importance lies.

A milling crowd gathers at a distance to watch him. He first performs *Kurnish*, by placing the palm of his right hand on his forehead and then bending his head forward, as if cradling his head in his palm. It is the way the Emperor is saluted, an act of putting one's mind which is the seat of one's intellect, into the humility of one's hand. It is an offering; a kind of promise made to the Emperor that the person would do all that is expected of him, without any questions or doubts. From the rider, Aurangzeb takes the robe-of-honour offered to him and then the epistle. Father has finally recognised his credentials. He holds the epistle as if it is a copy of the *Holy Quran*, touches it fervently with his forehead and walks away from the camel taking backward steps, all the way to the place from where he had started.

Mirza Abu Talib, known in his title as Shaista Khan, the 'cultured one' has avoided the *farman* ceremony. Instead, he waits patiently near his nephew's tent. He is the *subhedar* of Khandesh region. City of Buhranpur on the banks of Tapti is his headquarters. But he has come to help his nephew to take over the Golconda kingdom. After his arrival at Hyderabad, he had noted the celebrations over the conquests. Mir Jumla, Mohammad Sultan and the other officials had let their guards down. After four nights of feasting and revelry, the men had finally got back into their battle spirit. But his nephew, Aurangzeb had stayed put in his tent in the military camp, praying, reading the *Holy Quran* and ruminating. Aurangzeb had always been so, even as a young man, always grave, never caught laughing aloud. It was as if his youth had had met its untimely death.

There was a chance that Golconda Fort would fall into their laps without a fight, only by inspiring fear and showing them the extent of the imperial artillery. But, now, all depends on the farman. Shaista Khan, too, is curious to know the contents of the Emperor's decree. The sudden sound of footsteps interrupts his thoughts. It is Aurangzeb, his face flushed, striding towards the tent. He goes in without bothering to look at his uncle. Shaista Khan follows him in, apprehensive and worried.

Shaista Khan loves his nephew, Aurangzeb, like his own son, despite the fact that Aurangzeb is a staunch Sunni and he an austere Shia. And despite Aurangzeb is almost forty and he, just fifty. There are reasons for the affection he feels for his lonely nephew forsaken by his father Shah Jahan. Shaista Khan hates his sister's husband, hence loves his sister's son so disliked by her husband! But this is not the time to think about the past. It is time to watch the present as history unfolds around him. Outside, thousand cannon carts have taken their allotted positions. The artillerymen wait for orders from Mir Jumla and Mir Jumla, in turn, waits for Aurangzeb. The air is heavy with intangible energy. Thousands of swordsmen, crouch in the trenches and brave the scorching sun, eagerly looking forward to explosives smashing the wall of the fort.

However, all depends on what the Emperor's farman says.

Shaista Khan offers some privacy to his nephew. He gazes out from the window as the wind kicks the dust from the mounds of earth piled near the trenches. His mind ruminates over the past as well as in the future. Every Mughal Emperor's sons have fought for the throne, blinding or murdering their brothers. Even his brother-in-law, Shah Jahan had either slaughtered or poisoned his brothers. Shaista Khan's late sister's bones may be resting in the most expensive tomb called the Taj Mahal but her sons cannot escape their destiny. Only one of her sons will become the Emperor and the other three are born to be killed or maimed. Dara Shikoh, the forty-two-year-old first prince has been given the viceroyalty of several rich provinces. All he does is sit in his libraries, translate Hindu scriptures in Farsi, and hold seminars either with Hindu pundits or Sufi saints. Shah Shuja, the second prince is the *subhedar* of Bengal and a man of battles. He is given to women, hundreds if not thousands, mostly captured from villages of Bengal, and some gifted to him are from Persia and Europe. Aurangzeb, the third prince, the *subhedar* of the Deccan, is silent and religious, and has spent life in the battlefields, in the midst of death and despair. The Emperor regards him as the competition to his favourite son Dara Shikoh. Murad Baksh, the fourth prince is the *subhedar* of Gujarat. His senses are blunted by wine, and his mind, blinded by flatterers. Only a few pegs of fine wine are enough to entice the fourth prince and lure him to do anything.

'We cannot fight this battle,' says Aurangzeb, his voice cracking. Shaista Khan turns around, walks towards a wooden divan kept near Aurangzeb's charpoy and asks, 'Son, what does it say?'

'Read it for yourself,' Aurangzeb hands over the farman. He can trust his uncle, in fact, he is the only one left in the family whom the third prince can trust.

It is a short letter. Shaista Khan's brows form furrows as he reads, drawing the paper closer to his eyes. The letter reads:

My son, it is proper for the emperors and their sons to have lofty spirits and to display courage and military might to take on new frontiers. Time is of essence. The Deccan kingdoms had declared their vassalage years ago. They are technically the vassals of the Empire, our tributary states and are under our protection. This is not the right time to annex Qutbshahi. I am in touch with Abdullah Qutb Shah and have promised him cessation of hostilities from our side. They will pay revenue, and that money must directly come to the central treasury at Agra. Retreat immediately and cancel all your future battle plans.

'Strange,' murmurs Shaista Khan, wiping his brows with his stole. The air in the tent has suddenly turned hotter and more humid.

'What do you think, *Mamajan*?'

Shaista Khan waits before answering. He has spent all his life with the imperial family. His father and grandfather have been the grand *wazirs* of the empire. His aunt Nur Jahan was Emperor Jahangir's queen consort, his sister was Emperor Shah Jahan's queen consort. But what he has witnessed is unbelievable. Dara Shikoh has been given a glorifying yet unprecedented title of *Shah Bulund Iqbal*, the king of lofty fortunes. Never before had any of the past emperors allowed their sons to sit in their courts on a golden chair, kept only at a small distance away from the throne. For Aurangzeb the rules are decidedly different. He has been kept away from Agra and Delhi for twenty-two years now, and transferred from one difficult province to another. The Emperor has made sure that his third son is always short of reinforcements and funds. Aurangzeb's transfer to the Deccan for the second time too was a deliberate conspiracy. The Mughal-occupied areas of the Deccan, like districts of Junnar, Ahmednagar and Aurangabad give Aurangzeb less than ten million rupees a year as land revenue. Corruption is rampant and the collection, a hassle. It is a revenue-poor region. In the beginning, Aurangzeb had required support from the central treasury even to sustain his army, leave alone equip them with better arms. The treasurer at Agra reported to Dara Shikoh who was quick to blame Aurangzeb for arrears. If now, Aurangzeb annexes the Golconda kingdom and adds it to the imperial dominations, his income will increase several fold. The financial autonomy will set Aurangzeb free to develop his army. And with his killer instincts, he will also be able to build the strongest force as compared to all his brothers. In short, Aurangzeb will then become a real threat to Dara Shikoh.

'The Deccan kingdoms may have been the vassals of the Empire, but they have stopped paying tribute for the last ten years. The farman does not make sense. This shows that your father does not want you to be more powerful than Dara,' he says truthfully.

'He has gone blind,' murmurs Aurangzeb. His dream of taking over Qutbshahi is lost.

'All these years,' the third prince says cautiously, 'Darabhai has been busy with cerebral pursuits and philosophical discussions on infidels with men of theory, while we, you, me, and many others, our military officials and soldiers have suffered on the battlefields of Multan, Balkh, Gujarat and Deccan, wrestling with dust storms, floods, famines and plagues. While Darabhai has sought intellectual pleasure, we have fought battles of expansion and pushed the borders of the Empire, in north, south and east. We have slept on the ground, gone sodden with blood and have broken *rotis* in the midst of the dead.'

Shaista Khan nods and wonders, *How can the Emperor of Hindustan lack insight? And how can he be so passionate in his love for one son and hatred for another, both born to the same mother?*

'He has been more vicious towards me after my *Ammi's* death. He loves only the two of them, Jahanara Didi and Darabhai, both of whom look like *Ammi*.' He hears his nephew's words and looks at him. Aurangzeb seems to be talking to himself, as if in a trance, oblivious to his presence. He looks like a lost little boy without his favourite toy.

The uncle's mind goes back to a particular incident, just before Shah Jahan's accession to the throne, the only time when Shah Jahan had displayed his affection for Aurangzeb.

The winter morning had been bright and the waters of the Yamuna, greenish blue. The city of Agra had gathered in sheer anticipation to watch the sport. A large arena had been set up in front of the mansion occupied by Shah Jahan. The sand was levelled, the arena, fenced. The elephants had then arrived trumpeting, their trunks flying in the air. Once the fight had started, the enormous elephant bulls had grappled and shoved and locked their trunks. Men, women and children had squealed, cheered and yelled. In the midst of their combat, one elephant, the smaller of the two, had started bleeding. For a moment the animal had stood rooted with terror and the next moment he had fled towards the river. The other, seeing his opponent vanish, had turned furious, trampled the fence and charged towards the crowd. People had instinctively started swaying, stumbling and running like hares. Dara, Shuja and Murad had vanished. Only Aurangzeb had remained calm on his horseback, only to be thrown on the ground by the enraged elephant's whipping trunk. But the third prince, instead of fleeing, had drawn his sword and gazed at his own death. That might have been his last breath but for the quick intervention of a mahout. On that day, Shah Jahan had held Aurangzeb close to his chest, calling him Bahadur, *the brave one. Next day, the doting father had Aurangzeb weighed against the gold bars and had given him gifts worth two hundred thousand rupees. His bravery was celebrated by court singers in Urdu and Persian. This had been before the death of Shaista Khan's sister, Shah Jahan's wife and Aurangzeb's mother Anjuman Banu. Things had changed since then between the father and the son.*

'What have you decided to do? What about Mir Jumla's family?' Shaista Khan asks softly.

Aurangzeb looks at him, dark shadows of finality fleeting across his pale eyes. 'You will see,' he says calmly and continues,

Who can clasp the arms of a bride called kingship?
Only the man who can plant a kiss
On the lips of an eager sword
And bind its blade with his life
Firm, like in a kinship!

'Did you pen it?' Shaista Khan asks in admiration.

A disturbing noise at the entrance prevents Aurangzeb from responding. His personal servant, eunuch Mutamad, has brought in the Emperor's messenger who wants to know if the prince has a message to send. He does not look up but falls to his knees, his eyes downcast. The air turns heavy with bitterness and doubt.

'How is his Majesty, Shah Jahan, my father and the Emperor of Hindustan?' asks Aurangzeb.

'By the grace of Allah, the Emperor, *Padishah*, is hale and hearty,' answers the messenger nervously, sounding like a parrot. He holds his hands together in so tight a grip that his knuckles turn white and the veins on his wrist swell with bluish blood.

For a while none has anything to say to the other and silence grows within the tent. The messenger glances slyly at the prince. He sees a lithe man with a trim beard sitting on a gem-studded metal charpoy. With a posture unusually erect and head slightly thrown back, Shah Jahan's third son looks different from Dara Shikoh. This one is much leaner, and his tanned face is covered with sun wrinkles. His embroidered muslin Jama lined with green brocade matches the emerald-studded turban. A few daggers with jewelled hilts hang from the golden sash supported by a narrow leather belt. The messenger gingerly raises his eyes and looks into Aurangzeb's. They are pale grey. A shiver runs down his spine. The cold stare hints at a molten core of violence boiling in the mind.

'I will call you when my letter to the Emperor is ready,' says Aurangzeb, dismissing the messenger.

'Cancel the offensive, ask our men to retreat,' Aurangzeb tells his uncle.

The third prince remains alone in his tent for the rest of the day counting beads and shifting between his charpoy and prayer mat. Only eunuch Mutamad is allowed in, that too to bring the food. The eunuch watches intently as his master dips his fingers in the curry or tucks into his favourite cheese in spinach. Mutamad knows what's bothering the third prince. *The sorrows of the royals are as pompous as their lives,* he thinks, despite the genuine affection he feels for his master. He remembers his own life, his lovely childhood as well as his sinister past. That was another world, another time. He was a little Hindu boy named Venkat, whose ancestors fought wars for the Vijayanagar empire. After the fall of the empire they worked for Adilshahi. His neighbourhood had temples with ornate sanctorum, many pillared chambers and barrel shaped gopurams. They still lived in an enormous palace built on huge plinths made of granite. He remembers his last day of that life. He had been playing chess with a servant in a chamber that had countless pillars of wood, each opulently carved. The courtyards had shrines and one even had a tank embellished with a spout of a carved Nandi Bull with a gaping mouth that flung jets of water into the tank. His ears still ring when he remembers his mother's screams. 'The Mughals have come,' she had yelled. He had noticed her in the antechamber. She had turned ghost white. He could see the men entering his courtyard, mounted on huge horses. 'Deen, Deen, Deen, Deen,' they had screamed angrily. He had watched in horror as a horseman had picked up his mother and as another wrenched his small brother from her hand and flung him towards the wall. He could hear the skull crack. The screams, the blood, the limbs of of his grandparents, bodies of their guards and then the peace, his world had melted into a nightmare. His chessboard was drenched in blood. For some reason he had fainted and had woken up with a severe pain in his groin. 'You are a eunuch, and your new name is Mutamad, and Mutamad means trustworthy,' a man had said to him. 'He is so beautiful. A goldmine!' someone else had said.

Mutamad's master is too busy to notice his servant's face darkened with thoughts of the past, he is busy mulling over something else, something far more important. 'The reply, how must I reply to father's farman?' It is only late in the evening that he decides to entice his father with Mir Jumla's wealth. And extract maximum tribute money from the stupid king of Golconda. He summons his scribe and dictates,

What the esteemed Emperor has, most kindly, written with your gracious pen, concerning this slave has come like a revelation from the heavens. I shall act according to your wish and retreat. I shall send Mir Jumla of Golconda to you to be employed to serve the Empire. As the Emperor is aware, he is the richest man of the Deccan. His jagir *fetches him four million rupees in revenue and he owns some of the world's finest diamonds. He also has a five thousand, well-mounted and well-equipped cavalry and ten thousand infantry. His expertise in the field of artillery will enhance the might of the imperial army. And he, Mir Jumla wants to present you with a priceless diamond and 'one thousand one hundred and one' ser of pure high quality gold worth one and half million rupees.*

The other letter is to Abdullah Qutb Shah, the king of Golconda. It reads,

Be advised. We have already taken Hyderabad, and soon head for Kollur to capture your diamond mines. You could safeguard your kingdom from

total ruin if you release Mir Jumla's family. Do not forget that twenty years ago you had declared your kingdom as a tributary state of the Empire. Make haste; pay up the arrears. Keeping the current exchange rate in mind, the tribute of two million rupees, in pure gold, (either in your newly minted hones or in our Ashrafi mohurs) is due. The transaction will be carried out between you and me. And when this is done, we will give our consent to the marriage that you have proposed. But again, that will only happen if you cede the Fort of Ramgir and the territory around it, yielding a revenue of six hundred thousand rupees a year to me and this transaction too, must remain strictly between you and me.

***

Dark clouds gently slither into the southern sky of Javali. A flock of herons flies westward in the direction of Sindhu Sagar, the Arabian Ocean. The Koyana river cuts through the valley, its water a darker shade of olive green. On its banks, high above a steep and rocky hill, Shivaji's dream slowly moulds into reality. His vision takes shape in stones and mortar. A fort is being built on the hill's crest, half a mile above the valley. Shivaji has already named it *Pratapgad*, the fort of brave deeds. Bhorpya hill is girded towards the top, and has a table that is flat. It is about forty guz in length and breadth, a perfect place for a citadel, or upper fort. At its centre, the walls of a large court and private apartments have already risen above a large plinth. Around it, labourers busily lay large basalt slabs, finely squared at their edges, in lime mortar. At the southern side of the table, a few stonecutters hammer away in frenzy, making a deafening sound that echoes in the valley. Shivaji moves towards the northwest, almost sprinting, as if he cannot wait to reaffirm the gut-clenching feeling one gets as one nears the cliff. Moropunt Pingley follows him half-walking and half-running. Behind them, a few of Shivaji's guards march briskly to keep pace. Some workers have noticed him. They fall to their knees and slyly regard him from the corner of their eyes. He is younger than they had thought. Unlike many other employers, he glances at them, and accepts their presence. They catch the glimpse of his face – sun-swept yet fetching. His nose is like an eagle's beak. His large brown eyes are curious and responsive, not aloof or scornful. He has a short beard and a light moustache. They like his saffron turban that seems like a slanting temple spire with the few pearl strings attached to its apex. They admire his silky, pale, knee-length robe worn over tight breeches and his long woollen stole. His golden sash seems real. Some of them are moved by the way he looks at them, his eyes filled with warmth, an emotion that they had never encountered from men of power before. They feel him regarding them as men of flesh and bones, with minds and feelings. It is a strange sensation for them who have lived their lives like cart oxen, born to trudge, be whipped and breed to produce more resources for the men of wealth.

It does not take too long for Shivaji to reach the western edge. He staggers, trying to balance his feet against the blustery wind blowing mercilessly like a wailing beast. He tries to walk ahead without stumbling, as his robe balloons behind him. He leans over the newly built parapet and peers down. The northwest side of the hill looks like it has been hacked down by an infinitely huge axe. The vertical rock, black and shining has plunged straight into the coastal Konkan. Far below, the earth unfolds before his eyes, hilly, ridden with ravines, covered with patches of wild bushes. Despite the clouds, it is a clear day, without the usual mist that gathers around the mountains. The ghats skirting the hills look like serpents clinging to the slopes. Miles away, at the edge, the grey blue skyline has sunk into a thin blue line perhaps due to the emerald waters of Sindhusagar, the Arabian ocean. Not a single mountain stands so high that it can block his view of the sea.

'This spot lets you look into the horizon and watch all that takes place between Pratapgad and the sea,' he says. 'And from this side no one can enter the fort,' Pingle asserts, trying to balance himself as the wind continues to blow fiercely. 'Even if they ride on the waves of their imagination,' Shivaji replies with a smile looking at the stocky Brahmin. He continues, 'Unlike our other hill forts around Pune, this one cannot be besieged from all sides.'

Even as he speaks, Shivaji moves towards the south and passes by the stonecutters. The lower fort and its extensions suddenly rise into the range of his vision. More than a thousand men labour on the flat expanse of the lower ridge. He notices some women near the lime kilns. The bastions of the main entrance facing the south are halfway through. To the east, a long arm of the lower fort extension seems like an enormous war ship suspended above the sea of valleys. At its south-western corner, diggers scoop out the earth to make an artificial lake for harvesting rainwater.

Shivaji nods approvingly and looks at Pingle who had initially worked along with him on the drawings of the plan of the fort. Ten years ago the man with the intense black eyes and brooding mouth had knocked at his doors. Shivaji had taken just a week to decide. The man who had come to him was quiet, and said very little about himself. He did not talk about others, unless it was his task to scout information. Neither was he overtly polite or ready just to please. He stubbornly stuck to his view when he knew he was right. Incidentally, he was a Brahmin. But unlike many of his clansmen he did not treat his Brahmanism as an accomplishment. Over the years, Shivaji had discovered his many facets – a leader in the battlefields, a negotiator who spoke many tongues, a planner who was good with numbers and an architect with a vision.

'It is proving to be an expensive fort,' Shivaji hears Pingle comment. His dark eyes are anxious and he knows why. Niloji Sondev and Anna Datto, his financial advisor and treasurer have written letters regarding the burgeoning costs of the construction.

After ransacking Chandrarao Moray's treasury stuffed with a thousand *ser* of gold and five thousand *ser* of silver, Shivaji had decided to invest in a fort. For a month, Pingle and he had scouted to find this enormous hill in the middle of the valley. Together, they had worked with fort engineers on the structural drawings. On paper, Pratapgad looked like an eagle perched on a large basaltic rock rising like an enormous column over the valley. The fort had been designed to defend and protect. Shivaji had visualised it clearly – the protective walls meandering over the cliffs and ridges, approaching them, impossible and climbing, inconceivable. The ramparts were designed so as to have umbilical defence of two walls. Provisions had been made for bathrooms too to prevent archers from leaving their posts. The main entrance of the fort was planned with intricate details. The approach ran parallel to the ramparts so that the archers would never miss an intruder. The main gate opened into a small area in the front with an abrupt fall into the valley's abyss. This was to make sure that it could never be targeted by enemy cannons.

'I hope this investment brings us returns,' says Pingle, sounding stressed even though a majority of the funds are being drawn from Moray's treasury.

'Moropunt,' Shivaji stops and fixes his gaze on the Brahmin's face, 'forts can be built everywhere, on the river banks, at the confluence, on the islands in the midst of oceans, in the desert, in the forest, and on a hill like this one. Hill forts are most difficult to reach. But the foothills of most of the hill forts can be accessed by enemy cavalry. Pratapgad is unique. It is an invincible fort in an impassable valley. Only an enemy backed by a strong infantry can reach here. And the kingdoms around us rely mostly on their heavily armoured cavalry. Military strongholds like this one may not make us infinitely stronger but they will make our enemy infinitely weaker.'

The Brahmin begins to understand. He says, 'The enemy may remain oblivious to his loss of power.'

Shivaji nods and adds, 'Letting the enemy revel in the perceptions of his power is the first step to victory. Creating 'space zero', or *ranangan*, the battle-yards that help us do so is a strategy neglected by our native kings.'

Pingle loves Raja's definition of of *ranangan*, he has never heard of 'battle-yard creation' before.

'But it is not all about the battles,' Shivaji says softly. 'It is more about making the valley worthy to live for the people who are now our ryots. Call the *watandars* of the valley to meet us. Tell them that the valley is now one of our districts.'

Pingle nods.

'The valley looks red; this kind of laterite soil depends on rain. The ryots will need help if the monsoons fail.'

Pingle smiles. Unlike many *jagirdars* his master is interested in the science of agriculture.

'I want to know how much land in the valley is under cultivation. Have you found out what are the important crops that grow here?'

'*Ji*,' Pingle bows slightly and says, 'When the rainfall is good, which is usually the case, the soil here gives shorghum, pearl millets, wheat, maize, groundnut, tur and fodder.'

'Keep the records of the net sown area, the exact proportion of land under the various crops at a given point of time. Tell the *deshmukhs* and the *patils* of the valley that they will henceforth report to our revenue officials.'

'*Ji,*' Pingle whispers, while following Shivaji down the steps leading to the lower fort, concealing the joy he feels at the new responsibilities he is expected to fulfil. But he has still not received the list of *mauza,* the villages in the valley. In Raja's *jagir,* every village is a small world in itself, with boundaries carefully defined, encroachments avoided. *Paraganas* are divided into *tahsils* or *taluks. Tahildar's* office that keeps land records reports directly to Raja Shivaji. Tillable land is divided into fields; each registered in the name of the ryots, the cultivators. They are given interest free loans, and when the rainfall is low, the reveue collected from them is reduced accordingly. Even the land surveyors, who are regarded as outcaste by the society, are treated with utmost respect. He has seen them offering their food to Raja and Raja gladly eating it. Pingle will never do such a thing. But Raja Shivaji has his own definitions. The powerless always suffer, it is not just about protecting them, it is more about making them powerful.

Pingle knows that a thousand odd villages in Raja's *jagir* generate three hundred thousand rupees per year, with each village on an average giving three hundred rupees in cash or kind. This accounts for barely two hundred and fifty *ser* of gold per year. With Javali under them there will be considerable increase in the state income. But one thought has nagged Pingle for a while; he asks warily, 'Some of the valley's local *watandars* are men of wealth and power. If we push them, won't they turn into enemies?'

'Some might. Think about the ryots who have been the victims of the Moray's tyranny for too long. Coax the young amongst them to join us as soldiers; they can defend us in seasons between sowing and harvesting.'

'*Ji.*'

'There is something more. Dhondiba, the peasant beaten by Moray's men is still recovering. Give him oxen, farm tools and a field hand who can help him to till his land this season.'

Pingle nods.

Shivaji leaps over the last steps. He turns to his right and then marches towards the main entrance. To his left, a bunch of women are busy assisting their men folk. Their bodies are barely covered with grubby, frayed saris. They have noticed the men descending from the upper fort and have signalled the other women behind them. All of them then quickly scramble behind the parapet of the kiln. These women have been eking out a living in the open, at work sites, also bathing, cooking, and delivering children under the roving eyes of their employers. It is not uncommon for a younger woman to disappear and never come back or be found bleeding to death or dead, mostly naked, thrown in the wilderness at the mercy of the jackals. But the man who, they have heard is the new ruler of Javali, is young and respects women. But they can never be sure.

Between the kilns and the eastern extension, under the shade of a few banyan trees, Shivaji notices a few hammocks hanging on the lower branches. He sees a toddler, yelling, and a bunch of half naked children playing in the dirt, as cold winds continue to blow. Beyond them, billows of smoke rise above the canopies of the trees, making the air thick with the aroma of freshly baked roti made either from flour of pearl millets.

'Moropunt, get some warm clothes for the women and children. Remember, those who work for us are under our care, even the labours who work temporarily. Charge the amount to my account,' Shivaji says, his eyes full of concern.

They march towards the main entrance. A man has entered through the main gate. A few guards follow him.

'Mhadu!' Shivaji exclaims.

The man comes closer, his dark face flushed and his breathing strenuous. His body slowly adjusts to the stress of climbing the mountain and the thin air.

'What news?' Shivaji asks looking at his informer's tired face, dishevelled turban and soiled clothes.

Mhadu bows and steadies himself quickly. 'The Mughal armies have started moving northwards from Hyderabad to Aurangabad.'

'Where is Mir Jumla?' probes Shivaji.

'Probably in Agra. People in the camp say that he is carrying loads of diamonds and jewels to impress the Emperor. They speculate that he might be offered the coveted position of *mir atish*, an artillery commander in the imperial army.'

'Umm,' ponders Shivaji. The religious conflict between the Sunnis and the Shia is once again raging in the Deccan. Aurangzeb may be heading to his Deccan capital Aurangabad, but he will soon come back to attack Adilshahi. The time is just right. The kingdom has been weakened by the death of Mohammad Adil Shah, its ruler of thirty long years.

'And what is the news from the city of Bijapur?'

'Adilshahi is on the brink of chaos and is bursting with rumours. The Badi Begum is somehow coping with the death of her husband and also looking after the state's affaires. Her stepson Ali helps her in the matters of the court. Bijapur's grand *wazir*, Khan Mohammad, has taken military affairs into his hands. His rival, one Afzal Khan, has started inciting the new king against us,' Mhadu announces looking pensive, as if hesitating to say what he wants to.

'What does he say?'

Mhadu looks at him, his dark eyes clouded with shadows of uncertainty. 'It is said that he is keen to either eliminate us or tame us.

He says we are traitors, and he wants to spill the blood of the traitors to irrigate the hills of Maval.'

'And what does the Badi Begum say?'

'She wants to wait and watch. She is more worried about Aurangzeb returning to strike again.'

Shivaji does not comment. He has noticed Mhadu's feet – they are dry, cracked and full of blisters. The strap of his right sandal has come off. Shivaji's stomach churns. Thousands of scouts and informers have given themselves to him, to his cause: some are tanners, some honey-collectors, some village artisans. Their chief, Bahirji, has taught them different languages. They are the eyes and ears of his enterprise. Their feet walk miles without stopping, are bitten by serpents, bleed with sores, and are shackled if caught. But they walk his wishes, his aspirations.

'Wash your feet with warm water and apply clarified butter on your blisters. We have some stored here with the *mukadam* for the workers. The supervisor will also get you a new pair of sandals. It is dangerous to wear broken ones, you will fall and be hurt,' says Shivaji as Mhadu's eyes well up with tears.

It is only late in the night when Shivaji finally rests. He has eaten his evening meal along with Moropunt and Mhadu. Icy winds bluster with a shrill whistle as cloth panels of his tent flutter wildly, as if threatening to fly away and leave him exposed to the elements. Through the thin panels, he can see flickering lights of fires lit by his guards and can faintly hear their banter. Between him and the cold earth, there is only a small quilt made out of sheep's wool. Using his hand as pillow he looks at the dark sky through a small slit and notices that the southern clouds have drifted overhead. Various thoughts swarm in his mind even as he prepares to sleep. He notes them slowly,

Afzal Khan, the nobleman in the Bijapur court wants to annihilate us.

But there is another twist. Aurangzeb wants to swallow the Deccan. He will soon start another war, perhaps with Adilshahi. It is just a matter of time before the Mughal armies flood their borders. And if Aurangzeb annexes Adilshahi, a large part of the Deccan south of Bhima river, including the jagir *will become a Mughal terrain. If Aurangzeb renews the old peace treaty with Bijapur, the allied forces will prove dangerous. History might repeat itself. It is the right time to start diplomatic relations with Aurangzeb, the third prince of the Empire. It is the right time to form an alliance with the mighty Mughal. It is the only way to keep Bijapur armies at bay. It is the only way to get funds for our campaigns to seize part of Konkan under Adilshahi.*

***

Twenty-five miles south-east of Pune an enormous mountain rises three quarter miles above the Sahyadri plateau. The hill fort of Purandar on that mountain table is enveloped in darkness. One of its rooms is dimly lit by the pale rays of the moon. At first Jija Bai thinks she is dreaming but then she hears it clearly, the knocking sound. She quickly throws off the blankets as frosty air slices through her old bones. Gathering the *pallu* of her sari to cover her head, she moves towards the door trying not to stumble over anything. A million dark thoughts race through her mind. She pushes the wooden crossbar to a side and opens the door. A maid stands outside, holding a small lamp covered in a glass bulb, her face ashen with fear. A veil of soot and a strong smell of burning ghee linger.

'Sayee Bai Sahib is in trouble,' the maid whispers, her teeth chattering in the cold.

Without a word Jija Bai follows her to the chamber of her son's first wife. They walk through an open corridor joining the women's quarters, and are almost blown by the wind by the time they reach. It is warmer inside, a few earthen lamps burn in the alcoves of the walls made of stones. Jija Bai is alarmed to see Sayee sitting on her bed with her hands clasped around her stomach even as three little girls wrapped in woollen mufflers fidget at the far end of the room, almost on the verge of crying.

'Your mother is fine. I am here now,' she whispers keeping her voice as calm as possible and signals the maid to take them away.

Sayee moans in pain. Jija Bai rushes to her bed and asks, 'Is it bad?'

The young woman raises her head, and looks up as tears roll down her cheeks. 'Ma Sahib,' she says sobbing, 'I don't want to lose this baby. I know it is a boy.'

Jija Bai sits on the bed facing Sayee who has grown far too thin. It is her fourth pregnancy. The lustre women acquire when heavy with a child is distinctly missing. Her eyes have sunk into dark circles and her face looks gaunt as of a starving human. *How playful was she when I brought her home as a bride! And how seamlessly she had grown into a beautiful young woman,* thinks Jija Bai regretfully and mutters, 'Sayee, the astrologer has told us that you will carry this baby full term. You are also on asparagus powder of Shatavari. Have faith in our physician.'

'These spasms take my breath away. Only when they are unbearable do I ask the maid to call you.'

Jija Bai misses her son and feels guilty somewhere deep in her heart. In the past her loneliness had made her jittery. She had sought eight marriage alliances for her Shiva even before he was fourteen. She had made her home full with eight brides - Sayee, Soyara, Putala, Laxmi, Kashi, Saguna, Gunwanti and Sakwar. This had brought eight kulin Maratha families into her fold, the Nimbalkars, the Mohites, the Palkars, the Vichares, the Jadavs, the Shirkes, the Ingales and the Gaikwads. But she knows that her son loves his first wife Sayee, and she is his true friend. The others do feel neglected. And now, all of them are compelled to live in the residential quarters of Purandar Hill Fort for security reasons. And despite her pleas, Sayee has been fasting, eating only one meal a day as atonement so that a son is born to her. Jija Bai sighs. She remembers her home in Pune, the warm red stone building surrounded by temples and rice fields.

'Ma Sahib, do I worry you too much?'

She gently pats Sayee's stomach and says, 'Worry about him, he is your priority.'

The corners of the room are shrouded in darkness, as the light from the lamp fails to permeate the clinging, enveloping gloom. Jija Bai's gaze falls on a lamp and its flame. She wonders if her life has been like its wick – one end dipped in oil and another burning itself away. Her son is struggling, fired by the dream she had made him see.

'We will get through this, will we not?' She hears Sayee ask.

Jija Bai does not reply. Her Shiva is busy at Pratapgad, his military base in Javali. 'Without military strongholds, you will share the futile destiny of your warrior father,' she had once said to her son.

'My son, he will be fine, won't he?' she hears Sayee repeat her concern.

Jija Bai feels anxious and uncertain as she thinks about the destiny of the child growing inside Sayee. What has happened to the men of her family in the past, what will happen to to them in the future? Some have died fighting battles for their Muslim rulers, some have been murdered, and some are serving the Muslim kingdoms. She was born into a warrior family of Jadhavs who served the Nizamshahi. The last Nizam Shah was a shadowy king. His *wazir* Malik Ambar was a warrior and a good man. After Ambar's death anarchy reigned and noblemen started fighting with each other for power. Her father and brother had decided to join the Mughal. But before they could act upon their decision, they were beheaded in Nizam Shah's court. That was twenty years ago when Shah Jahan had personally arrived in the Deccan. Annexation of Nizamshahi and her husband's defeat in the hands of the allied forces of the Empire and Adilshahi had axed her small family into two pieces. Her husband was forced to relocate to Karnataka and serve the king of Bijapur. Their older son, Sambhaji was forced to do the same. She and her Shiva had continued to live at Shivaneri fort, near Junnar. The region had become unstable and was set to become a Mughal territory. Every day she had heard stories of slaughter, abduction, rape and murder. She was not sure of their fate till they had left Shivaneri in the dead of night and crossed the Bhima river to come to Pune.

Jija Bai looks at Sayee who has fallen asleep. The lamp has dimmed and the room has turned darker. She covers her daughter-in-law with a quilt and continues brooding.

Till today, for the past twenty years her husband has served Adilshahi like a loyal warrior. He is responsible for annexing the remaining parts of the Vijayanagara empire for his Muslim master and has become popular in the Bijapur Court. His fame has resulted in a political lobby against them. The head of the lobby is Afzal Khan, Bijapur's *subhedar* of the Wai province. The man has devastated Jija Bai's world, not once but twice. Afzal Khan had instigated the king and blamed her husband for kindling the fire of Shiva's rebellion. Her husband was captured. They had shackled him, paraded him through the avenues of Bijapur and had made him beg for mercy. At the same time they had attacked their *jagir*. Her Shiva had fought the enemy from Purandar and defeated them. Her husband was forced to publicly disown her and their Shiva before he was pardoned. Immediately therafter the king, Mohammad Adil Shah had fallen ill and remained bedridden with paralysis. In the absence of a strong king, noblemen like Afzal Khan had become powerful. His prying eyes had fallen on their son

Sambhaji, who had grown into a strapping young man. Afzal Khan had ordered him to annex the kingdom of Kanakgiri. Her son had led his men to the trenches near the fort and had waited for the reinforcements that had never arrived. During the ensuing battle, her twenty-five-year-old firstborn was killed. A cannonball had struck him, crushing his face to pulp. People say that Afzal Khan did not send the help on purpose. Some even say that Afzal Khan had bribed the king of Kanakagiri to kill her first son. Her husband had not dared to ask questions. Who could or would he approach? The king was on his death bed. There was no case and no justice. Her first son was a victim of political conspiracy.

'Freedom,' she had told her Shiva when he was a young boy, 'is life. Serving them means the end of it.'

She would ask young Shiva to note the hills, pointing to the surrounding mountains while in Pune, and say, 'There are forts up there. You will need several such military strongholds and at least ten thousand men trained in swordfight and archery before you can even lift your eyes to challenge the old order.' Her warnings had rung clear. 'You must change the definition of your karma and fight at frontiers never encountered by your father or his or even my father. These new frontiers will define you, the frontiers of your karma,' she had told him several times, always deliberately maintaining a steely expression in her eyes, unsure if her young son understood her words or not.

FIVE | THE COUNTERMOVES

Circa 1657

Three hundred miles east of Pune, the fort city of Bidar that stands on a high plateau, is always regarded as the north-eastern stronghold of the Bijapur kingdom. It is surrounded on all sides by a wall that is more than a mile in circuit, and is cut in solid rock and strengthened by bastions loaded with huge cannons. The city boasts off mosques, palaces, Turkish baths and a mint. It is believed to be impregnable to assault. But the Mughals have proved it otherwise. They have broken the wall at places by their explosive shells. The city burns and is surrounded by ugly trenches dug by Aurangzeb's men. The last of the trenches is wide enough to pitch tents. One of them belongs to the third prince.

'If only...' mourns Shaista Khan, sitting on a wooden platform and studying a map, holding the paper close to his narrowed eyes.

The map has been clearly drawn. For more than five hundred miles, the Bhima flows from the north-west to the south-east. Its roaring waters cut through the Deccan till it meets another river, the Krishna in Andhra. The Krishna is the Empire's southern border, and regions of Maharashtra and Karnataka, north of Bhima, belong to the empire. Adilshahi's north-east stronghold, the fort city of Bidar, has already fallen. Only Gulbarga needs to be axed away from the kingdom. 'If only the Emperor had allowed them to take Hyderabad as well as the Golconda fort, the entire Deccan north of Bhima would have been the part of the imperial dominations,' thinks Shaista Khan ruefully as he glances at his nephew, who is busy looking outside through the entrance of the tent.

The entrance to the pavilion is wide. Aurangzeb, sitting on a high divan, can see Bidar from his dugout – its protective walls fallen at places and two bastions turned into mere rubble. Inside the fort, some of the buildings still burn with a raging intensity. His job is done, despite all the political moves of his brother to stop him from annexing the Shia kingdoms. He had argued about the illegitimacy of Ali Adil Shah and sought permission from the Emperor to annex Adilshahi. His father had first refused but later had a change of heart after Mir Jumla had gifted the priceless *Kohinoor* diamond to him. That was Aurangzeb's idea. Funds and reinforcements had arrived in time. Mir too has now returned to the Deccan with the latest artillery recently bought by the imperial army.

'The Maratha diplomat is here,' Shaista Khan hears Aurangzeb murmur.

It is a spring morning, with a wispy mist settled on the earth. Aurangzeb has a long day ahead. Local landlords who have assured the third prince their support have been called for a meeting. Some of Aurangzeb's military officers who nurture new ideas of battle tactics have been called in the afternoon. But before anything else, they need to meet Shiva Bhosale's *vakeel*, an elderly Brahmin called Sonopunt Dabir.

Shaista Khan follows his nephew's gaze. A thin man wearing a red *pagari* turban emerges from the fog and walks briskly, businesslike. His face is grim as if he wants to discuss something terribly important. Two armed guards follow the frail guest. One can never be sure of the Marathas.

Aurangzeb glances at his uncle and smiles mockingly.

Sonopunt, the dabir of Shivaji who is assigned to look after the external affairs of the budding Maratha kindom does not miss the scornful smile. He bows deep, slyly glancing at Aurangzeb. The third prince sits very straight and busily counts the beads of his rosary with eyes half-closed. In the yellow light of the oil lamps, Aurangzeb's features appear sharp; he looks virtuous in his white brocaded robe and his embroidered *patka* turban. It is hard to imagine that this man is responsible for the Bidar massacre. Dabir is proud of the fact that he can judge people's characters just by looking at them, but until now he has not seen such a contrast – a refined facade hiding a dangerous mind! The truth tumbles out when Aurangzeb opens his eyes. A shiver runs down Dabir's spine. At first he thinks the third prince's eyes are empty but realises that they indeed have pale gray irises in them.

'I, Sonopunt Dabir, the advisor to Raja Shivaji Bhosale, bow to the mighty prince of the Empire and *subhedar* of the Deccan. I stand here with a humble heart,' says Sonopunt in Urdu tinged with a slight Deccan dialect.

Aurangzeb does not respond, filling the silence with invisible yet physically tangible impatience, as if he is in a hurry to get rid of the old sunken-faced Brahmin who speaks Urdu with a terrible accent. And why is this man, a *diwan* of a lowly *jagirdar* of Adilshahi, here?

Finally the third prince looks up, 'Say what you want to. Make it quick.'

'Raja Shivaji sends his humble greetings and a letter to my imperial prince. Raja looks forward to serve the Empire in the capacity of a regent and help the imperial forces conquer the rest of the Bijapur Sultanate. In return, all he wants is a formal recognition of his right over the land and forts in his possession,' speaks Dabir unhurriedly, empasizing each word clearly.

Aurangzeb feels an uncontrollable urge to laugh loudly. These uncouth mountain folks! He, the *subhedar* of the Mughal-occupied

Deccan, does not need any Shiva, and men like Shiva will not fit in the Mughal system. He wonders if Shiva knows the rock solid structure of the Empire. The head is the Emperor followed by his sons and the *wazir*, the Prime Minister. Decisions regarding the military appointments are taken by the *mir bakshi*, the army chief and the mir atish, the artillery chief. Provincial heads, the *subhedars* are assigned certain numbers of military officers called the mansabdars. High ranking *mansabdars* are given *jagirs*. But they are liable to be transferred. This is to ensure that they do not remain at one place for a long time and develop alliances with the local populace, a definite means to become a rebel. Rajputs are the only exceptions to the rule. They are allowed to keep their ancient kingdoms but are always kept busy at far off frontiers, thus preventing rebellion from their end.

'Why doesn't your Raja Shivaji go to Bijapur instead? It is easy to get an assignment as a regent with them,' says Shaista Khan with a serious face. It is his way to deflate the man's price and ego.

Dabir blinks. He cannot think of a proper answer.

Something flashes in Aurangzeb's mind. *Jagirdar* Shiva wants to rebel against his own king. In the Deccan, *jagir* holders are independent of any king, even when these estates fall into the terrain that officially, on paper, belongs to a kingdom. These *jagirs* are also claimed by inheritance, like Shiva's. They are allowed to have their own little courts and even thrones. The king is regarded as a mere overlord or a person above them in the order of hierarchy. Some of the *jagirdars* dodge paying revenue. Some become wealthier and more powerful than their kings, like Mir Jumla.

'Say in brief what the letter says,' demands Shaista Khan.

'The letter says that Raja Shivaji wants to help the imperial army as an independent regent. He is already in possession of the districts of Pune, Supe, Chakan, Indapur, the valley of Javali and the hilly Maval, along with the hill forts of the region. North Konkan is under Bijapur. If you allow him he will wrench the region from them.'

Shiva believes that we are retarded, intellectually compromised humans! thinks Aurangzeb.

'Shivaji Bhosale has, over the years, mustered more than ten thousand horsemen. He has created a fast-moving light cavalry, a perfect war machine for the hilly regions of the Deccan. He could even offer protection to the Empire's Deccan territories,' the Brahmin leeches on.

Aurangzeb searches for hidden motives. Shiva wants imperial protection to his *jagir* that, as of now, falls within the Adilshahi's territory. He is securing his *jagir's* future, when and if the entire region comes under the imperial rule or the old peace treaty is renewed between the Empire and Adilshahi. Shiva also wants to expand his *jagir*, take the coastal Konkan that, as of now, is in Adilshahi's terrain. The region has markets like Kalyan where wealthy merchants operate to feed supplies to sea freight, and salt to the rest of the country. Shiva wants to collect those taxes as well, all under the imperial protection and with the help of the imperial funds. Not bad at all!

'The benevolent prince has recently taken a regent of Hyderabad. That has kindled hopes in the heart of Raja Shivaji.' The fidgeting *vakeel* persists with an expression of optimism lathered on his face.

Aurangzeb's fingers work furiously on his rosary beads. The clever Brahmin is referring to Mir Jumla. What do these dimwits know? Mir Jumla had a weakness. His family was languishing in the dungeons of Golconda Fort. To ensure their release, Mir had been ready to do what Aurangzeb had wished for. Shiva's case is different: he has no infirmities. Shiva comes with strengths like his hill-forts, repaired and strengthned for battles. Once Shiva garners power under the imperial protection, he will surely bare his fangs. One needs special skills to hunt leopards that have the expertise to climb trees.

'How is Shiva's father?' asks Aurangzeb, suppressing a yawn.

The presence of two men with naked swords, breathing down his neck makes Dabir nervous. But Aurangzeb's question alerts him. He decides to answer briefly, fewer words, less problems. 'As my esteemed prince must be aware, Raja Shahji Bhosale is serving Adilshahi as a regent.'

'It is a good reason for Shiva to serve the king of Bijapur!' says Shaista Khan derisively while Aurangzeb jerks his head to show disgust. The action is involuntary. Petty *jagirdars* like Shiva and Shahji call themselves Rajas, the little kings without real kingdoms. The Shia rulers of the Deccan humour them because they are at their *jagirdar's* mercy in times of war. The entire military system of the Deccan kingdom is in a mess. Men like Shiva Bhosale must be made to feel like scorpions without their stingers, and tigers without their carnassials. It is easy, if, like his father, Shiva is removed from the hills of Maval and made to work in flat regions of Adilshahi, he will then be like an eagle without its killer talons.

'Uh Raja Shahji!' Shaista Khan snorts in disdain, pronouncing the word 'Raja' as if it were a derogatory term. 'How will Bijapur rulers react when they know that their regent's son wants to be a part of the imperial army to fight against them?'

Sonopunt Dabir glances at Aurangzeb's uncle whose eyes seem to blink with mock surprise. He says softly, 'Raja Shahji has disowned his son in the court of Bijapur.'

'He may even disown himself to survive!' the uncle pokes fun at the *vakeel*.

'People do anything for power!' Aurangzeb comments wryly.

Mutamad, who now stands behind the third prince, smiles ruefully.

The Mughals are constantly at war for more power, they call them 'wars of expansions'. The imperial invasion into the Deccan had turned his life into a hell. That war had killed his family and made him a slave, a eunuch and a child prostitute. After he was awakened from the deep sleep of opium dose and an excruciating pain between his thighs, he was allowed to rest for some weeks before he was brought to Aurangabad. He had no permanent home and was taken to the palatial houses of the *mansabdars*. The daytime had been peaceful with good food, special baths and good clothes. The nights had been nightmarish in the large bedrooms where huge men cuddled him first and then did something terrible. The pain was so severe that he could barely walk the next day. The soreness, the hurt, the humiliation, the shame and the insults made him comtemplate suicide. Eventually he was no longer a small boy. He was shifted to a large house where many like him lived. There, in that orphanage, an old caretaker took pity on him and started teaching him Arabic to read the *Holy Quran* and he memorised it.

'The old Bhosale has wizened with age. His son must learn from him,' Shaista Khan says while rolling the maps.

Dabir stares at the handsome man with a white beard wearing a headgear laden with jewels. He knows that it is tricky to challenge him. The ex-*subhedar* of the Deccan wields considerable power over the Mughal policies of the region.

'Or must we teach Shiva a lesson just like how his father has learnt?' asks Aurangzeb slyly.

The *vakeel*, also an advisor to Shivaji in matters of political affairs, has been in a tight spot many times in his life. He has never taken such insults and has always given a piece of his mind to those who've been cheeky. But the two men standing before him are the two most powerful military men. And he must focus on his mission as has been clearly outlined by Raja Shivaji. 'History may repeat itself. Our king, Ali Adil Shah will soon lose his north-eastern strongholds like Bidar. He is likely to buckle under the pressure. He may renew the old peace treaty and surrender some regions to the Mughal prince. He may form an alliance or declare a total defeat. Such situation may prove dangerous for us. If we are supported by Aurangzeb, we will be safe for a while, till we gather some more strength, some more manpower.'

'*Moshekeli, mushkeli!*' Shaista Khan murmurs in Farsi, his eyes shining with glee.

Dabir understands what the Khan has whispered and why he is delighted. *Moshekeli* means 'difficulty' or 'problem' in Farsi. It is because the Khan thinks that they have managed to shut him up, as it is difficult for him to answer Aurangzeb's question. He has heard that the imperial royals always resort to Farsi or Arabic in the Deccan if they do not wish the others to understand them. It is time to beat them in their own game, without hurting his objectives.

'*Maen ra babaekhsh,*' Dabir says to Aurangzeb in fluent Farsi. 'Forgive me' is what he means. The Brahmin continues to speak the language of the high and mighty with ease. 'I am just a humble *vakeel* of my master. It is not in my capacity to answer your question, my respected prince. I am here to carry your esteemed message to Raja Shivaji.'

It takes a while for the two men to get over the shock.

'*Aaghel, aaghel,*' an irritated Shaista Khan calls the *vakeel* 'wise' in throaty Farsi, his tone sounding an insult, and waves his hand in the air probably to show annoyance or to flash his diamond rings. 'Stick to Urdu,' he orders and continues, 'if your Raja wants to serve us, he will have to join our military ranks and become our *mansabdar.*'

Dabir smiles at the irritated Shaista Khan; men who like to tease do not take kindly to someone else teasing them. But that is the least of his problems and the real crisis is the uncle's proposal. A *jagirdar* in the Deccan is like a lion in the forest and a *mansabdar* in the Mughal army is a circus lion. Potentially defiant *mansabdars* are sent on the most difficult campaigns at perilous frontiers like the extreme north-eastern or north-western borders. Thus, they remain at the Empire's mercy for the vital supplies. The third prince may send Raja Shivaji to Assam, infested with savage tribes or to Peshawar where killer gangs of hill-men roam the narrow valleys.

The cannon thunder has stopped. An iora is letting off its vociferous repetitive whistles from the shallow valley to the east of Bidar. The bird calls sound more like an alarm than music to his ears.

'And there is another problem. The Javali massacre is still fresh on everybody's mind. We need time to think,' says Khan.

Dabir's face turns red, Shaista Khan's comment is utterly shameless. What about the Hyderabad and Bidar massacres? Siddi Marjan, the *jagirdar* of Bidar and his sons have been killed by Aurangzeb's artillery attacks. All his family members have been hounded out of their palaces, chased and slaughtered. Thousands of women from the city have already been dragged out of their homes into the Mughal camp. The third prince is known to keep away from women but his soldiers are granted the lease to please themselves.

'Meanwhile, tell Shiva Bhosale to behave. For Deccan will soon be the Empire's terrain. And the rebels and their supporters will soon be dead men. He will be responsible for the deaths of thousands,' mutters Aurangzeb.

Dabir wants to laugh out loud. Is that a threat? Men have always died in battles. Does Aurangzeb hold himself responsible for the deaths of his own soldiers? Or are the rules different for him?

When Dabir's palanquin had entered the Mughal camp, along a row of smaller tents to the right, he had heard men crying hoarsely, like stressful mooing of cattle. Alarmed, he had peered through the open slits of the dust covered panels. The sight had made his stomach churn. Men, bandaged with soiled rags blotched with crimson blood, lay all around the cramped space. A few caretakers, perhaps medics, were trying to calm their patients who were writhing in pain. He had noticed piles and piles of the dead, thrown in the open without even a shroud; probably the bodies were waiting either for a burial or for a cremation. *'How does it really matter after one is dead?'* he had thought, while out of curiosity he had looked carefully at the human carcasses, into which thousands of bulky rodents were sinking their teeth.

'We shall let you know,' says Aurangzeb, his eyes half shut. 'Technically, the territories of the Deccan Shia kingdoms are already a part of the Empire. And we do not need anyone to protect us from our vassals.'

'Remind Shiva that in the long history of our Empire, no one has dared to cross our borders and attack our terrains,' the uncle lashes out.

The *vakeel* tries hard not to wince in spite of the cramps in the calf muscle of his right leg. He bows deep, hands over the letter to one of armed guards and asks, 'What must I tell my master?'

'Tell him that capturing the valley of Javali and killing its ruler was criminal. From what we have heard, it was an act of premeditated, cold-blooded murder for personal gains. Not pardonable since it was not done in self-defence or on an impulse as a result of a heated argument. How do you think we can take such a criminal into our folds, even as a *mansabdar?*'

The meeting is dismissed almost immediately. The Brahmin's old frame quivers as he steps out.

Aurangzeb knows what jabs the Brahmin's head. The pesky intellectual! He knows how to hit them without warning, and leave them feeling humiliated. When the Mughals destroy and kill, it is war of expansions. But when others destroy and kill, it is crime! The third prince is not ashamed to tell that to the world.

***

The day has turned bright and the mist has disappeared. Mutamad gets busy. He has already organised four men. They hold fans made of peacock feathers to keep the royals cool and to flap the flies away.

Aurangzeb has forgotten about Shiva's Brahmin, and thinks about his full bladder and empty stomach. But he decides to get over with the meeting that has been arranged with Mir Jumla before taking a break. Shaista Khan, eyes closed in a state of bliss, holds the metal pipe of his hookah in his hands and hurtles rings of smoke in the air. A strong smell of mint envelops the tent.

When Shaista Khan opens his eyes, he notices Mir Jumla, grinning from ear to ear. The Persian artillery expert seems to be in an exuberant mood. His family is safe in Delhi and he is the new *mir atish* of the entire imperial army. The new artillery advisor has shown how the new cannon can be pulled by a single horse onto the field as opposed to the old cumbersome ones that required at least sixteen horses or oxen. The new weapon of fire changes the very means of combat, especially when enemies, like that of the ones at Bidar fort, enjoy advantages of long ramparts and countless strong static cannons.

'*Voila*,' Mir Jumla who loves to use French expressions throws his hands in the air and cries, 'time has come for my prince to enter Bidar as a victor.'

The victor and the vanquished are Aurangzeb's most favourite words. He smiles for the first time. There is another reason. The vaults of Bidar fort are stuffed with gold and silver. With that kind of funds, he can buy thousands of Bijapur's soldiers. The throne in the court of Siddi Marjan is made of solid gold, and it is laden with precious stones. The estimated cost of the throne is not less than forty million rupees.

***

It is been just a week since Dabir's return from Bidar. Raja Shivaji has suddenly called for an urgent meeting in the land fort of Chakan, just a few miles away from the Bhima River.

As the summer night descends like a raven waterfall, the land fort disappears in the darkness. A waning moon appears in the inky sky as ashen shapes of its light cut through the trees. The drawbridges have been raised over the moat and the gates are closed shut. The archers move soft-footedly on the ramparts. Scouts, assembled on the surveillance turrets built on the bulging bastions, try hard to scan the surroundings, as the loud droning of countless cicadas sweep across the forest floor.

Adjacent to the dark, sprawling courtyard is a *sadar*, the official meeting place. It has a room, the *khalbatkhana*, a den for secret discussions lit by two torches hung on its walls. Now, men fill its every corner. They sit on a thick *jajum* and watch Shivaji who stands near a wooden platform. Sonoji Dabir, Dabir's son Trimbak, Tanaji, Yesaji, and the fort keeper Firangoji Narsala look puzzled, almost confused. Cavalry captains, Minaji and Kashirao, prefer to stand near the lone window. Moropunt Pingle has come all the way from Pratapgad.

'The peasants in Javali need oxen and steel ploughs. We have emptied our treasury and given them interest free loans because once the monsoons arrive it will be too late. An empty treasury will not support our Konkan campaign that requires a thousand war-horses equipped with saddles. We also need battlefield allowances and supplies. We had hoped that the Mughal would fund our campaigns against Bijapur, but Aurangzeb has refused to form an alliance with us.'

Dabir nods in confirmation.

'We can still make them, the Mughals, pay for our campaigns.' Shivaji announces cautiously

'How?' asks Dabir.

Shivaji deliberates for a moment before he speaks again.

'Aurangzeb has deployed all his military at the north-east borders of Adilshahi, leaving his other territories in the Deccan exposed and vulnerable.'

'Who will dare attack their territory?' Yesaji questions, glancing at Dabir for approval. The elderly Brahmin, wrapped in a woollen shawl, does not say a word. He simply leans back on a large bolster, specially kept for him. Lately, even the coolness of summer nights has been aggravating his mild asthma.

'We shall,' declares Shivaji.

'It is banditry,' snaps an obviously nervous Pingle.

'Then all of them are bandits,' retorts Dabir. 'The Shahis of the Deccan have destroyed the remnants of Vijayanagara empire and looted the temple cities of the south. Twenty years ago, the Mughals had attacked the Deccan kingdoms, Nizamshahi was destroyed, and the other Shahis had become the tribute states of the Empire. In the recent past, Aurangzeb has plundered Hyderabad for extra funds to support his army. And if you had seen the devastation of Bidar, you would never have said what you just have.'

'The imperial terrain is regarded as sacred,' persists Pingle.

'By whom?' asks Shivaji as a faint smile plays on his lips. 'Bidar is three hundred miles east of us. The imperial army is busy invading deeper parts of Adilshahi. The region around Junnar and Ahmednagar is left without military forces.' His gaze fallen to the ground, he starts pacing and then announces, 'Tanaji, Yesaji and I will lead our men to Junnar while Minaji and Kashirao will go further north to Ahmednagar.'

Dabir is suddenly worried and bites his lip with his toothless gums. After Humayun recaptured Delhi a hundred years ago and re-established the Mughal Empire, no one has dared to mess with the imperial terrain. At present, they have two hundred thousand cavalry and more than three hundred thousand infantry. The Empire only fights wars of expansions. They invade but are not to be invaded.

'It is summer now and the nights are warm. We intend to live in the forests to plunder even the smaller villages of the imperial territory. The campaign may last for a few weeks.' Saying this, Shivaji rests as he is done with his task. The wind, encircling the courtyard, enters the *khalbatkhana*, making the flames of torches splutter in frenzy. Shivaji stops pacing while his eyes move towards the window. He notices a flock of white birds flying into the night sky through the patch of night sky visible from the window. Their wings rise and dip, then turn and twist. He watches till they become a white speck. *Even the birds have their freedom*, he broods.

'We need to grow strong to retain our liberty. When the time is right, the new king of Bijapur will strike us. There is a valid reason why they have not attempted so after their defeat at Purandar. Mohammad Adil Shah was bedridden for ten long years before dying recently. His son Ali was too young to take military decisions. In the recent past, Ali was too anxious about the imminent Mughal invasions to bother us. At present he is busy battling them.'

'You mean to say we have just been lucky to escape because Bijapur had its own share of problems?' Pingle asks wryly.

Shivaji watches his men. They know the truth as well as he but no one wants to admit it. It is the right time to put it in words. 'What else then? This kind of luck may not last for long. Politics is like a chameleon, it changes colours to survive, and in the Deccan, it may turn bloody for us, in an instant.

'To begin with, I have stopped thinking of myself as a mere *jagirdar*. And you must stop considering yourselves mere rebels. A rebel is one who defies an authority and undermines an establishment. Against whom or what do we rebel – against the ghost of Nizam Shah or our king Ali or the Mughal Emperor Shah Jahan?' Shivaji asks sardonically. He continues, 'They are the invaders, the intruders. We fight for our land, our freedom and emancipation for our people!'

'Their dynasties have ruled us for centuries.' Dabir utters wryly.

'Only because we have let them. Emperor Shah Jahan has blinded or killed six of his step-siblings. Our king, late Mohammad Adil Shah had captured his older brother Darvesh and gouged out his eyes. To disqualify his younger brothers from kingship, he had ordered the amputation of their ring fingers. I definitely do not want to bow to such men or the sons of such men.' There is a shadow of finality in Shivaji's eyes as he bangs his right fist on his left hand. 'We must now prepare for an offence before they do.'

Dabir looks worried. It is not as simple as Raja makes it sound. All the native Hindu kings have perished while defending their kingdoms. It has seemed like only the invaders have the right to be offensive. He remembers that their aggressions were opposed tooth and nail by the Rajputs for centuries. Eventually the warriors from the sands of Rajasthan have proved ineffective. History has repeated itself in the Deccan. The Hindu kings have perished as well, one by one.

'We must beat them at their own game,' says Shivaji and pauses for a few moments to watch the expression on his men's faces.

'Our need of funds is just one reason. The mighty fort of Bidar has fallen. Adilshahi's north-eastern frontiers may soon lose some more military strongholds. Aurangzeb is arrogant and evasive: he will either swallow Adilshahi or form an alliance with them. Both the situations are dangerous for us.'

Dabir agrees with what Raja is saying about the third prince's conceit. Aurangzeb's letter for Raja was given to him just before he left the ruins of Bidar. The letter said: *For now, we let you retain territory that is in your possession. This is the time to show your loyalty. As you are aware, the fort of Bidar, which was hitherto regarded as impregnable, and which has opened the path to conquer other parts of the Deccan, has been reduced within weeks to ruins by us. For any other man, it would have taken a year to do that which we have achieved. Soon we will blind the Bijapur rulers with fear. We will either flatten their kingdom or turn them into our eternal vassals.*

'We will be safe only if Adilshahi forces keep fighting with Aurangzeb. If we attack the Mughal terrain it may infuse courage in the minds of Bijapur rulers. They may continue fighting with the imperials.'

'You are playing with fire,' speaks Trimbak for the first time. He looks like a younger version of his father, Sonopunt Dabir, with his fair skin and sparkling eyes. Shivaji stares at his childhood friend and says, 'In the darkness, only fire gives out light. One must light it, kindle it, fan it, fuel it, or even play with it to keep it burning.'

'So will you again cross the waters of the Bhima?' asks Sonopunt Dabir with a smile.

Shivaji does not smile back but says, 'I shall do so without any guilt. We had the hereditary right to collect the revenue from the *deshmukhs* of Junnar and Ahmednagar. It was not a Mughal terrain; it was a part of our *jagir* in the past.'

Dabir closes his eyes; he knows that it is the beginning of a long drawn out war. Outside, the moon has reached the middle of the star laden sky and the air has turned frosty. It smells of woodsmoke. The midnight wind blows fiercely across the forest. The howling of the wolves has stopped.

A few miles away, to the north of the fort, the waters of the Bhima gush eastwards. On the river's northern banks, in the imperial terrain, a few men from Mang community have started beating drums, its echoing sound rattling through the woods, defying the borders of the kingdoms. The drumbeaters are born tanners, who collect people's waste in barrels at nights and carry them on their heads to dispose off far away from the habitat. They can also be hired as assassins. They work as Chandals, who behead the prisoners on death row. They are the forsaken children of the country. The sound stirs Shivaji's memories of other musical sounds – the wooden clapping of *kartals* and the metallic clanks of cymbals.

Shivaji was ten. The stone house had started buzzing with activity. It was now known as the house of jagirdar *Shahji Bhosale's wife. Villagers had started dropping by to talk to his mother about their problems and she patiently listened to them. They talked about the staple crop of sorghum and pearl millets, locally called jawari, bajra and rai. But even those had become scarce. The monsoons had failed for several years. In some years, it had rained a little and the sprouting cobs had raised their heads only to shrink and wither away by the scorching sun. But Shivaji had started liking the place. With his friends, Tana, Yesa, and others, he would roam the terrain on their ponies. It was a usual sight, the boys galloping away, some standing on the stirrups, as the ponies moved crazily across the dusty stretches. The air would tremble with the sound of their squeals, laughs and yells. The dust devils would not bother him any longer and he would not be afraid of dead animals and their bones. Something had intrigued him. He had noticed flocks of men with saffron flags going north. Always banging their* kartals *and cymbals, singing* abhangs *of a saint called*

Tukaram. He had heard people talk about this saint. He had wanted to follow a group and find out more about the saint.

One afternoon he and his friends had bolted across the parched lands, following the throng of pilgrims about to disappear behind the hills. They had galloped, cutting through the dust, leaping across the broken land. Something had made Shivaji glance at the sky. A large cloud, dark and heavy, had arrived from the south, dwarfing the hills of the southern skyline. It was dusk when they had finally caught up with the pilgrims who had camped at the foothills of a small hill. Shivaji and his friends had sat singing around the campfires. They had brought their ponies to a halt as saint Tukaram's poetry floated in the air.

जे का रंजले गांजले त्यासी म्हणे जो आपले

तोचि साधू ओळखावा, देव तेथेचि जाणावा

Shivaji had tried to hang on to each word, as if they were his scaffolds to reach some place that did not exist or he was yet to discover. He could see the pilgrims in the glow of their fires. Their faces had swayed with their music of kartals *and cymbals. A loud thunder had shaken him awake from his trance. He had felt the raindrops. The water had made his turban heavy. He had stuck his tongue out to lick a few droplets, relishing their sweetness. It was raining, it was indeed raining! He had looked ahead. The flames of the fires had vanished, doused by the rain. But they had still sung in the dark. The music had turned richer with another sound, the sound of raindrops. His heart had ached with a strange tenderness, the meaning of which he would know only in the future.*

The words had remained etched in his heart and mind.

The one who deems them as his own

The ailing and the dejected

The destitute and the rejected

That one is a real saint, that one is God.

***

The scorching heat of the summer morning remains trapped between the mountains around Junnar. Standing near the western gate, Salim and his men check the oxen carts, horsemen and palanquins entering the town. It is past lunchtime and the last cart has gone in. The carts stuffed with goods have come from all over, from the imperial cities of Agra, Delhi, Gwalior, Ujjain, Aurangabad, and Ahmednagar. Salim is already tired but his duty will be over only in the evening, after several hours.

'I envy the night guards, bloody *haramis*,' he snaps looking at his men. He is new but has managed to join as the head of the morning watchmen of the western gate who guard the town of Junnar.

The others chuckle, the night guards are indeed bastards. At night, with the market closed, they play cards and smoke their chillums. Most of them drink, and snore the rest of the night. The merchants, who illegally smuggle in alcohol into the town at night, bribe them with drinks. Salim looks inside – the plaza is filled with milling crowd. The famous market in the Deccan is bustling. Today is particularly a busy day, as loaded carts try to find their way through the moving throng. Their drivers shout abuses at the people blocking their way. It is noisy, with children running about, screeching. Beggars yell for alms while some sing praises of merciful god in throaty voices. Coolies, bending with loads, move behind traders. Richly attired buyers cluster around stalls filled with carpets, *jajums*, *shatranjis*, and pashmina shawls. Beyond the textile market there is the jewellery souk. Behind the souk stand rows of stables, where horse traders gather to sell their animals.

'Here he is again,' Salim hears one of his men.

The beggar, in an oversized grimy robe torn and darned at places, walks as if he is wading through knee-high slush. The sores on his face ooze with whitish fluid. His fingers are bandaged. He stinks like a dead rat.

That he may be a leper is a thought that Salim has already planted in his men's mind. Since then they remain away from him, disgusted and terrified to go near and ask questions.

The beggar moves on. He has noticed the reaction of the gatekeepers. He does not bother to look at them and is happy with the alms he gets. For the first few days, he just begged and got enough coins to buy food and it was later that he made friends. The beggars here accepted him when he told them that his wounds are not leprosy. He had removed his bandages and shown them his fingers, whole and healthy, not stubby and fallen. At night, they gather and gossip especially about rich merchants, their daily collections and places they hide their cash. Today, under the scorching sun, he trots from shop to shop, dragging one of his feet. A tiny copper coin or some leftover food from the shopkeeper's lunch or even a piece of a duster will do. He accepts everything with a smile. He moves towards a lane full of Turkish shops, overflowing with carpets hung on wooden stands. Their floral and geometrical designs overshadow the vibrant colours of their wool and silk. He stops in front of a particularly large edifice and stares at a rich customer, an African wearing a long white robe. He wonders whether the man is new, as the owner talks to him about the genuine and the fakes. His assistant unfurls one carpet after the other, first flinging them in the air with ease and then letting them fall on the floor with flamboyance. The customer drinks black kava, the aroma of its roasted coffee beans wafting in the air. The beggar moves his eyes away from the customer and the carpets. He turns to watch the shop accountant shoving pouches filled with coins into a large trunk.

The accountant notices the tramp drooling at his pouches from outside the door. He feels uncomfortable, jumps a step towards the beggar and gesticulates, asking him to vanish, and then spits at him, saying 'Let your good eye that casts a spell on our collection go blind!'

The beggar disappears, dissolving in the milling crowd like sugar in water. He is not seen by anybody even as night falls and the shops start closing. And nobody misses not sighting him.

***

Shivaji leads his horse carefully as the river Bhima whirls around his feet before flowing downstream. A thousand Mavali horsemen follow him. The soil of the Mughal terrain that was previously a part of his father's *jagir* feels strange to touch after the river water. He and his men mount their horses and kick them to get into a canter. A crescent moon hangs overhead as Shivaji and Tanaji lead their men to Junnar. Within a few hours of riding in the dark, Shivaji finally spots it - the silhouette of a hill, rising three quarters of a mile above the plain. No one can really guess that the fort Shivneri is perched on the hill's crest. A strange pain cuts through his heart. He was born there. His earliest memories are of his brother's face, mischievous yet smiling. He had not seen his Dada Sahib for twenty long years, and he will never see him again. Yes, that is what he called his older brother, whose face was blown off by a cannonball. His brother had become the victim of Afzal Khan's hatred for their father.

Shivaji gathers his mind and brings it to the present. At the end of the northern skyline, a shadow of Junnar's outer wall is clearly visible. They are already thirty miles into the Mughal terrain. It is strange that they have faced no resistance yet. No one seems to have heard the hoofbeats. But Shivaji is not surprised. His scouts have been roaming the terrain for months. The Mughal have become smug, and confident. They fear no invasions and even believe that their region is sacred. At last, at the northern horizon Shivaji notices an outline of a wall. Beyond the wall, the night sky glows pale yellow. The morning star of Venus shines bright in the east when they reach the base of the wall and gallop along its shadow. The outer wall is not fortified with a moat and there are no drawbridges to cross. As his scouts have already informed him, there are no archers or guards on the ramparts. He senses Tanaji slowing down his horse. Time has come to enter Junnar. They halt at a particular point, near a gate facing east. The tired and thirsty horses have started snorting. The animals are quickly taken away by caretakers who have ridden with Shivaji. Men with iron hooks and ropes are already at work. He waits as Yesaji hovers behind him. The ropes are flung. In the light of a single flickering torch held by Tanaji, the shadows of his men start scaling the wall.

'Clear,' Shivaji hears Tanaji as he moves towards the wall. The wall is not high and the ropes are thick, easy to hold and grip. The ramparts soon are crowded with his men. Some of them begin to scale down the wall on the other side to enter the town. Shivaji jumps over the flat terrace of the western bastion to scout; he likes to see for himself even though his men consider it as a security hazard. Below, between the market and the gate, a few men, probably guards, lie flat around the dying fires. They look very still, probably dozing on wine. The plaza is deserted and shops shut but the place is well lit by a number of torches placed in sand filled iron baskets. Beyond the market, residential buildings stand clustered, dark and aloof. A few minarets and temple spires rise above them and glimmer in faint moonlight.

His men move across the plaza, noiseless, like predators. It is time to enter the wealthy town, now a part of the imperial territory. Tanaji is waiting for him to descend. He moves towards the rope and scales down facing the wall and taking short backward leaps. A shiver runs through his body as he puts his feet on the ground – Junnar, the town his father loved. His eyes wander eagerly. He notices a beggar, standing with Salim at the market entrance. The beggar waves his hand and darts towards him, pointing at the eastern gate. Shivaji wants to know what the beggar implies. He notices gatekeepers scrambling to get up, their minds still in a drunken stupor. Some have started yelling. Tanaji along with a few swordsmen run towards the unsteady guards. The yells grow louder while the imperial dust is sodden with blood of the imperial guards for the first time in history.

Shivaji waits with the beggar while Salim joins them. The leader of the Maratha marvels how his scouts have seamlessly transformed into a beggar and a Muslim guard. Bahirji's men have surpassed all his expectations. Tananji and his men return, their swords dripping with blood. The beggar disappears with them. He seems to know the shops of cash-rich merchants in the market. They break open the wooden shutters and go straight for the iron vaults. The town seems to have woken up and the air vibrates with screams of the residents. The beggar turns up again, wielding an axe, and gives Shivaji a signal. Shivaji wrenches out his sword from his scabbard and runs behind the beggar as Yesaji follows them. They stop in front of a large shop, its wooden doors closed shut. Before they can kick the door, it is opened from inside and a few men jump out brandishing swords. They are not trained swordsmen and thus, it takes only a few moments for them to fall. Shivaji enters the shop that is lit by a small oil lamp. With his axe, the beggar breaks open the trunk to spill across the floor, countless *Ashrafi mohurs* of high quality gold.

Behind the market, two hundred Arabian horses are taken from the stables. Such fine horses are hard to come by. Tonight the fine animals will be used as the carriers of the plunder. Stolen Mughal horses will carry the stolen Mughal wealth to Shivaji's terrain.

Six | An Ant Flies to the Sky

Circa 1657

Jija Bai has been nervous for the past few weeks. Every day seems like a punishment. The thought of her son in the Mughal terrain is far more torturous than she had imagined. Many hours are spent in praying, many nights lying awake in bed. But her excruciating wait is finally over. Her son has come back from the Mughal territory, along with the yearly monsoon from the south-west. The rain clouds cruise above her like flying elephants on a mission. But her eyes long to see her son. She waits for him at the western side of Purandar Fort. The Kedareshwar temple of God Shiva stands on a hillock rising above the Purandar hill. She stands forlornly near the statue of God Shiva's mount, Nandi, as her ears pine to hear her son's voice. She has purposely kept her maids away. She needs to speak to her son in private.

'Ma Sahib...' She hears her son call out to her. Her frail body shivers.

'Do you want to ask something?' he whispers, touching her feet. She stares at him – he has become thinner and darker. She notices fine lines under his eyes. Her stomach churns. While she lives a comfortable life, mostly within the walls of their hill forts, he stays in the wilderness of enemy terrain, sleeps in the open, spends his days galloping under the sun, with the shadow of death looming over him. A sob chokes her. She waits till her throat becomes clear and says, 'You have plundered the terrain of the imperialists.'

Shivaji remains silent with his eyes fixed on his mother who had recounted to him the stories of the invaders. He remembers what she had said long time ago while her eyes had shone with rage and helplessness 'They have two weapons – one, their mind, pitiless, remorseless and empty of scruples, and the other, our mind, servile and fearful.'

'How could you not think of the consequences?' she asks. He had not told her about his plans. *It was easy to tell him about creating new frontiers when he was a small boy, safe under her wings,* she thinks.

'You have sowed the seeds of new frontiers in my mind, Ma Sahib, and they have turned into golden cobs of fearless dreams. They are seeped in ideas of freedom,' she hears her son say, as if he reads her mind and then frames his replies, 'will the armies of the empires and the kingdoms be kind if I refrain from doing that which I have?'

She fidgets uneasily and wraps her shawl around her shoulders. The wind has turned gustier. She knows what he means. Once she had told him the story of eastern Kabul, ruled by Maharaja Jayapala of the Hindu Shahiya dynasty, six centuries ago. The Turks had started gnawing at his borders. His cavalry of countless elephants had crushed the marching armies. Then Mohammad Ghaznavi had arrived with his fifty thousand soldiers. Jayapala had declared truce, paying heavy ransom. Within a few years Ghaznavi had returned. He had stormed, pounded, and seized seventy million coins and seven hundred thousand carts of gold and silver. The bloods of men, women and children had flown into every stream, river, well and lake. There was not a drop of colourless water to drink.

'If you fight them, they kill you; if you declare truce, they deceive you; if you kneel, they behead you. Now you choose your option,' she had told him a few years ago.

'After Maharaja Jayapala's fall, the dice of destiny was thrown against Hindustan. The invaders had arrived. They did not need provocation to be rabid,' her son whispers.

'I am worried about the present. The Mughals may not waste time. They may soon come, within days,' says she, not wishing to let go.

He points at the sky. 'Mother, look at those dark clouds. They are on a mission. It is pouring in the valley. The rivers and streams are flooded. The trails and tracks have disappeared under water. They will have to wait for three long months to enter this hilly region.'

She smiles nervously. The *goorav* seems to have finished his ritualistic prayer. He emerges crouching from the small door of the temple and comes towards them. His salver has a silver lamp, its flame flickers in the wind. She holds her hand on the flame of the lone lamp and then touches her forehead, seeking blessings from the fire used in worship. As the *goorav* turns toward her son to offer fire blessings, she glances at the sky; the clouds indeed seem ready to pour. She quickly enters the small temple. The linga, adorned with freshly plucked mountain flowers glows in the light of several earthen lamps. The power of God Shiva, of destruction and creation, has turned tangible in that small space. It is almost as if Jija Bai can touch it or even take some of it away with her. Her son has followed her. Shivaji kneels, his hands folded, his eyes closed.

I have done what I had to do. They will do what they have always been doing. And you do what must be done, he prays in his mind.

When they come out, he tries to hold her hand to support her on the steps but she is quick to jerk her hand away. He smiles, and knows that she has always cherished her independence. Her freedom and her self-reliance had been and continue to be her most prized possession. He stares at her - the large pearls in her nose ring and the huge red vermilion *kumkum* on her forehead makes her face look small, like it has shrunk. Her skin has gone pale and is freckled. Her eyes look tired with large dark circles around them.

Misty clouds whirl around them making the world invisible. She is not done yet. 'After the monsoons Aurangzeb will unleash his squadrons. Our small region will soon burn in fires of arson. Peasants will flee. Women and children will be taken as slaves,' her voice cracks with a sob in her throat and her eyes shine with tears.

'The Mughals think that it is their imperial right to invade under the patriotic title of war of expansions. They do not need any provocation,' says Shivaji, his eyes reflecting a steely finality that she has not seen before.

'Your father left us to serve Bijapur twenty years ago. Your father's rival in Bijapur court, Afzal Khan, killed your brother by not sending him reinforcements, on purpose. Shivaba, I cannot lose you,' his mother tugs at her last defence.

'Death is final yet fickle. I do not have to be in the Mughal territory to die. I can die here, in the safe confines of Purandar, of snakebite!'

Jija Bai winces. 'But offending Aurangzeb is like stamping on a snake, it is suicidal.'

'Do you think that living a coward's life will make me immortal? Ma Sahib, think, what will happen if Bijapur's Queen Begum and her son Ali Adil Shah renew the old peace treaty with Aurangzeb?"

Jija Bai does not say a word, she can no longer hold back her tears. The alliance between the Empire and the Adilshahi sultanate had once proved disastrous.

'We plundered the Mughal terrain because we needed the money to expand our military. Also we wanted to kindle the fire of courage in the hearts of Bijapur rulers. We wanted to show them that one can fight the Mughals,' he says. 'And, despite our efforts, the renewal may take place. Peace at one front promotes war at the others. And if that happens, guess who may march in to get us?'

'Who?' Jija Bai asks anxiously.

'Either Khan Mohammad, the General of Bijapur or Afzal Khan. Ali Adil Shah has grown up into a clever man, he will take the enmity between Afzal Khan and Pitaji Sahib into consideration. Afzal Khan is also the *subhedar* of the Wai province to which Javali once belonged. Once the peace prevails at their north-eastern frontiers, Afzal Khan will be free to deal with us.'

Streams of tears wet Jija Bai's cheeks.

'But I am prepared, Ma Sahib,' Shivaji says and smiles mysteriously. And together they walk to the place where the bearers wait with her *mena* and his palanquin.

As the bearers climb another hillock called Rajgadi, he muses quietly. He has his own laws of war and they say that the imperials are not gods and their terrain not sacred. If his men, even as much touch a woman, there is only one punishment: the perpetrator is pushed down from a steep cliff, into the abyss. This is done without blindfolding the criminal, so that he sees his death before he vanishes into the valley!

On reaching their private apartments on the Rajgadi hillock, Jija Bai says, 'I want you to meet our very special guest. We had sent a message about his arrival when you were in the Mughal terrain.'

***

It is dark inside the stone buildings, and warm. Seeing them enter, the maids busy with their morning chores quickly cover their heads with the *pallu* of their saris. A few disappear into inner chamber. Two are back within moments, holding a bundle. Excitement runs through his body, and it is divine, akin to seeing thousands of little lamps in a temple. He is scared to move, or even make any sound. Jija Bai takes the bundle in her hands, so carefully as if it contains her own, still pulsating heart, freshly wrenched out of her body. She gently shows what she holds to her son.

He stares at the small face of his son, his first son. Tiny, as if carved by a sculptor out of fine, alabaster marble, using a toy hammer. A short mop of curly hair stands on his head like a crown. His slender lips quiver as if he is about to smile or cry. His eyes are closed. There is a big dot on his forehead made with soot to ward off evil eye. Shivaji gingerly touches the boy's face with his index finger and is shocked by the tenderness of the baby's skin. The twenty-day old boy starts to smirk and opens his eyes at once; they are not brown like his own. The boy has black, limpid eyes, like his mother's.

'Go meet his mother,' nudges Jija Bai.

Shivaji enters the birth chamber as several maids, sitting around a bed, scramble, bow to him and exit hastily. The pale light of a few oil lamps fail to reach all the corners of the room. Mercifully, a sudden burst of rain starts pounding on the roof, driving out the stubborn stillness piled up around his wife. In that large foyer meant for women to deliver their babies, his Sayee sits on a huge mahogany bed, wearing a peacock green sari, the colour he likes. He removes his turban and stands in front of her, letting his mane fall on his shoulders. She looks up and stares at him unbelievingly; he looks handsome, his brown eyes, his gently curling tresses and the corded muscles of his shoulders visible through his *angirkha*. Her heart fills with enormous pride, and she feels scared that it might just burst. It has been a few months since she had set her eyes on the man she has loved ever since they were married, when she was ten and he, a year older.

'Did you see him?' she asks, smiling.

He looks at her without blinking as his body shudders with fear. What he has heard is true. Her illness seems so real now that he is with her. Her doe eyes have dark circles around them and her collarbones jut out from near the hemline of her blouse. She has not bothered to cover her head with her *pallu*. He notices that her long curls are all gone, taken as pillage by her illness. He takes her hands in his own, they have lost their softness. He raises them to inspect closely, they look as if they belong to an old woman. The skin has shrivelled making the bluish veins look swollen, like rivers in the valleys seen from the hill forts.

'He is beautiful and he has your eyes,' he whispers, looking into her dark, moist eyes, shinning with mysterious happiness.

She frowns and says, 'I hope he is born with your vision."

'And your wit,' he intercepts and asks, 'have you and Ma Sahib decided on his name?'

She hesitates and says, 'I thought Sambhaji will be best suited. We have lost your brother, respected Dada Sahib. Our boy might fill the void thus formed in Ma Sahib's life.'

Shivaji stares at his young wife. She wants to name her son after his slain brother. He draws her closer. Sayee rests her head on his chest. Her eyes slowly fill with tears. She does not want him to know that during childbirth she had bled excessively. The fort midwife has warned that such bleeding could lead to something far more serious called the 'childbirth malady'. It claims half the women before their baby is two years old. But he knows and knows more. The fort medic suspects tuberculosis. Shivaji feels utterly helpless as he tries to hide his knowledge. He is as powerless as a soldier who has lost his sword on a busy battlefield.

'I am glad our son has been born in Purandar. This fort has taught you that you could stop them,' she murmurs.

'It is true,' he says, remembering Musekhan's defeat.

'You need to go, we shall meet later in the day,' she whispers, trying to push the sobs down her throat.

She is right. Today's meeting is crucial. The pillage from the Mughal territory has been brought to Purandar. They need to plan how to put the funds to use. The construction of Pratapgad proved to be expensive. After Javali's capture, the number of his horsemen has risen to more than ten thousand. They are directly paid from the state treasury. He also plans to expand his infantry.

'Are you worried about the Mughal attacks?' he asks her softly.

'The Sahyadri Mountains in the monsoons offer divine protection. No one can enter this region. You have time,' he hears Sayee. Her words render him speechless. Lying here, while her life is drained out of her slowly but steadily, she even contemplates the military consequences and their solutions.

'Sayee,' he barely whispers still holding her close to him, 'you surprise me.'

'I cannot do anything else but think. And I cannot think of anything else but you,' she admits candidly. 'Please do not have doubts. Earnest and truthful karma is pregnant with wonders. Do you remember Mukta Bai's *abhang*? Isn't it so relevant even after centuries of having been written?' she asks softly, as her lips quiver with memories, 'When we were children we used to sing it often.' She pauses for a while and starts humming.

मुंगी उडाली आकाशी, तिनि गिळिले सूर्याशी
थोर नवलाचे झाला, वांझे पुत्र प्रसवला …

Shivaji smiles. Sayee has this habit of saying what she wants to through verses of famous saints. And she has memorised the writings of Mukta Bai, the younger sister of saint Gyaneshwar who had risen above superstitions and rituals of Hinduism. Mukta Bai was the sibling of this original philosopher. Her verses are Sayee's favourite. Especially this one is so meaningful. An ant has flown to the sky and swallowed the sun. A miracle has taken place; a barren woman has borne a son.

'You live in my heart, Sayee,' he says softly.

'Mukta Bai says, His spirit lives in our soul and only He is the abode of our hearts,' replies Sayee.

Shivaji knows. She is preparing him for her death.

He is reluctant to leave; there is so much to say. But men are waiting for him. Today he is to announce the names of his central ministers. Moropunt Pingle will be rewarded with the prime-ministership, and will henceforth be called the *peshwa* of the Maratha kingdom. Nilo Sondev will continue to be the *muzumdar*, and look after the financial matters of the state. Anna Datto, the scholar of mathematics, will assist Nilo Sondev and also be the *surnis*, the man responsible for the revenue collection. Yesaji Kank will be the commander of Maval infantry. Tanaji Malusare will head the infantry garrisons at Konkan. Sonopunt Dabir will continue to be the *dabir* and look after the external affirs. Raghunath Ballal will be elevated to the position of the state *subnis*, the paymaster general who will work with the *peshwa*. And Netoji Palkar will be the *sar-e-naubat* – commander-in-chief of the Maratha army. Most of these men will also command Maratha squadrons in battles and defend the state in times of war. Shivaji remembers that Netoji Palkar has to meet Murarbaji, the new fort commander of Purandar to orient the new *quiledar*.

'Ma Sahib has made special food, chicken rassa with lots of pepper and *basundi*, for desert. It is sprinkled with saffron just the way you like it. She will not eat her dinner without you,' he hears his wife's plea.

Shivaji's heart aches. He pays his men every month. It is not a big amount, but they do not complain. The cheerful, mostly balute men eat dry and even stale *roti* made of bajra, with onions and salt to taste. When on the move, they live only on poha, flattened rice flakes and wash it down with water. His war-horses and mules, sometimes, have to starve, take the blows of the blades, and die in the battlefields. However, their loyalty never falters. These men and war animals form the foundation to his dream. In their honour, he has vowed to become a vegetarian and eat only one meal a day.

***

The enormous bastions are made of black stones, one a little bigger than the other. When Murarbaji had approached the bastions for the first time, he was surprised to discover that a gate to enter the fort was hidden between them. The ramparts of the fort wall run above the gate where a few archers march with large quivers on their shoulders. They know that he has come to the fort just the day before and that he might be their new chief. They wave at him, smiling. Few rain drops fall on him suddenly. It is a good omen, he thinks, looking at the sky. The wind has turned wild, making it difficult for him to stand still. For a moment, his eyes blink; a lightning breaks across the sky. It thunders, making the hills tremble as sheets of rain start falling on the steps between the bastions. He runs for cover and stands under the massive stone arch of the gate along with a few gatekeepers stationed there to mind the entrance.

Javali was his past. That moment when he had collapsed unconscious on the battlefield had been the end of his old world. He had woken up with a huge vertical gash on his shoulder and an unbearable pain. His wound had leaked and smelt of pus. He had almost died. But it was Raja Shivaji who had come with the medic every morning for several days. The medic always carried a large pot of old clarified butter. The young man had watched without any revulsion, as the medic washed his wound and smeared it with butter. Every day before they left, Raja had said to him, 'You will stay alive. I can read the invisible lines written on your forehead. I can see you fighting for me, leading my men to success.'

It was not an easy decision to make. He had lost his parents in a pox epidemic. He was small and weak, his brothers even smaller. Moray family had given them shelter and food. His corded muscles were brimming with the rice, bread of pearl millets, soups of lentil that had come from Moray's kitchen. Someone had once commented about his natural talent and it was Chandrarao Sahib who put him up for training. He had tried to repay his master by being loyal, and obedient, complying with the master's wishes, without asking questions. But when he had seen Pratapgad being constructed, his mind had changed. His master Chandrarao Sahib had never thought of building one such fort despite the mountains and the money. A hope had sprouted in his heart, to live for a bigger cause, and die for one.

Murarbaji is brought back to the present as rain lashes him from one side. The downpour gets stronger. While he thinks of a way to remain dry, he notices a tall figure standing to his right.

'Scared of the rain? Let's move,' his ears pick up Netoji Palkar's gruff voice. Palkar has already moved inside the fort and has turned left. Murarbaji's ego is slightly hurt. He runs behind to keep pace with Palkar's long strides. To their left, he can see a hill rising high. A hill above a hill! One can see quarters on its crest, partially blocked by a bastion. Palkar stops abruptly. Murarbaji almost bumps on him.

'This hill is called Rajgadi, the king's seat and the large house hidden behind the bastion is Raja Shivaji's home. Let me brief you about the fort first. Purandar means Indra, the Emperor of Gods. Fifteen miles southwest of Pune, from the point of Kondana Fort, a branch of the

Sahyadri turns towards the east. The same extension of the range is called the mountains of Bhuleshwar. These hills are named after the innocent avatar of God Shiva. This range has many hills, and on one of the hills stands this fort, a mile above the sea-level and three quarters of a mile above the plains at its foothills. '

'Which is the nearest town?' Murarbaji asks, cutting through Palkar's barrage.

'The fort is barely a few miles southeast of Sasawad. It is a famous market in this region.' replies Palkar, almost shouting to be heard.

'How far is Purandar from the Adilshahi's borders?' Murarabaji raises his voice.

'Eighty miles east is Indapur, our last eastern region. Beyond is Bijapur's Wangi province. Thirty miles south of Purandar is Bijapur's Wai province. Your Javali was once a part of Wai, before it was given to Morays a hundred years ago. I hope you know that much,' says Palkar. He is curt and wants to stick to his agenda.

Murarbaji knows about the Wai province and its *subhedar* Afzal Khan Sahib. His late master was afraid of only one man. Chandrarao Sahib used to say, if we can save ourselves from Afzal Khan Sahib, even God cannot touch us!

Palkar moves towards the east but waves his hand pointing northwards. 'As you will later see, it is easier for the enemy to enter from the north despite the steep slopes. The cliff drops to a short distance. The wall fortifications are stronger here. Remember the watchtowers need to be manned at all times.'

Murarbaji listens with keen interest, not bothering to wipe the rainwater that rolls down his face. He has heard about Palkar. This tall and middle aged man with heavy brows, giant whiskers and a grim face loves very large turbans. He has been a military officer of Bijapur. It is said that he rides a horse as if the animal is his slave and the earth his carpet. His swordfights are legendary. Palkar, the master of guerrilla warfare, is Raja's guru. He trains his men to cut off the enemy's food chains and water supplies in order to kill thousands by sheer dehydration and starvation.

According to the recent news, Raja has chosen Palkar as the *sar-e-naubat, sar* for head and *naubat* for squadrons, the commander-in-chief of the Maratha army.

While on the move, Murarbaji is told about the Chowkies or the check posts dotting the hill, and about the watchtowers built in stone, called *Nishana Burj, Shendri Burj, Hatti Burj,* and *Konknya Burj.* The rain has dwindled to a drizzle. He is taken to a large stone chamber near the *Konknya Burj.* It is bare and has just one huge window. A dark man armed with a large cleaver guards the window. Murarbaji peers down and immediately his head spins. The window opens to a cliff of smooth and vertical black basalt plunging down into the valley.

'Criminals sentenced to death are thrown from here. They are rolled in blankets, but their head is not covered, on purpose.' He hears Palkar's chilling words.

'Which crimes are punishable by death?' Murarbaji is curious.

'Mainly treachery, but recently two of our soldiers were thrown down for molesting women,' answers Palkar calmly and before Murarbaji can recover, he walks away. He is shown some more chambers of granaries, ordinance depots and stockyards.

It has stopped raining

Palkar's dark eyes, surrounded by webs of wrinkles, bore into Murarbaji's and he says, 'Remember, we have decided to hand over Purandar to you. You are its *quiledar*, the fort commander. This fort is hardly forty miles south from Bhima. Beyond the river is the Mughal terrain.'

Murarbaji's chest swells with pride. Raja has given him a strategic fort!

Palkar notices pleasure fleeting across the newcomer's eyes. He says tersely, "You are not the only man in charge of the fort. Three men have been assigned to manage each of our forts, a *quiledar* and two others. The two others include a *subnees*, usually a Brahmin to help the *quiledar* in clerical work and the other is the *karkhanees*. He is primarily a commissary of grain and stores. There will be other officials responsible for gate passes, patrols, watchtowers, stores of ammunition and weaponry. They will report to all three of you.'

'Who guards the foothills?'

'Tribals like Ramosis, Parwaris and Berads are our foothill sentinels. Balutes from Mahr and Mang communities are our foothill watchmen. Raja calls them *gadkaris*, the garrison men. And remember, nobody is allowed to treat them as untouchables, they must be treated with utmost respect. They are on permanent assignments in Raja Shivaji's army. They have been given rent free lands between the forts to till and make a comfortable living.'

Murarbaji has never heard anything like this before.

'If you and I are the ramparts and bastions of the fort, they are the foundation. If you and I are the branches of the trees, they form the roots. We are more expendable than them.'

He just nods quietly. Palkar continues, 'There are a number of temples and lakes on this fort. *Gooravs* have the *watans*, the hereditary right to mind the temples. A fixed amount is given to them. The fort may change hands but they remain and are the oldest inhabitants of the fort. These *watandars* and their families are directly under the care of the fort commander. This fort is a world in itself, it is equipped to face months of enemy besiegement.'

Murarbaji starts feeling the pressure of enormous responsibility.

Palkar walks towards the east saying, 'We need to climb a hillock. I need to show you something.'

Murarbaji is eager to ask something that is not related to Purandar. He gathers enough courage before they reach the foothills. 'Have you been to Delhi or Agra? Are these cities really real?'

Palkar turns back and glares at this rustic man who speaks Marathi in a strange accent. *A real ghati from the ghats of Javali, despite being a Prabhu the man is as stupid as a mule*, he thinks to himself, barely concealing his smile. *The hills are full of village idiots like this one.*

'I have not been to Delhi and Agra but I lived in Bijapur for a few years,' he snaps. *What did Raja see in this man, just the swordsmanship?* Palkar thinks and starts walking.

They come to the foothill of a large mound. Palkar climbs a slushy path holding the liana vines hanging down from the cliff like ropes. Murarbaji follows him, his clothes soaked and heavy. It takes them a while to reach the top of the hillock. At the end of the upward trail, is a watchtower. The wind is at its strongest at this point. He sees a bastion over the hillock and notices a few archers pacing the tower.

'This hill is called the Kandakada. From this watchtower you can see the Vajragad Fort. Vajragad is Vajra, a weapon protecting Purandar.'

Murarbaji looks down towards the north and notices a ledge. It is hardly about four guz wide and is strengthened by two watchtowers at its north-east corner. The towers rise high above the wall. One is painted white and the other black. Between them, on the rampart joining the two, is a large cannon mounted on a platform.

'These towers are vital to launch an attack if the enemy reaches the smaller fort. Below those towers is an underground vault to store cannonballs and explosives.'

Murarbaji glances at another hill beyond the watchtowers. It is separated from Purandhar hill by a ravine that is not very deep. 'If the Mughals come from the north or the Bijapur soldiers march in from the east, they will first encounter Vajragad. But the hill of Vajragad seems easy to climb. If they reach the top of that hill, they can bring down the black and white watchtowers with explosives. Then it is just a matter of crossing the shallow ravine and reaching one of the gates of Purandar,' he rattles.

'That's a remote possibility,' replies Palkar hesitantly. *Well, the ghati is not such a simpleton,* he thinks.

'Vajragad terraces are at a much lower level than the Purandar fortifications. It is not easy to bring the towers after down,' Palkar says.

But it is not impossible either, if the enemy is clever enough to put the cannon on scaffolds. The weapon of Purandar can turn into its weakness, Murarbaji broods as some unknown fear grips him. His left eyelid has started twitching and that is not a good omen.

SEVEN | THE POWER GAMES

Circa 1657

The Delhi monsoon has been delayed. Afternoons in the imperial capital have turned unbearably hot. Khus curtains have been taken out from the attics, sprinkled with water for coolness and fragrance. The poor are seen heaving carts on the roads or carrying loads at the city's numerous construction sites with waterskins tied to their backs. The rich prefer to be indoors at noontime. The capital wears a deserted look as its lonely streets languish under the listless trees. Mirza Raja Jai Singh's mansion in the elitist area of the imperial capital is surrounded by a lush garden. It is hedged with woody cestrum shrubs, covered with clusters of white tubular flowers. This sweeping building with arched corridors and a single massive, enormous dome stands on the banks of a placid lake, a relief in this scorching weather.

A rider has arrived from the *quila-e-mubarak*, the blessed fort. Emperor Shah Jahan wants to see Mirza, now! As the house servants fuss over him, the rider waits in the courtyard sipping sweetened milk laced with crushed almonds. The gardens, the arabesque marble statues, the fountains, and the flower beds – he has seen it all. But what surprises him is the temple in the courtyard. Its spire rises high over carved marble patio resting on two gold pillars. On top of the gilded pinnacle, ripples a saffron flag with unnerving pride and fearless impatience. Mirza Raja Jai Singh is the blue-eyed *mansabdar* of the Emperor. He is even allowed to hoist the saffron flag – saffron, the colour of blood and fire, regarded auspicious by the Rajputs.

Inside, on the second floor, Mirza is in a hurry. The fifty-year-old descends the stairs to the courtyard with the agility of a young man. A servant appears with a stallion. Leaving behind the wide, tree-lined streets of Jaisingpura, a suburb named after him, he gallops behind the rider. He is concerned as all sorts of rumours about the Emperor's illness have been making their rounds in the city, like vultures encircling the sky above a battlefield, sinister yet sure. Some say the Emperor's illness is terminal. Mirza has not seen his master for a while. What worries him is that the Emperor has not indulged in state processions in a long time. Shah Jahan loves to show off his wealth and military might.

He can see, hear and smell the spectacular processions: the fully armoured elephants followed by a dense mass of horsemen, the proud bearers on the elephants, holding huge, silk embroidered banners of the crouching lion eclipsing a bright sun. The cavalry is followed by men in brocaded robes. These noblemen carry the Emperor's metal symbols like the sun, an upraised hand, a fish, a tiger's head, horse's head and scales of justice. The drummers and trumpeters come after them, the sound of their instruments sending ripples of excitement in the hearts of the onlookers. Smartly attired infantrymen march with the rhythm of the music. The musketeers, the rocket throwers, the shield bearers, and the camel riders follow. The Emperor arrives at last, on his elephant that is covered in rich trappings, and behind the Emperor sits one of the princes. It is usually Dara Shikoh. People gather on the rooftops and balconies to get a glimpse of Shah Jahan, he who is the 'Shadow of God on earth!'

Mirza wonders if he will ever again witness such processions of Emperor Shah Jahan. He has to slow down his horse when they reach the busy shopping arcades of Chandni Chowk. The open plaza between the market and the fort is crowded. The jugglers perform in the midst of a cheering crowd. A derveshi makes his sloth bear clap in front of a few urchins. People have clustered around men in grubby clothes selling amulets as charms. Some sit on their haunches near men claiming to be astrologers, each on a dusty piece of carpet, to look into their future through mathematical instruments made of some metal.

The fort wall is made of red sandstone. Its turrets and bastions gleam in the golden light of the afternoon sun. The gate and the path leading to the courtyards are well guarded. As they move in, the sight of many-pillared *divan-e-khas* reminds him of the Emperor's court in progress when Shah Jahan sits on the peacock throne that has a pearl-fringed canopy, supported by gold columns glittering with diamonds and rubies. The princes, the grand *wazir*, the *mir baskshi,* the *mir atish*, the clergy, the *mansabdars* and the ambassadors from far off countries stand with their eyes downcast. But Mirza loves to gaze at his master, whom he considers as his father. He thinks of how Emperor Shah Jahan's fair skin shimmers with health and his fetching features gleam with confidence when he bestows titles, promotions, honours and awards.

It has been quite some time since the last court was held.

Mirza is intrigued when the rider takes a right turn towards the private apartments of the Emperor. Shah Jahan never holds meetings in his quarters. He is to be surprised again. A contingent of tartar women encircle the royal quarters. The muscular women belong to a warrior tribe whose ancestors lived on the banks of Volga river. The Emperor trusts them to guard his forts and palaces. The women soldiers wear armour, trousers and helmets and seem unmindful of the bright sun. Their faces are covered with thin, transparent veils, their hands hold long spears, with sharp steel heads. Their kohl-lined, emotionless eyes dart in Mirza's direction without blinking. These women are trained in hand to hand combat and one can easily handle several men at a time. The messenger nods at one of the women, and the circle breaks for the men to enter. But they move only after the horses are taken away.

It takes a while for Mirza to adjust to the darkness. It is much cooler in the room. Huge satin sheets sway above them to produce arterial air currents.

He understands the gravity of the situation only when he sees the Emperor. A large bed is kept in the middle of the enormous chamber. The curtains are drawn. A poorly lit chandelier hangs at the far corner of the room. It is the only source of light and it infuses a strange dullness into the chamber. The Emperor lies flat on his enormous bed; the first prince sits by his father's side with his hands folded in his lap. Two medics whisper to each other in a corner, their eyes occasionally darting towards their patient. The smells of strange herbs pervade the room.

It has been almost eight months since Mirza has seen the Emperor. An epidemic had ravaged Delhi and the nearby areas. The air had reeked of rats lying dead on the streets, in the houses, and on the steps of the mosques and temples. Even the tanners were afraid to collect them. He had heard that people had died like flies. Some had developed large swellings in the groins or armpits before they had breathed their last. The city's avenues had come alive only when the dead were taken for cremation or burial. The rich had fled the city. The Emperor had sailed a hundred miles in his royal yacht to live in his palace at the base of Sirmur hills.

Mirza has also heard of a gala function that was held at Sirmur to mark the three decades of the Emperor's reign. The recently polished seven hundred and fifty six carat diamond called the *Kohinoor* had been kept on display for dignitaries to admire. Mirza had not attended the event as he had taken his family to Jaipur to avoid the epidemic.

He moves softly into the path of the Emperor's vision and bows deep. 'Accept *salam* from this *nachiz Jahapanah, zohr bekheir Jahanpanha,*' he urges the Emperor to accept the greetings from him, the insignificant one, and wishes the Emperor a 'good afternoon' in Urdu and Farsi. He always addresses his beloved Shah Jahan as *jahanpanha*, meaning 'the Sanctuary of the World' as the Iranis call their Emperor, *Shah Abbas,* and Mirza's master loves it.

The Emperor, who controls an army of half a million men, painfully adjusts his eyes to see his most trusted Rajput *mansabdar* and speaks slowly, 'We need your help.' The Emperor has to gasp while speaking. Mirza does not remember his master ever asking for help in such a pathetic manner.

He keeps a stoic face. The Emperor has given his utmost all his life. The entire ritual of 'giving' seems to take place before Mirza's eyes that very moment. As the *diwan-e-khas* shimmers under the massive chandeliers, Muslim *mansabdars* wait to receive the title of 'khan' or very exclusive titles such as 'khan-e-khanan'. The Hindu *mansabdars* wait wondering whether their new title will be 'raja', 'rao' or 'rai'. Some even expect very coveted titles like 'rai-e-rayan', 'maharaja' or 'mirza'. The beaming Emperor distributes *khilats*, the robes of honour, *serpech*, the turban ornaments, rings engraved with titles, jewellery, hunting dogs, race horses, war elephants and even *jagirs* or *mansabs* as gifts. The receiver performs a *kurnish*, bowing three times as he approaches the throne, bending down to the ground so that the back of his right hand touches the floor. The man gets up and touches his forehead with the back of his hand, as if offering his mind and body to the Emperor.

But now the Emperor seems to be losing *his* mind and body. The grim-looking *hakeems* have started discussing agitatedly. Mirza's ears pick up some of their Persian words – swollen feet, loss of appetite, urinary stones, water retention, pain, prognosis and treatment.

'Shhhhh,' Dara Shikoh quietens the noisy medics and looks at him, 'we need all the help we can muster,' the first prince whispers as his pearl earrings dance. The forty-two year-old Dara looks younger than his age with his child-like skin, oval face and softly curved nose. His beard is well groomed and seems shorter than that demanded by the norms of shariah. He is undoubtedly the most handsome among his brothers. Mirza's eyes dart back to the Emperor who stares at Dara, his eyes filled with worship and esteem for his first son.

'The shadow of war looms over us,' mutters the Emperor helplessly.

Mirza feels sorry for his master. *The life of an emperor is such an illusion, like fireworks that dazzle in the sky for a brief moment.*

That brief moment has lasted for over three decades for Shah Jahan. The man lying on the bed, who controls eight thousand *mansabdars* and their two hundred thousand horses looks nothing like an Emperor. Wobbly, with his skin covered with moles and hanging listlessly under his chin, he looks like an old tramp. His usually henna-dyed, neatly oiled hair stands on his head, vibrantly red but greying at the roots. The king of Jaipur, Mirza, has grown up under the care of the Emperor. At a very young age, he had walked away from his kingdom, to join the imperial army. For the past several years, the Emperor had depended on him to head many wars of expansions from Afghan in the north to Deccan in the south and from Kandahar in the west to Mungir in the east.

'The Emperor's illness is supposed to be a state secret. Only these *hakeems* and very few noblemen know about it. Even my sisters at Agra have no clue. But I am not so sure about my brothers,' announces the first prince gravely, his limpid, *surma* smeared eyes, boring into Mirza's. A large gold *serpech* fixed on Dara's turban dazzles in the dim room.

'In what world does the first prince live?' thinks Mirza. The rich and elite of Agra have already started gossiping about the Empeor's illness. But he takes the situation into account. The man before him is Dara Shikoh, the first prince backed by undue privileges. Who can challenge Dara Shikoh, who stands like a wall between the Emperor and the world? The vassal kings, the high ranking *mansabdars*, and even offenders waiting for justice, need to seek his permission to meet the Emperor. Dara Shikoh, the star of his father's eyes, has been made immortal by a hundred miniature paintings, commissioned by his father for sums unknown. People call him the 'Crown Prince'. If Mirza says something deemed inappropriate by Dara, will God help him from the humiliation that he will face? Mirza does not want to get into any trouble in times like these.

'What you say is true, my prince,' Mirza murmurs.

'We have consulted astrologers. My father is destined to live long.' says Dara Shikoh confidently. 'But even the mere news of his illness will drive my brothers to the capital to claim the emperorship. Battles may rage around us.'

Dara knows well that his family history is bleak. Mirza nods in agreement. The sons of the Emperor have only three choices – either to be the next emperor or be murdered or live a million deaths in the dungeons. Humayun had two brothers. One was sent to Mecca where he mysteriously died and the other, who had dared to struck coins and proclaim himself as the next emperor, was blinded. His eyeballs were wrenched out of their sockets and the empty holes filled with salt water. Mere blinding was not enough, Humayun had to exorcise his brother's spirit, rob his longings, his dreams, and his hopes. Humayun's son Akbar mercifully had no brothers to kill or blind. But there was a cousin who had died in the notorious political prison of Gwalior fort of opium overdose. Emperor Akbar's sons drank themselves to death. Only, Salim alias Jahangir had been lucky to survive his drunken orgies and opium bouts. His throne had been threatened by his own son Khusro, skilled in military training. Emperor Akbar doted on his grandson. After his father's death, Jahangir had crushed his own son's uprising, had blinded him and thrown him in the dungeons. And Mirza's master, Shah Jahan had no alternative but to kill or blind uncles, half brothers, cousins and their sons till his empire was cleansed of all the men who could or would aspire for the throne. Some were forced to go into exile to Iran. Even the little son of the blind and imprisoned half brother Khusro was slaughtered in his sleep. One of his half brothers, dying of syphilis, was allowed to live.

'We have decided on a strategy to stop them from coming closer to the capital. When their heads are filled with ravenous hunger and their muscles with murderous energy, it is best to keep off or keep them off. It is time to don the armour, Mirza; you will go east to deal with Shuja,' says the Emperor softly.

'Shuja Bhai seems to know. The news is that he has planned his coronation ceremony, as the next emperor, in his constituency. I had to let father know this shameful news.' Dara Shikoh's words shock Mirza. He looks at the Emperor. Shah Jahan's eyes shine with tears. The second prince wants to declare himself the next emperor when the Emperor is still alive. There is nothing more agonising in the world than the realisation that your son wishes you dead, even so for a man who owns the world.

'In this campaign against Prince Shah Shuja, Prince Suleiman Shikoh will be in command under your leadership,' says the Emperor. One is aware of the hurt he feels, the pangs of sorrow for Shuja who has already started acting like an emperor. The second prince has planned to bestow titles on his officers and enlist a large number of new ones. Soon his treasury will be empty. It is then that he will march towards the capital. Shuja has changed – twenty years in Bengal and his independence has emboldened him.

'I will be ready, *Jahanpanha*,' says Mirza, his face fails to belie the pride in his heart. Dara Shikoh's son Suleiman, the most favourite grandson of the Emperor, is to take an assignment under him. This does justice to his status. Rajputs are the true Rajas of Rajasthan. They are the kshatriyas, those who hold kshatra, the weapons, and hence, are warriors by birth. Mirza is a kachhwa Rajput, a *suryavanshi*, born into the solar lineage that links him to the descendants of God Rama. Among the Rajputs, he considers himself superior to *chandravanshis* born into the lunar lineage or the *agnivanshis* born into the fire lineage or *nagavanshis*, born from the serpents.

Dara Shikoh knows how Mirza's mind works. The truth is that Suleiman will go along with Mirza to keep an eye on him. There is a chance that Mirza may suffer a change of heart and decide to join Shuja. Loyalty is as fickle as the mind that bears it. With Suleiman in Bengal, they will get the news of Mirza's movements. If he does decide to turn traitor they can take his family into custody, even if the family is in Jaipur. Mirza will have no control over the situation. He will have to cut across nine hundred miles of terrain to reach his home to save his family and this path passes through Dara Shikoh's provinces.

The silence in the chamber is chilly. Then suddenly, it is interrupted by the Emperor's bout of cough. Dara leaps to hold his father who shudders violently. Before the medics reach to the bedside, the Emperor has thrown up. Dara Shikoh's hands are full of his father's phlegm. It is dark yellow.

The medics take charge. They put spoons of mint flavoured syrup in the Emperor's mouth while their patient makes loud gulping sound. Mirza watches in panic as the Emperor's Adam's apple, gone prominent with age, moves up and down with each swig.

'Even Murad Bhai has been acting strangely,' says Dara Shikoh who has come back after cleaning up. 'The news from Gujarat is beyond reckoning. As you are aware, Murad's drinking companions hate all those who are honest. Especially Ali Naqi, the upright finance man who had handled cash with an iron hand. The news is that they had hatched a plan along with some cunning court eunuchs. Letters of deceit signed by the honest minister had appeared in the *daroga-e-daak,* the imperial post. One fake document was made to fall in Murad Bhai's hand. That was enough for my impulsive brother whose mind whirls in wine. The minister was dragged and brought to the court where my dear brother jammed his spear through him.'

Mirza is at a loss for words. 'Who will deal with Prince Murad Baksh?" he asks softly.

'Murad is not a threat. The real peril is Aurangzeb. He has collected millions of rupees from Qutb Shah of Golconda and has not deposited them in the Empire's treasury,' snaps the Emperor, his head now resting comfortably on silky pillows. There is a fleeting shadow of pain in his eyes. His fourth and youngest son Murad has grown up to be a foolish and a pleasure-seeking drunkard. In the battlefields when the carnage rages around him, he lets himself drown into the delight of mindless slaughter. Such a man does not have brains to plan his strategies. But his third son, Aurangzeb has the intelligence, cunning and wherewithal. His most dangerous weapon is his calm and practical mind that remains unfazed. But Aurangzeb hates Dara and if he becomes the Emperor, the first prince will surely be put to death. Shah Jahan's stomach churns with anxiety and his mouth fills with bitter acid. He gulps it to curb another bout of cough. 'One is *anntar* and another, a *heyvoon!*' he whispers, calling Murad a baboon and Aurangzeb a beast.

'Does Aurangzeb know about the illness?' asks Mirza warily.

'We don't know,' admits Dara Shikoh.

'What has been planned to stop him?'

'What do you suggest?'

Mirza ponders for a while. It is not an easy question and there cannot be a single solution. He feels uncertainty for the first time in many years. It is a new emotion for him. 'To begin with, it will be advisable to call back the reinforcements.'

'That has been done. Nasiri Khan, Rao Chtrasal, Mir Jumla, Kartalab Khan and others have been contacted directly. They will soon get our farmans and leave for their northbound journey along with their squadrons.'

'Who goes to south to stop him?'

Dara does not want to give away any names. He knows that the Rajputs are strong military men, each supported by thousands of their warrior clansmen. If he fails to handle the one who stands in front of him, he can never be the Emperor. But there is a weakness. These warriors from the sands of Rajasthan can turn insanely jealous of each other. Dara Shikoh has learnt to play one against another. And he will do so when and if the war of succession breaks out.

'Is it Jaswant Singh Rathod?' asks Mirza directly.

'May be, but we have not yet decided,' says the Emperor truthfully.

Mirza stands quietly. Jaswant Singh, the king of Jodhpur, is hardly his son's age but in military ranks, he stands higher. They have bestowed him with the title of 'Maharaja' meaning a great king, while his own 'Mirza' means 'son of a king'.

'My last wish on this earth is that my first son, my Dara becomes the Emperor after I am gone,' whispers Shah Jahan. The whole world knows it, and the Emperor has made it clear through his actions. But it is the first time that Mirza actually hears it from his master's lips. *When strong men wish, their wish is a command. When weak men wish, their wish is a vain hope. But when strong men gone weak hang on to their old wishes, what do you think happens?* wonders Mirza and looks at his master. Shah Jahan, the king of the world, reminds him of a lost sparrow with a fractured wing.

'*Abbajan*, you are not going anywhere for a long time,' says Dara, who cannot bear the thought of his father's death. His words ring true.

'That Is not possible. It is the law of nature. And I have chosen you: you are that drop that turns into a pearl. My *morvavid*!'

Dara replies:

Why must I seek to be the emperor?

When I can be a free creature?

And let my mind unfurl without caution

Why must a drop be a pearl?

When it has a choice to be the ocean?

'*Masha Allah!*' Mirza says in Arabic. The praise is genuine; Dara's poetry is always effervescent and deep in meaning. The Rajput too wants to breathe in the chaste and divine air that surrounds the Emperor and his son. He thinks of his ancestors and their purity. In the past the Rajputs, the true warriors had lived strictly according to the codes, in war as well as in peace. The 'codes of war' were especially stringent. An unarmed man must not be killed unless he begs to be killed due to his injuries. A woman should not be touched unless she challenges you as a warrior. One must never flee from the battlefield. If one accepts someone as one's master, one must seek to die for him. A traitor should never escape death.

After Mirza leaves, Dara Shikoh gazes at his father who has fallen asleep. He wonders about Aurangzeb, and the fact that his shrewdest brother does not yet know about Father's illness. What is he up to, at this very moment?

***

In the north-eastern frontiers of Adilshahi, thirty miles west of Bidar, dust kicked by thousands of war-horses mixes with clouds of smoke from the artillery and muskets. It is difficult to see anything. Aurangzeb knows that he is trapped; his small Rajput detachment of two thousand men is surrounded by the squadrons of the Bijapur General Khan Mohammad. His *mansabdar*, Rao Chatrasal and his *hada* clansmen stand like a granite wall to protect him. Bahlol Khan of Bijapur has burst forth with his men but the Rajputs around Aurangzeb fling themselves in reckless fury vowing to slay or be slain. To his dismay Afzal Khan's squadrons gallop in, but Aurangzeb holds his ground, not afraid of dying in a fierce sword fight. He has learnt to remain calm in such dire situations. Hundreds of battles fought for the past twenty years have taught him that a battle, however much planned or strategized, is like a game of dice. It changes every moment. Nothing is certain or final till the last breath. One of his soldiers shouts in his direction. His other *mansabdars*, Ikhlas Khan and Mahabat Khan, have arrived. Aurangzeb remains in the field for six more hours, fights without food or water, just like all his soldiers.

The battle ends favourably. Bijapur's Balhol Khan is wounded. A fuming Afzal Khan is forced to retreat. Aurangzeb knows that squadrons under Mir Jumla and Diler Khan have moved on, invading the region around the Kalyani fort. If the second military stronghold of Bijapur falls in his hands, it will make way for an advance on Bijapur, the capital of the Sultanate.

Aurangzeb decides to go back to Bidar. The news from Ahmednagar has left him disturbed.

***

The long awaited monsoons have finally arrived at Bidar, offering relief from the oppressive summer. The walled city that stands on the higest point of the eastern Deccan plateau looms over a shallow valley with gently rolling hills. The slopes have turned brilliantly green. The fort at the eastern face of the city is protected by another mile-long high wall and a deep moat. Cut in solid rock, it is twenty-five guz in width. Palaces, mosques, Turkish baths, a mint, weapon stores, courtrooms and many other buildings fill the fort's courtyard. The enormous gates, battlements and palaces are awash with rain and sparkle in the evening light. The open spaces between the red buildings are filled with lush green lawns and manicured flowering shrubs.

The main courtyard has neatly piled red lateritic stones. More than a thousand labourers on the scaffolds repair the bastions and the fortifications that have been damaged in the recent battle. It still drizzles when Aurangzeb walks out of the sixteen pillared mosque, his favourite place in the fort. However, his heart is in rage. Within a month of his meeting with Dabir, Shiva has raided the imperial territories. The first attack had been on Junnar. They had taken away more than ten thousand gold coins, countless sacks of jewels, clothing and two hundred priceless war-horses of Arabian breed. Thereafter Shiva's horsemen had spread in all directions, cutting off supplies, and ransacking wealthy villages. The entire region had become unsafe for travellers. Merchants had stopped trading in the area. Many shopkeepers had fled. Even the city of Ahmednagar was not spared. But fortunately all the people, along with their valuables, had shifted inside the land fort of Nagar.

When Aurangzeb looks at the main entrance of the fort, he notices a few horsemen enter through the main gate. He knows they are the men from Samarkand. He quickly turns to his left and rushes towards the palace apartments. Mutamad, holding an umbrella over his head, starts running to keep up with his master. After crossing the many-arched corridor supported by enormously massive pillars, Aurangzeb moves towards a foyer lit by countless tall brass *shamdans* and a chandelier.

Kartalab Khan knows why he has been summoned. When he enters the foyer, he finds his employer sitting on a throne made of ebony and covered with plates of pure gold. It is a huge chair, about three guz in length. Its gold plates are embellished with countless precious stones. The foyer is large and roomy and the surrounding walls are draped in heavy brocaded curtains.

The imperial prince sits with his rosary in hand and eyes half-closed. Two guards, armed with javelins stand behind him. It is rumoured that the third prince changes his personal guards every alternate day or, sometimes every day. But that is not Kartalab's business.

'Our terrain has been disturbed by Shiva and his bandits. I want you to join our other *mansabdars*, Nasiri and Iraj, to restore order.' The Mughal prince narrows his eyes and continues, 'Slaughter everyone, take captives and drag them to our camps. Teach Shiva's men a lesson. Make them writhe in such agony that they beg for death.'

If he could, Aurangzeb would have loved to flog the Maratha with a whip made of raw hide, in public, till he would fall at his feet. Instead, a blade of fury cuts through his body. He shudders, as a feeling of violation shakes him. What they have taken is utterly insignificant in terms of money. It is a question of the universal perception of the invincibility of the imperial territories. It is about keeping the flames of fear burning strong. But Shiva is showing them dangerous possibilities. The lambs of the Deccan may grow carnassials and turn tigers.

Karlatab Khan nods rather vigorously. He has heard that Nasiri Khan was successful in driving away the Marathas from the imperial region. But it was also said that it was the heavy rains, more than the bravery of Nasiri, that had made the Marathas vanish. In fact, it was rumoured that that precisely had been the plan, to vanish just before the rains.

'Prepare your men to march into Shiva's territory,' orders Aurangzeb.

Kartalab wonders how he will march into the hilly region in this season. He has heard that the continuous downpour has lashed the hills and valleys of the region. The hill forts illegally occupied by Shiva have become more remote to the plains.

'Have no mercy, ruin his *jagir*, burn his villages, kill, enslave, do what you please,' says Aurangzeb. He wants his squadrons to go berserk with violence.

'Life is a *djalyab*,' curses Kartalab Khan softly in Turkish, calling life a bitch, in his mind. Just before he was to meet the third prince, people had warned him not to promise a monsoon invasion. They had said that the rains in the western Deccan turn brutal. The rivers in the hilly region become so aggressive that villagers frequently spot the wild waters hurtling elephants downstream along with mere twigs.

'Yes master,' says Kartalab Khan and bows deep.

The man from Samarkand hates to agree with his master on everything, but he has no alternative. He is an Uzbek. The region beyond Afghanistan and Persia had lost its major source of income when the Europeans had opened sea routes. The trade between Hindustan, Arab Lands and Europe had thus moved away from the Silk Road passing through his region. Men from Uzbek, Tajik, Kazak, Turkmen, Kyrgyz ethnic groups had been out of work. People had opted for the military jobs, either in the empire of Persia or the empire of the Mughals. Kartalab had been lucky. Now, the third prince has made him a *mansabdar* of two thousand horses, and may even offer a *jagir*. Life has been comfortable, more so because he, like most from his region, is a Sunni and speaks Farsi. He is also tall, fair and has light eyes!

'I will do all I can, even face death to fulfil the wishes of my imperial prince,' mutters Kartalab, bowing more deeply than usual.

***

Riding from the north-eastern frontiers of Bijapur, it takes Afzal Khan several hours to reach the city, the capital of the sultanate. He has abandoned the battlefields littered with his dead soldiers, for a purpose. The imperial dogs have outnumbered his garrisons, and have slain and captured thousands. He and the other Bijapur commanders have lost everything. The Mughal beasts have wrenched their arms, transport cattle, cannon, gunpowder, slave girls and horses. Villages after villages from Gulbarga, south of Bidar, to Kalyani, west of Bidar have been razed to dust. Not even a trace of tillage has survived the imperial gallopers and their roving eyes. The northern strongholds of the kingdom like the fort city of Bidar have fallen. But that is not the reason Afzal Khan has come all the way to Bijapur. He has come to the capital to remove a thorn from his path.

He stares at the wall surrounding Bijapur. It is massive and strong. He knows that it is ten to fifteen guz high and seven guz wide. It is fortified with continuous ramparts and ninety six bastions, apart from the ten at the gates. The ramparts are protected by battlemented curtain walls from the inside, and are designed for artillery and small arms. He smiles wearily, kicks his stallion to a trot. Banda Sayed is riding parallel to him. Fifty armed guards follow their master silently.

He chews a betel leaf nervously while they move towards the Alipur gate guarded by two circular watchtowers. Above the gate, the platform enclosed with battlemented walls is crowded with archers and the gate is shut. Countless oxcarts loaded with grains and livestock have assembled, waiting to enter the city. Their frustrated drivers stand in small groups, either smoking or talking loudly. He can hear them curse the officials behind the doors for the delay. But the enormous doors made of thick wooden beams, fastened together by iron clamps, strengthened by massive bars and bristling with long steel spikes are quickly thrown open for him. The sentries kneel in his honour. Someone informs Afzal Khan that the Badi Begum has been informed and she wants to meet him.

Bijapur always makes the Khan feel at home. His kohl-lined eyes wander to the eastern edge of the city where enormous timber scaffoldings rise as if to touch the sky. Tiny figures of labourers are seen hanging over them. They have been building a mausoleum for the past fifteen years. It has the largest dome in the entire world. A faint outline of a dark gray giant cupola is seen through the scaffolds. The structure is his master's tomb. He cranes his neck and gazes at it till he can see it no more. Afzal Khan's heart aches, he misses the dead king of the Sultanate.

'The world was a different place when King Mohammad Adil Shah Sahib was alive,' he says to Sayed in Deccani Urdu, his eyes distant.

Sayed nods. He knows his master loved the late king and is also loyal to the Badi Begum. But there is a problem. The Badi Begum loves her son Ali more than anyone in the world, despite him not being born of her womb. Even the old courtiers do not have a clue regarding the boy's origin. Adoption of a child is not recognised by Islam, so Ali is not their real king. And Ali does not trust Sayed's master the way his father did.

They pass through markets, streets lined with elephant stables, temples and mosques. The shops are opening for the morning business. When he was very young and very poor, Afzal loved to walk through these markets, admiring the objects displayed on the shop windows.

Jeweller's shops have special displays where daggers, knives and other precious items are neatly arranged on satin covered shelves, rising one above another. Afzal Khan glances at the perfume shops, stuffed with China vessels, crystal glass bottles, and costly, jewel-encrusted cups filled with essences of all kinds. 'They have no clue what's happening at their borders!' spits Afzal Khan in disgust.

Some places teem with beggars and wretchedly poor men and women selling berries or flowers, desperate to earn some coins. Sayed remains alert, scanning every building and its windows like a hawk. His quiver is full, his bow hangs over his left shoulder and his *pata* sword is safe in his scabbard. Sayed knows his master hates crowds. 'It has taken me half my life to get over this rotting smell of food,' Sayed hears his master say. He has heard this before and knows why. He glances at Afzal Khan, who looks straight ahead, his eyes shining, perhaps with tears, or with memories.

Afzal Khan appreciates Sayed's silence. Nothing has come easily to him. Little Afzal had to run and jostle for every bit he had achieved. He had shed tears and slogged for things other boys had taken for granted. His mother had worked at the palace. While she had washed and cut mountains of vegetables, he had run errands to get meat or spices; while she had cleaned roomful of pots and pans, he had dried them with a cloth till his hands had ached. Sometimes heavy containers had slipped from his hands and fallen on the floor. His mother had thrashed him mercilessly, till all the broomcorns had fallen off her broom brush and his skin had turned blue black. In that kitchen, sometimes the leftovers lay piled up like a mountain and its stink had cut through his brain, and the mere memory of it still gives him nausea.

'The late king has given me a new life,' he murmurs.

Afzal was going through a phase of severe depression which was abated only by eating. However, that had slowly turned him into a fat lump. This had gone on until one day, Mohammad Adil Shah spotted him and urged his queen to remove him from the kitchen and put him up for military training. Afzal had loved the camp and had enrolled to learn construction and demolition tasks, wrestled with charging bulls, dragged wheels at the oil mills to turn his bulk into hard muscles. When other boys' fathers had come to see their sons' progress, all had scrambled to show their skills in sword fighting and archery. But nobody paid any attention to him, the dark and unusually big boy who was a maid's son. The other boys had teased him for he was large, maybe abnormally so. Outwardly he had taken no offence but in the wrestling arena he had crushed them hard and had broken their bones. Sometimes he would hold them by their limbs, whirl around, spin them in the air and then fling them over the fence. As the years went by, almost everyone feared him. The day he was appointed a soldier he went to meet his mother. But she had been dead for a long time and nobody had bothered to inform him.

'The late king used to call me a *farzand*, a son,' he says wistfully, glancing at Sayed.

Mohammed Adil Shah had done more than that. He had asked Ranadulla Khan, the then General of Bijapur, to take Afzal under his wings. Afzal had worshipped the General and the General had also liked him. He had honoured Afzal Khan by first making him the *subhedar* of Karnataka and then of the Wai province in Maharashtra. But the General had passed away. Khan Mohammad, an African Muslim, was made the grand *wazir* and the general of the Sultanate. The new *wazir* hates Afzal Khan and he is also a Bhosale supporter. A single stroke of fate had changed Afzal Khan's destiny. His dream of going up in military ranks was shattered. And as long as Khan Mohammad lives, his dream will remain shattered.

They march through the wealthy suburbs lined with banyan and tamarind trees waiting thirstily for the rain that has already arrived in the mountains. Residential quarters made of local basalt with hues of brown are visible on either side of the street. Beyond them rise hundreds of domes, towers and cupolas, some dainty and some enormous. The avenue finally ends at a huge moat running along another massive wall that protects the royal citadel. They cross the drawbridge that is opened for them and enter the royal gardens lush with fruit trees. Peacocks leap across their path. Afzal Khan gazes at the massive central arch flanked by two narrow arches. Travellers say that it is the highest and widest in the whole world. Through the arch, an ornate palace rising seven stories above the ground is visible, *gagan mahal*, the sky palace.

Afzal Khan dismounts as a few men waiting for him at the entrance rush to take his horse. He enjoys the nervous glances he earns from them. He alone is allowed to go. While rushing towards the enormously high arch to enter the ruler's court, the Khan prays for success. The many pillared court is well lit. Twenty-year-old Ali Adil Shah sits on the gilded throne, his dark skin gleaming in the yellow light from the twinkling chandeliers. Beyond the semi-translucent curtains, he can make out the silhouette of the Badi Begum. They are waiting on him. He first bows in the direction of the curtain, and then to the young king.

Ali watches the *subhedar* of Wai. Bidar has fallen and other cities are under threat. What's the reason, what's the hurry for Afzal Khan to rush to the capital?

'*Khosh Amadid* Afzal Khan*ji*, speak,' Ali welcomes his warrior in Farsi.

'*Merci*', Afzal Khan, who has painstakingly learnt the language, thanks his king before speaking, 'I have rushed from the frontiers with a news that is far worse than the defeat that we have suffered at the hands of the imperialists.'

Ali blinks. His head buzzes with doubt.

'Speak your mind,' the Badi Begum from behind the curtains.

'I need privacy,' Afzal Khan darts his eyes around the court. Claps are heard from behind the curtain and soon the court servants scurry away soft-footedly from the many pillared court of the Sultanate.

'We had once succeeded in besieging Aurangzeb and his squadron, cutting off their water and food supplies. Soon they would have had to surrender to us,' says the warrior, choosing each word with utmost care.

Ali stares at his enormous commander whose voice is effeminate, a contrast to his appearance: bull necked, dark skinned, abnormally tall and muscular.

'I do not quite understand,' mutters Ali.

'A message had come from Aurangzeb, I have seen the epistle. I was there when they read it loud. The imperial prince had begged to be let off. He had promised to retreat,' Afzal Khan waits for some comment from either the mother or the son but the duo seem speechless with shock. Khan glances around with unease. 'Go on,' Ali quips. He is irritated by the deliberate delay in providing full information.

'A strange reply was drafted. It said, *Early next morning, get your men ready, make a forced escape. We will let you go.*'

There was a loud gasp from behind the curtains. An excited Afzal Khan continues, his eyes blinking.

'Our siege was broken at places. Aurangzeb was allowed to escape. Very few from our camp knew the real truth.'

'Who signed the order? Who was in command?' screams the Badi Begum. What a waste of an opportunity! Years of tension, millions lost in keeping the Mughals at bay, Aurangzeb's humiliating letters calling them, the Shia rulers, the heretics, the misbelievers...

'It is not easy for me to spell his name. I have already endangered my life by having a major argument with him on this issue,' he says evenly.

'You have our protection. Spit the name,' retorts Ali, thumping his right hand on the throne's railings.

'Khan Mohammad Sahib, the Sultanate's esteemed General and the grand *wazir*. But for him we would have had Aurangzeb in our hands, like a lamb,' he says loudly while wiping his forehead with his large hands. A dazed silence engulfs the court.

'*Fetne kardan!*' Ali curses in Farsi, accusing his General of instigating sedition.

Afzal Khan expects a barrage of questions and one mistake might take him where he does not want to go. He needs to change the subject quickly. He suddenly grows taut and says confidently, 'Shiva Bhonsle and his men have attacked the Mughal territories.'

'We know of that,' snaps the Badi Begum.

'Afzal Khan*ji*', he hears Ali Adil Shah's words laced with scorn. 'Had Shiva Bhonsle been with us, we may not have lost strongholds like Bidar and Kalyani.'

EIGHT | THE BEAUTIFUL CAPTIVE

Circa 1657

The rider is tired, he has been on his horse for nine days and has managed to make forty miles of southward journey a day. He has spent his nights in the forests and hasn't had a decent meal in a long time. His back-pain has worsened, and his body is sore. Inside his leather jacket, the epistle is tied to his body with strings. He had collected the message at Burhanpur, the Mughal capital of Khandesh. The *subhedar* of the region, Shaista Khan had personally given the message to him. They had met secretly on the banks of the river Tapti. There seems to be some dangerous urgency in the epistle he carries. They had never before asked him to ride nonstop or to this part of the world. The rider hopes that he is on the right track. His horse has started blowing forcefully through its nostrils. The animal is hungry as well as tired. The rider fears that the horse may collapse while speeding and send him crashing to the ground. It is an upward climb, albeit gentle. The only solace lies in the fact that he has probably taken the right route and Bidar is not far off. He narrows his eyes to look ahead and clearly sees the outer wall of the city. It meanders mutely towards the skyline, becoming smaller and then gradually melting into the horizon.

It is a rainy morning. The courtyard of Bidar Fort is busy with labourers finishing the repair work. They talk in Kannada and Urdu in a strange accent. A bunch of large, black-faced, grey langur monkeys sit on a watchtower to keep company to the Mughal archers. A few armed-with-swords guards stand in arched patios of stately dimensions.

Inside the courtroom Aurangzeb sits on the late Siddi Majan's throne, worth forty million rupees. The third prince glances at his scribe who sits behind a small wooden desk, surrounded by piles of papers. He winces. All those letters written and received to and from his military officers are as good as autumn leaves. His fierce battles with the Shia kingdoms have been an utter waste of time.

Aurangzeb's mood is as gloomy as the weather outside. Something is seriously wrong. He has received a farman from the Emperor telling him to stay put at Bidar. His *mansabdars* like Mahabat Khan, Rao Chatrasal, Nasiri Khan, Kartalab Khan and his artillery chief Mir Jumla have been contacted directly and have been called back along with their contingents. They are already on their way to Delhi. Shaista Khan has been asked to go back to his province and is already at Burhanpur. The Emperor has also played dirty by directly establishing a contact with Bijapur rulers for the tribute money. He, Aurangzeb, the *subhedar* of the Mughal-occupied Deccan, he who has struggled to get military strongholds of Bijapur like the fort cities of Bidar and Kalyani, has been sidelined, as if he bears no significance. He will have no manpower, respect and funds in an enemy territory. He will be a military destitute and that is the worst insult for a prince.

'There is a rider at the gate. He wants to see you in person, my prince; he says that the epistle is only for your hands,' Aurangzeb hears Mutamad shout.

'Let him come, with our guards,' replies Aurangzeb. The message has surely not come with the *daroga-e-daak*, the official imperial post. An official postman will never insist on delivering the mail personally to him.

Several moments pass before Aurangzeb hears footsteps.

'My prince, the message is from Delhi, given to me at Buhranpur by *khan-e-khanan* Shaista Khan. It is tied to my chest.' The words are spoken by a man, completely worn out by his task.

Aurangzeb glances at the man. The messenger has fallen on his knees. His turban is filthy and his jacket is soiled. On a signal from him, the guards pull the man up like a rag doll, make him stand and pull out his jacket. The strings run from his shoulder to his back. One of the guards shoves his fingers below the strings and yanks hard. The messenger cries out in pain, as the skin near his neck is pinched. The epistle is free. The guard hands it over to the third prince.

'Take him away,' says Aurangzeb curtly. His hands tremble when he reads. *The Emperor is ill, kept in a curtained chamber at his private quarters in* quila-e-mubarak. *Only two* hakeems *are allowed in. The area is heavily guarded by armed tartar women. Dara Shikoh spends most of his time with the Emperor. The* farmans *that have the Emperor's seal are probably written by the first prince!*

There is a sign of a crescent moon where the signature should be.

Aurangzeb knows instantly that the letter is from Isa Beg, his trustworthy envoy from Delhi. He starts shivering, in fury and in shock.

That evening Aurangzeb reads the message several times in the privacy of his apartments in the *Rangeen* Palace. What must he do? Obey the Emperor's latest farman and stay put at Bidar? But that may give Darabhai time and the means to muster an army. It is risky not to obey the official decree. What if Father has recovered? What if the farman had been really sent by him?

Aurangzeb tries to calm his mind while he paces like a caged tiger. Suddenly, his new acquisition, the Bidar fort, feels like a dungeon, a pit. He needs to get away, go north to Delhi. He wants to be a bird and fly this very moment to *quila-e-mubarak* to know what has happened to his father. Is the old man really sick or already dead?

The intricately carved wooden pillars throw long shadows on the mosaic floor. They look mysterious, as if beckoning him to find answers in their bellies. Something flashes in his mind. What if he finds a legitimate reason to leave Bidar, a reason strong enough to overrule the royal decree? Is it possible?

'*La ilah ilallah,*' he prays loudly, *There is no God but Allah.* He is startled to see eunuch Mutamad walk in, again with another epistle. This time, the man is sobbing. Aurangzeb instinctively knows what the message is. He stands below the chandelier to read. His hands feel a slight tremor as his eyes move from one word to the other. She is dead. The woman he had gradually fallen in love with is dead. The mother of his three daughters and two sons has become 'beloved of Allah'. His Persian wife Dilras Banu, his only Muslim consort, whom he had married in a grand ceremony twenty-four years ago, when he was barely seventeen, has died of 'childbirth malady' in Aurangabad. His children born by her, including their newborn son who still is unnamed, need him direly. Aurangzeb feels tears streaming down his face. The woman he loved and who loved him has posthumously offered him the possibilities of escape. He has finally found a perfect reason to leave Bidar, so faultless an alibi that even the Emperor's *farman* will fall weak in its wake.

He wants some fresh air and moves towards the pillared corridor of the *Rangeen* Palace. Innumerable torches flicker in iron baskets mounted over small marble platforms. Beyond the garden, walls encasing the fort and their battlements gleam in the dim yellow light of the torches. Just a few months ago, this palace and its private gardens had been littered with the bodies of Siddi Marjan's family members. They had run like rabbits, screaming and yelling before the blades of his soldiers had hunted them and struck them down. Before he shifted here from his camp, they had to wash the blood-stained walls and floors of the palace. It had created ripples of fear in the Sultanate. And fear is a weapon that he loves to use.

He hears footsteps. It is Jaffar Khan, his regional *mir baskhi*. The paymaster general has probably heard the sad news. Before the man can say something, Aurangzeb raises his hands and stops him.

'I will proceed to Aurangabad. We have a million rupees in the vaults of Bidar. You stay put here. Establish contacts with the *jagirdars* and the *deshmukhs* of the region. Pay them huge amounts and win them on to our side. Whoever agrees to be with us, send them and their armies to Aurangabad, for we need the military support.'

After Jaffar Khan leaves, he looks towards the sky. The moon, almost full in its circle, hangs over the eastern skyline, its silvery coin afflicted by pale shadows. Looking at the moon, he remembers something faintly, something that Dabir, Shiva's *vakeel* had said. That they had plans to invade the Sultanate's region in the North Konkan, the region that initially had belonged to the Nizam Shah of Ahmednagar! He strides towards his official chamber, crossing several closed corridors lit by torches. The guards are surprised to see him. They scramble, throwing their chillums away, and stamping the burning sticks with their sandals. The third prince arrives at the courtroom where his scribe is still at work in the company of a lone *shamdan* lamp. The clerk is about to call it a day and is surprised to see his master at this hour. He takes a fresh paper and opens a new inkpot. Aurangzeb starts dictating. The letter is for the Badi Begum of Bijapur.

Our association goes back to your late husband Mohammad Adil Shah agreeing to be the vassal of the Empire, and pay the yearly tribute, as was agreed upon, to us. That makes Bijapur Sultanate a tributary state of the Empire. Keeping that in mind, we would like to renew the old peace treaty. I, as the imperial subhedar of the Deccan, assure you that my army will stop further invasions on your terrain. If you agree you must do two things on emergency basis. Clear all the old tribute dues. And cede some of the Nizam Shah's territories occupied by you to us, the port city of Kalyan and the surrounding territories in the north Konkan. Remember that the regions you hand over to us must include the jagir *of Shiva Bhosale. Do not establish contact with the Emperor by bypassing me. I have been kind enough to recognise your adopted son as your legitimate king, despite the fact that it is not recognised by Islam. Obey or else.*

***

The hills of Sahyadri gleam in the evening sun. Five hundred men led by Abaji Sondev move gingerly through a narrow trail adjacent to the frightening cliffs of Tailbaila rocks. His eyes hover around to catch any movement in the thicket and his ears strain to pick up even the faint sounds echoing in the hills.

He has received the information from tribesmen of Telbaila village that the *subhedar* has planned to take this route. His scouts had sneakily followed the caravan from Kalyan till Sudhagad fort. The caravan is coming from Kalyan and has to cross the mountains to arrive at the plateau. They will then travel more than two hundred miles southeast to reach Bijapur. But that is not his plan. He wants to take the caravan back to Kalyan. Raja Shivaji has given him his first major assignment and he has to do it right. Feeling agitated, he leans back to balance and lets his horse canter through the steep grassy cattle trails. It is then that his ears pick up what he is waiting for: human voices and the rattling of carts. The caravan has arrived somewhere near the temple of Goddess Waghjai, less than a quarter of a mile away from him and his men. His heart pounds with excitement as he stops his horse and dismounts. He ignores the angry snorting of his horse and signals his captains. There is a flurry of activity as half his horsemen dismount and quickly tie their horses to the nearby trees. The others, the backup force, remain on the saddles of their mounts.

Mullah Ahmed, the *subhedar* of north Kalyan sits drowsily in his palanquin. Five hundred armed horsemen in metal helmets and chest armour ride ahead of him and about two hundred follow his caravan. It was his idea to use this mountain trail. Most of the mountain trails from Kalyan to Bijapur either pass through the Mughal terrain or through Maval. This one is a lesser known one, not frequented by the caravans so the dacoits do not usually wait here in ambush. Plus he has his armed horsemen. He is not worried about the journey; he is worried about the future that he and his family might have to endure. Kalyan has been his home for past several years. The region is the merchant's paradise and the tax collection is good. Over the years, he has created wealth for the rulers of Bijapur. Now the same rulers, to save their fort cities of Bidar and Kalyani, have given away his beloved Kalyan to the Mughal. The old peace treaty has already been renewed. The Badi Begum has signed the document. A Mughal *subhedar* is soon to arrive. So his king has ordered Mullah Ahmed to return to Bijapur in a hurry.

'The *haram* politics of the royals,' he mutters angrily under his breath. It was not his doing that the Bijapur army has failed to protect their north-eastern strongholds. His head throbs as acidic bile sloshes in his mouth. A thought comes to his mind, like a sneaky scout looking for escape: so what if he is a Shia or a Turk? He is a Mullah, a scholar of theology and Shariah law. He has spent hours delivering religious sermons. He can always try and join the imperialists. And even come back to Kalyan. He has heard that Aurangzeb is very religious and may even be pleased to take him.

The comforting thought is suddenly broken. His ears pick up swoosh and cracking sounds as his slaves whip the oxen carts that follow his covered palanquin. He sticks his head out from the small window to look back. Yoked together with large wooden beams, several pairs of beasts try hard to climb and bear the lashing mutely. The cart drivers seem oblivious to the contents of swollen sacks they transport. The sacks contain all the gold, silver and precious stones from his treasury. Several *zanana* palanquins follow the carts. He can see his son riding parallel to them to watch over the bearers who carry the women of his family. Something makes him glance ahead, something weird. Their track ahead has taken a turn only to disappear into a thicket. The *subhedar* of Kalyan is suddenly filled with a sense of foreboding. The rising hills looming over the trail, the dense woods, the strange jungle sounds and the frighteningly lonely path make him edgy. He notices his son's horse trot ahead, crossing the caravan, and catching up with the horsemen riding in the front. He hears some people shouting. He watches as his horsemen stride ahead with caution, removing their swords from their scabbards. Anxious now, he observes some of his horsemen turn left and disappear. But something is seriously wrong. A bunch of strange looking men emerge from the bushes. Terror makes Mullah Ahmed's bones go rigid. At least two hundred men have suddenly jumped out from the woods like kernels popping out of fire. The short, muscular and dark men wearing folded turbans like Turkish caps scramble like infuriated honey bees. He sees them running after his horsemen. They hop and sprint, taking strange stances with their swords. Mullah Ahmed can hear their cries, rhythmic, almost a battle cry. Their shrieks ride on the wind and echo in the valley. His horsemen return in haste. The enemy have started dancing around them, like tribals around a fire. The well-bred, delicately nurtured Arabian horses start neighing in panic. Some stand on their hind legs, some step backwards to retreat and some stumble and collapse, throwing their masters on the ground. He watches as the strange footmen hit their swords in vertical blows, striking his horsemen on their knees or ankles, parts of the body that are not covered with armour. His men try hard to reach the footmen by slumping forward, but their curved blades are too short. Some of the enemy footmen wrench out his men's metal helmets in frenzy, hold their swords upside down and strike the hilts of their swords onto their exposed heads. The hilts seem to have spikes. His horsemen fall on the ground, limp. Some horses have lost their riders; they run about in a state of confusion. It is a chaos. His men, who try to crawl away, are caught. His palanquin bearers have stopped, as if frozen with fear. He jumps out, holding the hilt of his sword gritted to his belt. But before he can pull out the blade a few men pounce on him. He is soon shackled. He trembles as he notices his son being surrounded by men brandishing swords with those long, fearsome blades.

It is probably the darkest night in the life of Mullah Ahmed. They have been captured. The captors drag his caravan and him to some place. It is only at dawn that he realises that they are taking his caravan back to Kalyan.

Thirty miles north, from where the *subhedar* of Kalyan has been taken as a captive, Shivaji has arrived near the edge of Kalyan at dawn. From a slight elevation, he can see the port town beyond its short outer wall with narrow ramparts. To his surprise, there is not a single scout or an archer visible on them. Beyond, the enormous waters of Ulhas River shimmer like molten iron, reflecting the crimson rays of the slowly emerging eastern sun. His scouts have already informed him that the last of Bijapur's garrison have gone with Mullah Ahmed's caravan. Kalyan is awaiting their new Mughal *subhedar*. He watches the south-facing gates open. His horsemen, standing behind him, make a large semicircle and advance towards the gate. They move ahead of him through the overgrown shrubs and bushes. He kicks his horse and enters the main gateway. He is a picture of daring and delight with his carefully chosen silk robe with flower motifs ballooning behind him, his saffron turban with a pearl aigrette gleaming in the morning sun, the hilts of daggers gritted to his belt sparkling with rubies and emeralds, his brocaded scarf flying in the air and his wide sash glittering like gold. A hundred men ride behind him, attired in equally fancy robes. It is a chance and he will take it. It is a chance to capture Kalyan without bloodshed. A few sleepy gatekeepers notice him and his followers. They straighten up rubbing their eyes in disbelief. The Mughal *subhedar* seems to have arrived. Flummoxed, they try to undo each other by bowing deeper than the others.

Within an hour, the gate fortified with iron spikes are manned by his men. The ramparts are crowded with his archers. By the late morning, his men have occupied the fort. At noon, the news has reached the nearby villages that the new governor has arrived, as several local landlords, wealthy fishermen and village headmen from the countryside put the saddle on their horses and gallop towards Kalyan.

It is late in the afternoon when Shivaji climbs the steps of Kalyan Fort that leads to the official court of Mullah Ahmed. The paths leading to the fort bustle with Mavali men with crimson coloured Turkish turbans. Shivaji is proud; his 'Mavali men' look like a regiment in uniform of saffron coloured mantles of quilted cotton worn over white breeches.

He crosses the courtyard as the residents of Kalyan look on. The salty riverside breeze feels warm. He walks towards the courtroom through an open corridor lined with his men. Yesaji Kank follows him. Before Shivaji enters the building, he looks at the open courtyard of the fort that is filling up with people who have come to see their new subhedar. The courtroom too, is full of local men, perhaps local Hindu and Muslim landlords or officials. He walks briskly to the throne, and occupies it as if it is the most natural thing to do. He leans forward, elbow on his knee and palm cupping his chin as he gazes at the people, eyes wandering from face to face. Yesaji stands behind him. Men look at Shivaji, suspicion and doubt fleeting in their eyes. They whisper into the ears of others standing near them. Whispers slowly grow into a loud murmur that ripples across the courtroom. He watches them and hopes he can capture their hearts too.

The street leading to the Kalyan fort is crowded. Two shackled prisoners, their sweat trickling down their foreheads, their eyes downcast, walk barefoot in the afternoon sun. Sometimes they drag their feet as if they do not want to move and are shoved from behind. It takes a while for the people to recognise them. They have seen those men riding ceremonial horses through the streets of Kalyan. It is their old *subhedar* and his son, tied in chains. They are being paraded like criminals. The older man stumbles twice and falls flat on the street like a drunkard. The crowd turns noisy as onlookers become wary. There is something wrong. The news spreads through the town and there is a stampede as women and children run to the safety of their homes. The caravan is back from where it had started, at the fort steps leading to the yard.

Shivaji watches them entering the already crowded court. He looks at one and all, especially Abaji Sondev. The man has successfully carried out the task assigned to him. The stress of a long journey and of bringing the prisoners as well as the pillage, does not tell on him. The men assigned to him move purposefully and seem well adjusted to their captain. Only the path from the entrance to the throne is free of people. Abaji's men start pouring the contents of their loaded sacks on the ground. Small mounds of gold coins, some Ashrafi Mohurs, some Bijapuri Hons, rise on the carpeted floor.

'Raja, there is something else,' Abaji speaks diverting his eyes to the entrance.

The patch near the doorway is bathed in the golden light of the western sun as long shadows of high pillars run over the Persian carpets leading to the throne. Shivaji follows Abaji Sondev's gaze. A veiled, handcuffed woman cuts through the crowd and trudges towards him. Two Mavali men push and shove others away from her, as if she is made of glass. The tiny mirrors on her long skirt shimmer in the evening sunlight. Behind her, he notices two more shackled prisoners. The men are tall and very fair, probably Arabs or Turks, wearing conical turbans and ankle length robes. Their footwear is missing. He can make out that they are men of battle and they usually show defiance as prisoners. The terror in their eyes puzzles him.

The men in the courtroom stare at Shivaji to gauge his next move. They now know who the man is, who has occupied the throne of their *subhedar*. There is no mistaking, as some of them have seen him in the past. They have heard about his Javali conquest, and incursions in the Mughal occupied Deccan terrains. The men are curious. It is not the first time that they are witnessing the ordeal of a woman. They have seen it many times, mostly poor peasant women being taken by wealthy landlords. They have seen raiders from the north sorting out women from fallen villages as if they are cattle. The gangs of African Siddis from the sea-fort of Janjeera hunt down girls from the nearby coasts to feed their slave trade. The official numbers run in thousands every year.

They are interested because they have heard that the man from the Maval Mountains is different. But some temptations are hard to resist.

The packed courtroom is eerily silent. It is broken only by one sound, the bells from the woman's anklets. She is now placid, like calm before a strom. The other two captives stand behind her.

'Allah,' she suddenly yells and bursts out crying.

'Let her go,' the younger man in shackles shouts.

The older captive falls to his knees. His shackles make a harsh metallic sound.

Shivaji feels his temper rising. It is the first time a woman captive has been brought before him. He can only guess what she must be going through, so shamed, humiliated, and shocked. He has seen his mother live in terror when father had left them alone at Shivaneri Fort. The region was taken over by the Mughals. Things had turned scary especially after one of his mother's young relative was abducted by an imperial *mansabdar* called Mahabat Khan. It had happened in Nasik, north of Bhima. The region was already under the Mughals. The young girl had vowed to take a holy dip in Godavari River for her husband's long life. The Mughal cavalry officer, Mahabat Khan had spotted her. Their paths had crossed only for a moment. He was leading his horsemen to capture the nearby Anjaneri Fort. He had tied her to the horse and pulled her along as if she was a rag doll. Many had seen it happen and many had heard her cries. 'If women from warrior Maratha families are taken in daylight what must be the plight of the poor?' Mother had asked him when he was too young to understand. 'They have blamed her karma for what has happened to her, for that is the easiest way for men who could have saved her to get away.' She had told him so. It did not make any sense to him then, but it is now. Shivaji shudders with rage. He glances at the captive. Her clothes are made of expensive silk, finely cut. Her skirt makes a circle around her. Her cuffed hands have countless gold bangles embellished with rubies.

'Stop crying, don't be afraid,' he says loudly. She shudders with fright but her yells turn onto whimpers.

'Abaji, tell me who this woman is?' Shivaji stares coldly at his man.

'She is from the *subhedar's* family.' Abaji rattles. The rage in his master's eyes sends shivers down his spine.

'Be more specific.'

'She is his son's wife,' Abaji stammers.

'And who are they?'

'The elderly man is the *subhedar* of Kalyan and the younger one is his son.'

'Why is she here?' The voice is soft but Shivaji's eyes shine with fury.

'She is a part of the pillage.' That is the blatant truth.

The leader of the Maratha keeps a stoic expression. Who can blame whom, when the emperors and men of power have already set an example? The Muslim invaders regard women and children as war booty. The Mughals alone have done enough damage. Babur, in his own accord, had killed thousands of men and made their women captives. Akbar had mustered five thousand female slaves in his harem. His small time general Uzbeg had boasted of converting and selling half a million humans, mostly women. Akbar's son Jahangir had sold two hundred thousand children within a year's time to the Persian Emperor. As per his memoires, he allowed his *subhedars* to take sons of the peasants if they failed to pay taxes. One of his noblemen, Sayed Chaghtai, had one thousand two hundred castrated boys, kept for pleasure. The current emperor Shah Jahan has taken countless women in his harem and has brought in thousands of tartar women as guards or sex slaves. Shivaji has heard from the travelers that they have seen wives and children of destitute peasants being sold in markets and fairs in the north. Just a year ago, the Mughal soldiers had taken thousands of women from the city of Hyderabad and Bidar, as battle perk. The Hindu kingdom of Vijayanagar had its own stories. Some of the Hindu rulers used to demand any beautiful young girl from her parents, and had kept themselves busy with battles fought for women.

'Since when have we started considering humans as pillage? Abaji, if we behave like them why dream of a Swaraj?' he asks sadly.

Abaji shudders and casts down his eyes.

'For us crime against women is as serious an offence as treason. We have either chopped off the perpetrators' limbs or pushed them off the cliffs if they have even touched a woman lustfully. And now in my domain such a criminal faces death penalty, and you know that.'

Abaji does not look up. The men in the courtroom hold their breath. Turbaned, armed men, tall and rugged, some hardened by battles, most carrying swords and daggers, some Hindus and some Muslims, some wealthy, some poor, young and old, stare at Shivaji unbelievingly.

'A peasant is the centre of the world. He produces grains, and hence the revenue. Everybody's life depends on him – the balutes, the soldiers, the *patils*, the *deshmukhs*, the *jagirdars*, the *subhedars* and even the king. Only a woman is above the peasant, she is the centre of his family, rather anyone's family.'

Abaji nods.

'If she is safe, her sons are stable in mind, if they see their mothers, sisters as subjected to crimes, they grow up as criminals. And the foundation of a strong nation cannot be built on the shoulders of such men. Why think of a Swaraj then?'

'Allah, bless this young man,' Mullah Ahmed, who is the first to understand Shivaji's words, says and raises his shackled hands skywards. He is still kneeling.

'Unshackle them and take them to their quarters. Abaji, the *subhedar* and his son are our guests.'

Abaji seems relieved.

'Whenever they wish to leave send a hundred escorts to take them to Bijapur territory. Treat the *subhedar* son's wife as a family member; give her clothes, bangles and enough food to last for the journey. Do everything for her, as you will, if your daughter's caravan is set to go on a long voyage.'

The *subhedar* stands up, he has a smile on his face. The young woman falls to her knees, quivers and says, 'Shukran,' meaning thank you in Arabic.

Yesaji, standing behind Shivaji all this while recalls something that had happened fourteen years ago. It was not unusual for the king's military men or the landlords to take whatever they fancied from the poor and helpless. An elderly Brahmin had come knocking at the gates of Raja's *Lal Mahal* at Pune. 'He has taken her, dragged her from our home, in front of my wife,' the poor Brahmin in a torn Dhoti had said in between the sobs. Raja, then a fifteen-year-old boy, wanted to know who the Brahmin referred to.

'The Patil, he took my daughter and disappeared.'

'Yesa,' Raja had roared, 'go immediately to Ranjhe and find the girl.'

'It is of no use; we have found her, dead, floating in the village well,' the Brahmin screamed. He had kneeled in despair.

Yesa had glanced at Raja, whose eyes had grown cold. 'Bring the Patil in shackles,' he had shouted.

'The Patil denies what he has done, he has even insisted on lighting my daughter's funeral pyre. The villagers had watched mutely. No one dared to question. Now her soul will roam in misery without Moksha.'

'We will give her soul the reason to seek the cosmic freedom,' Yesa had heard Raja's words before he left. He had ridden a few miles to Ranjhe along with twenty horsemen. The villagers had stood silently, watching the riders go to their chief's house. Their eyes had told the story. The Patil was busy meeting people in his courtyard. Seeing them barge in the village, he had started cursing, and had refused the allegations. But Yesa and his men had bundled him and brought him to *Lal Mahal*.

The criminal was locked up for the night. The next day the courtyard of *Lal Mahal* was full of people. The Patil was brought in shackles. He had fallen prostrate and screamed of his innocence.

'She has lost her dignity before she has lost her life,' Raja had said for all to hear. 'So this Patil has to pay by giving up his dignity.'

Everyone was anxious to know what would happen thereafter. There was a law against such crimes but no one had punished anyone for ages. Yesaji remembers each word Raja had spoken. 'Patil of Ranjhe, Taraf – Khedebare, Babaji Bhikaji Gujar has committed an act of offence while serving in his office. The report of his actions has reached us. Thereupon, as per our orders, chop off his limbs.'

The Patil had started screaming. 'Six months in the dungeons is the punishment,' Babaji Bhikaji Gujjar had started begging.

'It may not be enough any longer,' Raja had announced, his voice cold and resolute. The punishment was carried out right away. People had shuddered seeing the handless and legless torso of the Patil. It was a message to all the men of power in the region.

***

Night has fallen over Bijapur. Only the men minding the street lights scurry with their ladders to light them with torches. A few strays howl in the dark. The avenues leading to the Badi Begum's palace are deserted. Khan Mohammad, the grand wazir and the general of the Sultanate is worried. *Why would the Badi Begum summon me with such urgency,* he wonders. *And why would she send her royal guards to the north-east frontiers just to make sure that I come? Or is there something more?* He wrecks his brain as his palanquin moves towards the palace. *She never summons her noblemen at such unearthly hours.* The African warrior is anxious.

He has given his life to the services of the late king and is as loyal to the Badi Begum. His wives and children live in Bijapur. The kingdom has given him wealth and fame beyond his reckoning. Life has been tough in the recent past. Aurangzeb and his army had been on the rampage. The Mughal had caused colossal damage to the cities, towns and villages of the Sultanate's northeast frontiers. But he has tried to do all that was possible.

He struggles to fight despair when he picks up a faint sound of gallops. It is not from his horsemen, he knows that they trot, and the sound of hoofbeats belongs to the gallopers. In an instant he knows and breaks into a cold sweat. His pulse races as he looks out and sees shadows of horsemen beyond his own horsemen. The street is dimly lit and is lined by trees. The shadows lurk beyond those. Khan Mohammad pulls the sword from his scabbard and jumps out. The weight of the palanquin tilts. The bearers buckle and lose balance. The palanquin crashes loudly. The General's horsemen have sensed danger but it is too late. Before they can gather their wits they are surrounded by fully armoured horsemen. They are heavily outnumbered and the fight lasts only for a brief time.

Khan Mohammad tries to run away but his fear makes him unsteady. His feet slip on the ground, gone wet with the blood of his people. He tries to get up, holding the hilt of his sword but trips again and falls flat on the ground, eyes gazing at the sky. Within moments someone jumps over him to pin him down to the ground. All he sees is the shadows of men around him. Several swords go up in the air. He struggles but sees the gleaming blades come down on him.

'Allah,' is the last word that he speaks before his blood forms streams on the street of his beloved Bijapur.

NINE | THE MUGHAL THRONE

Circa 1658

The early morning prayer of Fajr is over and the muezzins from the nearby minarets have long gone back into the mosques. The eastern sky beyond the rocky hills turns orange. Aurangabad, the capital of the Mughal-occupied Deccan, shimmers under the early morning sun. It is spring, and the birds have gone berserk with their calls. When Nizamshahi was at its glory, Malik Ambar, the grand *wazir* of the kingdom, had transformed a small village called Kirki to a paradise. Like an artist he had painted its skyline with arches, domes, temple spires and minarets. Like a water god, he had created aqueducts to provide running water to mosques, palaces and gardens. When the Mughals had annexed Nizamshahi, Aurangzeb, then just twenty, was made the *subhedar* of the Mughal-occupied Deccan. He gave a new name to Kirki and called it Aurangabad, the city of the throne, and made it his headquarters.

Aurangzeb, standing in the balcony of the Naukhanda palace built on an elevated ground, stares at his capital. He loves everything about the walled city of Aurangabad and even its surroundings. It reminds him of his youthful days spent climbing the hill of Dawlatabad fort, visiting the caves of Ellora or shooting the tigers from nearby forests. The valley of the watershed was his favourite haunt, where serene blue lakes reflected the azure sky covered with white herons. Those herons always reminded him of his little bird, his Sher-baz.

Twenty years ago, at this very palace, on his first day at the court, a scrawny tribal had waded in with a hooded hawk perched on his fist. The bird looked striking with its ash coloured plumage marked with large grey bars. Even the guards had no heart to stop the man who had come in just a loincloth. 'My prince, this is for you,' the man had rattled in broken Urdu and offered his bird with so much pride as if the bird were a large diamond. 'It is Sher-baz, the tiger hawk. It kills smaller birds better than the big falcons,' he had insisted. Aurangzeb had gingerly unstuck the bird's hood and looked into the yellowish eyes of the little savage. The haughty hawk had stared right back at him. The little pest was caught in the hills of Afghanistan and trained in the forest at the foothills of Dawlatabad fort. For a few years Aurangzeb had enjoyed flying Sher-baz at partridges and the little brute had never let his master down. Aurangzeb will never forget the day he lost his pet. The sky was clear and he had flown Sher-baz. Within moments, the hawk had caught a baby crow that had just learnt to fly, and had veiled it within its wings. Moments later a mob of crows had risen from somewhere like a smoke, as the air trembled with the harsh din of their cries. The black birds had darted forth in the direction of Sher-baz. To Aurangzeb's horror, some of them had circled dangerously over his hawk. A few had rapidly descended with outstretched wings and pecked and clawed the bird-of-prey that had taken one of their own. The third prince had learnt a lesson that there is a thin line between being a victor and a victim. He had penned a verse back then:

The world changes
In a twinkle, in a breath
A moment ago it was life
Now it is death.

His poem reminds him of Shiva Bhosale. The bloody rebel has

entered the north Konkan and gone wild. The *kafir* is becoming a habitual plunderer and needs to be eliminated in a breath, before he spreads havoc over the Deccan. Aurangzeb has dealt with such men. He remembers a Bundela king called Juzhar and how he had chased the *kafir* fugitive through forests near Deogarh. Juzhar was soon captured and slain, his older sons were slaughtered in cold blood, and his younger children were converted to Islam. Aurangzeb had witnessed his father Shah Jahan choosing some young queens of the *kafir* to fill his harem. Juzhar Bundela's country was seized. Aurangzeb had toured through the region, viewing its glorious palaces, ancient forts, manmade lakes and forests full of game animals. Satisfied, they had then travelled hundred miles southwest to reach Dwalatabad. It was then that his father had announced his promotion; Aurangzeb was made the Mughal *subhedar*. That was twenty years ago.

Aurangzeb has the urge to burn Shiva Bhosale alive, or crush him under the feet of elephants trained in execution. But this is not the time to hound Shiva. More urgent things await him in the north. It is actually meaningless to think of the Deccan politics. What happens in the north will decide his future: it is either the throne or the grave!

If Darabhai becomes the Emperor of Hindustan, he, as the new Emperor, will be symbolised by *awarang*, the throne; *chatr*, the umbrella; *shamsha*, the sun; *alam*, the flag banners and *kawakaba*, the gilded globes. To challenge him, his name or anything that represents him, would be a crime of sedition, punishable by death. The Empire's bureaucratic machinery will be his slave and the *mansabdars* will lick the floor he walks on. The jury at the shariya court will twist the law in his favour. Darabhai's brothers, including Aurangzeb, will be put to death, and their children will breathe in the gloomy dungeon air infested with rats and lice. They may be forced to swallow large doses of opium and left to die rolling in their own filth.

A very sullen Aurangzeb leaves his chamber and marches to cross one arch after another. Three thin girls, their auburn curls shining in the morning sun, dash towards him. To him they look like butterflies in their sumptuously pleated silk skirts. His daughters from Dilras cling to him and start weeping inconsolably. They know their father will be leaving for the camp. Feeling numb, he kisses their heads, then peels them away and walks towards the inner part of his dead wife's palace. As he crosses one cusped arch after another, countless teary eyed eunuch slaves stand in rows and bow to him as deeply as they can. Aurangzeb does not bother to glance at the slightly feminine turbaned slaves dressed in sober coloured robes who have been his late wife's confidants. He enters the opulent chamber of late Dilras Banu. His wife's bed is empty; a plump elderly woman sitting on the carpet near his wife's bed gets up hastily. The infant she is holding is jolted out of his slumber and protests by screeching loudly.

'Allah,' she exclaims and bows as much her fat body allows, straightens up to stretch her hands to show him his fourth son who is yet to be named. The baby is all wrapped up in woollens. The six-month -old boy who is a Sunni from father's side and a Shia from mother's side has suddenly stopped wailing and has opened his eyes. Aurangzeb peers into those two brilliant pools of innocence and feels calm.

'I will name him Mohammad Akbar, after my great-great grandfather.' This baby may turn out to be my most suitable successor; the thought flashes across his mind as his eyes wander beyond the woman who holds his infant son. From behind her, seven-year-old Azam stares at him. Aurangzeb leans forward and tumbles when he tries to touch his first son born to Dilras. The boy jumps with fright and disappears. There is not much left to do, but to meet his second wife Nawab Bai. He crosses a few courtyards to reach the house of Mohammad Sultan's mother. Seeing him at their doorstep, the guards kneel. He has no time to nod and rushes in to face his second wife. Aurangzeb finds her looking old, her upper lip turned in a slight curl. 'Is she snarling?' he wonders and cannot believe that he once thought she was beautiful. He shakes his head in dismay and moves to sit on a large divan. The foyer is huge, covered with hand knotted, sapphire blue Kashmiri rugs and filled with carved furniture made of walnut wood, wrapped in ruby red tapestry.

Nawab Bai stands in front of her husband of twenty-two years who sits awkwardly on her gilded divan as if he is being punished. Bitterness wells up in her heart, filling her with resentment. She tries hard not to show her emotions – it is the irony of life. A man's love for a woman or vice versa does not always grow with time but hate persists and swells. Just a few years ago, she had pined for his gaze and would outline her eyes with antimony powder, drawing lines up to her hairline and thicken her lashes with soot from oil lamps. Her gaze would leap and sprint, sometimes falling at her feet and sometimes resting on her husband's face.

'Our Sultan won the battle of Hyderabad,' she says hoping that that might stir some emotions in him.

'With the help of Mir Jumla,' he comments wryly.

He treats even their boy with contempt, his own flesh and blood. Her eyes bore into him. He is visiting her after many years and had looked different then. Time has changed him without mercy: his face gaunt, almost vacant, his nose on the verge of resembling a knife blade, his brows starting to beetle. *Life lived in the battlefields,* she thinks about him but is overwhelmed with self pity. This man has avoided her, as if she were a redundant creature, lusted for but never loved. He has reduced her to being just a number who lives in the imperial harem, an old forgotten hag. She is shunned by the other women in the zenana who are Muslims by birth and who do not consider her to be a natural member of royal seraglio. They call her a second wife, making it sound cheaper than a concubine. But she has two sons to prove her legitimacy. It had not bothered her as long as her husband came to her apartments. But things have changed now.

'Now say what you want to,' he says, getting impatient.

Between man and wife all cannot be put down in words. Dilras's death has brought new hopes. She fidgets, as her wide and flowing long skirt sways. Is she being penalised for being born a Hindu? But that had not daunted him from spending nights and sometimes even days in her lap, as her long curls had covered him like the panels of a tent. Her being an *infidel* did not deter him when she was young, when he took her like a fervently possessed, never satiated predator. Her *religious infidelity*, her being a born *kafir*, did not bother him when he seeded her with two sons. She feels a new surge of anger rising in her and looks at him, the man responsible for her loneliness and isolation.

'I have heard that you are going north...'she says, not knowing what else to talk about.

'Is that why you called me here? Where I do not want to be?' he cries, getting vicious.

She feels humiliated and glances at his hands resting on his lap; they look rough and dark. Those hands had once touched her bare body. Just the memory makes her hair stand straight on her skin. Despite her rage, she longs for that to happen again. Like in the past, she longs for that look in his eyes, severe with craving, yet shining with interest. She has not forgotten how she used to chew beetle leaves to redden her lips and suck some musk pastilles to sweeten her breath. For the past months, she has been smearing herself with sandalwood paste to improve her complexion.

'It has been years since you have set foot in my apartment,' she murmurs, walking two steps ahead.

He winces, wondering if there is any sarcasm in her voice but finds none. This makes him uncomfortable and forces him to almost pity her. He regards her for a moment; she has not tied her hair and let it fall on her hips. The aroma of meat kebabs, roasted gosht and fried cashews wafts in the air. He looks at her. This is the woman who is responsible for his Dilras's death. This is the woman who had gossiped about Dilras being cursed and thus bearing only girls. She is the reason why Dilras insisted on having more children, hoping they would be sons. Dilras had already become weak after bearing him three girls. Aurangzeb had married a local girl called Aurangabadi purely for physical needs. He had decided not to touch Dilras again, not because he did not love her, but because more pregnancies would have proved dangerous. And they eventually did!

'Some yogurt mixed with honey?' she asks, hoping he will agree.

'I will be leaving for the north in the next few days,' he says coldly.

She freezes for a moment, jerks her head back in defiance, as a kind of riposte to her husband. She is the daughter of a king from Kashmir.

'Sultan will go with me,' he sounds curt and is up to leave.

'I am sorry about the Begum,' she says softly.

He stares at her this time, his pale eyes colder than ice.

'You hated her, didn't you?'

She says nothing as she watches him go. He has shattered her illusions. She does not hate Dilras as she hates the men in her life. First it is her father who had shamelessly surrendered to the Emperor Shah Jahan and turned into a mere vassal. Then it is her grandfather who had weaved the story of her birth to marry her off into the imperial family, done so that the men in her family are showered with titles and rewarded with high military posts. Her grandfather's story is the most disgusting tale that she has ever heard. A Muslim saint named Syed

Shah Mir had come to the hills of Rajauri, his kingdom in Kashmir. He had offered the saint his maiden daughter, a virgin of fifteen. They had had children and one of them had been Nawab Bai. The saint had later disappeared into the Himalayas. This was said to prove that Muslim blood gushed through her veins.

She shivers with indignation and falls to her knees, closes her eyes and prays fervently. She prays for the victory and welfare of the man she hates the most, her husband! The safety and life of her two sons depend on his capabilities. She prays to Allah and the long forgotten Hindu gods of her childhood. A guilt rises in her mind; *will God answer her prayer and why should he?*

***

'That's decided then, my prince?' Najabat Khan asks politely.

Aurangzeb eyes the tall and muscular *mansabdar* who stands before him and nods. It has been ten days since he has shifted to his camp. His tent is roomy but almost empty with just a wooden couch in the middle and a scribe's writing desk in one corner. The camp brims over with the clamour of the soldiers, yelling of servants, rattling of carts, hammering of weapon-smiths, neighing and trumpeting of animals. The racket makes him feel at home. His nostrils tingle with the reek of urine. Sometimes the wind brings in the aroma of meat boiling in large earthen pots kept in the open. Even the smoke of firewood does not bother him.

Mutamad stands behind his master but his eyes are fixed on Najabat.

'We have mustered quite a number of horsemen,' Najabat states, looking at Aurangzeb, who sits on the divan and counts beads.

Aurangzeb frowns at Najabat's serious expression. He glances at his scribe, sitting behind a low desk, surrounded by mountains of papers. The man is staid, a stereotype, talks less and never smiles, but is blessed with a sharp memory. The third prince asks, 'How many men have come from Bidar since last week?'

The scribe does some quick calculations with his fingers before replying in a low voice, 'Five thousand, my Prince.'

Jaffar Khan, the man managing Bidar after he had left, has been doing his job well and has already lured more than ten thousand of the Bijapur soldiers with the tribute money paid by their own Badi Begum.

Najabat Khan scratches his chin through his beard to clear his head. Even though reinforcements sent by the Emperor have left, they still have a few hundred *mansabdars* assigned for the Deccan. Combined with Bijapur soldiers, they will have twenty-five thousand cavalry troopers.

'You must hear what my youngest brother has written,' Aurangzeb says to Najabat with a sneer on his face. 'Read the letter from the viceroy of Gujarat,' Aurangzeb orders his scribe. The scribe finds the paper quickly in the priority folder.

Bhai, waiting seems so eternal while our enemy is growing stronger. Brother, make haste and move northwards from Aurangabad. If we delay our heretic brother, our father's most favourite son, Darabhai, will have time to muster more and more men. I want to join you to fight againt Darabhai, I will go with you. My further actions depend on your orders. In the depth of my heart I know it is our beloved Darabhai who is running the affairs of the Empire, from behind the throne. I want to see him dead, beheaded, his torso rolling in his own blood, the mulhid haramzada, *the bastard atheist pretending to be a Muslim!*

Najabat is amused. To start with, Murad Baksh is a drunkard and has recently murdered his loyal minister. The good-for-nothing youngest prince has already crowned himself the next emperor and his latest antics is the plundering of the Empire. He has hastily sent his personal army of eunuchs to Surat, the Empire's most famous port where the British and the Dutch ships anchor. It is stuffed with imperial treasure, the collection of custom levies. The basement is hired by the local merchants as a safe deposit vault. Murad's eunuchs have blown up the parts of the defending wall and have robbed the treasure that is meant for the military expenses. Like a dying atheist who conveniently resorts to God, the same Murad has suddenly remembered that he has a brother in Aurangzeb. Countless mails have arrived from Gujarat, filled with abuses and plans to murder Dara Shikoh.

Aurangzeb knows what his most trustworthy *mansabdar* thinks. He says softly, 'Darabhai is on another trip. He tries to be a liberal and wants to be another Akbar; my great-great-grandfather was also a born military general and a gifted administrator. Darabhai is a military-lliterate bookworm, basking in the reflected glory of his wealth that has come easily to him.'

'Orthodox *mansabdars* assigned to do court duties are already weary of the first prince's love for the *kafirs*. They hate him for giving importance to Hindu pundits and propagating Sufism among the fellow Sunnis. The *mullahs* and *ulemas* fear the loss of their importance if the first prince comes to power. They will not support him in crisis,' states Najabat.

A mysterious smile appears on the third prince's face.

Najabat smiles too and asks, 'What is the latest news?' Aurangzeb glances at his scribe who knows what his master wants. He picks up a note from the collector of Agra. The man is an orthodox Muslim and hates the first prince for his liberal views on Islam. The scribe reads aloud, *Prince Dara Shikoh has recently shifted the Emperor to Agra and guards his apartments like a tigress guarding her cubs. Only Padishah*

Begum Jahanara, a few grave looking Hakeems *and some eunuch slaves are allowed to enter the chamber of the patient. Padishah, the Emperor himself never appears in public, giving room to speculation. People throng in front of the window of the special court, every day to see him, but go back, the jharoukha remains empty. Even I have not seen him for weeks.*

'Father loves *jharoukha-e-darshan*, the ritual of of appearing in the balcony to take salute at the march past, to show himself to his subjects and see them perform *kurnih* with his own eyes. And now, it is of paramount significance that he shows himself to his people to crush the rumours of him being an invalid and to prove that he is alive and well.'

'We should go north immediately. I have a request: if and when we do start our northward journey, we must not halt for more than two nights at any place, because if we do, it will only embolden them,' Najabat says.

Aurangzeb raises his brows. Nobody else talks to him the way Najabat Khan does. And he does not take such comments from anyone else other than his uncle Shaista Khan. But Najabat is a man of firm loyalty and great daring.

What Aurangzeb does not know is that he is also a man who desires very young boys and who would know that better than Mutamad? It was before the third prince had taken Mutamad as his personal attendant. Najabat had a harem, four wives and countless slave women. But Mutamad remembers the nights he was forced to spend with Najabat; painful nights that made him weak with agony. Mutamad shudders to think that, thankfully, Najabat has no idea that the small boy he molested is now his master's personal servant. He has decided never to share his past with the third prince, who, in the eyes of Mutamad, is a man akin to God.

Najabat has noticed Mutamad, the beardless, well-groomed eunuch wearing cloths made of expensive silk. He has a tall and thin body with narrow shoulders. And the skin is very fair, almost alabaster. There is something very familiar about the face, feminine yet a bit broad for a woman. As Najabat tries to remember, a shiver runs through his spine.

'First tell me how and then I shall give my views,' Najabat hears his master's question.

He is quick to respond: 'I have heard that Mirza Raja Jai Singh and prince Suleiman have gone eastward with more than twenty thousand men to stop prince Shuja from advancing towards Agra. They must have thought of blocking our path too. If we halt, we give them time to march southwards.'

'*The essence of my strategy is divide and defeat.* I want them to come. Half of Darabhai's army will be forced to guard Agra and half will march southwards to intercept us. We have better chances to win two battles with two smaller armies than one battle with against one single massive army. If we halt for a fortnight before crossing the Narmada River, they will have time to advance towards us and stop us,' Aurangzeb gives his perspective with a strange smile on his face.

'Do you think the first prince will come personally or send someone else?' Najabat Khan, his eyes shining with interest.

'I hope the intended heir-apparent who has induced Father to recall the reinforcements from the Deccan comes to meet me in the battlefield. I have got the news that the coward, sitting safely in Agra forts, has established a direct contact with Bijapur's king and offered him peace for a large indemnity. I hope this time he leaves the safe precincts of my father's forts and meets me in the battlefield,' Aurangzeb says tersely and then suddenly breaks into recitation:

A man far from his asylum,
Helpless, needy and forsaken

Stalked by a hungry death
Then he pleads and then he cries and then he rants
While the lions are shredded by fishes
And crocodiles are devoured by ants.

Najabat Khan looks at his master with reverence.

'Khan Sahib,' Aurangzeb declares while his fingers count the beads of his *tesbih*, 'our halt is not to while away our time. The halt may give us the time to see which of our *mansabdars* are worthy to undertake such a long and dangerous journey. To reach Agra, we will have to travel six hundred miles through the sands of Rajasthan and dangerous hills of Chambal in blazing summer. When we halt before we undertake the perilous expedition, we will use the time to watch our *mansabdars*. Those who show reluctance will be left behind and dealt with later. Wars like these cannot be fought with burden of betrayal on your shoulders. *La ilah ilallah*,' the third prince murmurs, 'there is no God like *Allah*.'

In a flash, Najabat Khan darts towards his master and falls prostrate. He takes Aurangzeb's feet in his hands and kisses them gently and says in a quivering voice, 'God alone shows the way to one on a prophetic mission!'

Mutamad smiles bitterly.

After an overwhelmed Najabat Khan leaves, Aurangzeb checks if Mutamad is near the entrance, ensuring that his personal guards are out of earshot. He starts dictating to his scribe. The letter is for Murad Baksh.

My devout struggle to rip off the wicked roots of idolatry and infidelity from the realm of our Islamic Empire is already planned and in place. And my brother, you, whom I hold dearer than my own heart, wishes to join me in this holy endeavour. Your wish has renewed the confirmation of faith and teamwork, based on promises and oaths. I shall consider our losses and gains as one. I shall favour you more once the Mulhid, the idolater is plucked out and removed from our path. You cannot imagine what I have in mind for you. I crave to see you sitting on our father's peacock throne.

Aurangzeb stops. He has said all that he wanted to. That night he wanders through his camp. His mind shuttles between the Deccan and the north. *What is Shiva Bhosale up to?* he wonders.

***

Raghunath Ballal Korde is busy with his second military assignment seventy miles south of the port city of Kalyan and twenty-five miles east of Sindhusagar, the Arabian Ocean. The not-so-steep hill he climbs is enveloped in mist. Above him south-westerly monsoon winds shove the gigantic clouds towards the north. Raghunath hopes that it doesn't start raining, for in this region of Konkan, rain falls like a million waterfalls plunging from sky cliffs. The faint foot-trail has gone miry, sometimes forcing him to waddle through the knee deep sludge. He looks back; the mist swirls over the lush green slopes. Raghunath and his men have reached the edge of the Ghosal village. It is very early in the morning and a few birds nestling in the canopies above have started tweeting. The mist vibrates with another sound. Bells in the nearby Ganesha temple toll for the day's first prayer. The deity is famous, and the villagers vouch that the deity's followers have increased manifold over the years. He wishes he could see the idol and fall prostrate. Instead he crouches, darts from one tree to another, hiding behind trunks to enter the wooded area behind the temple, unseen. It is a patch of dense forest, grown over the last stretch that takes you to the fort at the hill's crest. He glances back and sees no one, just the lonely rain trees with enormous branches to hold their canopies. His men surely know how to conceal themselves and advance.

Raghunath and his two thousand men had ridden from Kalyan, with a speed of forty miles a day, had met a few fishermen en route and hired a hundred *dinghies*, to reach the island fort called the Janjira. The news is that the small row-boats have already gathered at a quiet corner of the creek, away from the prying eyes. But his first agenda is the hill fort of Ghosal. He has kept a thousand men at the base and has decided to climb the hill on foot with the rest.

'Janjira!' he sighs. The island-fort is the root cause of all the trouble. Raghunath has done his homework. Built on twenty-two acres of an oval shaped rocky island, it is a mile into the choppy sea. Its several *guz* high walls are fortified with nineteen rounded bastions with massive cannons mounted on each. Cannonballs fired from these have repelled countless enemy battleships, sinking some of them. The fort is a township, with palatial citadel overlooking the sea, quarters for officers, and two huge sweet water tanks. There are underground vaults, more like dungeons where the Siddi, the African chief, keeps the captured slaves. People are branded and shipped to the desired destinations, and countless young men and boys are castrated and made eunuchs. More than two thousand Siddi soldiers live in there, pirates at sea and raiders at land. Janjira is at the mouth of Rajpuri Creek, the biggest in this part of the shore. It is an anchoring place for Siddi's vessels. They also rule over the surrounding mainland including the Ghosal Fort. It is here that they keep their horses to raid nearby terrains. The Muslim rulers are least bothered, because Siddis supply them with slaves and protect their ships carrying royal pilgrims to Mecca. A fine nexus of imperialists, Bijapurians and the pirates!

Raghunath and his men have reached the outer wall of the Ghosal

Fort. He has been informed by his scouts that the northern ramparts are empty. More than a hundred years of peaceful life has made the Africans smug. Raghunath waits for the other scouts, who have scaled the walls, to return. Overhead, the clouds have turned darker. A few of his men appear from behind the tree trunks and the overgrown shrubs. He looks at the fort wall and notices two small figures, his scouts, running towards him. There is no garrison in the fort; its quarters, chambers, vaults and courtyards are empty but for the usual staff of servants and a few guards minding the granaries that seem well stocked. The scouts have checked all the western trails for ambushes. Apart from some urchins playing on the hill's western slopes overlooking a wooded area called the Khoryache forest, there is no movement on that front.

Feeling safe, his men, dark and wiry with scabbards hanging to their belts, gradually gather around him. He makes a quick decision. Most of his men will stay put at the fort. He will go back to the base and ride towards the creek a few miles south, along with his men waiting at the base. Then he would venture into the sea for the first time in his life and sail west over the waters of Sindhu Sagar, towards Janjira.

It is almost noon when the boats carrying him and his men finally float over the sea waters. It has started to drizzle. Raghunath eagerly scans the skyline while holding on to the hull as his boat bounces ahead, its bow rising and diving with the waves. As two fishermen frantically row the boat, his heart beats faster as he notices a long wall rising above the enormous rocks of the island. It is so massive that it looks like a sea-beast riding the ocean. He has read how the African sailors had managed to whisk the island from the *kolis* or the fishermen who were its original inhabitants. More than a hundred years ago the Siddis had gotten hold of it by fraud. They had sailed from the port of Surat, their ship loaded with fine wooded chests, embellished with gilded gold designs. They had asked the fishermen to permit them to store their goods on the island, saying that the chests were stuffed with wine and silk. To celebrate their alliance, the Africans had thrown a big party. The fishermen had got drunk. At midnight the chest had popped open and a thousand armed Africans had emerged like ants and done away with the entire *koli* community of the island.

Raghunath narrows his eyes to see the tiny figures of men scurrying on the ramparts of the fort. As his boats near the fort, the thunderous roars of the waves crashing on the rocks make his heart pound. Soon everything is a blur as the rain falls in sheets. He can only see one of his boats. A harsh crashing sound rises above the sound of waves and rain. Something has hit the boat. To his horror it sinks, taking a few of his men along. The deafening sound of cannons continues. Sea-men minding his boat lose their sense of direction and the boat meanders violently. After a while it stops raining but he is soaked and dizzy. The fort has vanished from his sight. It is just the gray-blueness of the waves around him. *What is inside that sinister looking fort?* he wonders.

Inside Janjira, it is business as usual, especially in the dungeons. The room is dark and cold like an operating room with only one wooden table in the middle. Two men swab the floor, the water in their metal buckets turning a deep shade of red with every wash. A small child lies on the table, naked, sobbing softly and staring at the low ceiling with his large eyes. From a vent near the corner of the room sunlight falls through cutting the darkness with its straight path. Two huge candles burn on a *guz*-high wrought iron stand. Its pale glow falls on the child, his thin hands folded over his ribs. A few turbaned men wearing white robes stand around the table. Their faces crowd in over him. One of them strokes his head and tenderly pinches his cheek. An old man with a bowl of green paste tries to soothe the small boy, an anxious patient.

'Apply the neem,' someone snaps as the old man mutters something apologetically and starts applying the paste on the child's penis, scrotum and testicles in circular motion. One of the men brings out a long flexible metal wire from the bulging pocket of his robe that is covered with blotched red patches and ties it loosely around the child's organ. Another man holding a knife seems ready and waiting impatiently. The old man backs off. In a moment, the metal strings are pulled tight and the barber's knife cuts through in a swift stroke. The surgery is over. The operation room is filled with the agonising cries. Blood splutters vigorously. The man who has tied the strings takes a twig out of his pocket and pokes the area oozing with blood as if searching for the right spot. He pushes the twig in once he finds the hole for the urine to discharge. 'Keep him awake for forty hours,' someone tells the old man as he gathers the child in his arms to take him away.

It is not every day that you get a boy who is fair. If the boy comes out the ordeal alive, he could be sold for a very good price, at least several times more than the price of an ordinary slave. The profits run high, even if eight out of ten boys bleed to death after the operation. It is a seller's market, the demand is bigger than they can supply. The requirement is huge and runs into thousands per year. Eunuchs are needed by all, including the royals, noblemen, and military officials. There is less competition in this business. The centres at Goa do not produce them in big numbers as in the past. Only Golconda Kingdom has some slave merchants supplying thousands of castrated boys a year. It is considered such a noble deed, a grand service. The Muslim kings and their large zenanas, the seraglios that contain hundreds or even thousands of women, grandmothers, mothers, wives, daughters, aunts, maids, need these men. The harems filled with courtesans, concubines and sex slaves are indeed a security hazard. They are pit-holes of affairs, gossips, intrigues where assassinations and revolts are planned. It is a humungous task to control the young women in the harem. Keeping men to watch them is as disastrous as keeping butter near the fire. The king needs attendants and guards and they cannot be men, or women.

The young boy will have a new life of a *hijra*, meaning divine soul. One day he might become a senior eunuch and possibly be known as a *nazir* or a *khwaja Saras* and may have a number of junior eunuchs to supervise. The boy is rather fair and is blessed with good features and perhaps may become the king's lover or a confidant.

Ear-piercing cries are heard in the dungeons below the operation room. The sound rattles through the corridors, simple tunnels lit by a few torches. In a gloomily lit passage, a few young men with their hands tied behind them are poked and prodded with iron rods and are driven by blows of a belt made of hide. On either side small rooms are barred with iron grills and are stuffed with huddled women and children, all shackled in iron chains. Some are weeping and some have fallen into a trance of dread.

'Wash them all and send them to the ship,' a man shouts at his servants from the end of the tunnel and climbs the staircase to come out in the open. *It is better to sell them fresh, before they are infested with lice or scabies or infect everyone before dying of some disease in the dungeons,* he thinks while rushing across a coconut grove towards a round pool. The rain has almost stopped. His wives and concubines, some African, some European and some local women dressed in short skirts and even shorter cholis are having fun at the shallow end. They giggle while splashing water on each other. Their pleated skirts make circles around them and they look like colourful water lilies. Siddi Kashim grins, removes his tunic, flings it away before diving into the deeper end. On the poolside, his smaller children romp around, black, brown and some pale, with heads covered with woolly or straight hair. He tries to remember the number of his children but gives up the effort; just looking at them makes him feel good about himself, his virility, his manhood. He lowers himself in the water enjoying its coolness and then floats on his back to stare at the faraway ramparts that rise high beyond the wall enclosing the pool. This is his unbeatable sea-fort, built by his forefathers, standing on an oval shaped rock a mile away from the shores of Konkan. In the midst of women's laughter and shrieks, he hears a guard calling him from beyond a wall built for privacy. Usually no one dares to disturb him unless the reason is a compelling one. He swears and swims to the edge, shoving away his youngest concubine, who has glided to be near him to press her body onto him. As he comes out, a eunuch slave, dark as basalt and thin as reed, appears from behind a fern bush and hands him a towel.

He walks across the gardens wiping himself and opens the door brashly. The guard is scared of his master who is a large man, with muscles corded like the bark of a banyan tree and eyes sharp like a blade. He has a habit of flying into a rage. His fury is legendary; when it possesses him he kills people by blows of his fists, or kicks them to death.

'Chief Yakob has a message for you.'

Siddi Kashim stares at the guard and nods, giving him permission to speak further. The message is from his younger brother. The dark man wearing a black turban and a short tunic rattles, now with some relief, 'The Marathas have taken Ghosal. But when they tried to attack the fort by sailing in small fishing boats, many sunk after our cannonballs hit them. Some of the boats toppled, sending many to their water graves.'

Siddi Kashim smiles and slams the door shut.

On his way back to his pool, he laughs at Shiva Bhosale and his men. The idiots have attacked his fort in fishing *dinghies*. Like frogs getting at a crocodile or turtles attacking a killer shark. If only they knew the strength of this sea-fort, Janjira, they would have sunk their pathetic boats themselves. They are also ignorant about his men, with their strain of African blood, trained sailors and soldiers, fit as stallions, one equal to ten natives in strength. As long as these empires and the kingdoms lack naval power, he is safe and at nobody's mercy. In fact, it is them who are at his mercy. They need his help to sail to Mecca. They depend on him for slaves of good quality.

The tightly packed ship must have reached the deep seas, he thinks before he jumps back into the pool.

The ship has indeed reached the deep seas. Balaji Avaji and the hundreds of men around him can hardly move, as one man's ankle is shackled to another's. Some are chained to the deck by their necks or hands. It has been a full day since their confinement. His body is numb and his stomach rambles in hunger. The burning pain on his right shoulder is acute. They were branded with red-hot iron before being thrown on the deck like goats or horses. The ship has hit rough seas and is rocking like a swing. His mind goes back to his father, mild tempered, an eye opaque with cataract, sinewy neck fixed on a prematurely bent spine, working long hours as an accountant and scribe for the masters of the Janjira fort. It was his karma to work for the Siddis. Only once in his thirty long years of service, had he broken the karma protocol and tried to protest against the sinister operations. A sin was committed. The Siddis had suspected him to be the traitor, leaking information to the Marathas. The consequence was that his father lay at the bottom of this ocean, stuffed in a gunny bag made heavy with stones and knotted at both the ends.

Balaji's body convulses with sobs. Someone behind him has eased himself and the stench is unbearable. There is a small tank full of water to wash up but they cannot reach it easily. They are tied down by heavy chains. The man next to him has started vomiting. He closes his eyes and starts weeping. He is just seventeen. His dream of becoming a scribe is over. It is his fate to be a slave. *Or a eunuch,* he thinks and shudders.

The man has stopped vomiting. He glances at him: the man has fallen back and his shackled legs are twisted. He looks like a dead grasshopper. Someone screams, saying there is a dead man among them.

Two sailors appear from the deck; these huge men with long matted hair do not bother to check if the man is indeed dead. They discuss something, letting strange syllables fly in the air while unshackling him. It is difficult to drag him through the crowd.

The ship starts rocking even more violently as the rain hits the deck. One of them looks at Balaji Avji for a moment before bending and unlocking his shackles with just one click. The sailor signals him to lift the dead man.

He gets up feeling giddy, his legs are numb. Somehow, he manages to pull the limp body over his shoulders. Some more fluids leak out of the dead man's mouth, its stench making him sick. He moves unsteadily through the rows of chained men with the weight on his shoulders, and almost tumbles as the ship rolls over the wild waters. Many have started retching, and the wooden floor has become slippery. He knows about ships and this one is broad-decked. He spots a formidable gun behind her foremast. They drag him near the railings and push the man resting on his shoulders over the board and into the sea.

Balaji stares at the sea mesmerised. He has never seen such giant waves, like mountains of water moving towards him. For a moment he does not know where the sea is or the sky. The sailors try to wrench him back to his place and chain him again. As they yank him, he looks at the sea for the last time and notices a mighty wave hitting the deck. The ship first shudders, twists violently, and then topples over.

He only remembers waves, gigantic, like surging, fluid mountains. He let goes, but tries to stay afloat. The last of his memories is a *dinghy*, and a few men shouting to help him.

Ten | Birth of His Navy

Circa 1658

It is winter. A few miles west of Kalyan, Shivaji and his men, Niraji Rauji, Abaji Sondev and Tanaji Malusare stand in the compound of an enormous shipyard. The leader of the Marathas looks at Niraji and smiles. The forty-year-old Brahmin is a scholar in subjects like law, history and finance and has been working for him as an advisor for several years. His advice is now needed direly. It's the beginning of the Maratha navy. The investment is huge but the returns are not immediate. Shivaji slowly shifts his gaze towards the Ulhas river. He is fascinated by its wide girth, a perfect waterway for sleek, predatory vessels to enter the wide expanse of the open sea, guard the coast and come back quickly for safety if such the need be. It is a moment of triumph. This river, the surrounding forests of teak, and the twenty-five hill forts of north Konkan were initially a part of Nizamshahi. After its annexation this region had become a part of Adilshahi. Now the Adilshahi rulers have traded it off to the Mughals in hope of an elusive peace. But there is trouble in the north and Aurangzeb has reached Aurangabad. Many of his *mansabdars* have been called back to Agra. Circumstances have given Shivaji a chance to take over the north Konkan, without the interference of the mighty Mughal. 'Swaraj is really His wish,' he says as the ship-workshop glimmers in the noon sun behind him.

Niraji agrees with his master, more so because they have acquired the region without much bloodshed, even the hill forts have been easy conquests. Adilshahi officials had not bothered to keep their military strongholds of the Konkan well-manned or well-equipped.

'They have never understood the strategic importance of this region,' Niraji says softly. For a while he has been studying the military importance of Konkan and meeting the local fishermen to know more about the coastline and the pirate ships that prowl the waters. Niraji is surprised by the formation of natural ports in the terrain. After crossing Kalyan, the river splits into two further downstream. Its north branch joins the creek at Vasai, currently under the rule of the *firangs*, while its southern branch ends into a massive bay called the Bombay harbour, again used by the *firangs*. Even Salsette Island, lying between the two branches of the Ulhas river is owned by them.

Tanaji, who stands behind the scholar Brahmin, listens to the conversation between Raja and Niraji with interest. He has been on a mission to search for the remote villages at the foothills of the mountains to the eastern side of north Konkan. The region is covered with giant teak trees with layered leafy tops. The forest is intersected by rivers plunging down from the mountains. Along with his two thousand footmen, he has been busy laying tracks to improve the transport of fallen teak trunks to Kalyan. He is here to see their first shipyard.

Shivaji starts walking away from the river and towards the lone massive structure that stands in the middle of of the open yard. His men and a few guards follow him. Their eyes dart to spot trouble, a hiding archer or a spearman. It is stiflingly warm inside the enormous foyer stuffed with ship-building material. It is bright too as sunlight sneaks in through large, open windows. The roof is made of wood and is held by wide brick pillars, supporting parallel bays to park smaller boats. At the far end, countless logs of wood are neatly piled against the wall and the floor is covered with masts, oars, ribs, mallets, augurs and boat bases. A large wooden table in the middle is piled with paper sheets, compasses, measurements tapes, pensils, rules, inkpots, penknives and magnifying lenses. A few men are seen working around a wooden table.

They are so short, how do they ever handle those long swords? wonders Rue De Guevera, the Portuguese ship engineer, who has recently started working for Shivaji against the wishes of the Portuguese viceroy of Goa. The tall and fair shipbuilder looks smart in a mantle made of Indian silk, with a little embroidery near the collar. The colour of his cap matches his clothes. He loves to dress well and enjoys a carefree life. He has been warned that the Hindu man he works for is a famous outlaw and is considered a criminal by the Muslim kingdoms. The officials of Goa are not pleased with him and have complained to the higher authorities. Letters have been sent to Portugal but he does not care. Three year ago, the viceroy of Goa, the Portuguese Capital of India, was expelled in an internal coup, and the usurper was arrested by another man who had claimed to be the successor of the expelled viceroy. The successor too had died mysteriously. The current governing council of three men is hopeless. There is anarchy and most of his countrymen are therefore doing what they please.

This is the ship engineer's fourth meeting with his employer and he is all ready for the barrage of instructions. To his right, his assistants are busy drawing on papers spread on the table. Much to Guevera's irritation, it is still cluttered with compasses, rulers and drawing knives. He likes his men to keep mum in his meetings. All of them are mere technicians without an iota of business sense. But again this is not the time to admonish them.

People have started fussing near the entrance. Some of his Indian carpenters talk excitedly, as they always do when their employer, Shivaji Bhosale arrives with his men, their eyes looking at every overhanging shelf, searching for any suspicious movement. Guevera's assistants promptly leave their tools and stand at attention.

'*Bomdia*,' Guevera bows deep and greets the brown-eyed short man who wears a slanting turban embellished with pearl strings. Shivaji smiles briefly and starts talking rapidly. The translator, a native Catholic, who had been chatting with Guevera's men, jumps forward. His experience says that he is expected to catch the Marathi words that fly faster than popping kernels.

'As we have discussed, the frigates, must be lightweight, not more than a hundred and fifty tons, even smaller would do, so that they can seek refuge under every shelter the land offers, deep or shallow, and can anchor near every port, big or small. Make sure that they are driven by sails as well as oars. Make them as manoeuvrable as possible. Speed is vital. Have a deck or two that will be able to carry a principle battery of carriage-mounted guns and a hundred sailors and fighters put together.'

The interpreter, who has taken off his cap to wipe his sweaty head, is trying to keep pace, fumbling occasionally.

They have discussed the specifications before but his new employer wants to be very sure. Guvera does not mind the continuous hail of instructions. He likes the clarity as it gives him a clear vision of what needs to be done.

Shivaji puts forth a new demand. 'Make them as lightweight as possible, with not more than two masts. We must be able to tow them with row boats.'

'We need twenty such ships within a year,' announces a man an official manner. Guevera has not noticed him till then, a thin, immaculately dressed Brahmin wearing a huge red turban, and with eyes as brown as his master's.

The demand is stiff and the time short, despite his hundred

technicians and countless craftsmen. He quickly calculates: twenty ships made will cost one hundred and twenty thousand rupees which is equal to a hundred *ser* of gold. He and his men earn a hefty percentage. He wonders how rich the native man is. Guvera looks at his assistants, who, despite his warnings, listen in on the conversation. One of the bolder ones whispers, 'We would be able to submit the designs in four weeks.'

'Make your designs both on paper and as models carved in wood and iron. Send them to us as soon as you finish,' says Shivaji with an air of finality. The meeting is over. The engineer watches his employer leave, without goodbyes or adeus or even a hint of acknowledgement.

Niraji knows what the *firang* thinks. Following social etiquettes is really not his master's strong point, and especially not when the discussions are about specific tasks. As he follows Shivaji to the exit, Tanaji and his men walk behind them. Outside, in the yard, the air is not too clammy and a salty breeze blows from the west. They walk through the dock filled with the hulls of two half-built battleships. Noticing Shivaji, the workmen leave their work tools on the floor and spring to their feet to glance at their new ruler. Shivaji walks ahead. He is keen to inspect the supporting wooden framework around the hull. The scaffoldings have lattice work, distinctly *firang* in style. Shivaji gazes at the ramp, trying to gauge if he can leap over it. A labourer, applying caulking to the fixed panels, swiftly moves across and gives him a hand. The leader of the Marathas walks over the ramp built alongside the hull of one of the ships. Fascinated, he looks around as the entire yard unfolds before his eyes. At the far end, under the shade of a huge banyan tree, carpenters saw timber as workers carry heavy beams of teak laboriously on their shoulders.

Niraji and Abaji march alongside the ramp. Tanaji and the guards follow. Shivaji stops abruptly to touch a wood panel. 'I believed that only the hilt of a sword or the saddle of a horse talked to you when you touched them,' Shivaji turns and glances at the Brahmin, 'but even these planks of the ship have a lot to say.'

'And what do the planks say?' Niraji asks with a faint smile.

'They whisper that they are the parts of a powerful war galley. Within months, as a battleship, they will sail the waters of the Ulhas to glide into the ocean via the creek of Vasai. Despite fewer masts, once the sails are fully spread, the battleship, loaded with cannon, will cause ripples of terror in the waters of the Ocean,' says Shivaji, grinning.

Niraji does not comment. The *firangs* rule the sea; they have colonies from Cape-of-Good-Hope to Macau in Chinaland. Most of the important ports between Diu in the north of Konkan and Kochi in the south belong to them, with Goa as their capital. Niraji had once visited their shipyard in the southern part of Goa. It was enormous, built at the edge of the ocean. Thousands of native and European carpenters and coopers swarmed like ants around a half-built vessel that lay about three hundred *guz* across the yard. Its wooden frame looked like the gigantic ribs of a beast fitted on a wooden keel and planked with wooden boards. Countless blacksmiths hammered the dark metal to give it shape. The air was heavy with the smell of molten iron. 'It is a galleon, propelled by sails alone,' someone had whispered. 'It can carry sixty cannon and four hundred sailors and seamen.'

'I know what you are thinking, Nirajipunt,' he hears Raja's words. 'It is just the beginning for us. We will soon take over the trade, at least a part of it.'

Niraji has discussed this issue with his master. It is about the essentials of life. Salt is harvested and spice is grown in Konkan. They need to be transported from one port to another and then carried by the oxen to the cities on the mountain plateaus through the tracks that run through Javali. The merchants are mostly natives and are compelled to pay hefty fee for passports to the *firangs* to set sail. Siddi pirates attack their ships. *Jagirdars* like Moray fleece them when their oxen carrying goods cross the mountains. Raja dreams to provide the natives with merchant ships at affordable costs and levy reasonable taxes. He also wants to do away with the passports.

The men have reached the end of the shipyard. They stand under the coconut trees at the edge of the yard. Cool shadows of the enormous leaves dance on the ground. Despite winter, the breeze had turned warm and humid. Somewhere in the nearby bushes a lark repeatedly lets out melodious whistles.

'The shipbuilding is only the first step, we will have to take over the ports of Dabhol, Chaul and, if possible, Wasai by sword,' Shivaji announces.

Swaraj needs funds. The main legitimate sources of money are land revenue, road toll collection, and tribute paid by the vassal kings. Konkan is blessed with grooves of coconut. It has orchards of banana, mango, jackfruit, papayas, jamoon, gooseberries, and cashews. Here spices grow in abundance and quality salt is processed from sea water. At its hilly east, the forests are covered with trees. Teakwood from here is transported to different countries in order to build ships.

'Swaraj is His wish, but there are some realities that we must confront, especially when wish to reduce our dependancy on the *watandars*.'

'People with merit over people with hereditary rights!' Abaji comments for the first time adjusting his pagari turban.

'Yes, but that means we pay our military men and our revenue officials every month, directly from our treasury. Our horsemen get five rupees as a monthly salary. Ten thousand horses need sixty thousand ser of grain and fodder every day for survival. Our infantrymen too are on our payroll. The ryots in our regions are provided with farm animals, instruments and quality seeds. If monsoons fail, we wave off the revenue. Do your math, *Puntoji*.'

Niraji clears his throat but keeps mum. The present land revenue is enough just to maintain their tiny military. Konkan provides opportunities in terms taxes on salt, spices or wood. Textile industry has flourished in the natural harbour called Chaul famous for its skilled labour. The weavers spin silk and cotton stuff. Shiploads of their satin, taffeta and muslin bales leave the moors of Chaul for the rest of the world. They are sold mostly to the emperors and the kings.

'Another way to raise funds is to provide ships to our sea merchants. The money can be used to build ports, war-ships and sea-forts,' Shivaji says.

'We have failed to conquer Janjira!' Abaji whispers with shadows of regret in his eyes.

'We will take it one day, or build another equally invincible sea-fort in the near future to keep them under control. You have a lot of work to do Abaji. You will be our *subhedar* of Kalyan.' There is no hint of sarcasm in Shivaji's words.

Abaji's eyes shine with hope.

'That reminds me,' Tanaji says, 'Raghunathpunt has rescued a young boy named Balaji Avji from Prabhu community from the sea. He was on the slave ship of the Siddis. The boy has loafty dreams; he wants to work as a scribe for you.'

'How many could have been rescued, and how many need yet to be rescued from this beautiful coast with an ugly past!' Shivaji says bitterly.

Niraji Rauji closes his eyes as salty breeze from the west whirls around him. The blue green waters of Sindhusagar are tainted with the blood of millions of innocent lives. The land that once swayed with Vedic chants caved in under the Muslim aggressions from the sea and land. Thousands of Hindus were either culled or converted to Islam, and a new community of the Deccani Muslims was born. Then Vasco De Gama, the *firang* sailor, had arrived. It was purely business until Afonso de Albuquerque had set foot on the sands of Konkan. He started slave trade, slaughtered the old and the very young. The healthy children, men, and women had become his new commodity. Following his orders, the *firangs* had captured one port after another, Goa, Dhabol, Chaul, Vasai and Mumbai, and become too rich, too soon. Once the trade had flourished and the Masters of Portugal smelt opportunities, they incited the Church. The Jesuit evangelists had worked on the poor Hindus, first giving them free rice, followed by employment in their colonies and their military. These Hindus had then turned into insanely orthodox Jesuits, just to prove their loyalty. Those who had refused to convert were subjected to evil torture: victims were drawn on spiked wheels with weights tied to them, boiling oil was poured over them and burning sulphur dropped over their bodies. The most hideous punishments included wrenching out human foetuses in slivers from the wombs, the severing of the genitals of men in front of their wives, the hacking off of the breasts of women before their husbands and the piercing of their private parts with daggers.

'Religion, religion, it has become a most lethal weapon,' Shivaji whispers.

'People like Aurangzeb will make it even more dangerous, a weapon of mass destruction!' Niraji comments wryly while fanning himself with his shawl.

'The third prince of the Mughal empire is an enigma. Raghunathpunt has gone to Aurangabad to meet him. All sorts of rumours have been floating in the Deccan about the Emperor's health. People say that Aurangzeb may go north, to Agra. Without him in the Deccan,

Bijapur rulers will have time to deal with us. We need the Mughal backing more than ever before,' Shivaji says.

Niraji raises his brows. 'Will Aurangzeb entertain us?' he asks.

'I do not know but I hope so, no harm in trying.'

'We have plundered the Mughal terrain and we have also taken over the north Konkan that is given to the Mughal by the king of Bijapur. And above all, we are the *kafirs*.' Niraji Rauji narrows his eyes.

'We will try to form an alliance with Aurangzeb; if we fail we will think of something better. Nirajipunt,' Shivaji says with a bitter smile, 'the money we have taken from the Mughal terrain has helped us to pay allownces to our soldiers who have been battling in Konkan for over two months. '

There is a silence for a while.

'*Puntoji*, please say the *schloka* recited by Bhima where he talks about dharma to his oldest brother, the brother who is an austere follower of dharma but has gambled away all their wealth,' Shivaji requests softly.

Niraji clears his throat and says the Sanskrit verse with a slight musical intonation,

'सर्वथा धर्म मूलोर्थो धर्मा सुचार्थ परिग्रह
इतरेतर योनी तौ वधिर्धि मेघोदधी यथा'

'Do tell us what it means,' Tanaji asks with reverence.

The Brahmin obliges, '*Dharma* means religion. But here it refers to the right code-of-conduct. Amassing wealth without *dharma* is as futile as *dharma* of a poor man. What can a poor man do for the people, however good his code-of-conduct may be? But a wealthy king, if he is a follower of *dharma* can change his subjects' lives for the better. He can afford armies to protect them. He can change history! Similarly a wealthy man, who does not follow *dharma*, is nothing but a mindless beast backed by power. For the sake of good, Wealth and *dharma* are interdependent just as the ocean and the clouds. Water vapour rising from the ocean makes rainclouds which fill the ocean. One needs wealth to follow the *dharma*, and *dharma* to make the wealth worthy.'

'We use *dharma*, the religion, as a weapon, a sword to divide people. It is used as a tool to subject humans to unspeakable atrocities and mass slaughter. Muslims, Christians and Hindus are no exception,' says Shivaji scornfully.

'People of Konkan live in constant fear of the marauding Siddis. Many peasants have fled from Rajapuri area into the forests. Adilshahi *subhedar* could have helped them but he did not, because the victims were mere *kafirs*. And he did not want to clash with the Siddis. He and his masters need their help and protection when they travel by ships to Mecca.' Niraji Rauji comments.

'That is where they are wrong. Their interest comes first even when dealing with their own subjects. It is the people who make a country,' Shivaji says while he remembers his past and the lessons he had learnt.

He was eleven. The great famine was over. The monsoon had arrived in full swing. The denuded forest surrounding his stone house had turned green as leaves burst out from the twigs that had suddenly gone tender. Dust devils did not haunt the region anymore; instead, gushing streams had swirled and rushed over rolling cobblestones and danced around the giant boulders. Flocks of different birds had started frequenting the skies above them as if the lost souls with wings had, at last, found their sky. The days had gone by as he, along with his gang had romped and played about. They jumped in the muddy pools to dirty each other's clothes, rode their ponies standing on the stirrups, and followed the shadows of flying eagles. The number of his friends had grown, Tana, Yesa, Tana's brother Surya, Bhima, Bhika, Kavji Chimna, and Bala, some as young as ten and some as old as twenty. The only exception had been Baji Pasalkar who was an old man of sixty. But all that would change. He had noticed a very old man arriving in a palanquin along with Sonoji Dabir. 'He is Dadaji, the Diwan of your father's jagir and the surrounding hill forts,' his mother, sitting on a charpoy in the open veranda, had whispered to him. The men had bowed to her. Dadaji's red silk turban with a wide rim looked like a large umbrella on his head. His eyes were sharp, like a knife with a blade of steel. Shivaji had listened as they discussed something about the peasants who had run away and disappeared in the hills, about the earth that was tilled by donkeys, about the babul trees growing instead of rice and corn saplings, about wolves breeding like lice and snatching away livestock, about hunger despite the rain. 'People without a country and a country without its people,' Dadaji had whispered, this time his deep eyes had cut through Shivaji's soul. 'Raja, you will come with me to find the people of this country, they are yours, and you are their Jagirdar, *the protector of their children and their women.'*

Frail Dadaji could ride a horse through hills. Shivaji and his friends had followed him, had galloped through narrow cattle paths, and had walked where there were no trails. They had spotted men, emaciated, half naked, and hungry. Occasionally Dadaji had spoken to them, and they had invited Dadaji to their shacks, roofed with old tattered clothes, as bandicoots scurried around in fear. They were told, 'He is Raja Shivaji, your Jagirdar's *son. He will help you find your land so that you can till it.' Those unclean, lice ridden people had looked at him, their eyes sparkling with tears. Their children, covered with grime and scabies had stared at him too, with their large and vacant eyes. 'They are peasants of this land. Once upon a time,' Dadaji had explained to him in a grave voice, 'they had grown rice and millets on this earth. They can do so again. As a* jagirdar, *you will have a right to collect a portion of their produce as revenue. With those funds you can maintain a small cavalry, and help Bijapur rulers in times of war. You may, one day, become a famous nobleman in their court just like your father.'*

More than ten expeditions in the wilderness in search of the peasants had borne fruit. They had arrived from the forests, their children trotting behind them. Dadaji had declared that he had a hundred gold coins of a tola each, given to him by Shivaji's father. The money was enough for the initial expenses. Shelters had appeared behind the house. Mother had been busy ordering the maids to get enough water and food. Families were given new clothes. The maids had built large mud stoves in the backyard and had kept them smouldering by blowing air onto the fire with wooden tubes. Shivaji had watched the maids' hands holding the wooden beam of the grinder as it went round and round and the flour poured out like a waterfall from the gap of the round stones. It was collected in a large wooden plate, and kneaded with water to make dough. The women had made small round balls, flattened them and roasted directly over the fitfully glowing embers burning in the stoves. Its aroma wafting in the air had always made him hungry. The peasants and their families had watched wide eyed when they were served hot rotis called the Bhakaris with onions and salt. The hungry peasants had broken open the onions with a single thump of their fist. Within days their gaunt faces had turned cheerful. The air had started filling with sounds of squealing and laughing of children. One afternoon Dadaji had called everyone for a chat. 'Food will soon finish,' he had announced. 'You have eaten well and rested well. Your hands are strong enough to start tilling. The cursed earth when ploughed with donkeys will soon be blessed. Once Shivaji, our young Jagirdar, digs this very earth with a small gold plough, it will be your turn to clear the soil off babul trees, matted roots and weeds.' Their efforts soon turned the barren land into green fields

Groups of pilgrims going northwards, had started stopping for a while, their kartals *and* cymbals *silent. They had gazed at the fields swaying with tiny saplings of millets, their eyes shining with tears of joy, as if they had found some hidden treasure. A few of them had walked into the open veranda of his house to inquire. His mother had given them water and*

some jaggery. They sucked on the unrefined cane sugar candy with relish.
She had appealed them to sing an abhang that was very dear to their saint's
heart. The words of Tukaram had risen above the din of their kartals
and cymbals. One had played Ektari, made of dried pumpkin head held
between split bamboo and just one string.

शूद्र वंशी जन्मलो म्हणोनी दंभे मोकललो

घोकावया अक्षर मज नाही अधिकार

वेडे वाकडे गाइन परी तुझाच म्हणवनि

Those lines remain embedded in his heart.

Am born in a lowly kunbi family

So, thankfully, the conceit has left me

I have no right to learn

But God, I will sing to you

Without concern

My words may not be literary wonders

But God you must listen

Despite the blunders.

***

'Summon Shiva Bhosale's man, with two armed guards on either side, and keep the sentinels posted around the tent. Ask them to be alert,' Aurangzeb says loudly to eunuch Mutamad who is at the entrance. He gathers himself on his divan and picks up his rosary beads lying on a small table next to him, dropping his eyelids like flags flying half mast.

Raghunath is nervous. He has ridden one hundred and fifty miles northwards from Rajgad to reach Aurangabad. The journey had not been easy. But what he has seen after reaching his destination has made him weak with anxiety. It is a massive military camp, with the green tents of the Muslim squadrons and the saffron tents of the Rajput squadrons. There are foreigners in the camp too, tall and the blue eyed men hailing from Afghanistan and beyond and white men from Europe. The camp seems endless with long animal stables that run for miles. Raghunath feels overwhelmed on seeing the weapon-smiths and their portable forges, cartloads of cattle and goats that are fed on the camp, and the markets stuffed with all kinds of things.

But Shivaji's *vakeel* is surprised to see the bare tent of Aurangzeb, the viceroy of the Mughal occupied Deccan. Unlike a few Muslim men of importance whom he had met in the past, the third prince, with his long silvery beard, looks genteel. His divan lacks grandeur and he sits wearing a white, full sleeved robe probably made of chintz, and a matching turban. His fingers count rosary beads. His eyes are half closed, as if he is praying.

'I, the humble *vakeel* of Shivaji Bhosale, bow to the mighty imperial prince, who is also the esteemed imperial *subhedar* of the Deccan.'

Aurangzeb feels the visitor's gaze and knows that he is dealing with a cunning and intelligent man. Shiva's *vakeel* has come for some shameless diplomacy.

'My master, Raja Shivaji Bhosale, asks for pardon.' Raghunath does not waste time and bows as deep as he can. This is another Maratha trait that Aurangzeb hates. No small talk, no pleasantries, no foreplay with words. The Marathas are cunning, like sly foxes hiding in the shadows of tall grass, not showing themselves to the world but gauging it from afar.

Raghunath tries to look into Aurangzeb's eyes, concealed behind his drooping lids, for a hint of a reaction, hoping the prince will grace him by locking eyes with him but it does not happen, not then at least.

'Are you the one who killed the Moray man?' he hears a voice, deep and resonant.

'It was in self defence,' Raghunath says cautiously. Shiva Bhosale's *vakeel* speaks Urdu in a lowly Deccan accent. Like someone who first thinks in his tongue and translates his thoughts in Urdu.

'And the daylight robbery ordained by Shiva at Kalyan?' Aurangzeb asks brazenly, as if he has been waiting to ask this question for a long time.

'The wealth of Kalyan belongs to the imperial treasury, my prince. The Bijapur rulers had ceded the land to the Empire but their governor was a thief fleeing with the treasure,' announces the *vakeel* without wincing or showing any guilt.

'Is Shiva an imperial regent who must worry about us?'

'He is aspiring to be one, my prince,' Raghunath says. His dark eyes are fixed on Aurangzeb who suddenly raises his eyelids. His pale irises make the hair stand straight on the *vakeel's* skin.

'If he is an aspirant then he is not our enemy, he is our servant-to-be. And so his attack on the imperial terrain is akin to treason, an act of sedition, punishable only by death.'

Raghunath steadily replies, 'That mistake has changed my master's life. Since then he has started protecting the imperial interests as if he already is an imperial regent.'

Aurangzeb stares at the *vakeel* with disbelief.

'What he did is still punishable by death, enemy or a servant. He raised his sword against the Islamic Empire and plundered our region... it is like waging war against God.'

Raghunath bites his lips. It is futile to debate. The third prince might bring out a list of all that is punishable by death according to shariah law, the path to be followed. The first crime in the list would possibly be being an infidel, that is, he might say akin to defying the existence of God.

The *vakeel* clears his throat that is itching due to staying in the dusty camp, 'If the imperial prince could officially grant him all the villages and forts in Raja Shiva's possession, he would do everything in his capacity to guard the southern frontiers of the Empire in the Deccan.'

'Even depositing all the funds wrenched from Mulla Ahmed into the imperial treasury?' Aurangzeb cuts in.

'Yes, immediately after the official recognition is granted.' Raghunath is quick.

Aurangzeb shudders with rage. He wants to violently shake the *vakeel*, slap him, slay him and feed him to the wolves. But his priorities have changed. He must deploy his military force to tackle bigger foes. The Empire is at stake.

'*Mashallah*! Tell me what makes Shiva think that we need his help?'

'It is more about serving you, than helping you, my esteemed prince.'

Shiva Bhosale's *vakeel* is a clever scoundrel. And the whole lot of them, the Marathas, are like the mountain rats. Aurangzeb has heard that the rats survived due to their strong sense of smell. It helped them to gather information. It is possible that Shiva has smelt the Emperor's illness, and has as assumed that he, Aurangzeb, would be gone for a long time. In his absence, the Bijapur's army, free from the Mughal aggressions will turn their military against them. If he, Aurangzeb, yields now, showing solidarity, then the story might be different. Shiva needs him more than he needs Shiva. The *harami* wants time to get stronger.

'It is his wish to serve us then. Despite the grave crimes committed by Shiva we may consider his request. Put him and his cavalry to use, someplace somewhere. We shall send him an official letter, sometimes in the future,' Aurangzeb says in a voice devoid of any emotion while he counts his beads slowly and deliberately. This is his way to put off shamelessly persistent people by sounding utterly positive yet totally evasive.

After the *vakeel* leaves, Aurangzeb starts dictating a letter. The letter is for the Badi Begum of Bijapur. She needs some menacing advice. The woman has been writing to the Emperor to gain sympathy and support.

Be advised. Twenty years ago Adilshahi had become the Empire's tributary state. You have paid the initial tribute money. We have been ignoring the arrears. But now you have established a contact with the Emperor. You have promised him that you will pay all the arrears directly to him, casting me aside, I, the imperial subhedar *of the Deccan. What do you think? The Emperor will protect you from me? And that is not all; you have allowed the Deccan to become a breeding ground for the* kafir *rebels. Do not forget that you have renewed the peace treaty with us and have promised us parts of the Nizamshahi territory taken by you twenty years ago. But that region is no longer under your control. And now the north of Konkan is also lost. You are a typical Shia ruler who has allowed a mere* jagirdar *to become so powerful that he has turned into an adversary. Eliminate Shiva. How you do it is your problem. You may take the help from Shiva's enemies or forge an alliance with Siddis of Janjira if the need be. Make haste. You have committed many sins. You have defied Islam by adopting a son and making him the king. We can only hope that his natural parents are not* kafirs. *I may forgive you for all your sins. Do what I say, for if you don't, we will take over Bijapur by violent means. Your city will burn like a* kafir's *pyre, and your king will die a pathetic death in our dungeons.*

Aurangzeb is no longer worried about the consequences of his actions or letters. Despite the fact that he has received news from a very trustworthy source that his father has sent a farman to Maharaja Jaswant Singh Rathod, one of the mightiest *mansabdars*, to intercept him near Ujjain. Aurangzeb does not need to wait for Darabhai to divide his mighty army. The Emperor has already done it. He only needs to surprise Jaswant by reaching early. It is time to intercept the interceptor.

***

The horse carrying Shivaji flies like a javelin across the flatlands of north Konkan. Cool morning air whips past him as the ground thunders due to his five thousand horsemen. His scouts ride before him, leading him to Mahuli Fort, the only hill fort in the region of north Konkan that remains to be taken. It is also the only fort in the region that belongs to the Mughals. Aurangzeb has refused to help. Hence taking over the Mahuli fort is fully justified. Shivaji's eyes search the skies till the cluster of hills rise high over the northern horizons. The forest at the foothills teems with trees of teak, banyan, khair, kalamb, and bibla. As planned it is time to stop. His men slow down and gather around him. He looks at them, his eyes moving from one face to another: Moropunt Pingle, Abaji Sondev, Netoji Palkar, Tanaji Malusare, Yesaji Kank, Abaji Sondev, Sambhaji Kavji, Murarbaji, and Ibrahim Khan. They are of different castes, Brahmins, Prabhu, kulin Marathas, Balutes and one Muslim. They are all warriors, ready to bathe their swords in the bloods of his enemies. Death has stopped bothering some of them. Their fathers had worked for his father. Some had come to him seeking employment and he has chosen them from hundreds of aspirants. Some are his childhood friends, his soulmates. Ibrahim Khan is new, he has previously worked for Bijapur, but the

Afghan warrior is a veteran in matters of battles.

He slowly moves his eyes towards the Mahuli hill. It looms three-quarters of a mile above him. Enormous spurs rise above the mountain, strangely resembling giant humans. Near the hill top he can faintly see the outer wall of the fort. Twenty years ago his father had hidden behind this wall before the allied forces caught him and shackled him. Shivaji tries to imagine Aurangzeb's reaction to this attack and smiles. To the fort's west, is Vasai, a *firang* settlement around the Arnala Fort, looking towards the ocean. To its east mountain passes plunge down from the Deccan capital of the Mughals, Aurangabad. From the citadel of the fort one can keep vigil over all the crucial passes from Kasara to Umbraj, usually preferred by the imperial armies to enter the Konkan. It could also be his military stronghold to protect the shipbuilding dockyards scattered around Kalyan. It was the same fort where his father had sought refuge. Hunted by the imperial and Bijapur armies, it was here that he had begged the Portuguese to rescue him, who instead helped the Emperor to track him down.

He looks back at his men. They are waiting for his orders. He announces, 'Tonight, lay siege around the hill.'

Palkar is surprised. Siege craft is an arduous procedure, even a small fort protected by a few unyielding soldiers hold out for weeks or even months against the massive number of besieging men. The siege could block all the routes and cut off supplies leaving only two choices for the trapped men: surrender or die of starvation.

'We neither have the manpower to block the routes nor enough food to last for even two weeks,' said the new *sar-e-naubat* of the Maratha army.

'The Mughal garrison up there may be anxious to crush us with boulders. Let them think we are laying siege and they are not in immediate danger. On the fifth night, which is a moonless night, we

will climb the fort from all sides so that they do not know which end
to protect. In the meantime, send our scouts to study the routes going
up from Shahpur, from Machi, and from Asangao. Ask them to check
the slope that climbs from the northwest. It is covered with dense
forests of fragrant screw pine. The hidden path takes you all the way to
the top.' Shivaji shares his battle tactics.

The five days go uneventful. Sometimes they can see the small
figures of the Mughal soldiers on the ramparts of the fort, but it is too
high to note their actions. On the fifth night, four of the five thousand
of Shivaji's men start climbing the hill on foot, rising three quarter of a
mile, from all sides. The leader of the Marathas along with Tanaji and
Yesaji scale it from the west. The air is filled with the sweet smell of
pine. The hill is steep but it is not blindingly dark as hundreds or even
thousands of fireflies appear and disappear at random paces. The little
flying creatures light up the surrounding forest but their flickers are
not bright enough to expose the intruders.

When Shivaji arrives at the base of the fort wall, his men have already
gathered. Some of them have thrown the rope hooks and have started
scaling. To his surprise, there are no night guards on the ramparts.
Within moments, they encroach on the walls. Some have even reached
the ramparts. According to the plan, a hundred of his men blow the
trumpets. The ear splitting calls shake the mountain and batter at their
ears. The Mughal garrison finally wake up, utterly confused by the
sound. Actually, the Mughals should have been on the ramparts to
crush the Marathas with boulders and kill them with arrows. Instead,
Shivaji's men are on the ramparts. Arrows are showered on the Mughal
soldiers clamouring in the fort's courtyard.

He waits as Tanaji and Yesaji hover around him. It takes only an
hour before he hears shouts from the ramparts. 'All clear,' he hears his
sar-e-naubat bellow, 'they were drunk, and all are killed. The fort is

now in our hands.'

The main Kalyan gate facing the west is flung open and Shivaji clambers like a possessed soul. He knows it is more than a mere victory or a mere triumph. As he enters the courtyard strewn with the bodies, he breathes deeply. It was here at this very place that his father was defeated and shackled. At this very place, his father's fate as the future servant of the Bijapur Sultanate was sealed.

'Remove the Mughal banner,' Shivaji shouts. 'Let the orange flag fly on the pole.'

***

They have shifted to their new home, Rajgad Fort. It has become Jija Bai's favourite pastime to be in the watchtower rising above the fort's citadel. The hills of Maval bathe in the beams of the morning sunlight. A sharp winter breeze blows around the girth of Rajgad fort that is more than twenty miles in diameter. It rattles across the giant mountain holes swerving around the ridges and then flies through arched manmade tunnels dug across the mountain's belly. The hill continues to rise a mile into the sky. From its crest, its lower terraces that float over the surrounding valley look like trunks of giant elephants, one sprawling towards the west, another towards the east and the third towards the north. The wall and the bastions of the terraces are armoured by another parallel wall, separated by a deep trench. Jija Bai glances at the Padmavati terrace of the hill that runs northwards. The stone buildings of offices and granaries shimmer in the morning sunlight. A lake that looks more like an emerald pendant faces a lone building meant to store the weapons and the explosives. Beyond the building rows of market platforms are visible. Jija Bai walks to the corner of the tower and peers down. To her left is the

Mahadarvaja, the main entrance of the citadel. It seems to open to a sudden mountain drop of straight black basalt. There is only a small treacherous trail that comes up from the Padmavati terrace. Such a false visual perception for the enemy! Far below, the wooded slopes end up into a dense forest.

Her ears pick up the sound of a bell. Her eyes shift to a temple of Goddess Padmavati, an avatar of the Goddess of wealth, Lakshmi.

The guards have come with mena bearers to take her down to her apartments. It is time to see her ailing daughter-in-law. The news has come that Shiva is arriving from Konkan.

When she nears Sayee's chamber in the far corner of Daruni palace, a strange pain leaps from her heart only to settle down in the pit of her stomach. In the front yard four little girls play with sagar skittles. They fling one high enough to pick another from the floor and then catch the flung one before it falls down. Three are her granddaughters born to her first daughter-in-law Sayee and one is born to her second daughter-in-law Soyara. Besides them, on a charpoy, maids in colourful saris sit and whisper to each other. They look grave. They know that their mistress is ill. One of them has a little boy in her lap. The toddler's eyes gleam when, unexpectedly, his grandmother bursts into his view. His sudden happiness stirs the still, anguished air. With nose screwed, his dimpled cheeks swell with a smile of pure joy and he lets out a yell, raising his hands in anticipation. He leans dangerously towards her and violently bounces his body to set himself free from the maid's grip. She tousles his silky curls and pulls him in her arms. He feels like a soft cotton pillow. She buries her nose into his curls and breaths deeply, filling her lungs with the gentle smell of sandalwood oil. The boy starts laughing while his tiny body shakes, jerking himself as well as her. She looks into her grandson's dark eyes as her heart starts filling up with unbearable love. She kisses him softly on his nose. He is already playing with the vermillion mark drawn on her forehead, and then his attention quickly shifts to her nose ring. She finds him heavy to carry and walk. One of the maids leans forward to take him back, and the little one starts wailing. For a moment she holds him close to her bosom and then gently places him in the maid's hands, as if he is made of glass. The silence around them is torn by his piercing cries. She sighs and then walks softly into Sayee's chamber. The young woman is lying on her bed, almost still. The relentless cough that tore through her lungs seems to have given up. A yellow glow of a lone oil lamp heightens the gauntness of her once beautiful face. Four childbirths have exhausted her.

She walks near the bed and gently touches the younger woman's forehead. She whispers, 'Girl, listen, Shiva will be here in the evening.'

Sayee closes her eyes as tears stream down the sides of her face. She wants to get up, select the best sari from her collection, the peacock blue one, with orange mango motifs woven on its border. Wear the pearl nose ring that has a large ruby in the middle. Oil her hair to tie a bun, and get some jasmine strings, to pin them around it. Smear her eyes with lamp soot. And wait at the gate to welcome him. But that is not possible. Her body has become a pit of pain. It is hard to breath sometimes. Very few people come to see her. She knows that her affliction is a curse and the curse can be passed on to anyone who comes too close. Even the fort doctor does not linger too long. She has seen her death in his eyes.

She lies on her bed, trying to bury her sobs. Her mother-in-law has left. It is difficult to gauge how many hours have passed. The maid has come twice, once to pour some bitter medicine into her mouth and once to feed her lentil soup. But she has lost all her appetite. The fever has come and gone three times, making her sweat and shiver. Some slimy mucus gathers in her mouth. It makes her feel like throwing up. She is terrified. The last time she tried to vomit, she noticed bloody mucus. She does not know if she is drifting to sleep or death. Suddenly, she is woken up by ear splitting sounds of drums and high pitched trumpet calls. *He has arrived.* Her bed shudders, as though the hill sways beneath her. She can hear shots from the cannon on the ramparts of citadel. It will be a long time before he comes to her. And she is prepared, he may not stay with her, he will go to his chamber. She will also not hold him back. She has made up her mind. She will not make him unhappy by whimpering or crying. She will not show her crumpling self to him.

It is late in the night when Shivaji walks past the queens' palaces of Rajgad fort. In the evening, his other wives had come to receive him at the main entrance of the citadel. Draped in colourful silk saris they seemed eager to worship him with *arti*, to ward off the malefic influences of evil eyes of his enemies. They had giggled and nudged each other with their elbows covered with embellished bands of gold while impishly throwing glances at each other. In their eagerness, some had scrambled while holding large gilded trays filled with wick lamps, burning camphor, conch shells filled with water, tiny silver containers of vermillion and lit incense sticks. He had waited patiently till all seven of them repeated the same ritual. Their demureness had occasionally been overruled by their youth as they tried to lock their kohl-smeared eyes with him, gazing at him longlingly. He had responded to them while trying hard to hide the shadows of guilt.

Even before he was fifteen, he was married off to most of them. They had grown up with him, as friends. He knows that they are no longer the young girls he played 'hide and seek' with or teased by pulling their braided hair till they complained. Now they seek his love. He knows what they feel under the veneer of strict codes of behaviour expected from Maratha daughters-in-law. And they know his love for Sayee, and how mesmerised he appears at the mere mention of her name. Some of them have given him daughters. Sayee has given him his first son, and now, after three daughters and one son, she is dying.

He reaches Sayee's chamber with a heart heavy with sorrow. She was already succumbing to her illness when he had last seen her. He feels miserable thinking of how she will look, her body ravaged by tuberculosis. The room is lit brightly with several lamps. She lies on the bed, still as a log of wood. He goes near and gazes at her. Her untied hair has fallen over her chest. She stares at him, her limpid eyes large and moist, and her nose ring gleaming with pearls and rubies. He searches her face for the havoc that her sickness has wrought. Or, perhaps, to unveil the mask of death that shrouds her pretty face. Or to measure the time that remains. Unexpectedly she flashes a smile. It reminds him of tiny vinca flowers clinging to life even on dry, rocky and barren earth. Her eyes sparkle with joy and then suddenly the room is filled with waves of her girlish laughter.

He stands there, feeling foolish. Has she caught his eyes hunting for the impending doom?

'Was the Kalyan girl really beautiful?' He hears his wife's question, her voice mocking yet stern and her eyes full of mischief.

'I have not seen her,' he fumbles with words, and then bows to his queen.

Eleven | War of Succession

Circa 1658

The summer months have arrived. As the sun rises above the city of Ujjain, warm breezes from the sandy desert of Rajasthan blow eastward and sweep across the battlefield. A nervous Maharaja Jaswant Singh Rathod waits for Aurangzeb's army to appear at the southern skyline. He was told that his sole task at Ujjain was to scare off Aurangzeb. Jaswant would show off his army of thirty thousand cavalry and flutter thousands of imperial banners in the air. The Emperor's farman was clear. Shah Jahan wanted to frighten his third son enough to make him scurry back to the Deccan. His presumptions have turned out to be very different from the actual turn of events. Just two days ago, Jaswant was told that Aurangzeb had not taken a long halt before crossing the Narmada river as he had previously planned. At Burhanpur, Murad Baksh had joined Aurangzeb from Gujarat. The brothers and their armies had met on the northern banks of Narmada. People, present at the occasion, have told Jaswant that the allied forces look like an ocean of troopers, and their march seems purposeful and resolute. The enormous cavalcade has arrived a few miles south of Ujjain, a week before it was anticipated.

Jaswant had acted fast. His military formation stands cramped between two hillocks, on an island protected by ditches filled with water. For the last two days a thousand men were deployed to bring buckets of water from Shipra River to fill the ditches dug around the battlefield. The area is muddy and slushy. Jaswant has put his army in a strong defensive position. He plans to unleash his cavalry on the advancing army of Aurangzeb and Murad slowed down by the manmade mire, thus putting them in a weaker position.

A few miles south from where Jaswant and his army wait, Aurangzeb, sitting in the howdah of his elephant is wary but not worried. Darabhai has thrown the first dice. Bhai's trusted warrior, Maharaja Jaswant Singh Rathod, has come with thirty thousand men, if not more, to prevent him from going to Agra. He calculates that he has two things in his favour. Jaswant has not commanded such a large army in the recent past and Quasim Khan, the powerful *mansabdar* who has come with Jaswant, hates Darabhai's liberal views. There is more: Jaswant does not know what modern, light weight artillery can do. Continuous battles have taught Aurangzeb newer tactics and their impacts. As his elephant sways beneath him, the third prince's mind appraises the military situation. The enemy's battle formation, the core, the advance guard, the left and the right wings, has been done conservatively. Jaswant's army stands on a island, surrounded by a freshly dug ditch filled with water. The core of Jaswant's army is formed by his six-thousand Rajput cavalrymen from his own kingdom of Jodhpur. Two thousand of them rally around Jaswant's elephant. Ten thousand cavalrymen are placed in the advanced guard to face Aurangzeb's approaching cavalry. Jaswant's left and right wing have just four to five thousand horsemen, making his advance guard the strongest part of his military formation. Aurangzeb calls it heavy-in-the-front tactic. He has faced such situations and knows how to tackle them. Watching the dense mass of horsemen around him, the Mughal *subhedar* of the Deccan thinks about his battle formation. His advance guard has eight thousand horsemen led by his first son Mohammad Sultan; his right wing has five thousand horsemen under his second son Muazzam, his left wing consists of another five thousand horseman led by Murad. The rest of the cavalry of several thousand stands around him. By buying over soldiers from Adilshahi and uniting forces with Murad, he has outnumbered Jaswant. But the real power lies somewhere else. His conservative battle formation is infused with extra power that is beyond Jaswant's knowledge. Several thousand archers and musketeers back up his advance guard. His scouts have studied the battlefield and identified a small hillock. His artillery will be fired from an elevated position. It is also manned by *firangs* who have worked for Mir Jumla. Even though Mir has been called away by the Emperor, he has left behind his experts to serve the third prince who had saved his family.

Maharaja Jaswant Singh Rathod glances at his advance guard. The horsemen, dressed in ornamental armour, hold huge imperial banners made of embroidered silk. The moss green flags flutter and show off a rising sun partially eclipsed by a couching, angry lion about to break into a roar. Thousands of those lions and suns make Jaswant's heart pound with excitement and help him forget the power of the enemy, albeit for a moment. He narrows his eyes and watches. Aurangzeb's army slowly appears on the southern horizon. It is only when he sees the sea of troopers gliding down the gentle slopes, like evil shadows of ominous rainclouds sweeping across the earth that his bones turn cold. The mass looks energetic, despite the fact that they has travelled three hundred miles north from Aurangbad to reach the southwestern side of Ujjain.

Jaswant waits for Aurangzeb's advance guard to move ahead and fall into his trap. Instead, the earth starts shuddering with explosions. The third prince's gunners are swift, their shots precise, not wasted, never going wayward, and never exploding midair. The shots are fired from an elevated position in the right directions, landing in the midst of Jaswant's advance guard, causing acute infernos. Under the cover of this barrage, Aurangzeb's arches and musketeers move ahead. The skies turn dark with arrows flying northwards. The flying projectiles tear through the chain armour of Jaswant's horsemen. The musketeers move like lightning pulling triggers with their modern barrel loading weapons, the flintlocks. Chaos sinks in as Aurangzeb's orders his cavalry to burst forth. The air reverberates with harsh sounds of trumpets, drum beats and piercing battle cries, hailing the ways of Islam. But Aurangzeb has misjudged Jaswant's Rajput warriors who hail the power of God Rama with all their might.

The Rajputs seem ready to sacrifice their lives for Jaswant. Their deaths would elevate the status of their beloved motherland, Jodhpur. How can one compare that to the vassalage of the Mughal? They break away from their lines and gallop towards Aurangzeb's artillerymen, and start slaughtering the enemy gunners. But the *firangs* are trained in sword combat. They slaughter the impulsive Rajputs and keep firing. Aurangzeb notices that Jaswant's horsemen from his left and right wing desperately flee the battlefield, their horses stumbling and falling while crossing the water-filled ditch. He laughs as Jaswant's men try to get away from their own trap.

There is more to come, shame and humiliation. Jaswant has watched Aurangzeb's men come in waves, quick, and forceful towards the core of his battle formation. The imperial banners have fallen on the ground and enemy horsemen have ridden over the rising suns and crouching lions. Jaswant's men ask him to climb down from his elephant for his own safety. He is swift to dismount as the mahout tries to steady the beast. He takes a horse but fails to see a lone enemy horseman break the ring of his guards. An excruciating pain sears through his body. Blood gushes out from his right arm. His guards scramble and kill the attacker. But Jaswant is struck by sheer hopelessness and pines to gallop straight into the ranks of the advancing enemy to be mercifully slain. He does not want to be so defeated. But someone catches the bridle of his horse and drags him out of the battlefield, overpowered, injured and filled with rage. He remains alive only to be overcome, to witness the enemy grab his artillery, war animals, and weapons.

The battle is over in a day. Quasim Khan has disappeared along with his five thousand men. Jaswant's war animals and weapons are missing.

It is only in the evening, after Aurangzeb's army has marched ahead and disappeared beyond the northern horizon, that a vanquished Jaswant comes out of his hideout and visits the battlefield. He watches in horror as countless vultures glide across the orange sky without flapping their wings, like kites of death. The twenty-eight-year-old imperial commander of seven thousand horses is crestfallen. The Raja of Jodhpur province in the south-western part of Rajasthan walks gingerly, his gaze fixed on the ground littered with the dead. More than ten thousand of his men have been slaughtered. The terrain, three hundred miles south of Agra and a few miles southwest of Ujjain City, near Dharmat village, is sodden with blood. His eyes scan the western horizon. The sun sinks, the sky gets darker and soon night will engulf them all. The air stinks of rotten flesh. The smell is bound to attract packs of wild scavengers. Soon they will rip his soldiers apart. He imagines packs of wild dogs, wolves, hyenas, hovering like agents of death, their eyes glowing like embers, their jaws drooling with blood. He feels sick, turns back signalling his guards who look more puzzled than him. Their young commander, their Maharaja, has aged overnight, appearing ten years older. His turban is missing, his robe is soiled, his hair blows back and forth in the wind, and his hand is tied in a sling blotched with blood. But it is his eyes that worry them: glassy, blank, as if the spell of life lay shattered in them. They also know that none of his Muslim officials have kept their grounds. Most have fled after the third prince's gunners, archers and musketeers started mauling them. There is a rumour that they have joined hands with the third prince.

Jaswant's disheartened men wait for him so that they can return to their camp on the banks of Sipra River. They fear for him, and suspect that he might kill himself with his own dagger. He is a Rajput whose forefathers had left home to kill or to die. In anticipation, they had allowed their wives and young children to enter sandalwood pyres and turn into ashes. They had worn saffron robes, smeared their forehead with their loved ones' ashes and walked out of the gates of their forts. But Jaswant Singh Rathod has let his men die, let his enemy win and has himself survived.

**

Aurangzeb breathes in deeply, filling his lungs with a cool breeze. Thousands of his soldiers frolic in the muddy Yamuna river. He knows why. They have not bathed for weeks. He hears them scream, shout, and laugh. Downstream, elephants too cool off in the river, flinging jets of water on fellow elephants with their trunks. Beyond them, the shore is lined with horses thirstily lapping up the water. This summer has been particularly harsh with the past months dry and difficult. They had travelled three hundred miles northwards from Aurangabad to reach Ujjain and confront Jaswant. The battle had been a fierce one. Many of his men and animals had been killed, thousands wounded. He had not allowed them the luxury of resting and recovering. Instead he had quickly steered his victorious army towards the northeast, travelled through the bleak landscape of Chambal, and marched three hundred miles under the scorching rays of sun to reach Gwalior. Quasim Khan had deserted Jaswant and joined him. On his way to Agra, many a Mughal garrison had come to his camp. His uncle, Shaista Khan and his contingent of ten thousand cavalry had met them at Gwalior. They had rapidly traversed a hundred miles northwards towards Agra. But instead of going straight towards the Empire's capital, Aurangzeb had taken his army to the east, arriving at the southern banks of Yamuna. Villagers across the river have welcomed their third prince, and have sent him more than a thousand cattle as gift. Tonight his men will feast and rest.

He moves to the edge of his camp where his Muslim officers have started forming a large semicircle around a wooden platform. His son Sultan, brother Murad and his uncle have already arrived. He watches Murad talking animatedly to a group of people. He had wanted to speak but Aurangzeb has discouraged him. 'It is dangerous,' he had told Murad. 'I do not want you to be hurt by informers hidden amongst our men. They will pretend to be offended and turn aggressive.'

Aurangzeb notices a few men standing behind his uncle and whispering to each other. Some gesticulate to draw his son's and his brother's attention. On seeing him, they stop talking and are all ears for him. He swaggers unhurriedly, as if deliberately pondering over the decision he has already made. The battle ahead is not an ordinary one. The men bow deep, once, twice and then thrice. Eunuch Mutamad stands near the platform holding a speaker cone. Aurangzeb swiftly climbs the platform, his eyes sweeping over his men in a quick glance, as if he wants to regard them, judge them, measure them, and feel them. Like a blacksmith scrutinizing hot iron, fresh from his forge before he starts hammering. They look uneasy under his gaze, their eyes squinting under the glaring sun. They have been with him for so long that they have almost forgotten what their life was like before they knew him. He has led them to battles, made them live in dangerous battlefields, but has always stayed put in their midst. They have seen him praying five times a day, every single day. They have heard him recite the *Holy Quran* from memory. He had never gambled or indulged in wine or women. He is their prince among the princes and some of them adore him for he is the son of Shah Jahan whom they worship.

Aurangzeb's gaze wanders beyond the gathering. The terrain is covered with babul trees, their branches have disappeared in the webs of twigs that blanket the earth. Far beyond, towards the northwest, a bunch of arjuna trees with dusty green canopies rise more than twenty guz above the ground. They are filled with drooping yellow flowers that sway with the wind. He marvels at their ability to blossom in such scorching conditions. Beyond those trees he knows that Darabhai's army has gathered in large numbers, since the north-western sky has darkened by the clouds of dust. He looks down at Eunuch Mutamad who hands him the speaker trumpet. Aurangzeb nods briefly. Mutamad knows what he and his men have to do. The third prince is not willing to take any chances. He holds the trumpet near his mouth and starts speaking in Urdu that is mixed with Farsi and Arabic for all to understand.

'All of us gathered here are warriors, fearless, dauntless and ready to spill our blood for the Empire. We have done that in the past, many times over. We are born to die as martyrs. But we have a chance to depart this life in a more meaningful, more divine way. A death of a *mujahiddin* beckons us. A death of a holy warrior! We will slay for a higher cause, get slain for a higher reason. We must take our war to another level. We are the chosen ones to breathe in the vicinity of the divine.'

He stops for breath. Men look at him, confused. He ignores their expression.

'Life is a struggle and all of us die. Death as a *mujahiddin* promises unattainable things, like escape from the interrogation by the angels in the grave, the chance to bypass the purgatory uncertainty, to avoid the agonising wait to be pure before entering paradise. A *mujahhidin* is entitled to the highest ranks in HIS court.'

Aurangzeb speaks slowly with dramatic voice modulations as if each word is an ocean pearl, to be seen, felt, pined for and sought with hunger.

Many in the crowd nod vigorously, not knowing what lies ahead.

'What is the meaning of a *kafir*, the Arabic word which is active participle to the root K-F-R, the word that means 'to cover, to deny, to hide?' he asks. 'Is it a person who rejects Islamic faith and hides from the truth like an ostrich burying its head in the sand? Or is it also a person who is born a Muslim but wanders into the unholy turfs of infidelity, under the pretext of seeking truth? The truth exists in the *Holy Quran*. Revealed by Him to his chosen Prophet; our beloved Paigambar, Be Peace Upon Him. To seek truth elsewhere is to dishonour our Prophet '

He pauses to take a few deep breaths and to let his words sink in the minds of his men.

'A person who rejects Islam may either be blind or ignorant, stupid or mad. But a Muslim who shows interest in the faiths of the infidels is a *Shaytan*, evil to the core.'

He pauses again to see the expression on the faces of his warriors, who look utterly puzzled.

'Whoever helps a good cause becomes a partner therein and whoever helps an evil cause shares in its burden.'

Silence fills the empty space above the gathering. He knows that this silence can be far more potent than the dust clouds hovering over the north western skyline.

'Jihad,' he finally screams into the cone of the speaker trumpet. 'This is the only way to deal with these evil men. We hereby declare jihad against the infidel Dara Shikoh, the first prince, for disregarding Islam.' Aurangzeb makes the words sound like an explosive that has been just fired, 'A man who encourages *kufr* and hides from the truth cannot be our ruler,' he repeats again and again till his throat goes sore and starts itching. 'If your men fight for my cause they become mujahiddin, and if they die, they become *shaheeds*,' he says with élan as if doing a favour by offering the men a chance to become the holy warriors, the chance they will never get, and they must never let go. 'Jihad is essential to save our Empire from a heretic dog who aspires to be our next Emperor. How can he who regards the *Holy Quran* and the scriptures of the infidels as two sides of one coin?'

He strikes still deeper till the sharpness of his words slice the logic of some of his officers. In sheer disbelief, men of war listen what their master has to say. Somewhere at the back of the crowd, he hears sullen mutterings of disapproval. The sound infuriates him but he waits, standing still, without removing his gaze from them. This is one moment to lose or win a thousand hearts, to lose or win the world. Eyes filled with cynicism, doubt, confusion, anger and rage look at him. Whether for him or against him, for Darabhai or against Darabhai, he is not yet sure.

'*Anta turidwa-howa, yuriidwallaahyafthreeal ma yuriid,*' Aurangzeb says as loudly as possible in chaste Arabic. The men are smart to catch up. 'You want what you want, he wants what he wants but Allah does what He wants.'

As if by magic two clergymen in spotless robes and long, flowing, white beards appear on stage. They start reciting the verses that play out the orders to kill the *kafirs*. The hysteria now turns into a mass mania. Swords are taken out of their sheaths, their blades glittering in the sun, the reflected rays blinding them on that very day.

Like molten lava that erupts from a dead volcano, Mutamad and Najabat Khan are the first ones to raise their hands and chant, 'Deen, Deen, Deen, Deen,' alluding to the splendour of Islam. Within moments, almost all the men raise their hands and scream Deen Deen Deen Deen. The collective sound reverberates through his military camp, rattles above the babul twigs blanketing the terrain, shakes the canopies of arjuna trees and hovers over the north-western dust clouds. Its chilling resonance silences the voices of dissent. Hearts that had pounded with cynicism and doubt explode with the hysteria of pride that they collectively feel for their fidelity and brotherhood.

Mohammed Sultan glares at his father with eyes shining with astonishment and hurt. He has never disliked his Sunni father with so much passion. His father is surely not a man to be trusted. He is a man who wants to use religion as a weapon and he, Mohammad Sultan, may also be a potential victim of his father's fanaticism.

Murad Baksh too glares at his brother as jealousy eats into his heart. Aurangzeb has used his idea to instigate their warriors. He cannot accept the fact that his brother receives all the love and admiration of the military officers. It is he who deserved that adulation.

***

Battle Formations

| Chatrasal Hada | **DARA SHIKOH** | Rustam Khan |

Dara's Rajput Squadrons

Dara's Artillery

Aurangzeb's Artillery

Aurangzeb's Artillery

Murad Baksh

Mohammad Sultan's Heavy Cavalry

Aurangzeb's Rajput Squadrons

| Khan Dauran | **AURANGZEB** | Bahadoor Khan |

Ravindra Godbole, *Aurangzeb, Shakyata and Shokantika* (Deshmukh and Company Publishers Private Ltd)

Dara Shikoh does not want to think about the defeat of Jaswant Singh Rathod. He sees it as Jaswant's hesitancy, his reluctance to fight with the Empeor's third and fourth sons. But he, the general, the first prince will not hesitate to do what he deems right. He has turned a deaf ear to his war advisors telling him the dangers and the pitfalls of the delay. He had decided to wait for three long days, and he has. He did not want to launch the first offensive but waits for his younger brothers to march in. However, something nags the first prince: Why does he wait? Is it his reluctance or his fear of war or Death?

Dara wipes his face with a small towel. It is insanely hot. The sweltering sun, blazing sands and the blistering wind around them – his men and animals must be burning under their heavy metal armour. It is their third day. The marshalling of ranks is long over, battle formation has been done with and his army can be set in motion with one bark of his order. His gaze rolls over his army, the enormous elephants, wrapped in steel plates and strengthened with barb wires. Weapons like swords and spears are tied to their trunks. Their steel coated howdahs soar above the sea of horsemen and footmen, perhaps fifty, perhaps seventy thousand in numbers commanded by the Muslim Khans and the Rajput Rajas. The air is filled with suspended dust particles and rattles with the whinnying of restless horses and trumpeting of impatient elephants. Somewhere in the front, drummers standing behind the cannon make a racket. The cannon carts linked to each other by massive iron chains have formed a barrier, giving the drummers a false sense of safety.

A steel howdah specially designed for him makes him feel safe and sound. Its metal plates are thick like bricks, and cover him up to his neck. Above, it is secured with metal bars that reach up to its roof making the howdah look like a cage.   Footmen with javelins march from behind while countless swordsmen guard the beast's legs. Heavy iron chains with dangling steel balls are tied to its trunk. The tusker is trained to swirl them to kill men who come near it and use the axes to chop off their legs. But the first prince is disconcerted. A dust particle has invaded his right eye and it stings and waters. He knows that he has indeed made a mistake by waiting, thereby putting his army in a contingency mode for three successive days. His uncertainty has allowed his brothers' armies to move further eastwards and reach the banks of Yamuna River. He has given them the leave to rest and recover from the miles long journey across the dry plains, Ujjain to Gwalior and then towards Agra. The blunder has been committed, and he is aware that his men, horses and elephants are tired and drained under the veneer of banners fluttering in the air like rivers of silk.

He looks ahead. His *mahout* has stopped the elephant. Mir Jumla, the tall Persian stands before them, clad in chain mail armour.

'Do not worry, my prince, we are prepared.' Mir Jumla first bows and straightens up, his voice rising above the din of the battlefield. Dara Shikoh raises himself, resting his body on his knees and looks through the bars. Mir Jumla's dark eyes are looking up at him but they just twinkle, giving nothing away.

'Our plans are in place. The artillery, in a mile long line of cannon carts surrounded by cannoniers and rocketieers, stands right in the front, stuffed, ready to fire,' shouts Mir Jumla.

Dara Shikoh is not comfortable with Mir Jumla and other military officials. They are strangers to him, he does not know them as he has hardly fought any battles and is dogged by a nervous feeling that they are not under his control. He has been gathering *mansabdars* from far and nearby provinces. Their contingents are hastily equipped with armour and weapons with the arsenal from Agra Fort and they are pampered with huge funds from the imperial treasury. He is unable to deal with them decisively and does not know if they truly stand by him or not. A strange fear nibbles at his innards. The ill will between his personal army and his father's highly paid *ahadi* soldiers is obvious. Ahadi, in Arabic means 'stand alone', and these soldiers do not report to any *mansabdar*. They are not used to taking orders, have not fought any battles in the recent times and are good only for a parade. The mutual jealousy between the Rajput and the Muslim military officials suddenly bothers him. Aurangzeb's victory and Jaswant's defeat have suddenly created a new equation in the mind of the people. With one single blow Aurangzeb has brought him down from the position of the crown prince to a prince. But what hurts the most, according to Dara's suspicion is the fact that some even think of him to be lower in position than Aurangzeb. He is no longer sure how to be the General of this war, or of any war for that matter. He swallows hard; his mouth feels dry and the blisters on his tongue burn with pain but what he notices makes him forget his physical pain. The southern horizon is darkened with dust, it seems that his brothers on rampage have reached.

He looks down. Mir Jumla is staring back at him, his eyes waiting for orders.

'Fire when you see them,' he shouts, pushing his hand out of his howdah through the bars and waving it like a banner. He cannot decide if his orders will come sooner or later.

Mir Jumla does not comment, but only turns back and disappears.

Shaken, Dara Shikoh narrows his eyes and stares ahead. The entire southern horizon has come alive with footmen, horsemen and elephants. Banners flutter wildly in the air. It is unbelievable that his younger brothers have gathered such a large force. He feels the ground shudder beneath him. Between his and his brothers' armies, the plain explodes as a thick cloud of smoke rises like a dark curtain. He looks on, aghast. Mir Jumla seems to empty the stock of their explosives even though the enemy has not walked into the firing range. The explosives hit the barren land between the armies. A curtain of smoke rises, blocking his view. He waits as his elephant raises its trunk in fear and trumpets as his *mahout* struggles to control his fidgety animal with his *unkush*. Acrid smoke that rides on the wind makes him breathless while he suppresses a bout of cough by closing his mouth with his hands as the enemy starts emerging from the wall of soot. The enemy comes in waves and he is numb with shock as explosives, arrows, and javelins start raining over his men. Some arrows hit the metal plates of his elephant. One gets stuck into the barbed wires and he can see its shaft shudder on impact.

He looks down: one of his bodyguards has fallen, impaled by a javelin.

The war has begun. Dara looks to his left and shouts, 'Attack'.

His left wing is commanded by Rustum Khan. Thousands of horsemen pull out swords from the scabbards and charge at European artillerymen protecting Aurangzeb's right wing.

Dara looks at his right but does not say anything. His right wing is a sea of Rajput squadrons and is commanded by Chatrasal Hada.

Aurangzeb is not worried but Dara, not being used to battles, makes the mistake of using the same old tactic. Worse still, his army is a motley of hastily put together squadrons. Dara may be backed by numbers but his army is not at all a cohesive body. To face such a disorderly enemy, Aurangzeb has divided his artillery into two units, and put his heavy cavalry, commanded by Mohammad Sultan in the middle. The enemy is likely to attack impulsively, and will be intercepted by two pronged artillery attacks, while Sultan can advance towards the core of the enemy's battle formation. Aurangzeb has placed Murad Baksh and his army behind the left artillery unit.

Aurangzeb is behind Mohammad Sultan's squadrons and is surrounded by a mass of horsemen. He watches from his howdah as both the units of his artillery start firing at once, killing Dara's horsemen in large numbers. Mohammad Sultan's cavalry advances towards the core of Dara's army. Another mass of cavalry commanded by Murad presses forward towards Dara's right wing, with Murad sitting in an armoured elephant that marches recklessly into Dara's army. Suddenly, a sea of saffron-clad Rajput horsemen under Chatrasal Hada move towards Murad's elephant. 'You want to wrench the throne from the first prince Dara Shikoh?' they shout in chorus and lurch ahead like rabid dogs. The archers among them shoot wildly at Murad's elephant. The projectiles miss Murad but get stuck to his howdah and the tusker's armour. Soon his war beast looks like a giant porcupine. His *mahout* is hit, and falls down on the hot sands of the battlefield, dead!

Dara watches too and realises that Murad's reckless march has blocked Aurangzeb's artillery. Raja Chatrasal Hada and his thousands of Rajput horsemen from Gaur, Sisodia and Rathod clans have charged forward, wielding their swords, literally flinging themselves on Murad's contingent. He feels excited for the first time but his excitement is short lived. He looks to his left. Rustum Khan's elephant is nowhere to be seen. He notices Aurangzeb's horsemen wearing green turbans breaking into his domain, their swords cutting his men down as if they are goats. Aurangzeb's artillerymen are busy firing. Dara notices for the first time that his brother's artillery has a line of archers trained to use their composite bows to fire grenade like rockets. Flames rise from the midst of the dense body of his cavalry. Around him his men are shot down quickly by arrows and javelins.

'To the left,' he shouts at his *mahout*. He has to investigate. The *mahout* hesitates. His General is not supposed to abdicate his position.

'To the left,' he screams again.

As they move towards the left, his elephant lumbers forward through the sea of his army and he no longer can see his right wing, or what his Rajput commander is up to. He searches for Mir Jumla who has vanished. To his right, he sees a long line of cannon on wheels. His artillerymen have abandoned their guns. His elephant keeps moving towards his left and Aurangzeb's right wing. Dara watches with dread. The battleground is littered with bodies, broken blades, shields and hilts. Enemy horsemen have broken his artillery barrier. His *mahout* moves the enormous tusker through the hysterically fighting soldiers while his countless guards hover around his elephant. It is a long and slow journey.

It must have been just an hour, he muses. To his right, the earth is strewn with corpses and rolling heads, eyes staring into the dusty sky, and scattered limbs. Horses stand lost and confused near their dead masters, some of the animals are shot dead by the arrows. Injured men cry for help. Aurangzeb's frenzied riders move ruthlessly over those on the briunk of death. The stench of dirt and burning flesh stings his nostrils. The deafening noise of clashing swords, leaping hooves and the beastly cries of hysteric warriors din on his eardrums.

He was not born to do this. He was born to study theology, discover the real meaning of religions, and write books!

'Our advance guard has vanished,' shouts someone. Dara gazes at his right and a cold shiver runs down his spine: he is in the firing range of the enemy's cannon, one such that he had never seen before.

'Turn back,' he yells at his *mahout*, who too has noted the large and small cannon mounted on pivot over the wheels, surrounded by frantic white men. They swirl the guns in his direction. It takes his *mahout* a while to turn back the cumbersome beast and start moving across the front line towards their core. The cannons start firing violently. Aurangzeb's archers too have gone insane. He looks up and notices long, burning shafts flying above him. Its tiny embers enter his howdah, like a shower of molten drops of burning candles. His skin burns badly. He rubs his eyes and looks down to see some of his guards turning into bright torches, their high pitched cries rising above the din of the battle. Iron projectiles hit the targets carrying off heads and limbs of his remaining guards. He is still safe in his howdah, its thick steel plates resisting the crossfire, but he fails to notice a mysterious horseman appearing to his left. He holds a stretched composite bow to its fullest. The arrows are shot in succession, aiming for the eye holes of his fully armoured beast. He feels his elephant rock violently under him. Perplexed, he watches as his *mahout* tumbles down. The elephant raises its trunk to screech in agony, and then stands on its hind legs looking skywards. He holds on to the steel bars of his howdah to hang on and sees the trunk of his mount wriggling in the air, either to ward off the plunging death or to arrest the life that is bidding farewell. Then the animal suddenly slumps as if life is snuffed out of its enormous body. The howdah tumbles down and crashes, breaking into bits and he finds himself flung on the floor as dust starts rising around him. His fall is awkward, he falls face down. His metal body armour hits his jaw, breaking some of his teeth. His mouth fills up with something warm, something with a metallic taste. He watches his *mahout* disappear underneath the elephant and hears the crushing sound of bones. Someone drags him from behind, lifts him by the armpits and hurls him on a horse.

'The first prince is dead, our beloved Dara Shikoh is dead,' a horseman whirrs past shouting.

Dara Shikoh's army starts to scramble, there is a stampede crushing men, animals, artillery carts. Panic leads to mayhem and the pandemonium leads to crumbling of Dara Shikoh's battle formation. Kalil Ullah Khan from Samarkand, one of Dara's *mansabdars*, watches the fall of Dara Shikoh from a distance. He is least bothered, as he is forced to defend Dara Shikoh whom he hates. It is the same prince who had him beaten with a shoe for a trivial matter. The Samarkand warrior nurses ambition to work for Aurangzeb as he gazes at Dara Shikoh ride towards Agra, running away from the battlefield. Dara has noticed Kalil Ullah Khan staring at him with glee, but he is helpless. He spits to show anger and spews out a few of his broken teeth. He watches in horror as his injured soldiers drag themselves away from the field. The sky above is littered with vultures. He shivers and kicks his horse to a full gallop in the direction of Agra. His world of books, music, poetry and theological studies seems to evaporate in the heat and dust of his battlefield he has left behind where another drama of brotherly love unfolds. Aurangzeb has rushed to check on the injured Murad. 'Brother, my brother,' he cries while watching the best medic tend to Murad's superficial wounds. 'What will I do if anything happens to you!' he laments and keeps Murad's injured hand on his knee. He touches it tenderly and says, 'The war was fought for you, my brother and the future Emperor. You must take care as you are precious to me, much more than anything in the world.'

***

It is rather early for the monsoon but the rain clouds float over Agra. It is almost the sky's attempt to quickly wash away the blood of the thousands from the battlefield. Eleven days and eleven nights have passed after Agra has fallen into Aurangzeb's hands. Dara Shikoh, the holder of lofty titles such as *Shah Bulund Iqbal*, the king of lofty fortunes, *padshahzada i buzurg artaba*, the senior son of the Emperor, and *jalal ul kadir*, the superior and the most capable, has run away like a frightened rabbit, first to Agra Fort and then to Delhi. A smile appears on Aurangzeb's face. The Emperor has shut the gates of Agra Fort and Aurangzeb has cut off the water supply that the fort enjoys from Yamuna. The news that many of the fort inhabitants have died of thirst has been making the rounds. He diverts his gaze from the sky to the path before him and walks briskly through his camp at *Nur Manzil*, a far off suburb south of Agra, while his uncle runs behind him muttering a request. 'Son, do not get carried away by your father's sudden hail of love, it is a fake show of a well thought out diplomacy. Sending her is a part of that plan.' Shaista Khan insists with genuine concern. *He might be damn right*, Aurangzeb thinks, *Father has shut the gates of the fort on my face, and now when I have cut off water supplies to the fort, he is trying to be tactful.*

He does not utter a word but rushes towards his *shamiana*, made to befit the victorious prince. The floor is covered with Persian carpets and the panels are made of satin. At the far end, away from the entrance and facing a gilded chair, a woman, wearing a long white mantle and a thin veil, sits on the ground. At the far end Mutamad stands like a statue. It is the first time that he is looking at the famous princess, the Emperor's most favourite person in the world, who referes to her as the *Padishah Begum*, the Emperor queen!

The Mughal princess hears her brother's footsteps but avoids looking up, even after he occupies the high backed, gilded chair before her. The third prince stares down at her, wondering what he must say. His eldest sibling, their father's heartbeat, *Padishah Begum*, sits near his feet like she is his *ghulam*. He watches as she takes off her veil and looks up, her greenish blue eyes staring at her younger brother. His sister's once beautiful face is covered with fine wrinkles, and her hair has streaks of henna dyed red. He jerks his head backwards, just to show her that he is now in command. She looks like a matron in a mantle with a high Chinese collar. He knows what she hides behind her clothes, ugly scars of severe burns.

She cannot bear the silence any longer, starts crying, her thin frame convulsing with each sob.

'Sister, sister, Begum *Sahiban*,' he mutters not knowing what else must be done. He has always seen her dressed in gowns, made of silk and chintz, wearing the best of what the famous jewellers of Hindustan could offer. She, Jahanara, the Emperor queen, has always been in control, always in command, always amazing people with her philosophical rhetoric. He and his brothers would hover around her, amazed at her grace. But that was many, many, years ago; he has not met her for a while and feels like a stranger now.

Still sobbing, she stretches her hand, hands over an epistle to him and whispers, 'It is from father.'

Father is a beaten man now. His letter is no longer a farman.

He rips it open with total disregard and takes the Kashmiri silken paper out to read. Father's Arabic is chaste; he has written a verse in black ink.

My son, you are my champion,

I, the Emperor, backed by a half a million troopers

Am a beggar

My fate, slapping me hard

Made me a prisoner, a mere ward

Remember, not a leaf falls from a tree without Allah's will

And still

We remain proud of our triumph in this perishable world

Lying in a drain called life

Like a worm eternally curled

I praise the Hindus who put water in the mouth of the dying

You, my son, a chaste Muslim, are starving me of the elixir of life,

It is akin to slaughter and slaying.

The third prince wants to laugh. For the first time, his father speaks like a commoner, without orders, arrogance or accusations. He throws the paper away. He watches his startled sister and quips, 'Now I have become his champion, uh, now that he is left without a choice.'

'Bhai,' Jahanara speaks, her voice quivering with emotions, 'what is happening to our family, to us and why?'

'Our family?' he says scornfully and wags his index finger at her. 'You and your Darabhai should know 'why' better than I do, Begum *Sahiban*, you have lived with father, in the palaces adorned with riches. For you, far, far away has been the world of battlefields sodden with blood and filled with the stink of rotting dead. That world has never touched you, that world has been my home for years.'

'Why did you do what you did?'

'What have I done? I was on my way to see my sick father when Jaswant intercepted me with his army. Is it a sin to come home when your father is ill?'

'I am talking about your declaration of jihad against Darabhai, why jihad against your own blood?' Her voice is clear.

'Do you not know?'

'Kindly enlighten me,' Jahanara whispers trying hard not to sound scornful. He stares at her, searching for even a slight shadow of a snigger but she looks sincere and grave.

'Once Darabhai made his intentions clear by sending Jaswant to stop me, I started to think,' he snaps. 'What must one call a man who draws parallels between the holy Quran and the Upanishads of the *kafirs*? What must one say about his public statements such as infidelity and Islam are twin sisters? You must agree that his deeds make him an enemy of Islam. Will this enemy of Islam rule our Islamic Empire? What must a chaste Muslim like me do when he happens to be my brother? You must agree that it is my duty to fight him. And what must one call this fight against the enemy of Islam? You must agree that it is called jihad.'

For a moment she is speechless. 'The *Holy Quran* talks about tolerance, even towards the followers of other religion. Here we talk about our own brother, a Muslim, a liberal Muslim at that,' she whispers.

'That's your interpretation,' he cuts her off.

'And if your interpretation of jihad is to kill even the liberal Muslim, what happens to your tolerance then?' she asks softly.

'Dear sister, under the circumstances, what kind of jihad should I have followed, by words, or by sword? I would have started this spiritual fight by words but Bhai had not given such an opportunity. He prepared for war.' Aurangzeb pulls out a *tesbih* from the pocket of his robe and starts counting the beads.

She listens, her eyes fixed on his beads. Words form in her mouth like froth, to gulp or to spit. Spitting them out may mean death, by poison, opium overdose or by a serpent bite. 'Jihad,' she says bitterly, 'and all for the bloody throne.'

'Talk for Darabhai, you do not know me. I am not interested in your throne,' he says calmly.

'Who then would be the next emperor?' she asks coldly. Her gaze has fallen to the carpet near his feet.

'How is father?' he asks, ignoring her question and her coldness.

'He is recovering,' she says defiantly. In the depth of her heart she knows that father's recovery is politically insignificant. Darabhai's loyal warriors like Chatrasal Hada, Ramsingh Rathod, Bhimsing Gaur, and others have been killed. Thousands of *mansabdars* who had fought for Darabhai have joined the victor, including Mir Jumla, Maharaja Jaswant Singh Rathod and Diler Khan. The news is that even Mirza

Raja Jai Singh has left Sulaiman Shikoh and is on his way to Agra from Bengal. The orthodox Muslim warriors have joined Aurangzeb in large numbers.

'If he is well enough and decides to punish the infidels like Darabhai, he may continue to rule by the dictums of the *Holy Quran*. Otherwise, both Murad and Shujabhai have already got the *khutba* to read in their names. They have also minted the coins... how can I vouch for their actions? Both of them want to be the Emperor.'

'Murad?' Jahanara mutters to herself and keeps silent. Murad had always been a difficult child, destructive and unmanageable. His favourite game had been hurting swans with his catapult and rolling on the ground laughing when the birds had screeched and fluttered, bled and sometimes died. The palace servants had been his targets too. He would fling pebbles and even rocks at them, till they begged him to spare them and cried at his feet. She had hoped he would grow out of it, but even at the age of thirty-eight he had remained the same. A failed viceroy of Balkh and Gujarat, an alcoholic, wasting his time in the court intrigues of his sycophant noblemen.

Aurangzeb keenly watches his sister's face. His lips curl into a sceptic's smile.

'Then, who do you think? Do you think Shah Shuja will be a better choice?' Aurangzeb asks contemptuously.

'Why not Suleiman?' Jahanara blurts and then bites her tongue with deep regret. Twenty-four-year-old Suleiman Shikoh is the pride of her family; Darabhai's eldest son has been born with beauty and bravery. He is the star of her father's eyes.

'Where is his father?' Aurangzeb asks as his eyes bore into her eyes.

She shudders and knows that he knows. The night of the defeat was one of the darkest. The streets of Agra were hushed like a graveyard. Everyone at the Fort lay silent, as slaves and servants moved through the corridors and courtyards like lost spirits. The escapees from the battlefields started arriving in the city, the hoof beats shattering the ominous stillness.   Darabhai who had left shouting slogans like, 'Victory or Grave,' had returned, vanquished yet alive. He had not come to meet them but she was told that his face had blisters, his eyes were swollen and his clothes were covered with soot. She could hear the wails and cries of his wives from his apartment. Darabhai had to leave, vanish before he was captured. Father ordered mules loaded with gold and silver coins to be sent with him. A farman was dispatched to the governor of Delhi to open the fort and treasury for the beaten prince. She watched from her balcony as the first prince left for Delhi, shadows of horsemen, palanquins, mules and slaves moving westwards. She had run towards her father's apartments, her father had been watching from his balcony. The thin old man with long face, grey beard, and his bleary eyes stood staring as shadows of his first son and his tiny convoy dissolved into the night.

'I will leave for Delhi tonight,' she hears her third brother speak. She is terrified, she must dispatch a message, Darabhai must know. Aurangzeb watches her face like a cat looking at a mouse.

'Don't bother. The coward has already fled from Delhi.' She hears Aurangzeb's words filled with derision and exhales in relief but cannot resist speaking further. 'So chase, bloodbath and death – are these the fate of our family?'

'That,' he says with contempt, not moving his eyes away from his sister, 'you should have asked Father before he advised your beloved Darabhai to wait for me at Samugarh with fifty-thousand soldiers.'

'I had begged them to consider,' she says feebly.

'Did they pay any heed, your beloved father and your *mulhid* brother? And now you want me to follow what you say, you, who concurred Darabhai's heretical views and exalted his image by preaching his philosophies that were against Islam.' He relaxes his body on the back rest of his gilded chair and counts his beads faster.

'I do not preach his philosophies as I too believe in those ideas. In fact, I had asked to translate Hindu scriptures like the Upanishads into Farsi,' she says without cringing.

'I do not want to argue with you, just agree to the fact that it was father's and Darabhai's idea to send Jaswant to intercept me near Ujjain. Even the battle near Samugarh, was well planned.'

'What could they do? You were advancing towards Agra with yours, and Murad's armies.'

'Is it a crime for a son to visit his ailing father?' Aurangzeb asks blandly. 'Is the Emperor afraid of his own army governed by his own sons?'

Silence lingers for a long time as Jahanara mulls over her victorious brother's words.

'Father begs you to keep your brothers from harm, they are your own flesh and blood,' she whispers softly, her tears falling on the carpet.

'Father is in no position to cast morals. Have you asked our dear father what he had done to his uncles, half brothers, cousins and nephew? He murdered them, blinded them, and expelled them'.

'Had he not done so, we would not be alive. In fact it was done primarily to save you and Darabhai from the clutches of our stepgrandmother, Empress Nur Jahaan, that snake of a woman.'

'And if I had not done what I did, what kind of fate would await my family?'

'For his love for *Ammi*, our *Ammi*, please spare him the anguish of seeing his first son die.' Jahanara plays out her last weapon.

Aurangzeb can no longer maintain his gravity but bursts out laughing.

'Love for *Ammi*? That man is a cannonball of lust, ready to explode between his thighs at the sight of any woman. Can you count the number of women he has taken after *Ammi* is gone? You should know better.'

Mutamad shudders. *What is his master trying to imply?* He has heard the rumours about the Emperor and his first daughter. He looks at the princess. He cannot see her face but he knows that she has started to sob.

'And what is the cause of his illness? Is it not the overdose of aphrodisiacs as I have heard? Is the senile old man still hungry for the female flesh?'

She closes her eyes with indignation, as tears stream down her face.

'Entire Hindustan talks about his erotic endeavours, who would know better than you, sister?' he insists mockingly.

Mutamad squirms, he has never heard his master talk so explicitly. Not even to him, a lowly eunuch slave.

The words sting Jahanara and bring back agonising memories of the past and the night that had changed her life.

She was in her twenties, living a life of a beautiful princess, and she was indeed so. She would walk in the palace gardens, under the silvery light of a full moon, the stars twinkling like jewels that adorned her body. Her girlfriends would play the flute or tambourine and fill the air with soft music that matched the cascades of water streaming out from the lit fountains. She remembers that the flower-decked gardens had looked different then, and she had danced wearing fashionable caps with egret feathers, while her friends dressed in organza skirts had matched her steps. The large anklets covered with tiny bells had created their own music, as they had sung the songs of love together. One night that dream had shattered.

Jahanara remembers the night as if it was just yesterday. The corridors of *dulatkhana-e-khas* were silent. Candles had burned silently in gilded and enamelled brass shades hung on the wall – giving away a pale yellow light around the oil paintings framed in gold borders. Outside, the courtyards were bathed in the silvery beams from the sky. It was her favourite time to take a walk. She had tiptoed so as not to startle the palace staff. Before reaching the gardens, she had heard some hushed voices. She had not intended to eavesdrop but they had been talking about father and her, and their desire for each other. The malice had stabbed her heart. She had retreated backwards and accidentally hit a shade that hung on the wall. The burning lamp had fallen on her. She had looked on in horror as her fine clothes made of chintz and silk had caught fire – and the flames had risen too soon. She had done nothing to save herself and looked defiantly at the blaze, 'This is my trial by fire,' she had thought. The air had soon filled with the smell of her charring flesh.

She controls herself and brings her mind back to the present.

'Father wants you to come to the fort and meet him.'

He nods affirmatively knowing that he would never do so. She suddenly gets up. He realises that she is far too frail, almost like a reed wearing a gown. She looks into his eyes and says evenly, 'The true meaning of jihad is to declare war with our inner demons.'

'*La ilahilallah,*' he whispers. 'There is no God except Allah.'

He does not want to offend her anymore and must think like the Emperor. Father has given her the port of Surat in Gujarat as a gift. The revenue generated from the trade from that prosperous city supports the imperial army. She has donated huge funds to Muslim clergies to build mosques. For her deed she is held in high esteem in the religious circles of Mecca. It is rather untactful to offend her, especially where philosophies of Islam are concerned.

Mother is dead. The wife he loved dearly is also dead. Father has been a hypocrite and spitefully partial. One brother is a pseudo intellectual, one a womaniser and one a drunkard, and all are hungry for power. His family is utterly dysfunctional. But he has lofty dreams for the future of the world. Aurangzeb is sure that one day he will impose his ideologies on the very world that has tormented him. His vision is that of an empire spanning from Afghan in the north to Ceylon in the south where people follow his perception of Islam. His mission is to remove the Shia kingdoms from the atlas and eradicate the *kafirs*. To achieve his goal of religious cleansing he must become the next Emperor! He has already strategized; he has executed some of his plans and needs to accomplish some.

Murad Baksh no longer suspects Aurangzeb. His big brother has proved his loyalty by sending him a gift of one hundred and fifty thousand Asharfi *mohurs* and two hundred and fifty Arabian horses. 'We must rejoice in our victory, my brother and future emperor,' Aurangzeb has written.

Murad agrees to have dinner with him. *Why not?* he thinks. *I am surrounded by my ten thousand troopers.* The *shamiana* is lit by a hundred polished and shining brass *shamdans*. The ceremonial tent is covered with colourful Turkish carpets. Smell of roasted *gosht* or meat kebabs wafts in the air. But Murad looks forward to the several silver ewers filled with wine that beckon him. His brother has managed to get glasses made of rock glass. Murad has decided to drink, and he is not worried about his safety. His guard Nirudin Khawas is with him. Nirudin does not drink and will die for him if the need be. As Aurangzeb empties small cups of Turkish coffee, Murad empties glasses of wine.

Murad does not remember the rest of the night. When he wakes up, he finds himself shackled in a palanquin. He tries to shout, but his mouth is stuffed with pebbles. They have also taped it shut.

Twelve | Bijapur Obeys the Emperor-to-be

Circa 1658

Shivaji glances at Moropunt Pingle whose face is flushed with excitement. They have crossed Mahad, a small town of narrow lanes and huddled houses at the north end of Javali. The wind howls, sounding eerily like a wailing woman. His *kathiawadi* horse canters through the uneven trail. The land is covered with luxuriant vegetation. Gleams of sunshine sneak from the broken masses of rainclouds. Near the skyline, huge hills wait like beasts, their girths gigantic, their peaks shrouded in clouds. One hill is largest, sitting smug in the midst of others. Like a lion bounded by its pride.

'That one, the mother hill, looks like someone has axed it away from the Sahyadri Range,' he mutters.

'That is the hill of Rairi, it is special,' Pingle responds quickly.

'It is just fifty miles away from the Arabian Sea and three to four days by horse from Rajgad fort,' he comments.

'That's only a part of it,' Pingle says without explaining

It does not take much time for them to reach the base of the hill. Pingle seems to know the path, so there is no need to look for one. As they start climbing, their horses slow down. He notices a large cliff hanging over their heads, like a raised hood of a giant snake. Moving a little ahead, a huge cascade bursts into his vision. It plunges from the cliff into a deep ravine. He wrenches the reins to pause for a brief moment. Water has always fascinated him. Here it is compressed between two giant rocks jutting out from the crag, only to leap down with a roar, forming a foamy torrent in the gap and spraying the path with milky effervescence. The thick canopies of the tall trees seem to emit a strange green light around them. On the enormous branches of those trees bulbuls, myna, hornbills, parrots, egrets and sunbirds chirp, screech and call their peers with high-pitched whistles.

'The real surprise lies ahead,' Pingle declares as his eyes shine.

He smiles and guides his horse through a slushy patch as a hundred men silently ride behind them. He looks ahead and sees the trail becoming narrower and steeper. His horse climbs slowly, cautiously taking one step at a time. He grabs the saddle horn to keep his weight forward and notices the earth below, uneven, covered with mud and stones. As they pass bamboo and teak forests covering the slopes, he spots pugmarks of tigers. Half-eaten carcasses of goats are seen too. They cross a glade with a small pond in the middle. As they move further up he notices something move in the thicket.

He glances at Moropunt Pingle and then at his men who follow them. Within moments their swords are out of their scabbards. The horses stop and start snorting; even the animals have sensed a presence in the woods. They jump down from their horses. It is easier to defend oneself on foot in the mountains. A few men wearing grubby loincloths, their bare chests covered with tattered blankets scurry out from the bushes. They are dark and thin, their chiselled muscles forming slender cords over their limbs. There is hardly any flesh on their faces, yet their dark skin gleams, perhaps with enthusiasm. They hold their hands close to their chests as though hiding something precious.

'Show what's in there,' Pingle shouts.

They shiver and hold out the cusp of their hands to reveal red, ripe, wild raspberries.

'For Raja Shivaji,' one of them says in a low, barely audible voice.

Shivaji pulls out his shawl from his shoulders and unfurls it. He holds it in front of the tribal.

'They are Katkaris, they eat everything, even rodents,' Pingle blurts.

He ignores the *peshwa* and says, 'Give them to me as I love the berries.'

The men come forward; their eyes shining with tears. They empty their hands into the folds of Shivaji's silk cloth, one by one.

'How did you know about us?' he asks, surprised.

'We know everything that happens around this hill,' the man who looks like a leader replies shyly.

Shivaji stares at his face. The man has fine sun wrinkles. His head is covered with frayed, white hair. The man looks at him, without blinking. His eyes plead for something his lips are afraid to utter. Most of these men are exploited by the rich landlords as cheap labour to work in the fields, to chop trees and to wash cattle. Sometimes, out of hunger and desperation these men are forced to rob and even murder.

'Come and meet me at the fort tomorrow morning, all of you,' he says softly and turns to Pingle, 'We will meet them tomorrow and select some of them as scouts.'

Shivaji eats a few berries and gives the rest to Pingle to distribute. His shawl is empty; he throws it over the man's shoulders.

'It will keep you warm,' he says.

As they resume their journey, he waves at them till they become specks and vanish from his sight. Gradually the weather grows mistier. After a particularly treacherous bend they are suddenly blinded by strong sunlight. The mist has vanished. He looks into the valley; the world below is submerged in the dark clouds as the world above basks in the golden rays of the afternoon sun. The surrounding mountains have risen above the blanket of clouds. They are smeared with several white streaks of rain water torrents pouring from the sides. His horse has chosen its own path to climb the last stretch before they reach the crest. It is a miles long flat table. An enormous hill looms over him and his men, rising above the mountain table like a horn on the head of a giant. He kicks his horse to a gallop. The boundary of the black basalt against the backdrop of the blue expanse creates an ethereal suspension. Countless eagles fly, drawing circles in that suspended space with serene dignity, carefully guarding the rock from the bending sky.

'The fort is on top of the rocky hill. Prataprao has been driven out. It is yours now Raja,' Pingle finally announces.

The horses are left behind with a few men to water and feed them. The upward climb will be on foot. A few local herdsmen are to guide them. Their leather sandals with flexible soles prevent them from slipping down each time a stone is dislodged by their weight. They grab ledges and crevices, and sometimes tough vines as they push themselves upwards. He starts feeling a tingling sensation in his knees and looks at the Brahmin who is older than him. His *peshwa* shows no sign of distress. The air has thinned and the winds are cooler. The men need to breathe deeply to fill their lungs. It takes them a good hour to reach their destination. Shivaji looks on with fascination. A large plateau lies before him. As he walks past small stone structures and ruins of a stone wall, he sees a flat mountain crest, vast, and endless. It is a plateau more than a mile above the sea and overlooking the coast, with abrupt slopes plunging into Konkan. It is unlike anything that he has seen before.

'One can build a city here,' he thinks and turns to look at Pingle who is watching him, his eyes shining like jewels. 'This place will be the capital of our Swaraj, floating in the sky and overlooking the Sindhusagar,' Shivaji announces, his eyes dreamy.

The leader of the Maratha feels overwhelmed. He walks ahead and notices men practice with wooden swords. Two of them have strayed away from the others. They are quick and seem to sense each other's moves. They take stances with their swords, turning offensive or defensive as the game demands. One of them is large and stocky and the other, small and wiry. Each one tries to push his rival backwards over obstacles like rocks or shallow ditches. They move, shoving each other with their strikes, from the flat earth and climb over the rocky mounds. The stocky man starts losing his balance. Shivaji watches them fight, first with interest and then with fascination as their wooden swords bang on each other, especially when they block or parry each other's blows. The wiry man is far more nimble and seems to guess from which direction his opponent will deliver his blow.

'Who is he?' Shivaji asks Pingle pointing towards the wiry man.

'Jiva Mahalya,'

'I want to meet him after their fight is over.'

'He will come by,' Pingle assures him.

He watches them till they finish their fight as the wiry man finally manages to accomplish the leverage he was seeking for, his sword-hand moving swiftly, as the wooden blade of his opponent can no longer parry the attacks. The swordfight is over. He notices the winner walk towards them with uncertainty as streaks of sweat stream down his face.

'Give him your sword,' he shouts looking at Pingle and draws his own blade out of its scabbard.

'You have just finished a gruelling drill and I have just climbed this steep hill. We are equally drained of energy.'

Jiva Mahalya stands still, throws his wooden sword away and takes a real blade of a real dhop sword, shining and straight. He has fixed his eyes on the man with brown eyes. *Is he the man who he thinks?*

Mahalya is confused. The man who has challenged him wears a finely cut *angirkha* made of costly chintz and a saffron turban laden with pearls. Mahalya has not yet seen a man with such fair skin and sparkling eyes. *He is indeed Raja Shivaji,* Mahalya decides. He quivers with a strange excitement as Shivaji advances forward holding the sword at a lower level. Mahalya's opponent looks calm and his blade gleams under the afternoon sun. He holds his ground by keeping a wide distance between his feet and tries to guess the direction and the force of Shivaji's strike. He knows that the ability to think beyond one's mind saves one's life. Sweat dribbles down from Mahalya's forehead and into his eyes. It stings but it is dangerous to blink. He has heard that Raja Shivaji trains every alternate day, and has garnered incredible sword skills. Raja's strong offensive bouts make his enemies lose their ground and crumble. Mahalya holds his sword near his body. Only this way can he retain the strength of his arms to parry the strikes of his famous opponent. The thought of hurting Raja Shivaji unnerves him. As the distance between them shortens, Shivaji delivers a forward blow, gliding his sword horizontally. Mahalya avoids it by jumping backwards, away from the orbit of Raja's blade. Within a blink, Shivaji's backward strike brings the blade of his sword towards Mahalya's right knee. He jumps high, letting the blade slide beneath him, without touching him even the slightest.

An energetic fight explodes between them as the air vibrates with the clang of their blades. Many leave their drills and run towards the fighters. The spectators form a large circle around them. To their left Shivaji has seen a small spur with a slope on one side and a drop of two *guz* on the other. He increases the strengths of his blows and darts forward as Mahalya parries his attacks and moves away. Sometimes, unexpectedly Mahalya moves forward, cutting off the power of his opponent's blows but Shivaji manages to push him unhindered, towards the slope of the spur and within moments brings him to its edge. Mahalya immediately knows that he cannot retreat. It would probably be best to push the blows of his opponent and move forward but he hesitates. He simply buckles, falls back from the spur and crumples on the ground. A cold blade touches his throat. Mahalya closes his eyes. He has heard stories about sword games where rich men have killed for fun.

'Will you be my guard?' he hears Raja Shivaji ask.

'*Ji, ji, ji,*' Mahalya cries with happiness as he scrambles to get up.

'Put him up for *pata* training,' a breathless Shivaji tells Pingle, wiping sweat from his forehead.

'You don't know him, neither do I. He is a lowly Balute from an obscure village on the borders of Javali.'

'Moropuntoji, a sword is a great leveller. It kills the enemy and it also shatters disparity. For sword is then God and the holder its disciple. Some of these disciples of the blade live life by their own codes, codes that do not differentiate between life and death, profit and loss, wealth and poverty and our Mahalya is one such disciple. You will see,' Shivaji tells his *peshwa.*

'We need a thousand Mahalyas when and if they decide to march in,' Shivaji whispers as the sky above the hill of Rairi shimmers in brilliant sunlight.

Moro Pingle understands in a flash. Tukaram's words rush to his mind.

पुरजी तो पाईक ओळीचा नाईक पोटासाठी एका ऐशी तैशी
जातीचा पाईक ओळखे पाईका, आदर तो एका तयाचे ठायी

The Brahmin now knows the real meaning of those words.

A soldier who fights to fill his stomach

Is a servant sans passion!

Only a warrior knows another warrior
And the hearts that pine for a mission!

***

As the domes and minarets of Bijapur gleam in the morning sun, the palaces in the citadel take one's breath away. The Badi Begum bathes in her private *hamaam* on the second floor of her seven storied *hava mahal*, 'the wind palace'. Her slave girls carefully pour rosewater on her henna-coloured hair. The water in the enormous marble tub is lukewarm, just the way she likes it. The girls tending to her fear her fragility and hence are as nimble as possible. They also know that she is temperamental and even the slightest mistake in the bathing ritual can end up in flogging. But again, it is quite natural that she is short tempered. Managing the kingdom after her husband's death has not been easy. Ali's adoption, his education, and the effort to win his love were hard. Aurangzeb's repeated invasions had left her paranoid. He has seized her north eastern military strongholds including the fort city of Bidar. From there Bijapur is not far off.

As her maids soap her hair, she thinks about Aurangzeb's victory. The news heralds that he has conquered Agra and Delhi, which means that he will probably stay away from the Deccan a long time now. Something flashes in her mind; she knows that it is time to do that which will eventually keep her kingdom safe.

'Hurry,' she orders the girls. They pour some more water on her to wash off the lather, and wrap her in a towel. She rushes to her dressing room and within half an hour strides to the seventh floor. The palace servants look aghast, and bow as she walks past. She has never done this before; she has always been a strict queen who has stuck to royal protocols.

'Ali, Ali,' she calls, almost breathless. It is my age, she consoles herself, that makes it so difficult to climb these winding stairs.

Ali is puzzled as he sits in his library stuffed with manuscripts written by famous historians, as servants hover around him. *Rarely does Ammijan climb to the seventh floor to meet me,* he wonders. She always sends a messenger. He rushes out past his wives' chambers to the balcony adjacent to the main entrance, to his mother who waits for him near the parapet that overlooks the lush gardens.

'Badi Begum,' he exclaims in surprise and bows deep to his mother. She is tall and stands upright in a long gown with sleeves woven with pearls and rubies. Her deep brown eyes have fine wrinkles around them. She looks at him affectionately, notwithstanding the pain that reflects in them.

Ali calls her Badi Begum and not *Ammi* that she longs to hear. He knows that his childless mother cherishes him more than anything the world can offer. And the world has offered her everything that she has ever wished for. She is the sister to the king of Golconda, Abdullah Qutb Shah and was the queen consort to the late king of the Sultanate, Mohammad Adil Shah. When Ali had come to know that he had been adopted he had felt betrayed and disappointed, even though his *Ammi* loves him unconditionally.

'Ali, my son,' she says eagerly, 'Aurangzeb has taken over Agra, he is the Emperor-to-be.'

An overweight Ali, wearing a finely cut silk jama with flower motif, looks perplexed. He knows about it.

'He may not come to the Deccan for a long time,' she says.

The Badi Begum's excitement is not unfounded. Aurangzeb's second tenure in the Deccan as an imperial viceroy has brought her grief and heartbreak. Each night, for the past few years, she has stood near the arched window of her bedroom and stared at the protective ring that the walls had formed around her city. She has inspected the bastions guarded by armed men scanning the vast expanse for advancing enemies. When sleepless nights have given way to lethargic days, the Badi Begum has anxiously read Aurangzeb's humiliating letters written to her after the demise of her husband a year ago.

The most recent one is the most dreadful. If they failed to eliminate Shiva and hand over the regions under him to Aurangzeb, the third prince will burn Bijapur like a funeral pyre of the *kafirs*. He will let her beloved Ali die a pathetic death in the Mughal prison.

'We must wrench away our north-eastern frontiers from the clutches of the Mughal,' she says looking at her son, her eyes depicting shadows of retribution.

'*Ammijan*, we can get back the region either by fighting the Mughal or by eliminating Shiva. Our kingdom has been the tributary state of the Empire for long. We have also renewed the old peace treaty with them. Fighting them will be treason. Instead, we will do what the Emperor-to-be desires. We shall eliminate Shiva Bhosale.' She hears Ali's words and knows that Ali is being rational. Her army is also not in position to face the imperial army. Many of her military officials have joined the imperial army under the third prince. The exodus has weakened her kingdom.

'It's not easy. Shiva has the hill forts to hide, to launch attacks, to be invincible. And who do you think will hunt him down?' she asks gloomily as she looks around the balcony in search of eavesdroppers.

He walks closer to her and whispers, 'Consider Afzal Khan for various reasons. He is the viceroy of our Wai province, the frontiers of our western borders and is acquainted with the terrain of Javali and Maval. Also,' Ali lowers his voice further and mutters, 'he has a personal vendetta, he hates Shahji Bhosale.'

Ali has indeed grown up, muses Badi Begum. It is time to further test

Afzal Khan's loyalty and aptitude. Don't they still call him a *Farzand*, son of Adilshahi?

'He has helped us to annex the Hindu kingdoms of Karnataka either by sword or by deceit. Remember Kasturi Ranga, the chief of Sira and the way in which he was lured by Afzal Khan to negotiate a treaty? Don't you remember how then Afzal Khan had killed him during the meeting?' Ali's questions sound like resolute statements.

'How will Shahji Bhosale react?' the Badi Begum questions. She does not want to offend him. If he decides to revolt, her kingdom will be in deep trouble.

'I will take care of Shahji Bhosale,' Ali assures his mother.

Finally, she nods, accepting his suggestion.

Ali and his scribe spend their night in the library. A letter is written to Shahji Bhosale, each word thought over a million times.

Be it known to Maharaja Farzand Shahji Bhosale.

In the recent past you must have been tormented by the arrogance and treason committed by your son, Shivaji Bhosale. You need not live with that terrible burden. From the depth of our hearts we understand your plight. We know that you are in no way responsible for your son, Shiva's deeds. He alone is, and will be dealt with in our own way. We shall give you your Bangalore jagir as has been decided. We have also informed all the chieftains to assist you in all possible ways. If anyone behaves otherwise, he will be severely punished by us.

Afzal Khan's caparisoned elephant trundles to enter the city from the Ali Rauza gate. This western side has its own advantages. The *subhedar* of Wai likes to see the fifty-five tonnes of *malik-e-maidan*, and also avoid the crowded streets of the eastern suburbs that stink of rotten food. The giant cannon weighing fifty-five-thousand *ser* mounted on an enormous stone is the pride of Bijapur. Its muzzle is shaped like a lion's head, whose open jaw crushes an iron elephant to death. Before every battle Afzal Khan likes to tell men working under him that the 'Lord of the Plains' ejects cannonballs weighing more than him to smash the approaching enemy half a mile away. While he is busy admiring the gun he feels the gaze of people on him. They are staring at him in fear. He is a huge man, his head touching the roof of his howdah, making the muscular *mahout* look puny in comparison. Rumours are rife in the city that it is he, Afzal Khan, is the one who has instigated the Queen to murder Khan Mohammad, the late *wazir* of the Sultanate.

It takes Afzal Khan one hour to reach the royal court as the guards and slaves scurry around him, staring at him in awe. He swaggers with an air of arrogance as he enters the enormous court of Adilshahi's royals. He is careful to keep his kohl-lined eyes expressionless and roving. The court with its high ceiling supported by countless pillars that form overhead arches, has been redone. The massive windows embellished with carved wooden panels are covered with satin curtains heavily upholstered with gold brocade. Huge chandeliers dressed with rock crystals have been lit. The floor is covered with several Turkish rugs of different colours and designs. At the far end, on the gilded throne, with two lions made of pure gold squatting on either side like domesticated pets, he notices a pensive Ali. The young king's chin rests on the cusp of his right hand. To the right of the throne is another chair, partially blocked by a semi-transparent curtain. He can see the outline of his Badi Begum. There is nobody else in the court.

As she watches Afzal Khan walking towards them, a wave of relief surges through her body. She hates it. It is a sign of her weakness. It is undoubtedly true that he has been serving them devotedly for the past twenty years and has been a favourite of her husband. He has shown courage and bravery when he along with Shahji Bhosale had annexed the remaining Vijayanager empire. During her husband's long illness, he had obeyed her orders with reverence, as though they were the commandments. He has proved his loyalty once again by warning her about Khan Mohammad, whom she had so blindly trusted. Nevertheless, seeking emotional relief in one's military men is a sure sign of weakness.

Afzal Khan bows deeply first to her and then to her son.

'How is your family? How is Fazal Khan?' she keeps her voice sweet and motherly. He has fifteen official wives and countless children but he dotes on Fazal Khan, his eldest son.

'By the grace of Allah,' he murmurs again bowing.

'*Farzand* Afzal Khan,' she now speaks with loud intonation, her message uncomplicated, simple and straight. 'We have renewed the peace treaty with the Mughal. We have offered prince Aurangzeb our regions that include the Bhosale *jagir* as well as North Konkan.'

'We are caught between the devil and the deep sea. Shiva Bhosale is unlikely to let go of his *jagir* without a fight and Aurangzeb has written that if we do not do what we have promised he will burn Bijapur like the pyre of the *kafirs*.' Ali says and loses his composure. 'Our faith, Islam demands Shiva Bhosale's blood, the traitor cannot be left alive on the edge of our kingdom. He will destroy us,' the king shouts.

Afzal Khan stares at Ali and wonders, *Ali is so much darker than my master Mohammad Adil Shah. The new king is surely not his real son!*

'I understand,' Afzal Khan says after a while and throws his hands in the air. How would Shahji Bhosale react?' he asks, his beady eyes watching the excited Ali panting with anger.

'Shahji Bhosale has written a letter to us saying that we are free to deal with Shiva in whatever way we deem fit. The letter has his seal.' Ali snaps, 'It has been ten years since he has disowned his first family.'

'We must consider our future and not what Shahji Bhosal will make of this matter,' interjects the Badi Begum. 'We cannot delay it. We have heard that Shiva is on a horse-buying spree.'

'Most of his horsemen are *bargirs*. Shiva selects each one personally. He is not just cunning, but also has military intelligence,' Ali incites.

'Even a *shiledar* is directly paid from Shiva's coffer that overflows as a result of robbing and plundering. Netoji Palkar who previously worked for us has been made a *sar-e-naubat*! He has helped Shiva gather a few thousand such *shiledars*,' says the Badi Begum, sounding distressed.

Afzal Khan does not reply. Shiva Bhosale is indeed clever. *Bargirs* are well mounted, armed horsemen who are paid by the kingdom they work for. Even their horse belongs to the state. *Shiledars* too are horsemen paid by the kingdom, but they bring their own horse and equipment. It is an expensive military scheme. Even the Mughals have to depend on their *mansabdars* for maintaining cavalry. Most of them cheat the Empire's military system by keeping less number of horses so as to save and amass money. It is even worse in his country. Bijapur rulers have to threaten, bribe or beg their *jagirdars* and the *deshmukhs* for military support in times of war. They can never be sure as to who will stand by them and who will join the enemy. But a salaried cavalry, paid by the state will always be faithful. Its ruler will always be sure of the numbers.

'Shiva's system is against the *watandars*. Soon he will take away lands from the nearby *jagirdars* and *deshmukhs* and bring it under his revenue officials. He has done it in Javali,' Afzal Khan mutters.

'You can convince the Maval *deshmukhs* to join you. Tell them they will cease to exist if Shiva Bhosale prevails.'

'North Konkan is taken. His men have tried attacking the Janjira fort. He has also started work at shipyards, and tomorrow he may even build sea-forts. The man is dynamic. It is easy for him to enter our other regions, for example Wai, the province under your supervision that lies just east of Javali.' Ali's words are deeply humiliating.

'Shiva is amassing strength by the day. We have heard that our Ibrahim Khan has joined him along with his thousand African horsemen,' informs the Badi Begum.

'After returning to Bijapur, the dumb man Mullah Ahmed is busy singing praises of the *kafir*, Afzal Khan whispers to himself.

'After the takeover of Nizamshahi, we had allowed Shahji Bhosle to keep his old *jagir*. Whoever knew that his son would turn out to be a traitor and unlawfully seize the hill forts in that *jagir*? What have we done so far? We have recently lost more than twenty five forts of North Kalyan to Shiva. And two of our strongest forts of Bidar and Kaliyani that guarded our north-eastern borders have been swallowed by the Mughals,' says Ali sullenly

Afzal Khan raises his eyebrows. Is the king holding him responsible for the loss? He is not the military general of Adilshahi; he is just a *subhedar* of the Wai province! After the death of Khan Mohammad, who was the *wazir* and also the general, Ali has announced the name of the new *wazir*. But he is yet to name the new military general. And how can Ali hold him responsible? For the past ten years, he has been trying hard to expand the kingdom by taking over the Hindu kingdoms of Karnataka in the south and dealing with the aggression of Aurangzeb in the north. He has struggled in the battlefields, while his master, Mohammad Adil Shah has remained in bed, paralysed and stricken with bedsores. Ali was just a boy of ten when his father fell ill. Now this juvenile young man is belittling him. What does this adopted son of the late king know?

'If this goes on, son,' the Badi Begum intervenes, her voice soft to make up for Ali's rudeness, 'Shiva Bhosale will make us beg. With Javali in his hands, he controls the trade route of Dabhol on which our supply of salt, spices, wood, textile, and such other things depend. Shiva can starve our kingdom of those essentials.'

'We feel that you are the most competent to take up the challenge.' Ali's affirms.

Afzal Khan does not want to say anything amiss. There are traps within traps within traps but no time to unravel. He has cleverly gotten rid of Khan Mohammad, but there is a new *wazir* now. Khawas Khan, the African warrior is rather close to Ali Adil Shah. He needs to find out whether Ali is acting on his own or is being incited by Khawas Khan. Perhaps it is Khawas Khan's idea to send him to the peril called Shiva. But Afzal Khan thinks decisively. He will treat this as an opportunity given by Allah. If he eliminates Shiva, his court rivals like the new *wazir* will collapse inevitably.

'We have kept funds aside to bribe the *deshmukhs* of Maval,' the Badi Begum assures.

'If you can buy off Kanhoji Jedhe, the *deshmukh* of Bhor Maval, half your job is done. He wields considerable amount of power over the other *deshmukhs* from Shiva's jagir. He and his five sons are warriors, their cavalrymen are trained in the hilly region,' advises Ali.

'Am I the only man in control of this operation or will our *wazir* also be in command?' asks Afzal Khan sounds resolute.

'You are now the General of Adilshahi, and henceforth you will not take orders from anyone,' announces Ali.

Afzal Khan nods, his body shivering in ecstasy. He tries to conceal his excitement, raises his hands skywards and says gravely, 'My esteemed king, I promise you I will bring Shiva's head to your feet. If I fail, then sever my hands from my body.'

'We do not wish that to happen. We want Shiva Bhosale, shackled, standing in this very court, as a captive. If that is not possible, then severe his head from his body and bring it to us as a trophy,' The Badi Begam says as if it is an order.

After the newly appointed general leaves, Ali Adil Shah looks at his mother and quips in Farsi, 'Hope he is not, *poz-e-ali, jib-e-xali.*' The great boast and small roast!

On his way home Afzal Khan cannot help but think about his past, when he had saved Adilshahi from being wiped out. When the Mughal Emperor and his late king had joined hands to annex Nizamshahi and later to defeat Shahji Bhosale, his master had accepted the vassalage of the Empire. He had to also pay twenty million rupees as tribute. After a few years, Mohammad Adil Shah had started ignoring the protocols of the Mughal treaty. He was reprimanded by the Emperor for carrying out practices that were the prerogatives of only, well, the Emperor. Holding court in lofty places outside the citadel, witnessing elephant combats and using sovereign emblems fixed on a long gold spike, a sun, a fish, an upraised hand, and scales of justice. Over the years, Mohammad Adil Shah had broken the stringent protocols on various occasions and was reprimanded with the serious threat of war.

Afzal Khan still lucidly remembers the night of festivities. On an event to celebrate a battle victory over parts of Karnataka that was ruled by a few stray Hindu kings, a still robust and beaming Mohammad Adil Shah had thrown a lavish party. On the terrace of his seven story palace in the air, the drunken king had been enjoying with his favourite nobles. The very fair Turkish female slaves, carrying goblets of wine, had floated around seductively in silk tunics as their flaming hair streamed on their open backs. The fireworks had exploded over the skies creating designs with embers, in tandem with the musicians who had been playing the sitar. They were selected carefully from the 'army of Nauras' that had more than three thousand musicians on the government's payroll. The music was relaxing and calming the nerves of those who were already drowned in wine. As glasses were emptied, their hearts had sunk deep in the bliss of happiness. The aroma of roasted beef had wafted across the terrace as royal cooks barbecued the meat marinated in vinegar. His master had ears only for the sounds of revelry and laughter that had filled his beloved city, lit by thousands of street lamps. In a contemplative yet romantic mood he had called Afzal Khan and asked, 'Did Tansen sit or stand when singing in Emperor Akbar's court?'

Afzal Khan had no answer for his drunken master.

'Ah, leave that aside, you are not a connoisseur of music, like,' Mohammad Adil Shah had tried to recall the name of a man with whom he had always enjoyed conversations on wine, women, art and music. He raised his index finger in the air, and announced triumphantly, 'Farzand Shahji Bhosale.'

A cleaver of jealousy had lanced through Afzal Khan's body.

'Anyway, tell me what does Bijapur say about me, Afzal Khan *Ji*?'

'They are singing your praise, what else can they say?' he had replied cautiously.

'What does Shah Jahan think of himself? What will happen if we challenge the protocol of the Mughal Treaty, Afzal Khan *Ji*?'

He had looked around as noblemen drank, danced, caressed the slave girls and tore flesh from the bones of tandoored meat. He could have replied in sycophancy; instead, he had taken refuge in the truth, truth that could have cost him his life.

'If you do that my King, instead of the sounds of revelry, we will only hear lamentations of grief. The streets lit by lamps will be drenched in the blood of our men. Adilshahi will be a part of the Mughal Deccan.'

The master, even in his state of total drunkenness, had heeded his advice and had sent a letter of apology to Shah Jahan and saved his kingdom. Peace had reigned for ten long years until Aurangzeb had started his war against the Shia kingdoms of the south. It was time to protect Bijapur again. He had saved his beloved Adilshahi in the past and he would do so again in the future.

Thirteen | The Battle Looms Ahead

Circa 1659

Yesaji Kank stands inside the wrestler's *akhada*, barefoot, in a loincloth. The commander of the Maval infantry is a simple wrestler at heart. He intently watches two young men struggle in another mud pit and makes mental notes as their torsos and limbs twist and turn to lock their opponent in a python grip. He notices several flaws. For him every single move, every single glance, every single movement and even a moment of stillness is a move or a countermove. These youngsters, with muscles rippling down their arms and thighs, look strong. But they have not understood the importance of sequencing and how to sense the opponent's stances in advance. Suddenly, his ears pick up the familiar sound of hoof beats. He jumps out of the pit, covers himself with a towel and leaps towards the entrance. Some of his fellow wrestlers run behind him. The sound has stopped. His men minding the front yard scramble with excitement. He notices Raja Shivaji and his guards dismount from their horses. For a moment he feels joy but his instincts tell him that something serious has happened. The visitor is grim and there is that worrisome tightness around his mouth. The guards drag the horses away as he notices Raja rush towards his favourite spot, a far corner of the wrestling akhada. Barring a few men pulling shafts of wheels near a well to draw water, as a part of their fitness regimen, the place is empty. The tree stump stands still - it was used by them as a base point when they played hide and seek just fifteen years ago. But that now seems like an ancient past, just another time in another world. The visitor quickly sits on the stump, not bothering about the dust that has gathered on its surface. Yesa and some of his wrestlers circle around him. Above, through the gaps in thatched roof, a few rays of the noon sun sneak in and fall over their faces, revealing the shadows of concern in their eyes.

'The news is true. Afzal Khan has taken up the challenge. He is the new General of Adilshahi,' Shivaji whispers.

He takes a moment to grasp. This is the first time that the Bijapur rulers have considered a man of Afzal Khan's military status. It is a disturbing news. The Sultani calamity is about to march in from the east.

A shiver runs down Yesa's spine.

'Many of Adilshahi's *subhedars* have already reported for duty. Several *jagirdars* and *deshmukhs* have agreed to help the new general. They have all gathered at Bijapur along with their men. Afzal Khan has mustered ten thousand well mounted cavalry and equal number of infantry. We will get the precise numbers of his war elephants, camels and guns-on-wheels within days.'

Yesaji nods.

'We need new swords. Leave immediately and start meeting the blade-makers of the region. Find new swords-smiths if the need be. Explain to each one about the length, weight, balance, and sharpness of blades we need for our dhop swords, *patas*, daggers and javelins. Specify proportions and the dimensions of the blade. Change the design of the hilts. Add cushioned linings and bigger knuckle guards for a better grip.'

Yesaji knows what needs to be done. He has done it before.

'And yes, make the ridges of *pata* blades heavy. Ask them to add more metal to the blade near the hilt. That will bring the centre of gravity closer to the hand that holds the sword.'

'A few bladesmiths had visited Rajgad last week. They insisted that a little more carbon and chromium in the iron make the blades less bendable yet they do not break when they hit the bones.'

Yesaji counts his fingers. He must remember the number of instructions.

'I will send you a letter in this regard,' Shivaji smiles and says but soon turns serious. 'The rulers of Bijapur have opened the doors of their treasure in support of Afzal Khan. The number of soldiers deployed to finish us is huge. Soon, our small terrain will turn into a battlefield, a real one.'

Yesaji and his wresters remain silent.

'I need to go, *sar-e-naubat* is waiting for me. We need to send the letters to the Maval deshmukhs. Afzal Khan has already written to them saying if they do not join him he will dig them out from their hiding places, slaughter them and their family members to pieces and extrude their body parts through oil mills,' Shivaji relates.

'That's typical of him,' Yesaji murmurs and urges, 'Come home, mother has made ambil soup and mutton chops marinated in ginger.'

'You will bribe me with mother's food and then will want a bout of wrestling with me to break all my bones. I am a man now, am too old to be lured,' Shivaji announces as his brown eyes turn mischievous. There is a faint ripple of laughter. Food made by Yesaji's mother is a favourite among them. They can almost recall the taste and feel its aroma.

'I have been a vegetarian for over a year now,' admits Shivaji.

Yesa wonders why his friend has stopped eating the food he so relished. He stands near the entrance to watch Shivaji and his guards gallop away, leaving behind a minor dust storm. He stares till the horsemen become mere specks and then vanish from the range of his eyes. His mind goes back to his past.

As a child, his only preoccupation had been to play with others of his age. They had loved to run down the slopes, sprint over the stinging karvi bushes and swim across the shallow rivers. But that had changed when swordsmen, wrestlers and archers selected by Dadaji, the Divan of Bhosale jagir *had surfaced. He was bent on training the young jagirdar and his little warriors, for that was what people had called them. In the beginning, each of them was given a wooden sword. Yesa had learnt many new words: attacks, stances, lethal blows. One day, a military official of Adilshahi, who was then working for Raja's father, had arrived from Bijapur. He had come to show them how the swords and their blades ought to be handled. The man was tall with enormous coils of whiskers covering his face. Yesa and others had scrambled around him, eager to show him their new iron swords. They had waited, their eyes gazing at his stern face, their chests swollen with pride, waiting to hear some words of appreciation.*

'It is not about your sword; it is about how you handle your enemy,' said the tall man, his eyes moving from one face to another. They had stood in the veranda of Raja's stone house. The afternoon sky had darkened as lightening tore through the clouds and was followed by ear splitting thunder.

'Who is our enemy?' Raja had asked.

'It depends, son. We serve Adilshahi. This makes all their enemies ours.'

'Why do we serve them?' Raja had enquired again, this time with a tinge of sharpness. The man whom they called Netoji uncle had glared down as lightning and thunder had continued to rip the sky apart.

'Now that is a question. They are the Sultans, the kings. This land belongs to them. Even this jagir *falls in their territory. We eat food grown on their soil. They are our masters.'*

'It is the peasant who tills the land. We eat his food. Even the Sultans eat

his food.' Raja had been in tears.

'But the land our ryots till belongs to the Sultanate. Why just the peasants, even the jagirdars are the servants of the kingdom.' Netoji uncle had answered cautiously.

It had started raining in sheets. The fierce wind had flung the showers in the veranda.

'Who has given them the land?' Raja's queries had not stopped. His face had paled with anxiety.

'They have won it by sword.'

'And if the peasants can fight with swords can they take the land back from the king?'

'That is enough. Raja, you must learn to respect the kings. Not just respect, you must know how to bow to them with profound obeisance. You must also learn to answer the king's questions, with downcast eyes. You need to practise how to kneel before him when he gives you gifts.' Dadaji, who was standing near the steps leading to the house, had snapped.

Yesa had glanced at Raja, who was staring at Dadaji, eyes filled with a dark rage that Yesa had not seen before.

No one had spoken about the incident again. They were still training with padded swords and arrows, but these did cause injuries, and occasionally had broken their bones. Dadaji was strict. Missing a day of training had meant spending the entire night out in the dark, amidst the barks, howls, and snarls of the predators. The evenings had been spent in learning military subjects like the quality of the weapons and the war animals. They had also discussed the grips and pommels of the hilts, edges, and weights of the blades and how to preserve them from rust. They had learnt how to fletch and notch the arrows, what was the cheap way to make spears, why mares, not horses, were best suited to hilly terrains. The nights were spent around fires lit near Raja's home, listening to stories about raiders who came from countries beyond the mountains of Himalayas and their southern offshoot of Toba Kakar ranges. And the famous Bolan Pass from where the Turks and Afghans had entered Hindustan. Yesa's parents did not mind him being away from home. It was quite prestigious that their son was a friend of their jagirdar's son.

There was the night when the flames of bonfire had trembled in Raja's mother's eyes, when she had told them the story of God Shiva. 'Shiva is shakti, the power and the energy. The universe,' she had said, 'dances with him. When flowers bloom, when eggs crack for chicks to emerge, when a leaf appears on a twig, or when a calf is born of a cow, it is him dancing his anand tandava, his celestial dance of bliss. Shiva is like fire. It is in the lamps that remove the darkness, in the bonfires that warm up the wintry nights, in the stoves that cook our food. But when he is angry, the universe shakes in dread. That is when he performs his rudra tandava, the dance of destruction. He whirls as his braided hair become whips to dislodge the stars, he stomps his feet to quake the earth and he opens his third eye flinging out flames to set the oceans on fire.'

'And why does he get angry?' Wide eyed Tana had asked hesitantly, sitting on his haunches, his hands tight around his scrawny legs.

'It is us, when we misbehave and cause pain to others.' Raja's mother had tousled Tana's hair.

It was then that Yesa had told his friends about the Shiva temple hidden in the mountains, and had sought permission from Raja's mother to take the boys the next day. The day he would never forget, the day that had changed their lives.

Their ponies had flown towards the southwest, leaving behind rows of intervening hills and their velvety green slopes. It was for the first time that they were venturing out of the jagir. A year's training in swordfight and archery had emboldened them. Yesa had finally spotted what he had been looking for: Korle village lying cramped between two enormous mountains.

It was noon, but the clouds had cast shadows over the huddled houses and narrow lanes. They had dismounted and led their ponies to a lone house at the edge of the village. Peasants sowing waterlogged fields had first watched them with curiosity and then had gone back to their tasks. They had stopped near a house, almost buried in fallen leaves of the nearby trees. It had mud walls but no door. Its thatched roof had collapsed. Yesa glanced inside, eyes stinging with tears. The mud floor had become miry with rainwater. He had quietly led his friends behind the house where once his grandparents lived. A ramshackle animal shed had stood still on four rickety bamboos. Behind the shed the grass had grown wild and the old fence of trees stumps was covered with moss. The ponies had whinnied impatiently at the sight of food. They had removed the saddles and the bridles from the ponies and hid them in a dry corner of the hut.   The next bit was undertaken on foot. They had walked along the edge of the village, sometimes wading through waterlogged fields. They had noticed a line of oxen carts moving towards the east before they had reached their destination, the base of a hill. The slopes were vertical cliffs, along with rainwater streams falling forcefully. Yesa had moved a few paces, craning his neck to inspect the abrupt mass to find a less treacherous slope. Wiping his hands dry over the pleats of his angirkha for a better grip, he had touched the base of the hill. The spot had seemed suitable to climb. Soon, his hands and feet had gotten busy finding crevices, clefts and tough wood vines. After a while he had looked down to see the boys hanging to the sheer slope, clenching their teeth and lifting themselves up, grunting. The wind had made their pleated angirkhas balloon behind them. Panting with exhaustion, he had found a niche that had taken him to an edge. Soon all had stood on the ridge, hands and feet burning with scratches, leggings torn and angirkhas soiled. He had looked up and found a relatively easy foot trail going up and sighed with relief. Something had made him look down and then he had frozen with terror. A bunch of raiders had been flying in the direction of the ox carts. There was something sinister in the way the raiders had advanced. He had glanced at Raja, who was shaking, his eyes moving with the horsemen sweeping across clogged fields as jets of water had swirled behind them. Who were they, the Mughals or the soldiers of the Sultanate or the goons of the local landlord? Yesa had watched as strong winds whipped past him, pushing a huge cloud between him and the earth, blocking his view. For a moment he had thought it to be an illusion. But he could hear the faint screams of men, wailing of women and shrieks of children. He had waited on the ridge like a helpless bird with clipped wings, his new sword gritted to his belt.

'Had we been on the plains, we could have helped them,' he had whispered.

'Helped? They would have killed us too. And if they are not the enemies of Bijapur, they are not our enemies and we are not supposed to stop them,' Raja had almost shouted.

Disheartened, they had started climbing the trail to the temple. It had been a cave, its low hanging roof a natural, uncut rock, supported with massive manmade stone columns. Once their eyes had adjusted to the dark, they had slowly been able to make out a Shiv-Linga made of black stone in the dim light of a lone earthen lamp. The air inside was cool and smelt of burning incense. The boys were quiet, what they had witnessed while standing on the edge seemed to have numbed them. They had not even been hungry. Despite his promise of hot millet rotis *with blobs of fresh butter given to the temple visitors by the villagers of Rohida, nobody had mentioned food.*

Raja's eyes were fixed on the Shiva Linga. Then he had heard Raja saying, 'Let me tell you the story of God Shiva in my own words.'

The boys had scrambled around Raja : Wiry Tana, his brother Surya, dark and stocky Bhima, squinty eyed Bhairu, buck toothed Kavji, fair skinned Trimbak, youngest and the shortest Chiman and the oldest, sixty-year-old Pasalkar.

Instead, Raja had turned grimmer, swirled around and looked at each of them before speaking again. It had not seem like he had memorised the speech just to impress his friends.

'*God Shiva creates life, bears calamities, and ends evil. It had happened in the distant past when both, devas and asuras had started churning the ocean using a serpent called Vasuki as a rope. Just as butter floats when the cream is churned, they had hoped treasures would emerge from the ocean. Instead, a pot of poison, called halahal had surfaced. It was so potent that a drop was enough to finish the world. It had to be destroyed before it wiped out life forever. All faltered and wanted to hide their faces. The Gods and the demons had gazed at their own feet in fear and shame, but only God Shiva had dared. He had stridden over the ocean waters, lifted the pot over his mouth and gulped down the bluish green brew. A voice from the thunderous sky had warned him against doing so. But Shiva had even licked the last drop that had tried to sneak away from the rim and fall on earth to do as much damage as possible. Halahal had seeped down his throat, turning it blue. But he, the Neelakantha, the blue throated one as he was called later, had survived the ordeal, and he saved the world.'*

'*Friends,*' *Raja had lowered his voice and bitten his lower lip,* '*you call me a Raja, a king because I am a son of a jagirdar. But remember, all the jagir holders in the Deccan call themselves Rajas. We, the jagirdars are mere revenue collectors who work for the Muslim kingdoms. Our armies are meant to fight their wars. Our blood is meant to irrigate their battlefields.*'

The boys had looked on, wide-eyed.

'*The real rulers humour us when we call ourselves Rajas, like lions that ignore the barks of lowly dogs. The emboldened dogs may perceive that they are kings of the jungle but it is not true. We too live in such perception.*'

Raja had stopped for breath.

'*We are like the wooden swords used in the drills. They are called the swords but they actually are not. They have no blades to cut the enemy.*'

There was utter silence. Raja's words rung true in their ears.

'*We are even less effective than the wooden swords, as we do not know who our enemy is.*'

'*In the name of God Shiva I want to tell you that I dream of a Raj, a Swaraj, our own state that is ruled by us. I want our own military bases, manned by our armed garrisons in places that will be inaccessible to the Bijapur or Mughal armies and we will never have to bow to any of them.*'

Raja had spoken unhurriedly. Later he had turned around to look at each of them to see their reaction - a smile, a snigger or a mocking could mean that they had not taking him seriously.

'*We have seen the intervening hills of this region, and many have a fort built on their crest. I want them all. They will be our military bases. It is a difficult task, like God Shiva gulping down the halahal. Halahal actually refers to pain and agony that is beyond endurance. It is the pain of being skinned alive. It is the pain felt when eyes are gouged out or when a body is scorched by the fire. Today, in this ancient temple, I take an oath. My first step will be to acquire the dilapidated, neglected hill forts of Adilshahi standing in my jagir and repair them. These will be our military strongholds, the seeds of our Swaraj.*'

Yesa had watched as Raja had wrenched his new, real sword out of his belt, moved further towards the Linga, and held his left thumb over it. Before they could guess, he had raised the blade of his sword and made a sharp cut on his own thumb. Crimson droplets had fallen on the Linga.

'*I do not want to be a wooden sword, I want to be a blade, sharp and cutting, one made of iron. This is my first offering,*' *the young jagirdar had concluded.*

Each of them had followed him, bathing the Linga with their blood, thus binding by blood that they had spilled in the ancient temple of God Shiva.

***

Afzal Khan's horse trots through his military camp, a mile east of Bijapur. Sayed Banda and his men follow him vigilantly, holding naked swords in one hand and navigating the horse with the other. The drummers make a deafening racket as they rally before his procession. He is not an ordinary viceroy anymore but the General of Adilshahi. Never before has he experienced such public adulation, and never before has he been the cynosure of all eyes. He watches as the soldiers jostle and push, and shamelessly climb on each other's shoulders just to have a glimpse of him. This rise in the social ladder achieved at the age of forty is truly mesmerising. People who have never seen him before are stunned at his physique. He is indeed a big man, whose fully grown horse looks like a pony. His jama lined with silver brocade dazzles in the afternoon sun. And the kimoush turban embellished with emeralds makes him look taller.   He waves as some raise their swords to hail their new master and some scream and chant his name and the words written in his seal.

'Afzal Khan, Afzal Khan, *Katile Kafiran* Afzal Khan!'

The chants please him immensely and he caresses his long, henna dyed beard. The seal that he put on each of his official letters has been the subject of discussion in the Deccan. In fact, some of the Hindu landlords have gone cold in fear when they have received letters with his seal.

'*Katile Kafiran, Sinkadar Biniyade Butan*, the killer of the infidels and the destroyer of the deities.'

Afzal Khan is proud of his name, that means, superior, most excellent, and principal in Arabic. Impulsively, he turns to Sayed and shouts, 'Send notes of encouragement with my new seal to all my officers, and demand that they read it aloud to their respective contingents.'

Sayed nods with reverence as he is reminded of the words etched on his master's new pledge of assurance.

If you seek higher heavens

Then compare this Afzal, with the Afzal, the supreme, in the best of men

And when the beads of the rosary are counted

You will hear only one name, Afzal, Afzal, and only Afzal

'This is the time to show the snobbish men of power born in elite families that merit does count. Late General, Ranadullah Khan's son Ranadaula, proud Turani noblemen Waheed Khan, Yakut Khan, and Ankush Khan, African warrior Siddi Hilal, Afghan warrior Hasan Khan Pathan, Maratha heavyweights Bajaji Ghorpade, Mambaji Bhosale, Kalyanji Yadav and Rajaji Ghadge along with their contingents will take my orders. Never again shall I have to listen to anyone, it is my battle and I will plan the game. If I win even the new *wazir*, Khawas Khan, will be forced to bow before me,' broods Afzal Khan. However, rumours fly across the capital. One hears that someone has let out a lie, that it is not Afzal's merits but the secret of his birth that cunningly links his mother to the king of Bijapur.

Afzal Khan tries to wriggle out of painful memories, compelling his mind to focus on the present. As they reach the western edge of the military camp leaving the crowds behind, Afzal Khan frowns to himself. There is the last but most important place that he needs to visit alone. He looks at Sayed and nods, before kicking his dark brown horse to a full gallop in the western direction. Sayed is displeased, but he has to respect Afzal Khan's privacy and hopes Allah will take care of his master.

For a distance, Afzal Khan rides parallel to the moat infested with crocodiles and gallops along the outer wall of the fort city of Bijapur. The archers minding the enormously bulging, round bastions of Bijapur's outer wall recognise him and wave. He waves back to them in acceptance of their greetings while crossing the north facing Bahamani gate. Thereafter he kicks his horse to fly northwest through vast stretches of open farmlands. Some have been recently ploughed, and look like patches of earth edged in grooves and orchards. Beyond them stand quadrangular guest homes built by his master, Mohammad Adil Shah, for the travellers. It is evening when he arrives near a hillock. From its base he can see a low yet ornate building enclosed in a compound wall. He dismounts quietly, leads his horse uphill. The path is well looked after, hedged with flowering shrubs. Hundreds and thousands tread this alleyway, their hearts fluttering with the hope to their future. Afzal Khan quietly tethers his tired animal to a lone mango tree near the gate. It is evening and only a few torches burn in the marble stands near the entrance. He shakes off his sandals in haste before entering the building. A blind old man sits near the shrine covered in red and green brocaded velvet cloth, surrounded by heaps of roses and jasmine. The pleats of the man's long robe fall around him and his long, slivery beard covers his chest. He seems lost while counting his sandalwood rosary beads. Another man sitting behind the shrine hums rhymes to evoke the divine powers of the Sufi saint Hazrath Pir Amin Chisty who lived during the times of his master's Mohammad Adil Shah's father.

Afzal is not a scholar of his religion but knows that Sufism cannot be learnt easily and one has to first find a master, who has *izazah*, a sanction from another master. It is not a regular instruction but a divine transfer of mystical light from the master's heart to the disciple's, quite like sunlight illuminating the earth to welcome the day or a bud blooming to become fragrant, a fruit ripening for sweetness, the rainclouds sweeping in every year from the south. This mysterious transfer takes years, and sometimes an entire lifespan but once done, it is equivalent to knowing Allah, and loving him, as though He were a part of you and you Him. Some Sufis, their hearts brimming with divine light turn awliyas, or the walis. These divine men hover on earth to look after the ones who believe in them. Like a mother or even more, for awliyas are also blessed with inner vision that is eternal, not bounded by time.

'It that you? You have come after a long time.' He hears the blind old man whisper. It is known that the divine light was transmitted from the famous Hazrath Pir Amin Chisty's heart to the blind man's almost fifty years ago.

Afzal Khan removes his turban, hunkers down his body and put his head on the floor before the old man.

'Son,' the old man finally speaks in a quivering voice. 'Don't go, as in my vision, your body has been severed from your head.'

For the first time in many years Afzal Khan's heart misses a beat. He starts shivering and feels the touch of the old man's trembling hand on his head. The Sufi saint consoles him mutely, pleads him to accept Allah's decree.

On his way back, instead of going east towards the camp he rides further west, towards the hills of Torvi, riding past the enormous water tank built on a massive platform of stone masonry and connected to the Torvi river. The water reservoir is large enough to harvest rains during the monsoons to ensure uninterrupted water supply to Bijapur's countless gardens and fountains. But Afzal Khan remains oblivious to everything, even when huge domes and smaller cupolas of his summer palace on the edge of Takki village rise into his view. The high gate is thrown open to welcome the owner. His horse trots through the shady gardens covered with canopies of mango and tamarind trees. His head buzzes with crazy ideas and he fails to notice an army of kneeling servants. Dismounting hurriedly he rushes to his private quarters, like an enraged tiger leaping to its prey.

It is late into the night but sleep eludes Afzal Khan. Should he trust the blind man or should he just let it go? He curses himself for going to the Dargah to seek his future. But that was a done deed. And a seed of doubt has already been sown. As the chandeliers burn throwing golden light over his enormous bed, bleak thoughts fill his mind. He has to wind up his personal affairs before he leaves for his western campaign. He clutches his head with his hands as if it to banish the sounds from his large harem. The soft music, peals of laughter, faint crying of one of his countless children sound harsh to his ears.

His fifteen legitimate wives and their children are to accompany him. His twenty-year-old-son Fazal is to be his right hand. His concubines, picked from different parts of his country, bought from the slave traders or presented to him by his officers, will be left behind. A new stock of seventy-seven young women has been left untouched. The bloody battles with the imperialists and tensions of court politics have robbed him of both his leisure and libido. Who will have them if he dies in the battlefield? The girls will fill someone else's bed, sire someone else's children. Sheer jealously overwhelms him as visions of these virgins in other man's arms hammer his skull like an iron mallet striking a large metal bell.

'Bring Sarah,' he screams as eunuchs scurry outside his door. He waits impatiently, glancing at the door every few seconds. His youngest catch is almost thrown into his room as the door is bolted shut behind her. A slim girl with large eyes, long lustrous hair and wearing a transparent skirt with a very short blouse looks up at him. She is a wretch whom he does not even want to pull to his bed. He waits as she shivers, her hands trying to cover her breasts. She, the incapable bitch, has failed to stir his manhood. For a moment he disregards the fact that, in the recent past, all of them have. A blade of rage slices through his mind. He gets up at once and rushes towards her, with the confidence of a hyena lunging at an animal already killed by a jungle cat. Seeing him advance so rashly, she turns stiff with dread and then falls on the ground like a dry, broken reed. He lifts her by her hair, holds her in one hand and starts marching towards his private bath. She hobbles like a dead animal as he drags her across a long corridor lined with cusped arches. The main foyer has a large marble tub and a fountain spewing water jets at its centre. He kneels near the tub and places her on the water. She floats like a petal as he stares at her striking face, translucent skin, and small breasts. Her flimsy clothes flail around her like wings of a bird dropping dead from the sky. The faint sound of splatter echoes in the marble-floored bath. The mild scent of rose and khus wafts in the air. He watches her for a while as cool water brings her back to her senses. She suddenly jerks in his arms, thrashes her limbs about, like a calf on its last spasm before being devoured by a carnivore. He holds her hard with one hand around her waist and uses the other to drown her face. She struggles feebly and within moments is limp, her fourteen year life gone too quickly. Her kohl-lined eyes glaze for a brief moment as she sinks in the pool.

He has decided to kill the remaining seventy-five women in the next few days. They will drown in the same manner, in the same bath tub. He has also decided to build tombs of precisely the same pattern for each of them, seven in eleven rows. The tombstones will rise over a raised platform at the backyard of this very palace. He intends to name the place *satt kabar,* to let the world know his absolute passion.

***

Standing on the ramparts of the Rajgad citadel, Shivaji glances at the vast expanse rolling before his eyes. Swollen clouds have settled on the hilltops. From the eastern side, night descends like a raven waterfall. As he gazes at the abysmal slopes plunging beyond the western boundaries of Rajgad citadel, he notices the orange sun, half buried into the earth's horizon. *What will tomorrow witness, carnage or courage, destruction or daring?* he thinks. There is not much time left. The Bijapur's General will soon reach Baramati. From there he plans to proceed sixty miles northwest to reach the foothills of this very fort. The mighty Khan will break, smash and burn everything along his path. There is a chance to change the General's mind while he is at Baramati. He must cancel his northwest journey and go thirty miles southwest towards his Wai province.

Shivaji gazes at the distant hills of Torana and Lohagad forts and remembers how he had acquired them.

He was fifteen and the mountains beckoned him more than ever. He had three Maratha friends who would die for him, Tana, Yesa and Baji Pasalkar. His two Brahmins advisors, Sonoji Dabir and Dadaji Kondev, were by his side. And then there was Palkar. Moroji Pingle had just joined them. He had one hill in his possession, the hill of Murumbgad with the ruins of an ancient fort on its table. He longed for Torana, the fort above a steep hill twenty miles south west of Pune, at the source of Neera river. There were deliberations and discussions. Along with Yesa, Tana and Baji Pasalkar, he had galloped towards Torana. They had scaled the exceedingly difficult hill by foot, dressed in their finest silk angikhas and pearl studded turbans. Sixty-year-old Baji with his white moustache was made to look like a military official of Bijapur. They had held talks with the keeper of Torna, an elderly Muslim. They had pretended to be Adilshahi officials and had offered him a hundred rupees and ten Ashrafi mohurs. The man had seemed eager to leave the desolate place. The fort was in ruin, its outer walls had fallen, the quarters were damp, and the woodwork infested with white ants. Even the courtyard was covered with overgrown grass. The granaries were empty, and its ceiling had bats hanging upside down. Weather and erosion had turned the fortified bastions into abodes of predators. When Shivaji had ordered the repairing of Torana, there had been a miracle.

The diggers had discovered an old trunk full of ancient gold coins buried below a fallen turret. Some king had perhaps hidden his wealth wealth in times of war. With that treasure Shivaji could hire labourers working at Torana as well as Murumdev, now called Rajgad. They had cleared the hill tops of overgrown bushes, rebuilt the walls and bastions, cleaned the mossy water tanks, repaired the inner offices and residential quarters, and mounted new cannons on the ramparts. Soon the hill forts had men assigned to hold the fort in times of attack. The foothills were guarded by tribal living in the forests.

The news had soon reached the Bijapur king's ears. Shivaji's father had written a warning letter to reprimand him. Dadaji, now old, worn out and anxious was on his death bed. Shivaji had gone to see him and it had turned out to be their last meeting. 'What can I say? I am a mere servant of your father, and your father works for the king. You must be loyal to the king, but whatever you do, look after the cultivators, the real children of this soil. Do not put them in one basket. Levy taxes according to their soil, availability of water and what they produce. Think of variables like seasons, rains, and human errors, and do not rely on permanent land assessments. This soil is not a Khalisa land, she is our Kali Aai, our black mother.'

After Dadaji had passed away, the Adilshahi king had sent his army to eliminate him. He can never forget his first ever battle fought at Purandar. Bijapur was defeated but Shivaji had lost his old guard. Baji Pasalkar was killed while chasing the army of Fatte Khan.

And this is the second battle. Who will be the victor and who will be the vanquished?

Shivaji searches the sky as if to decipher God's secret message for him. Far above, between the clouds, a few daring stars blink like the pieces of life's puzzle. Around him, a strong draught of chill air slithers like a floating spirit of a brutally killed serpent - avenging to strike. He shivers at the thought of having to meet Sayee, perhaps for the last time. Tomorrow he would be gone to the valley of Javali. Walking down the stairs, his carefully constructed emotional fortifications collapse in a pile of sorrow. He walks towards the daruni palace dragging his feet as though they are heavy and bound.

When he enters Sayee's chamber, a strange pain shoots from his heart only to settle in the pit of his stomach. She lies on her bed like someone waiting for death to strike its sword. His footsteps alert her and she opens her eyes. Moving closer, he notices that her eyes exude grief, deep and longing.

'For Shambhu,' she whispers 'you are both his father and mother from now on. May God bestow upon you a long life and in the coming battle against the Sultanate, may you emerge victorious.'

'I hope so too.'

'Hopes,' she sighs and continues in a quivering voice, 'are the shackles of life, defiant to everything, including death. Death too bows down to these chains.'

'You always confuse me, don't you?'

'This is what you have taught me,' she smiles weakly and continues. 'But it is very simple. You are my God, the owner of my destiny, and the master of the vermillion that adorns my forehead. I have always hoped that it is you who must light my pyre. Women have this habit of making even their deaths a prisoner of their hopes.'

'I shall do all that you hope for.'

'I have no such wish now as I have set my death free from the fetters of hope. It has already granted me my most cherished wish that is longed for and prayed for by every Hindu woman. It is to die while her husband is still alive. Not to be left behind to live a wretched, inauspicious life of a widow. Not to die the sinful, miserable death of a widow. I am dying before you. I am dying with my forehead smeared with red vermillion.'

'Sayee,' he says, his throat tight, 'I haven't done anything for you. I have always been away.'

'It is about being a part of your life,' she says, her eyes shining with tears, 'it is about your life touching mine.'

'Even at a tangent?'

She keeps silent as if she is contemplating the greater purpose of her short existence. He can barely see her face now. The lamp has dimmed. He looks away in desperation in a hope that all that he sees is just a nightmare.

'Sayee! Don't go Sayee, please don't leave me,' he pleads while swallowing a rising sob.

'We always wish to control things that are beyond us and we always let go of things that are within our reach.'

'What do you mean?'

'Like my death and your life. It is time for you take control. This is the first time that they have not dismissed you as a mere rebel but have sent such a huge army. This is the first time that they have regarded you as a proper enemy. Regard that as a tribute to your rising power. I am glad that this has happened before I am gone.'

'What about Shambhu?' He hopes that their son's name will make her despise death and not embrace it.

'He has you,' she quips and continues, her words now barely audible, 'No leash however strong is of any use now.'

'Stop it Sayee, shh!'

He holds her close to his heart as her thin frame shivers with fever and weakness.

'Don't stop me please. There may never be another time,' she warns and persists, still gasping for air, 'When we married, we were just children. We grew up together. Your ideas initially surprised me. Our fathers worked for the Sultanate and you were born to serve the masters of your father that was your duty, your karma. But you charted a new path, drew new frontiers of Swaraj that did not exist.'

He looks down at his dying wife. He takes her hands in his and for the first time in eighteen years of their married life declares, 'I love you Sayee, I love you so much.'

Unexpectedly, the room is filled with Sayee's laughter.

'I have never believed you capable of saying such romantic things.'

He notices the familiar twinge of mischief in her eyes.

Shaken, he too, joins her and laughs, holding her hands close to his heart, oblivious to the fact that, hearing their laughter, in another chamber, someone fumes in anger.

Soyara indeed is outraged. A deep ache of envy cuts through her heart and smashes her patience. She is hurt for he does not remember her. The other wives are simple women, content to be pushed away from view, but she is different. She looks into a nearby mirror; her reflection fills her with self-pity as it reminds her insistently of her beauty and her worth. The pallu of her Paithani sari that covers her head has pink elephants woven in silk. A bow shaped nose ring studded with pearls adorns her delicate nose. Several heavy todas shackle her hands from her wrists to her elbows. Her neck that otherwise looks like a lotus stem is strangled with a peti, its rubies breathing fire into the pale glow of the oil lamps.

'He is leaving to fight a dangerous battle,' she thinks as her eyes well up with tears. 'It is so late; he may not even have time to come by. If only I had given him a male heir things would have been different. I will have to meet him when he eats his evening meal, amidst a thousand others.'

She goes to the window to see if her husband has left Sayee's room. She watches him walk out in a hurry, his face red and swollen. But he does not turn towards her chamber; he walks away, and goes to his mother's room.

Jija Bai is in her prayer-room, the pallu of her sari covering her head. A maid is busy severely chafing a tiny piece of sandalwood on round sandstone to make a paste to smear the deities with.

'Ma Sahib!'

She quickly turns around, as if she had been thinking of him all along. Despite her earlier resolve, she asks 'Are you sure that there is no possibility of declaring a truce?'

'No Ma Sahib, there is no choice now.'

He kneels besides his mother as his eyes take in the deity of Tulaja Bhavani, a replica of the original from the temple in the hills of Tuljapur town on the western borders of the Sultanate.

The Tuljapur Bhavani, the destroyer avatar of Goddess Parvati, God Shiva's wife, is known as the 'Shakti Peetha' - a source of primal energy. Her eight hands hold eight weapons but her eyes inspire dread and fear. He gazes into them and they, like the eyes of the original one, fling strange, unfathomable energy in his direction, making him tremble. The ripples of that vigour cause waves that cut through his body. His mind hovers between the real and the surreal worlds. Her huge kohl-lined eyes seem to cast out rays of invisible force, more powerful and more dazzling than the rays of the brightly shining sun. They seem to peel off the outer layers of his being and strike his soul. The force of her gaze becomes tangible, crushing all his doubts to pulp. His eyes are unable to withstand the power of her eyes, he closes them and oblivious to him, tears stream down his face. Deep in his heart he knows that Her energy has touched him, Bhavani has given him a 'kaul', her positive inclination that he must go to the valley of Javali and fight his second battle with the Adilshahi forces from Pratapgad.

Circa 1659

Despite a few stray clouds, the sky above Pratapgad fort is clear. The meandering wall fortified with enormous bastions creates an illusion of a crown of black iron metal fixed on the head of a tribal king. The gigantic fort extensions spread out like his long, muscular arms. Below lies the dense forests of the valley. At the upper fort, several sentinels carrying javelins have formed two semicircles around huge bastions guarding the citadel. *Peshwa* Moroji Pingle glances at the guards to be sure. They are smartly attired in their tight breeches and brocaded angirkhas. Their Turkish turbans look like small crimson boats on their heads. Satisfied, he goes back to the *sadar*, a large assembly chamber built with stones and supported by pillars. A few servants are busy placing tall brass samayee lamps in the corners. A short divan has been placed at the northern side of the room, near a large window towards the west. A small desk for the scribe stands facing the open window.

The first to arrive are Sonoji Dabir, his son Trimbak Dabir, and surnis Annaji Datto. A little later, chitnis Balaji Avji, the newly appointed secretary walks in with an ink pot, a notebook and a long feather with a nib. They have been called to Javali by Raja Shivaji. Their faces are flushed with admiration for the newly built fort. They wonder at the the pillars rising above the stone pedestals, strings of fresh jasmine and marigold draped around them, the ceiling of polished wooden beams, an enamelled glass chandelier bound to gilded chains, its light falling gracefully on the black basalt floor covered at places with carpets and

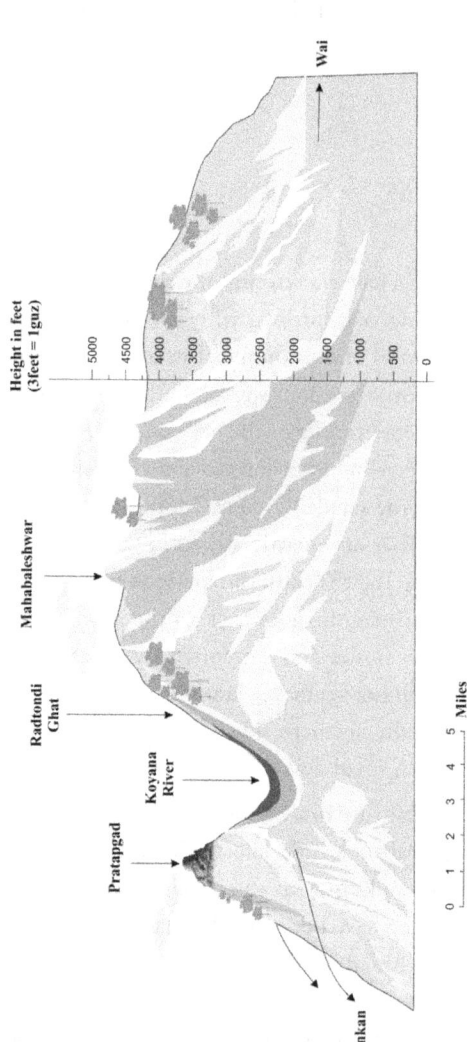

Dr Srinivas Samant, *Vedh Mahamanavacha* (Marathi) (Deshmukh and
Company Publishers Private Ltd)

the bolsters that are draped in silk cases neatly lined up near the walls. The nervous whispers of the men fill the room. Ibrahim Khan who has quit Bijapur service to join the Maratha army has come from Konkan dressed in a long green *zama* and a shining *kimoush* turban. *Sar-e-naubat* Palkar, infantry commanders Tanaji and Yesaji have arrived from Maval. The drums start beating and as the voices of the guards announcing his arrival wither in the air, Shivaji walks in taking long strides and stands before the board.

'Be seated,' says the leader of the Marathas. His men obey, they either sit cross-legged or on their knees, their gaze fixed on him. It is no longer a matter of plundering an isolated caravan near Kalyan, or fighting a small battle with *jagirdars* like Moray. It is facing confrontation with the Bijapur General and his huge army. There is the chance that they will perish, their families will be killed, abducted and enslaved. Tales of Afzal Khan's strength and merciless nature have reached their ears, and have filled their hearts with dread.

In the depth of his heart Shivaji knows that his men may urge him to make peace. He feels their gaze, and knows that they are searching his face for traces of panic.

'The time has come. Afzal Khan is already in our territory and has reached Baramati, a hundred odd miles north-east from this very fort. Soon his war animals will stamp our terrain turning it into a battlefield, sodden with blood, and strewn with limbs. Rumour says that after camping for a week in Baramati he intends to march towards Pune. If he does, his enormous cavalcade will destroy our *jagir*, the core of our budding kingdom. His archers have already turned easy with their bows, stretching them and letting the arrows fly to the peasants working in the fields.

'And we have done nothing to stop him,' snaps Dabir.

'What do you want me to do, venture out to oppose him in the open?' Shivaji asks with a sneer that he does not bother to hide. 'That is precisely what Afzal Khan wants.'

'A few things have already been done.' Palkar, who stands near Pingle, announces in a distinct tone. 'All our forts are well-manned. Our intelligence system has been put to work. Bahirji Naik and his men have infiltrated the General's army.'

Shivaji nods. His *sar-e-naubat* has been on the move for the past few months, visiting hill forts of Kondana, Purandhar, Torna, Lohagad and others. He has briefed each of the fort commanders to keep their granaries stuffed with enough grains, salt, oil as well as medicines and has made sure that they know about the caliber, mobility and range of the cannon mounted on their ramparts. He has personally inspected the garrisons, taken stock of the storehouses and checked the quality of the gunpowder and cast iron projectiles. During his innumerable meetings with the tribal at the foothills of those forts, he has made sure that they keep a constant vigil on the forest trails leading to the fort.

'*Subhedar* Abaji Sondev guards our western borders from Kalyan, Murarbaji, our eastern borders from Purandar fort and Firangoji Narsala our northern borders from Chakan fort,' Palkar assures.

'Are we then preparing for war? Is there no possibility of a treaty?' Pingle asks anxiously.

Shivaji just smiles.

'If he wants a treaty, we shall oblige.' Pingle has made his decision.

Shivaji stares at his *peshwa* and speaks, his words clear and loud, 'A treaty with Afzal Khan? Do you not know what had happened to Kasturiranga, the king of Sira when he had gone to Afzal Khan to make his submission, to my brother who had trusted Afzal Khan and waited in the trenches for the reinforcements to arrive or to the Bijapur's loyal *wazir*, Khan Mohammad? These men are all dead, brutally and cunningly murdered by him.'

'Then war is the only option,' Dabir says, his face shrivelled with worry. 'Now when we raise our sword against the king, the doors of any kind of treaty with Adilshahi are forever closed. In this world of Islamic empires and the kingdoms we shall have no one to turn to, to fall back on.'

Shivaji closes his eyes briefly and says in a steady voice, 'Speculating about the future will only lead to confusion. We must find out what Afzal Khan seeks, a treaty or my head. But while doing so we must also prepare for war.'

The *sar-e-naubat* takes over, 'The first step is to choose our battleground for it can turn into a dangerous zone, where people will be killed, houses destroyed, farmlands flattened and barns set on fire.'

'What do you mean?' Pingle stares at Palkar.

'I shall explain.' Shivaji intervenes as his eyes sparkle. 'In our *jagir* the samplings of sorghum, pearl millets, gram, and horsegram have already begun to grow. If the General takes his army towards Pune, the peasants will be slaughtered and their fields spoilt. Our ryots' morale, their livelihood, their families and their cattle will be trampled under the hooves of the Bijapur's war animals. We seek freedom and peace for our ryots and not at their cost. We raise our swords to protect them; they are the soul of our Swaraj. We must stop the General from entering the region around Pune.'

'Do we have a choice?' Dabir asks.

Balaji Avji, sitting behind the small desk tries to scribble the essence of the discussions. Shivaji remains silent for a while and says, 'We do.'

Dabir smiles doubtfully.

'What if Afzal Khan cancels his plans to go to Pune and steers his cavalcade towards Wai, the province he governs as a *subhedar*?' Shivaji suggests.

Dabir comprehends instantly. The young Maratha who stands before him is indeed an intelligent strategist. If the General wants to extract a treaty on his terms he will first destroy the region to show his might. But if he wants Raja Shivaji's head he will steer his army towards Javali as the valley is just twenty miles east of Wai.

Shivaji speaks again, 'The General knows I am here. He had sent a few scouts to confirm the news. The scouts were brought here by Bahirji's men who had posed as guides. And the General's men have seen me at the foothills of this fort. To be very precise, it was arranged that they 'see' me here.'

'What if he decides to proceed towards Pune? What then is our plan of action?' enquires the *peshwa*.

'That is unlikely and to analyse why so, we must look beyond what's obvious,' Shivaji says without blinking. 'The Mughals pose a far greater threat to Bijapur than we do. With Aurangzeb busy warring with his brothers, logically, the Bijapur king should have tried to recover his military strongholds lost to the Mughals. Instead, he has unleashed his army towards us. What does that say?'

The *sar-e-naubat* answers, 'This is crystal clear and not too difficult for anyone to fathom. There is a sequence. The Bijapur king has renewed the old peace treaty with Aurangzeb, reinforcing their status as a tributary state of the Empire. Secondly, it is well known that Aurangzeb is furious with us. We have plundered his region. He had ordered his *mansabdars* to waste our villages, slay our people without pity, and plunder the region thoroughly. But then he had to go north to fight the war of succession, so he must have commanded the Bijapur king to deal with us. Perhaps our elimination may be one of the clauses in their peace treaty.'

Shivaji's esteem for his army chief reflects in his eyes. He says softly, 'Aurangzeb is a man on a mission. I can actually see what his vision is, a vision of a large Islamic empire that includes the Deccan. Such a man will not accept the rise of a *kafir*. He must have given an ultimatum to the Bijapur king.

'May I say something?' Ibrahim Khan asks, his handsome face serious, his large eyes filled with disgust. He hails from Afghan and is a Shia Muslim. Previously a cavalry commander in the Bijapur army, he has witnessed many a court intrigues. He was in the court of Kalyan when Shivaji had shown his respect for the captive woman. It was then that he had decided to leave the king's army along with his five hundred pashton horsemen to join the leader of the Marathas. 'This religious zeal is an act. Had they been so spiritually inclined, they would have become *awliyas*, *pirs* or *fakirs*. When politically powerful men talk of religion, they use it as a weapon to gain power. Aurangzeb has incited the Empire's military men, especially the orthodox, against his own brother Dara Shikoh, calling him a heretic. He does not want the other powerful *kafirs*, for that is what he calls them, like the Sikhs, the Rajputs, the Bundelas, the Marathas and others to take cue and rise against the Empire. He wants to destroy the man who has set a dangerous precedent. He plans to achieve his objective through the Bijapur rulers. And the Bijapur king is eager to please the Emperor-to-be to keep his kingdom safe from further Mughal invasions.'

The others who still have trouble trusting Ibrahim gape at him while Shivaji smiles and says, 'What Ibrahim says is true. That is the reason why Afzal Khan will come to Wai. It is Aurangzeb's wish to capture or kill me, and his wish is the Bijapur king's command!'

'Afzal Kahn will reach Wai in a week or so. The monsoon season is upon us. It is impossible for any army to move in the direction of Javali from Wai. During rains, this valley turns into a water trap as its rivers are flooded, mountain trails blocked by landslides and slopes covered by wild vegetation. The locals say that even the wings of the flying birds turn mossy,' says the *sar-e-naubat*.

'This valley will be our *ranangan* zone, our battlefield,' Shivaji announces.

The *sar-e-naubat* walks near the board and points to the map and explains, his index finger forming a trail. 'Wai may be just twenty miles from this fort but to reach here, one has to travel forty miles across the mountains and valleys, hiking a steady climb to reach the plateau of Mahabaleshwar and then braving the abrupt descent from the ghats of Radatondi. As we know, Radatondi means cry-face. This trail makes even the hill men weep with dread.'

'Ummm, forty miles of death-defying voyage through ghats surrounded by dense forests and perilously plummeting rocks,' Dabir comments and continues, 'if Afzal Khan wants Raja Shivaji, he will come to Wai. But what will make him undertake the perilous expedition to reach the *ranangan* of our choice? Surely he knows the valley, considering he has been the *subhedar* of Wai for the past ten years. He may insist that he meets Raja in his den, at Wai.'

'Yes, he will want to do that. But we will invite him to Javali,' Shivaji says nonchalantly.

'All this happens only if Afzal Khan is a dimwit. It beats all logic,' says Dabir sharply.

Shivaji closes his eyes for a moment. His brother's face, crushed by a cannonball floats before him. For a very brief moment his mouth winces but he quickly recovers and says, 'Wars defy logic. Ali Adil Shah is too young and is a man of finance and not of battles. It has already been months since Afzal Khan has left Bijapur. He must have already spent a million rupees. By the time we invite him to Javali he would have wasted three more months of monsoon. The king will be impatient for the returns on his investment.'

'Will Afzal Khan's advisors let him jump into our trap?' Dabir challenges.

It is Ibrahim Khan who speaks while his eyes burn with the memories of humiliation. 'Afzal Khan is an autocrat and does what he wants. Nobody advises him. If someone attempts to, he makes fun of him.'

'How many men do we need and have?' Yesaji Kank asks hesitantly.

'It is not about how many, it is about the kind they are. That is why we want all of you to pick up hill men and the rock climbers from your forces and bring them to the field. We want numbers from each of you in two weeks,' retorts Palkar.

'Call for woodcutters, grain traders, butchers, and cooks from the nearby villages. Let it seem like we are expecting thousands of guests and have to supply the General's army with firewood, grains, meat, spices and even wine. No costs must be spared,' Shivaji slowly unfolds his plan.

'Are you planning to feed his army?' Anna Datto asks. Niloji Sondev, whom Anna Datto reports to, is a very strict finance man. The accounts are closed annually and balance payments due by the state are either paid in cash or by bills on the collection of revenue. This deficit caused by this sudden and huge expense has to be worked out by him.

'Not just the army but even his war animals.'

'It is an enormously expensive gamble,' worries Anna Datto as he knows that the number may run into thousands of rupees, if not hundreds of thousands.

'You seem to have even planned to provide him with servants, maids, and *shikaldars* to sharpen their blades to chop us swiftly!' Sonoji Dabir says with slight sarcasm.

'Yes, that's the plan. And if we win the battle Annaji will have no deficit, only surplus. Ideally, spoils of war must foot the bills of our wars,' Shivaji quips but Annaji does not look impressed.

'Annaji, when we built this very fort, questions were raised regarding the huge funds being invested. The fort's remoteness, its inaccessibility, its location in this perilous valley where enemy armies may not even dare enter were the issues. Remember, if we can win this battle because of this fort, just this battle, we will have been reimbursed. The fort has served its purpose. Military investments are not a gamble; they form the thin lines between victory and defeat.'

'And who will serve as the brilliant *vakeel* to hold meetings and discussions with the mighty General of Bijapur?' Dabir's interest is piqued.

'I have someone in mind,' Shivaji says and claps his hands.

Two guards came in, bringing a man along.

'For this operation, we have chosen him as our *vakeel* who will deal with the mighty General. He will tackle Afzal Khan and bring him to Javali, our *ranangan*, where the offenders will be forced to become the defenders and the defenders will get a chance to be the offenders,' announces Shivaji as the men sitting before him blink in disbelief.

Gopinath Bokil is a frail old Brahmin who has lost all his teeth, literally and metaphorically.

***

The rambling Shalimar Garden in the northwest suburb of Delhi looks freshly drenched by the recent bout of rains. The ponds and lakes are filled with clean blue waters, partially hidden under blooming lotuses and their large, round leaves. Arches built over the canals are decorated with strings of marigold while swans with snow white plumage float in pairs over its waters like sail boats. Large numbers of peacocks forage and leap in the shades of enormous fruit trees. The apartment buildings near the central Sheesh pavilion are crowded with personal guests invited by Aurangzeb. They are looked after by well-attired servants who prepare sherbets and black kava as welcome drinks and hookahs to smoke. The marble pavilions are spruced up for the most important event.

The procession starts with the deafening din of drums, tambourines and trumpets. The skirting of tree-lined avenue running through the sprawling garden is packed with people. A long file of ceremonial elephants adorned with gilded chains and dangling bells trundle from the garden's southern gate to reach the Sheesh pavilion. The *mahouts* are in red silk tunics and turbans, their javelins resting on their shoulders glitter with diamonds. Their ornately decorated tuskers carry an imperial benchmark of polished balls slung from a pole, the ensigns of the Ottoman Empire. The men on other elephants carry the various symbols of a Mughal emperor, made of silver and gold. The emblems are of the sun, an upraised hand, scales of justice, a fish, a tiger's head, and a horse head. Behind them, horsemen ride smartly, carrying silver maces. They are followed by the dense columns of uniformed footmen, musketeers, rocketiers, and the scouts. The cavalcade moves through the barricaded path. Throngs of noblemen, dressed impeccably in silk robes and colourful headgears walk solemnly behind the footmen. They are followed by others carrying hourglass, gong and hammer to tell the time. At the end trundles a huge, caparisoned elephant, carrying a gilded throne on its back. Aurangzeb sits on the chair as his eyes survey his subjects who jostle and push each other to have a glimpse of their master on his coronation day. Behind him, on a large wooden platform, an elderly man stands holding the backrest of the throne. It is Uncle Abu Talib, alias Shaista Khan.

But the Emperor-to-be is not exactly brimming with happiness. His heart is not filled with joy, and his head is full of worries. Murad has been sent to Gwalior under heavy security. Aurangzeb has ordered his men to put him in the opium cell. The warden is supposed to instruct the prison doctors to feed Murad large doses of opium everyday. There has been no news about him. He wonders if the prison doctors have betrayed him. There are more such qualms that do not allow him to enjoy the best day of his life. Darabhai has been seen wandering on the banks of Sutlej river in Punjab. The vanquished prince might have headed for the Bolan Pass, a thousand miles northwest of Agra and may across the pass to reach Persia. The Persian Emperor likes Darabhai and they both may form an allainace to attack Delhi. On the other hand, religious men, the Syeds, Mullahs, Imams and Fakirs of Mecca will not recognise him as the new Emperor if the former is still alive. He has already sent forty-five thousand Ashrafi *mohurs* to Syed Mir Ibrahim of Mecca. There are some things that need to be taken care of immediately. The liberal Muslims who have helped Darabhai ought to die. But that has to be done cleverly, within the precincts of the shariah law. The news from the Deccan is not so encouraging either. The Adilshahi General has steered his military cavalcade towards the Wai town in the mountains at the eastern borders of Javali. The news is that Shiva Bhosale has been holed up in the valley. There is status quo on that front.

The royal elephant stops in front of a lofty pavilion with bright coverings. It is decorated with tapestries of embroidered velvet, European screens and gold tissue from Turkey and China. As he alights, all the people kneel, some even fall prostrate. As he enters the pavilion, a hush prevails, as if people are even afraid to breathe. The astrologers have declared the time, three hours and fifteen minutes from the sunrise. When Aurangzeb finally climbs the steps of the platform, a sea of people has gathered blocking all the routes to the venue of his coronation. The air vibrates with tangible divinity as clergies recite the *Holy Quran* in their high-pitched voices. People notice that Aurangzeb's swagger has changed and he walks more like an emperor and less like a soldier. He even sits on the satin cushions of the coronation throne kept in the open courtyard like his father, legs folded under him, and the silk of his Jama falling around him. A turban bound around his head glitters with diamonds, rubies and emeralds. An aigrette with a nodding fringe adorning the front part of his headgear is special, worn only by the kings and the emperors. His name and titles are publicly proclaimed through the religious sermon. The Muslim clergies do not mind reading the *khutbah* in his name even when the old dethroned emperor still lives. Coins bearing his name are thrown on the waiting crowd. His titles are announced loudly, *bahadur*, the brave, *alamgeer*, the conqueror of the world, *padishah*, the Emperor, *ghazi*, the holy warrior. The final announcement is made in a verse:

The new minted coins,
Are stamped with his name
They shine like the moon
And he, Aurangzeb
The Alamgeer,
Will dazzle the world
Through day, night and noon.

***

Dara Shikoh looks in the broken mirror and shudders with self pity. He hates his reflection; it is that of a sick man with dark circles around his eyes and an unruly beard. His front teeth are missing and his head, wrapped in a soiled turban, is full of greys.

It is a desolate place called Dadur, nine miles east of Bolan pass near the Afghan border, and a thousand miles away from his home, Agra. His wife Nadira Begum has died. The last day of her life was spent gasping for breath, in his arms, asking for water that was not available. She, the mother of his sons, Suleiman and Siphir, had been groomed to be the empress. The scorching heat of this region that made the birds drop dead from the sky had put his delicate wife to death.

What has become of his family? This was not the life that he was supposed to lead! His palaces, the gardens, the pavilions, the plush apartments, his retinue of slaves tending to his need, his wardrobes filled with carefully chosen clothes, his libraries stuffed with rare manuscripts, pundits who came from far and near just to listen to his views, his countless concubines, one prettier than the other, his guards, his horses, his ceremonial elephants, iron vaults stuffed with jewels, and his army of twenty thousand cavalry and equal number of infantry – all have vanished as if they had never existed. If memories stab him like a dagger, guilt consumes him when he thinks of his father. He has left the Emperor in the hands of the murderous Aurangzeb. The future of his two sons is bleak. His dreams for Suleiman have shattered, the young prince now in his twenties stranded in Kashmir with his army. The last piece of news that he had heard said that Mirza Jai Singh had deserted his son and had run back to Delhi to join Aurangzeb. His second son Siphir is at least with him, sleeping in another room, but his body has been burning with fever due to this oppressive heat. Dara angrily wrenches the turban from his head and throws it away as tears fill his eyes. He slowly walks back to his bug-infested bed he dreads and slumps on it with a thud and starts wailing as his body shakes violently.

He has tried his best. Having lost the battle at Samugad and realising that Delhi was too dangerous for him, he had travelled hundreds of miles to reach Lahore and lavished whatever funds he had on whoever was prepared to join him. In a short span of time he had mustered twenty thousand men. But Aurangzeb's murderous army, full of vicious jihadis, had followed him. They chased him across flooded rivers, braving severe monsoons and treading swamped paths. His hastily collected soldiers had been slaughtered or bought over. He and his family had gone into hiding and crossed the frozen waters of Sutlej in Punjab. With a few remaining guards and eunuch slaves, they had spent an entire day in the open, shivering in their tattered clothes like vagrants. That had been the most dreadful day of his life and it was there that he had received the news of Aurangzeb's impending coronation. Everything was over, his life snuffed out. He had fled to Sindh, and then Runn of Cutch, borrowing money, food and clothes from people who once kneeled before him for favours. He had wept bitterly over his fate. He had finally fled to the region near to the borders of Afghan and had taken refuge in the camp of Malik Jiuan. The small Afghan Chief was once captured and brought to Agra as a fugitive and was condemned to death under the feet of an elephant. He had intervened and goaded father to spare the life of Malik Jiuan and even set him free.

Dara Shikoh's body shudders with sobs. He hopes that Malik Jiuan can provide secrecy and protection to him for a few days.

'Prince, wake up, please wake up, we must move,' he hears his personal guard. 'Malik Jiuan has turned traitor.'

He jerks his head and jumps out of his bed. How can it be? He rushes out to a small corridor, like a wounded deer chased by a wild cat. The night is dark and not a single torch burns anywhere. He runs to his son's room, kicks open the flimsy door and gathers the young boy in his arms. Siphir is hot, burning with fever.

'Call the others and get our horses,' he orders, carrying his son on his shoulder. It is dangerous not to believe his guard and wait to confront Jiuan. He has decided to go north, towards the province of Kandahar, and then flee to Persia. There is hardly any choice. The animals look tired and underfed. His horse protests by snorting when he tries to get it to walk and then kicks it hard to a gallop. They move towards the north. Only fifteen guards and eunuch slaves follow him on their horses. It is a difficult ride, holding the burning Siphir with one hand and managing the bounding horse with another. If he leaves his hand the boy will slip and fall on the rocky ground.

The faithful horses fly over the hilly region as the waxing moon throws enough light over the hills to form large, dreadful shadows. It is still hot; the wind hits his face like whips of flames. Within few hours, the morning star appears in the east, and the enormous hills of Bolan become visible on the northern skyline. So colossal, so high are the silhouettes that they looked like beasts waiting to swallow the world. As they ride closer, he is able to spot the pass.

The faint silvery light of the moon has cracked the enormous shadows of Bolan hills into two halves. They slow down to enter. The tired horses trot and pant with exhaustion. The pass is wide but feels dingy between the two hills looming on the either side. It is like a furnace and a blast of hot air greets them. They cannot breathe. He holds his son tighter, wanting to know if the boy is still alive. At places, the passage between the limestone rocks narrows to a tight trail, allowing only two men to ride abreast. The wind suddenly starts blowing through the winding path. He looks at the sky and notices that the stars have disappeared and the moon has turned pale. The first rays of the sun gradually turn the night into a day. He slowly diverts his gaze from the sky onto the path unfolding before him. Something makes him turn back. He notices small specks moving up and down at the far end. He narrows his eyes and realises that they are horses galloping purposefully towards him. His blood turns cold.

Then everything happens quickly, in the blink of an eye. The chasers take hold of him in the pass and Siphir is snatched away. He is shackled and put on another horse. His captor is Mirza Raja Jai Singh.

Dara barely remembers the thousand miles of journey back to Delhi. The ordeal of that humiliating voyage has become a blur, his mind wants to block out nights spent in shacks meant for animals. He wants to let the times when he was dragged for miles tied to a trotting horse while climbing the slopes or when the food was thrown at him as if he was a tramp, dissolve quickly. All he remembers is being hauled by slaves in the court of *quila-e-mukarak*, hands tied behind his back, feet heavy with iron shackles, along with his son Siphir Shikoh. He remembers his long unkempt hair not letting him see properly. He remembers not walking but heaving himself against his will.

He wonders about Aurangzeb's clear instructions. 'I want them to be paraded on the back of a female elephant through all the major avenues of this city, and do not forget to smear this elephant with dirt for that is what they are worthy of.'

The sun is harsh and it is extremely hot even for a Delhi summer. As the elephant sways, Dara looks at his beloved capital. He is not in a howdah; he is tied to the back of a small female elephant. The avenues look familiar. Thousands of horrified eyes watch him, some are full of pity. The elephant is not a magnificent male tusker, it is a measurable female smeared with mud. The animal is neither pompously caparisoned nor is it decorated with gilded framework. The first prince is not sitting in a howdah inlaid with gold and covered with glorious canopy that resembles a silver cupola. The first prince himself does not look like Dara Shikoh, *Shah Bulund Iqbal*, the king of lofty fortunes who always wears large pearls, enormous turban with gilded sirpech and embroidered coat. It is so utterly confusing for those walking by. Those were once his people, who looked at him with love and worship. Dara Shikoh hates to look up, he sits there like an old man with a bent spine, his matted hair on his face like a veil. He lets his shoulders droop and keeps his hands limp on his lap. At one turning when the elephant spins, he slides from its back that is slippery with mud. He is then tied to the elephant with long ropes, and feels like a dead, dried up lizard stuck to a wall. He is thirsty and fears for Siphir who is lying still next to him. He sees thousands of people, barricades keeping them off the street. He hears them scream and chanting his name. He slowly drifts to sleep and the screams of his people turn faint.

From the watchtower Aurangzeb too hears people chants Darabhai's name. He is livid, his subjects love Dara. There is a danger of a civil war.

'Call them all, whoever is in the fort,' he barks orders before marching off towards *divan-e-khas*. Mutamad is shocked; his master has lost his temper after many years.

The meeting takes place in the evening. Tiny oil lamps burn in the chandeliers hung in the patio of *divan-e-khas*. In that twinkling light, precious stones stuck to the pillars reflect rays in every possible direction, rendering hints of life to their floral patterns. Aurangzeb sits cool and composed. The beauty of his new home fails to kindle any cheer in his heart. Sitting on his father's peacock throne, he glances at the faces of his men from the corner of his eyes. He has to be careful, as per the royal etiquette, even his gaze is now a reward, a *mehernazar*, a giver of mercy. His uncle Shaista Khan who was always against Darabhai, Mirza Raja Jai Singh, Mir Jumla's son Mohammad Amin Khan whom he had saved from death in the dungeons of Golconda Fort, Bahadur Khan who is his loyalist, Danishmand Khan who was first a Dara loyalist but now has changed his mind, and Hakim Daud, the orthodox noble who considers Darabhai a heretic, are standing in front of him with sullen faces. Their expensive clothes, embellished with motifs of floral patterns, gold and silver ornaments and colourful turbans have no impact on him.

He does not start a conversation and lets the silence grow, waiting for his men to turn uneasy and then blurt out their thoughts.

'Spare his life,' he hears Danishmand Khan, his face flushed with anxiety.

Shaista Khan seems restless. His favourite nephew has made a big mistake, wanting to make Dara Shikoh look silly in public. But the tables have turned. The avenues of Delhi have formed gossip hovels. They cannot rule out trouble now that the people are fuming in rage. Anything can happen and it is best for all that his eldest nephew Dara, the Crown Prince is dead.

'Who are we to decide?' Khan says solemnly, his eyes filled with concern. 'It is up to the theologians of the Shariyah court to punish him for his heretic ways of life.'

'Kill him; he does not need a trial. His death will be lauded by Islam and the Empire,' spits out Hakim Daud.

'The Emperor must decide,' Mirza Jai Singh quips. He is the only Rajput in this meeting.

Aurangzeb has closed his eyes. The men vent their opinions and suggestions, discuss, and try to outwit others. Aurangzeb thinks of the reasons why his brother must die. Roshahara, his younger sister has sent a message that Dara must die. She has stated several reasons, the most important being the fact that the people support him, since they know him more than other princes who have always been away. But he, Aurangzeb has other things in mind. It is better to cut off a limb that has turned gangrenous. Public memory is short. In any case orthodox noblemen fear Darabhai's liberal views that may lessen their importance if Dara becomes the Emperor. He suddenly gets up and climbs down the stairs of the throne platform.

'It is our duty to give my brother a fair trial. Please find the people who have witnessed his love for the infidels' faith.'

That is all he manages to say. Now, he must wait, in silence and hope.

Aurangzeb spends a sleepless night. The very next morning, avoiding the *divan-e-khas*, he chooses a barren, curtained room beyond his private quarters for the trial. He stands in a corner, keeping low for fear of violent ends. The chamber mills with Quazis the judges, imams the religious leaders, and the muftis who issue legal opinions and also interpret shariah. Dara stands to his left, shackled, unkempt, looking like an old man, older than his father. A witness standing in front of him reads what Dara Shikoh, the Crown Prince, has written.

'I love this story that explains Vedanta. It is simple and easy. A tree has two little birds. The first one is on the uppermost branch. It does not hop, or swing but is serene and still. It looks so pleased as if it seeks nothing from the world. The other bird is restless and hops from one branch to the other, pecking at sweet and bitter fruits. When it tastes a bitter fruit it jumps one branch higher. After a while the restless bird finds itself on the same branch as the happy bird. Then a primal truth dawns on its soul. It realises that the first bird that seeks nothing from the world is, in fact, the real one. Its humble soul is a part of the absolute, the divine. And hence I have, in my most modest pursuit, written a book called *Majma-ul-Bahrain*, the Mingling of Two Oceans, as I find such similarities in basic truths stated in Hinduism and Sufism. That you are the divine and the divine is you.'

The witness has finished reading. Aurangzeb knows what the quazis think. His brother has wandered into the turf of infidelity, first learning Sanskrit and then going to Banaras, the Mecca of the Hindus to learn from the Pundits. He has gone to Lahore and has become the disciple of Mullah Shah, whose heart, people said was lit by the divine light sparkled in the heart of the famous Sufi Saint Mian Mir.

Another witness is called.

'Why did I spend years in writing the book *Mingling of Two Oceans*? It is because of my understanding of Yog Vasistha, the original scriptures where God Rama learns about the truth from sage Vasistha. It is enchanting when you can see a real snake while only looking at its image. You imagine it rearing its hood and striking like a whip. You see in your mind's eye, its fearful fangs, and are scared. The fear thrills you. But once you know it is just an image, it no longer seems terrible. The world is such; it is full of Maya, the illusion. Maya brings enlightenment through its own destruction. Once you know what Maya is, it is no longer charming. The world becomes flat and dull.'

The third witness reads out one of Dara Shikoh's poems:

May the world be free from the noise of Mullahs...

And their Fatwa

These 'learned' to the ignorant

And their ignoramus vents

Inflicting torments on true saints...

Aurangzeb watches the quazis and the muftis looking aghast. They exchange glances, shrugging helplessly.

Someone reads out the final verdict.

'Dara Shikoh, the accused, has to pay for his association with the Pundits. He has to pay for translating the Hindu Vedas into Persian. He has to be punished for writing a book called *The Mingling of Two Oceans* in which he preaches to unite Hinduism and Islam. He has to be punished for translating the book in Sanskrit. He has to be punished for studying Talmud, the New Testament of the Jews, and Sufi writings.'

'The accused is determined to disgrace Islam,' the quazis have declared their unanimous verdict. The muftis ask for a death sentence.

They have signed a decree on the ground of infidelity and deviation from Islamic orthodoxy that is punishable only by death. Their verdict clearly states that the criminal should be beheaded.

Aurangzeb walks out. It is risky to delay any further. The royal execution must take place soon. He waits under the arched pavilions till they take Dara away. He waits for some more time before going behind the trial room. It is the fort's prison. On seeing him, the guards give way. He walks through the dimly lit corridors. Dara is behind bars, his face devoid of any expression in his attempt to hold to the last dregs of his dignity. From another dungeon, the cries of Siphir ring out like the screeches of a trapped bird.

Strangely he feels vulnerable. Burning torches in alcoves give out black smoke that floats like a messenger of death. His brother's hatred for him hovers in the voids of those bare corridors, flooding the space. Suddenly, he hears footsteps and feels safe. The sound reverberates on those stonewalls and echoes in the empty space. The slaves have already arrived to take the convict to the gallows.

The door makes a creaking sound – the slaves push their hands under Dara's armpits and pull him up. For a few moments they wait for their new master's orders while the Crown Prince hangs between them, limp and weeping. He obliges and signals. He follows them to an inner chamber. It is dark with a single torch burning on a wall. The slaves scurry around the empty room, make Dara kneel, his hands on his waist. The convict grunts, as if he wants to throw up. The iron chains jingle sadly. The muscular slaves armed with swords surround him. Aurangzeb raises his right hand and the swords fly. The convict's head rolls on the ground as blood sputters in large amounts and the headless body is cut into pieces.

Aurangzeb is pleased. A *kafir* enthusiast is dead.

Fifteen | The Ensnaring

Circa 1659

Krishnaji Bhaskar is confident of his negotiation skills, but Shivaji Bhosale and his men are dangerous. 'Invite Shiva Bhosale to Wai and make sure he comes,' his master, Afzal Khan, has ordered. As the bearers of his palanquin reach the base of the hill, he narrows his eyes and looks at the newly built Pratapgad. Its gigantic walls rising above the cliffs in the midst of drifting clouds make his heart pound. The hill's velvety green slopes are broken at places with vertical plunges of naked black basalt. On top of this beastly hill, Shivaji has been holed up all along, while his master, Afzal Khan Sahib along with his army has been camping near Wai town for months. Krishnaji sighs. His hometown has been cramped with twenty thousand men and ten thousand animals. The butchers work continuously, swiftly cutting the throats of the cattle and goats and leaving them to bleed. The bloodless meat is halal, lawful to eat by the Muslims. The Brahmin's stomach churns as his olfactory nerve recalls the stink of bones and skin waiting to be disposed off. The soldiers defecate on the banks of Krishna River. Even the war animals bathe in the same water. Medics of Wai have been busy treating soldiers sufferimg from diarrhoea, a disease very so common in the monsoons. Rains are synonymous with immobility and this status quo has been unnerving.

Krishnaji's mind drowns in thoughts as his palanquin bearers cross the narrow lanes of Par village and climb the hill. This trail twists and turns to reach the main entrance of the fort. The newly built outer wall is awash with rain, its basalt stones gleaming in the sunlight. He is amazed at the massive ramparts and bastions. However, the fort itself is small, and can accommodate only a few hundred men at a time. The turrets over the ramparts are manned by archers. How can a mere *jagirdar* afford this? he wonders. Time has come to meet the most infamous rebel of the Bijapur Sultanate. Shivaji's sentinels, who have gathered around him to take him to their master, are armed with swords, quivers full of arrows and bows. Afzal Khan's *vakeel* is impatient to enter the massive stone structure built on a high plinth where Shivaji Bhosale awaits him.

The *sadar* is quite and cold as the mountain wind circles in its empty void. Shivaji sits on a divan, his hands folded in his laps. Gopinath Bokil stands near his master. Afzal Khan's *vakeel* has come with the invitation. They watch a tall and muscular Brahmin walks in. Afzal Khan's *vakeel* has a large moustache, and is dressed in silk dhoti and orange angirkha. His red pagari looks new. An embroidered shawl is thrown on his shoulders. He notes a sword gritted to his belt.

Krishnaji regards the two men. One is a short Brahmin with a naive face standing next to the divan. He guesses that it is Shivaji's *vakeel*, and finds nothing outstanding in him. But the man who sits on the divan is certainly not ordinary. He had heard about Shivaji's remarkable brown eyes. It is almost impossible for anyone to fathom the thoughts and feelings of this man by looking into his eyes. The face is serious, almost resolute, and the forehead is smeared with horizontal lines of sandalwood. Krishnaji admits to himself that the rebel does look like a king in his saffron, pearl studded turban.

It is when he looks into the eyes of the man that a shiver runs down Krishnaji's spine. Shivaji's sharp and piercing gaze bore into him. He feels a bit nervous, clears his throat, adjusts his sash, bows involuntarily and says, 'Afzal Khan Sahib is concerned.'

'I know, so are we,' he hears a humble voice. The gaze of his host is no longer sharp and cold. Instead, shadows of sadness have mellowed the rebel's eyes. Yet, the Bijapur *vakeel* is eager to say what he intends to. The rebel needs to know where he stands and what his status is.

'Raja Shivaji, I must tell you that one should know one's limitations. Can we at all compare ourselves with them?'

'The benevolent king, Ali Adil Shah is the sun of our skies. Our General is a brilliant ray of that sun and we are the lost shadows waiting for resurrection,' Shivaji says slightly bowing his head.

'That is a handsome comparison,' admits Krishnaji, wiping his forehead with his shawl.

'But you are the torch that will guide us through the darkness of night,' says Bokil, while nodding his head.

Krishnaji merely shrugs and declares in a plaintive voice, as if it pains him to see men like Shivaji wasting their time in rebellion. 'Nothing will be gained by rebelling against the king. If I were to advise you, I feel that you should enjoy the lavish life that only the king's court can bestow on you. Come to Wai and surrender to the General.'

'Do you truly feel that we have a chance to bask in Bijapur's glory?' Bokil asks earnestly, looking vulnerable.

'Why did I make such mistakes?' Shivaji laments. 'What had come over me all these years?' The Bijapur *vakeel* feels pity as he looks at the youthful face and says patronisingly, 'What are you fighting for? You are already a wealthy man, born to a *jagirdar,* and, with our hereditary laws in place, you are already a *jagirdar,*. You have the means to chart your own path to be a nobleman in the king's court.'

Shivaji casts his eyes down, his expression is withdrawn and brooding. He plays with strings of pearls around his throat and says, 'Men make mistakes. One cannot turn back wheels of time and undo what has already been done. One can only forget or forgive to a certain extent. But let me tell you truthfully that I have soulfully resigned to the fact that I am a mere servant of Bijapur. The proof lies in the fact that I have not troubled your General's army. I sit here, quietly, repenting and asking God for forgiveness.'

Shivaji's words ring true. Afzal Khan had tried all the tricks in the book to provoke the holed-up rat. He had even threatened the temple priests of goddess Bhavani at Tuljapur and extracted large amounts of funds from them. Afzal Khan had purposely called the *jagirdar* of Phultan region, brother of Shivaji's wife Sayee Bai Sahib and compelled him to convert to Islam. He had also struck terror by letting his archers take aim at the innocent peasants in Shivaji's territory. But they have met with silence.

Bokil clears his throat and says hesitantly, 'Grave mistakes have been committed by us. But we want the General to know that we have rebuilt and repaired the old, dilapidated hill forts and built this one. Our lands are generating a revenue of a million rupees a year. All will be surrendered at his feet for the benefit of the king. But we have kept personal gifts for the General: two hundred Arabian horses and a thousand of Mughal *mohurs*.'

Krishnaji does some quick calculations. A thousand Ashrafi mohurs would mean twelve ser of pure gold. 'Khan Sahib hates personal gifts. When do you intend to give them to him?' he asks casually, looking at Shivaji.

'We will give him personally, only when we meet, like a devote placing a petal at the feet of his favourite deity,' whispers Shivaji. 'You know Krishnaji,' Shivaji says with dreamy eyes, 'it may wash away some of our sins. To us, the General means more than the Bijapur king He is not an outsider, a Turani or an Irani. He is a Deccani, a native Muslim, a son of this soil. I am eager to kneel before him. He is one of us.'

'He is more than all of us,' Krishnaji's tone turns righteous, but somewhere deep in his heart he is pleased, at least Shivaji wants to meet his master. 'Our Afzal Khan Sahib is a self-made man. His father was neither a *subhedar* nor a *watandar*. It is not easy to rise to the coveted position that the Bijapur's general enjoys!'

Shivaji smiles at the the Bijapur *vakeel's* taunt guised in the veneer of graciousness.

'You are right. We are among the millions, but the general is indeed a man in a million. And he has chosen you to show us the light. It speaks volumes of your talent, intelligence and capabilities. How do we take things from here?' Bokil asks keeping both his hands on his chest.

Shivaji turns his gaze to his *vakeel* and says gravely, '*Puntoji*, as we have discussed, we know our goal, our journey ends at the General's feet.'

'I know you are anxious to meet Khan Sahib. I have come here to make your dream come true,' says Krishnaji, his hands locked in a tight fist.

'Let us hear what plans you have for us,' Bokil asks looking up at Krishnaji, his eyes brimming with hope.

The Khan's *vakeel* needs time. He looks around, eyes moving from pillar to pillar as he flings his shawl over his right shoulder. A lot of money has been spent on this fort. He diverts his gaze back to Shivaji and appeals, 'Afzal Khan Sahib was, at one time, very close to your father. He wishes to maintain the relationship. The General is keen to recommend your name to His Majesty, Ali Adil Shah, for ranks and titles.'

'*Ji*, it is the General's generosity. What is his message for us?' Shivaji asks politely as his eyes shine with optimism.

Krishnaji pulls out an epistle from under his belt and hands it over to Gopinath, who opens it carefully as if it is a gold chest containing precious pearls from the deep ocean.

The letter is in modi script, in Marathi peppered with Farsi words. He reads it slowly.

Your frequent impertinence has caused anguish to the King. You have the hereditary right only on your jagir. But you have taken the forts and seized Javali. Your men have brutally murdered Chandrarao Moray. You have plundered our subhedar of Kalyan. You have harassed the peace loving, religious Siddis of Jangira. You have unlawfully taken over the region of north Konkan. We had ceded some of that territory to the imperialists to maintain peace in the region.. Before I think of waging a war, surrender all your forts and provinces to me for that is what the king, Ali Adil Shah, wishes.

Krishnaji does not look away from Shivaji as the note is read. Shivaji's brown eyes look like lamps that have been rudely snuffed out by a storm. Finally the disheartened rebel darts a questioning look at him and says in a defeated voice, 'What do I have to do?'

'Come and meet Afzal Khan Sahib at Wai,' says Krishnaji magnanimously.

Shivaji stares at him, not responding to his proposal. After a long silence he says, 'This valley lies at the western borders of the Wai province of which Khan Sahib is the *subhedar*. In simple words this valley, including this new fort are the part of the General's region. He must come and claim it. The battle is already over; he is the conqueror and I the vanquished.'

Krishnaji does not want to say something that he might regret later. The man sitting in front of him is dangerous but what he says is not untrue either. His words imply that the General must come to his conquest as all conquerors do.

'By God Shiva, fear breeds hesitancy. And hesitancy means indefinite delays,' Gopinath says with a long sigh.

Krishnaji nods. If Shivaji hesitates to meet his master in Wai, it will be disastrous. Time is slipping away like a thief, snatching enormous funds with each passing day. Five months have gone by. The Badi Begam is impatient and has been asking for a probable outcome. He has read the letter she had written to his General. It says:

We have given you funds to buy the deshmukhs, we have raised your salary, given you allowances for thirty thousand troopers, a retinue of hangers on, and a fleet of war animals among other things. Now it has been months and there are no results. Whatever has happened to your lofty rhetoric?

'Your master is the brave one and bravery also means resolve. I am sure the general will decide. But it is not a thing that one can convey through a letter. A confrontation will do,' says Shivaji. Krishnaji is suddenly uncomfortable as a tinge of fear rushes through his mind.

'Please let me come with you to Wai to meet the General,' says Bokil apologetically while pulling the strings of the small satin bag that he holds. He takes out a heavy bracelet of gold embellished with stones, and ten Mohurs with imperial engravings.

'It is our humble way of honouring you.'

'That's not necessary,' Krishnaji blurts but takes the bracelet. The rubies and emeralds encrusted on it shine luminously. The General's *vakeel* tries to feel its weight in the cusp of his right hand by swinging it up and down. 'Not less than twenty tolas,' he thinks. He does not refuse the coins either.

'An Arabian stallion too is a part of our goodwill gift to you. It is waiting at the courtyard of the lower fort,' insists Shivaji.

'When can we leave for Wai? ' asks Bokil eagerly.

'Tomorrow should be fine,' says Krishnaji.

'Let me take you to your quarters. You must be tired.'

'When the heart is filled with fear, you fight or flee. It is worst when it is filled with shame, like mine is, as you are then bound with fetters of dishonour,' says Shivaji as Bokil and Krishnaji exit the chamber.

***

Jahanara is numb with sorrow. The red sandstone of Agra fort sparkles in the mild, early morning sunlight. The mighty walls with massive bastions that encase the fort stand mute. They remind her of the vanquished soldiers who have returned from the battlefield, some injured, some ashamed to be alive. The fort's courtyard, pavilions, mosques and gardens are crowded with Aurangzeb's soldiers. His personal slave eunuch Mutamad has taken over as their chief. She hears him firing orders. They have been accessing Darabhai's palaces that are within the fort and even those outside, she has heard. Countless trunks filled with his wealth are already on their way to Delhi. His two most beautiful concubines have been taken too. On their way one of them has disfigured her own face with a dagger, while the other is happy to be with the new Emperor.

Serdab, underground vaults built under the pavilion for royal seraglio, are silent. Her aunts, sisters-in-laws, ladies-in-waiting, slave girls, concubines, and courtesans living in the harem mourn. The underground passages that join the quarters of the royal women are empty. She walks across them and feels several pairs of eyes watching her through slits of the windows. She knows that the women here are desperately bored and live on hearsay. They pounce on any shred of gossip like jackals on a bloody carcass. Yesterday's incident has been the most horrifying, the most haunting. Jahanara ignores their gazes and walks along the garden, the Angoori Bagh. She climbs the stairs of her khas mahal to enter the extravagantly decorated foyer of her apartment. Two enormous chandeliers float in mid-air. Hundreds of tiny lamps burn in them, protected by small glass shades. Pale silk curtains billow inwards into her room creating pastel ripples in the air. She quivers and looks up at a painting hung on the wall. It is a portrait of her mother. The ageing daughter goes close to the painting and peers into her beautiful mother's eyes. But her mother does not look at her, she seem to stare out, at her own tomb, the Taj Mahal. Tears flood Jahanara's eyes. She walks mutely towards the balcony that rises above the outer walls. Her eyes wander beyond the luminous Yamuna, beyond the blurring sands and stop at Taj Mahal, the mausoleum that houses her mother's remains. Her *Ammi* is luckier than her *Abbu*, the dethroned, heartbroken Emperor who is now captive at Mussaman Burj, the octagonal tower that overlooks the magnificent tomb. Death has spared her mother from being a witness to despairing tragedies. Jahanara glances at the Yamuna. The river drifts gently, as if grieving over the fate of the royal family.

'He will not stop, he will keep flogging the shadows, forever, till they come alive with pain and he will burn everyone around him till their ashes become mere dust,' whispers Jahanara to herself. She has understood that it is impossible to hate anyone in the world the way Aurangzeb despises one who stands between him and the throne, even those he suspects to. No one and nothing is spared, even the dead.

Yesterday has been the darkest day of her life. A coffin engraved with holy text and sealed with wooden bars had arrived from Delhi. It was taken to the dethroned Emperor and opened while all in the chamber were weak with dread. They had a faint inkling what the coffin contained and hoped that their guess was wrong. As the slaves dislodged the nails of the bars with hammer and finally ripped open its lid, the smell of death filled the corridors of Mussaman Burj. Her beloved brother, her own flesh and blood, the son of this fort, Darabhai lay in the coffin, his matted hair covering his face and shackles still grasping his body. His eyes were wide open and looked glassy. His neck had been covered with sutures. She could not recognise him. 'People look so different when they are alive,' she had thought and glanced at her father. Yellowish green bile had streamed down from the corner of the dethroned Emperor's mouth. He had started flipping his hands like the wings of an injured bird and had choking. At that very moment she had looked at the distant marble mausoleum, the Taj Mahal, the iconic monument of love between her parents! Just a blur at first, it had then broken into millions of fragments. The fragments had flown gradually into the space above and looked like a cloud of marauding locusts. The marble cenotaph of her mother had gone missing, and Jahanara could see her mother's body. It had shuddered violently. The lonely minarets had suddenly appeared like four venomous fangs guarding her mother's mortal remains. Then, it was just darkness. She had fainted and remained so till the evening. When she had awakened and gathered her wits, words of the famous Sufi poet, Amir Khusro who lived centuries ago had sloshed in her mind. 'Even an infidel will not do what you have done. Is it halal to break someone's heart the way you have broken mine? Is it allowed by Islam?'

Late at night she scribbles in her diary, *I have survived the fire, to face something far worse. How many will die a brutal death, how many will turn into miserable spirits and how many will burn in hell under my family's curse?*

***

Bokil's sleep is disturbed by the incessant cries of an infant. He is at Krishnaji's house at Wai. Six days and six nights have gone by waiting for the Bijapur General to summon him for a meeting. He is awake when he hears a woman singing a devotional song. It is already dawn and he is late for his bath. He unknots his cloth bundle, takes out a new set of clothes and walks towards the staircase. A young woman cleans the front yard with a broom while an older one waters a tulasi plant in a large square stone basin. She sings about her undying, divine love of tulasi, the holy basil and its love for God Vishnu. The women, their heads covered with the pallus of their saris, do not bother look at him. He can hear voices from inside the house. They have been a good host. His food is served on time, by the young Brahmin helpers wearing sovale, the auspicious cloths purified by rites and rituals. He has made friends with them. They have told him that Krishnaji has been promised a large piece of land from Afzal Khan Sahib for bringing Raja Shivaji to Wai. He must never let that happen. Afzal Khan must come to Javali.

He goes to the backyard. Someone has already filled the buckets of water and kept them near the well. A round brass pot floats in one of the buckets. He gingerly pours cold water over his head. It is icy, making him cringe and shiver. His lips sing the praises of Ganges and Yamuna rivers, their waters washing away his sins, but he thinks of Afzal Khan: his traumatic childhood, his complexes, his desperation to be the *wazir* of Bijapur, his dedication to the Badi Begum, his past victories, his hatred for the Bhosale family, the cunning with which he had murdered King Kasturiranga, the jealousy he had displayed when he drowned seventy-seven of his concubines, and his unmatched physical strength. But does the Bijapur's new General do things in the heat of passion or are they calculated moves or a blend of both? Bokil is responsible for the answers. Raja has chosen him to tackle such an impossible man, and the Brahmin knows why. He has his strengths, he can analyse other people's thoughts, stay calm in situations that infuriate others. He can be firm when pushed to the brink. Also, the Bhosale family knows him for years. He has been in the services of Raja Shivaji's father even before Raja was born. He is a man who likes to keep a low profile. Almost retired, all he does is to occasionally help muzumdar Nilo Sondev, the financial advisor, and surnis Annaji Datto, the man responsible for revenue. But now, his master has placed on his shoulders the task to deal with the mighty Bijapur General and his snobbish *vakeel*.

Back in his room he sits on the floor to meditate, placing his right foot on the left thigh and left foot on the right one. He shuts his eyes and tries to stay clear of thoughts. It is a blank spot in his mind where thoughts, reflections, estimates, planning, questions and answers do not intrude. It is his private domain. Within an hour he comes down, with a silk shawl thrown over his shoulders. Seeing no one in the front yard, he decides to take a walk. It is still early, and the streets of Wai are empty. He is determined to do that which he has not done in the past few days: see the camp. After half a mile of brisk walk, the banks of the Krishna River unfold before him. The stone steps leading to the water are polished, flat and wide. The skyline is filled with spires of temples, built with black stones, the reflections of which shimmer in the gentle waters of the Krishna. He walks downstream, and hears horses neighing, elephants trumpeting and men shouting. He quickly climbs a small hill that blocks his view to investigate. The vast ground is covered with rows of elephants, horses, oxen and camels. An army of slaves wash, tether, and feed the beasts of war and burden. The stench of the droppings makes the Brahmin cover his nose with his hands. He turns back and notices Krishnaji running towards him.

'The General has granted you an audience, tomorrow noon.'

Relief surges through Bokil's body. These six days and six nights have finally been rewarded.

Next day, Krishnaji leads Bokil through the lanes of the Brahmin gulley floored with irregular stone tiles. Wai is a typical Marathi town. The localities are segregated according to the castes. The houses are huddled together. But one can see only bare walls and the wooden doors embellished with iron spikes or rings. Most of the doors are shut. The *vakeels* enter a narrow path, a lohar gulley lined with small brick houses. A few blacksmiths are busy either hammering iron or pumping their bellows to warm their forges. Naked children play between the forges, some dangerously close to the fire. Bokil notices that the blacksmiths make sword blades. He shudders as he follows Krishnaji. They enter a path that runs between the river and the fields covered with tiny shoots of sugarcane. Beyond the fields, away from the river, Bokil notices the slums of untouchables. What amazes him is the large fortress rising before him, very near to the banks of the river.

'That is Afzal Khan Sahib's residence,' says Krishnaji, speaking for the first time. Despite the fact that he is prepared for the meeting, a shiver runs down Bokil's spine. He tries to calm his mind and continues taking deep breaths till they reach a huge gate. A few guards stand chewing betel leaves, their mouths blood-red. They do not glance at the Brahmins.

'This is where I will meet the mighty Afzal Khan, face to face,' guesses Bokil. The entrance is not bolted and Krishnaji pushes it open, inviting his guest into the courtyard. Beyond the door stands a massive stone mansion, and a few steps take one to a many pillared patio. On either side of the steps, two fountains spray jets of water in circular stone tubs. On the patio a few swordsmen move in slow pace. They stop and bow to Krishnaji. The duo first enters an antechamber and then a large, pillared foyer.

At the far end a few people have gathered around a gilded chair taken up by an enormous man, who seated seems as tall as the men standing around him. Someone shouts, 'Khan Sahib, Shiva's *vakeel* is here.'

The huge man darts a look at Bokil.

Afzal Khan speaks in Urdu that is laced with a Deccani accent. In the quiet room, his voice roars aloud, 'Where is your Shiva hiding?'

At once everybody's attention shifts to Bokil. The short *vakeel* moves forward as men around the General make way for him. They watch him as he kneels, untying something from his shawl and placing it near the Khan's feet. When he straightens up, he sees a servant in a black tunic picking the gift and handing it over to the General.

A bejewelled dagger is a mark of the highest regard. It is given to honour a warrior, in recognition of his valour. A dagger can thrust, stab, penetrate and pierce. A gift such as this one inflates someone's ego. It has a sharp and shining blade made of steel. The blade is firmly fixed in a jade hilt embellished with decorative designs. So intricate is the work that a look at the hilt will convince a connoisseur that the dagger is not an ordinary one.

Afzal Khan rises from his seat with the dagger in his hands. He is a keen collector of weapons. Bokil stares at the General in astonishment as his headgear seems to touch the wooden beams of the ceiling. He feels like a midget. The General curls his upper lip and scrutinises his gift. Without removing his eyes from its hilt he says, 'Stolen eh?'

Some chuckle, while others sneer.

'May be ours, taken after seizing our valley,' a fat man standing behind the General suddenly declares, his voice full of hatred.

'Humm, is that so Prataprao, did this really belong to your brother Chandrarao?' asks Afzal Khan absentmindedly.

'Here is a letter from Raja Shivaji, my esteemed General,' says Bokil, trying to draw Afzal Khan's attention to business.

For the first time, the General bothers to, literally, look down at Bokil. He smiles indulgently, takes the letter, hands it over to Krishnaji, who first fumbles and then reads it out like a pupil duly reading out text after being admonished by his teacher.

ou, the General of Adilshahi, who has defeated the mighty kings of Karnataka and dealt with the rampaging armies of the Mughals, must know that it is our privilege to meet you. It is our fortune that you have come to bless us. Your bravery can only be compared to fire that has the power to destroy everything. We humbly invite you to the valley, the region that will soon be yours. We do not fear the kings or even the Emperors. We fear YOU, for men like you make them. Please come and claim your terrain. Kindly bring your army along, for we have no deceit in our heart. It is our responsibility to look after them. Please enjoy our hospitality that includes food, water, shelter, firewood and servants. After all, those too will soon be yours.

Bokil watches the General, who has gone back to his gilded chair, from the corner of his eyes. The *vakeel* suspects that the General is letting the silence grow in the chamber, on purpose, waiting for him to say something. The General's minions too wait with baited breath, ready to react according to their master's inclinations. The weather, outside, has turned cloudy, as a few drops of rain start rattling over the roof.

Afzal Khan is visibly irritated. His *vakeel* should have managed to bring the rebel to Wai. He clears his throat, shifts his gaze to Shiva's vakeel and asks harshly, 'Who killed Moray?'

Bokil knows that he must speak the truth.

'Raghunathpunt Ballal Korde,' he answers calmly.

'Who gave the orders?'

'Raja Shivaji Bhosale.'

'He killed my brother by deceit,' shouts out the fat man, thrashing his right hand in the air.

'And you want me to trust Shiva and come to Javali?' asks Afzal Khan.

Bokil takes some deep breaths as he knows that what he says now will lead to his success or failure. He must, without wavering or blinking, look straight into the General's eyes.

'By God Shiva, forgive me for being truthful. For hundred long years, the Morays had occupied the valley and amassed wealth through land revenue and road taxes. The benevolent kings of Bijapur had never asked for any kind of explanations. You, the esteemed General, had been busy either defending or expanding the northern and southern borders of Adilshahi, while the Morays had been filling their coffers without paying any revenue to the king. When we opened their vaults, we found trunks stuffed with gold and silver.'

Bokil waits to breathe. Krishnaji is shocked. This ordinary *vakeel* of Shivaji can twist and turn a story well, very well indeed.

Pratap Moray fidgets behind the General.

'A man of your years and wisdom should know that Shiva Bhosale has not paid a dime to us either,' says Afzal Khan, cutting off Bokil's argument with a blank face.

'By God Shiva, the esteemed General knows that Raja Shivaji's jagir was destroyed by the allied forces of the Empire and the Adilshahi kingdom. The ryots had fled. Thorny babul had invaded the soil where millets had once grown. During the same period, a famine had ravaged the region for three long years. It has taken us years to gather the absconding peasants to till the land. Only recently, after taking over Javali and parts of North Konkan, the lands under Raja

Shivaji have started generating good revenue. He is keen to surrender his terrain at your feet.'

Not a word from Bokil rings untrue.

'Shiva Bhosale has turned the hill forts of the region into his military strongholds.'

'I am glad that the wise General has brought this up. It is time to speak without fear. The fort commanders appointed by Bijapur had turned these military strongholds into brothels or gambling dens. While the late king, the benevolent Muhammad Adil Shah, had lain in bed, while you had fought battles at Adilshahi's north and south borders, the erstwhile wazir Khan Mohammad neglected the kingdom. All we did was to throw those pimps out and repair the forts to prevent structural damage.'

'Well,' Afzal Khan regards Bokil for a while. The Brahmin is shrewd, he has anticipated these questions and is doling out well-rehearsed answers. He must be thrown off the track. Afzal Khan suddenly asks, 'Why did Shiva attack Musekhan at Purandar ten years ago?'

Bokil does not blink but just clears his throat before speaking. 'Musekhan had come marching to attack. No talks or conciliation was considered. You are the first person who has hinted at the avenues of negotiations.'

'Shiva Bhosale has plundered our *subhedar's* caravan and taken Kalyan, pretending to be the Mughal *subhedar*. He has even seized all the forts of North Konkan. Now do not give reasons saying that it was done for some greater good.'

Bokil does not wait to answer. 'It was indeed a grave mistake. Then again, we had information that Mullah Ahmed was defecting. He had plans to run away with the treasure and join the Mughals. Where is Mullah Ahmed now?'

Afzal Khan smiles for the first time. Bokil realises that the bull-necked man with beady eyes does have a charming smile that can disarm the other person. There is a reson for all that charm. Mullah Ahmed and his family have recently gone to Aurangabad. Mullah's son is now a Mughal *mansabdar* of five thousand horses.

Bokil does not give in to the temptation and does not smile back. That would mean that he is just spinning a yarn knowing well that Mullah Ahmed has recently defected. Keeping a worried face, he rattles, 'General, please put an end to this. My young Raja is now ready to surrender. He trusts you. Please do not delay your decision. Raja Shivaji is remorseful and depressed. If he gives up the hope of your pardon, he may just become desperate and disappear into one of those hills. It will mean war, a loss of life, property and time. And then you may not find him, ever.'

Afzal Khan knows how perilous the valley is, a perfect hiding place for a rebel.

'Why can't Shiva Bhosale come here, to Wai? What is he so afraid of?' Afzal Khan says, his effeminate voice cracking.

'There is a simple answer to that. Raja Shivaji is terrified of you, not because he thinks you will harm him, but because he has no moral courage to face you. We may debate on this for hours, but the truth is that he will not venture out of the valley.' Bokil is resolute.

'He must know that I am like an uncle to him, his chachaji. Since his father and I fought have many battles together, I consider Shiva as my nephew.' Afzal Khan's voice is tender and his eyes soft. Some of his men, including Krishnaji nod vigorously.

Bokil retains his passive expression but allows a shade of regret to float in his eyes. 'My esteemed General, now that I know that you regard Raja as your nephew, let me tell you something. Knowing the path and walking it are two different things.'

'What do you mean?' blurts Krishnaji.

Bokil ignores him and goes on, 'Raja Shivaji believes all that you have said. Even then it terrifies him to act on his beliefs and come to Wai to pay his respects. He is unable to do what you wish him and what even he wishes to do.'

'What can we do to make Shiva walk the path?' Afzal Khan questions, his eyes losing their softness at an alarming rate.

'By God Shiva, I wish I knew,' Bokil says sadly, shaking his head with regret.

'What are the options?' Krishnaji wants to know, his eyes fixed on Shivaji's *vakeel.*

'The only option I see is for you to come to the valley, the region that Raja is so eager to surrender.'

'How many men are there on Pratapgad?' asks Afzal Khan. The wary and reluctant fish is taking the bait.

'The lower fort may have a few hundred and the upper fort is guarded by not more than a hundred men,' answers Bokil carefully.

Afzal Khan suddenly throws a question as his narrowed beady eyes regard the Brahmin.

'Can you take a sacred oath for our safety?'

'If only I could get a leaf of Peepal and some water,' replies Bokil calmly.

An oath of a Brahmin is a line etched by a knife on a rock of black basalt. If they break the oath taken, their seven generations burn in hell without any hope of a moksha, the cosmic freedom that releases their souls from the vicious circle of life and death. Disregarding an oath is moral treason, and for a Brahmin it is akin to betraying God. A Brahmin has to be sure of what he says before deciding and while taking an oath. If he envisages the opposite while he swears to God, he seals the fate of his soul, the soul that embarks on a sinful, endless voyage from earth to hell and from hell to earth.

Krishnaji looks at his master with admiration. Why couldn't he think of this earlier?

The servant in the black tunic runs to the courtyard. Shivaji's *vakeel* feels the General's gaze fasten on him, searching his face for clues that will reveal his thoughts.

The servant is back with a leaf and a small brass container of water.

Bokil sits on the floor, his legs folded in a *padmasana*, the leg position that looks like a lotus. As Afzal Khan, Krishnaji Bhaskar, Prataprao and others loom over him, he closes his eyes to contemplate. The leaf and the water are kept before him. A while later, he takes the leaf in his hand and crushes it as savagely as he can, declaring, 'God will crush me and my forty-two forefathers if I break my oath taken for the General's safety when he comes to the valley of Javali.' After throwing the crushed leaf on the ground he takes the water container in his left hand and starts reciting a mantra. During the recitation, he pours a bit of water in the cusp of his right hand and swallows it from the base of his thumb. He does it three times and for the fourth time holds the water in the cusp and declares, 'I embrace the divine water of Ganges in my hand. I swear by its divinity that I will be truthful to my oath for as long as I live.' Then he pours the water on the floor.

It has started pouring outside. 'Even the Gods agree, even they are pouring the water of my oath,' he says pointing at the rains.

Silence reigns for a long time.

'I will think over it,' declares Afzal Khan finally, wrenching out another dagger from his belt and chafing its blade on the blade of the dagger that has been gifted to him.

The noise of the screeching metal sets Bokil's toothless gums on edge. He mutters, quivering, 'I will never break my oath.'

Being a Brahmin himself, Krishnaji is sure of what his counterpart has muttered. A Brahmin will never in his dreams even contemplate breaching an oath.

'Betraying you is akin to betraying the Emperor now that the peace treaty has been renewed. Raja Shivaji is well aware of this,' assures Bokil and bows deep for one last time. 'Sahib, once you decide to come we will clear the mountain path from Wai to Pratapgad, and that is a promise of a Brahmin.'

SIXTEEN | THE COUNTERSTROKE

Circa 1659

Darkness fills the citadel housing the residential quarters of Pratapgad. The world has shrunk and turned into circles of pale light only around the torches. Despite hundreds of men on the fort, a deathly silence reigns. The fragile hush is occasionally broken by wailing of foxes or calling of an owl, somewhere in the woods of the lower slopes. Shivaji walks along the western ramparts of Konkan, the vast expanse of which is an abyss of darkness. It is been days since Bokil has returned from Wai but Afzal Khan has not sent any message. Incidentally, that is not what bothers Shivaj. He feels a strange premonition. He walks in a pensive mood as his ears pick up a sound of footsteps. Alert, his hand touches the hilt of his sword, but he knows what rather than who has come his way.

The messenger from Rajgad informs that Sayee has passed away.

Shivaji wants to let out a untamed cry, to weep openly, to sob and let go of his emotions but his eyes are dry. He has been expecting the news but somewhere deep in his heart he has wished for a miracle to happen. He was told of the diagnosis and the prognosis of the disease by the fort medic. It was a secret that he had never told her but suspected she knew. *Rajayakshma* or tuberculosis, the king of the diseases, had devoured her leisurely for two long years. She had already set her death free and now her death has set her free. His heart aches with guilt for not being able to be by her. The mother of his son has died alone. The cremation will soon be over. He wishes the fire would swallow his memories of her too.

Shivaji was thirteen, wide eyed. They had a new home, a large house built with red bricks. 'It is Lal Mahal and it is your new home. The peasants till the land, giving us grains. This house has been built from the revenue they pay us.' So he was told. He had sprinted through the ground floor foyer and had climbed the stairs. His friends had followed him in a file. The stairs had opened into a long corridor, large windows on one side and rooms on the other. They had bounded through the sunlit passage that had a ceiling of massive wooden beams. He was proud, this was his new home. There was a balcony and he had wanted to know what could be seen from there. He had gazed at the expanse and noticed hills at the horizon. Between him and the hills there had flown a winding river, swollen with water.

'Shivaba,' his mother had called him. There was some strange urgency in her voice.

There were people with mother, a tall man wearing a colourful turban and a woman who was perhaps his wife. As he had come to know later, the man was the jagirdar *of Phultan region near the valley of Javali. Behind the couple had stood a wiry, dusky girl, seven or eight years old. She was floating in a sari, head covered with her pallu. She had stared at him with big eyes, shadows of anger fleeting across them. A strange smile on mother's face had made him uneasy, and what she muttered had embarrassed him. 'She is Sayee, we have fixed your marriage to her.'*

His friends had giggled. This could not be true. He had to do or say something.

He had shot back. 'I don't like her, she is too dark.' His friends had stopped giggling. Some had even looked at him with respect.

'And I don't like him either, his nose is too big.' He heard Sayee's clear and fearless voice for the first time.

The memories have already started haunting him. He walks back to his quarters leaving the messenger. A few oil lamps burn mutely, and the shadows of flames dance on the ceiling, looking like beasts of sorrow, sorrow that mottles his throat, threatening the choking sobs to break free. Keeping his sword away he slumps on the bed, holds his hands behind his head and shudders with sobs. He lies there hurting, waiting for the night to slip away until he can hear the temple bells of the morning worship. As the sky beyond the windows turns pale, he pulls himself out of his bed. He moves towards the entrance and then to the steps that take him to the lower fort. He rubs his eyes that still sting and glances at the lower fort. He narrows his eyes to focus and notices a fort guard run towards him.

'News has come. Afzal Khan has decided to come to the valley,' says the informer, anting with excitement.

Shivaji buries his sorrow deep in his heart. He is expecting people to arrive from Hirdas Maval. It is only at noontime that the visitors arrive. When Shivaji enters the sadar, an old man with white beard stands near the door along with his five sons. His eyes shine with tears when he bows deep.

The man and his sons gather around Shivaji as he sits on the divan.

'Raja, we have heard the news,' the old man whispers. Shivaji sadly waves his hand to stop the visitor from talking about Sayee. He does not want to break down. This is no time.

'Kanhoji, you have received a threatening letter from Afzal Khan. But you have come to me. If I lose the battle, you will lose everything too, your *watan* and your family. There is still time. Go to Afzal Khan, help him.'

The old man's eyes fill with tears. He says in a quivering voice, 'Raja, it is not about my *watan* or my family; it is about saving my soul. You fight for our freedom, I place my *watan* at your feet. We are ready to die for your cause.'

'Are you sure?' Shivaji asks bitterly. 'Your neighbours, *deshmukhs* like Khandoji Khopade, Utravalikar, Kedarji, and Jagdale have gone to Afzal Khan. If Bijapur wins these men will be rewarded with titles, military posts and bigger *watans*.'

Kanhoji bows deep and whispers, 'They have gone, that is their karma. I have come to you along with Bandals, Silimkars, Pasalkars, and other *deshmukhs*. I have told them that Afzal Khan is deceitful, once his objective is over he will ruin us all. While the Maratha kingdom is ours, it is our Swaraj.'

***

Under a bright noon sun, the river Krishna flows playfully with loud gurgling sounds. Something is afoot inside the Afzal Khan's fortress in Wai. People have gathered in the main foyer. They are worried, some are angry with their General's decision. His most trusted men, son Fazal, *vakeel* Krishnaji, the late General's older son Ranadhaula, chief guard Sayed Banda, officers Yakut and Mambaji Bhosale, the first cousin of Shiva's father stand around his chair. When Afzal Khan had left Bijapur, he had had strategies and tactics in mind. Those had worked with the Hindu kings of Karnataka. *Kafir* men of power had a weakness, they could either be subdued with fear or provoked to turn hostile. But Karnataka was a different region. It was not hilly and Afzal Khan could confront the enemy who refused to meet him.

Shiva could not be provoked.

The mere sight of his enormous cavalcade of ten thousand horsemen, an equal number of footmen, five thousand artillerymen, a thousand camels, a hundred elephants, and five hundred cannons on wheels, thousands of beasts of burden, countless slaves, women, traders and hangers-on has already struck terror in the hearts of people. His bards have done the rest. They have gone from village to village and sung hoarsely, exaggerating his and his army's strength. When some of the *deshmukhs* from Shiva's *jagir* had meekly come to him, he had accepted them graciously. He had moved leisurely through the terrain, camped near the famous temples, threatened the priests and forced them to part with wealth from their treasuries. But *kafir* Shiva had refused to be provoked as he had hoped. Shiva's wife's brother, the jagirdar of Phultan was captured and circumcised. Even that had failed to infuse rage in Shiva's heart. Raiding some of Shiva's territories, random killings of villagers, nothing had worked to bring the coward in the open. That is when Afzal Khan was forced to think about new battle tactics.

The new Emperor, Aurangzeb wants Shiva's territories in exchange for peace in the region. Afzal Khan's king is clear: he wants Shiva, dead or alive. And he, Afzal Khan has decided that the hunter and the beast ought to meet. It has become imperative to seek the alpha wolf, because the beast with his pack cunningly avoids the hunter. The hunter has to seek, even if that means walking into the den of the wolves in the dangerous hills.

The king and the Badi Begum are getting impatient now. It has been six months since he has left Bijapur. More than a million rupees have already being spent on this expedition: the heavy salaries of royal cavalrymen, bribes given to the Maratha landlords, food and fodder needed to feed twenty five thousand men and thousands of war animals. There is another problem. Kanhoji Jedhe, despite dire threats, has decided to help Shiva Bhosale and has convinced several *deshmukhs* from Maval to join the rebel. Their infantries are trained to fight in the mountains. It is a great loss indeed. Further delay may mean more *deshmukhs* joining hands with the enemy, albeit not openly!

'Sahib, isn't there any other way?' Sayed, standing to Afzal Khan's left leans forward to be properly heard.

'Sayed, you should be the last person to be wary,' thunders Afzal Khan.

'Sahib, you think I am scared?'

'Are you not?' Afzal Khan sounds angry, but the next moment he modulates his voice to the mournful pattern of a man who has been sinned against, 'What is wrong with all of you?'

'Father, we are all concerned about your safety,' declares Fazal whose cherubic face has blackened with exposure to the sun.

Afzal Khan regards his twenty-year-old first son with dismay. The boy is a good horse rider and has learnt sword fighting from famous masters but has grown up in the safe confines of palaces. He is yet to rise to the harsh realities of life. 'Javali is not as dangerous as we think,' says Pratap Moray, speaking for the first time and waits for a glance or a nod.

'Say what is on your mind,' replies Afzal Khan.

Pratap curls his moustache nervously and rattles, 'I know every corner of the valley. With our mighty army, what harm can befall us?'

'It is not about Javali, it is about Shiva Bhosale. My nephew is a dangerous man, just like his father. They say one thing and do the other,' objects Mambaji Bhosale to Pratap Moray's statement while blotting his face with his shawl.

Afzal Khan looks at the aging Maratha for a while and says, 'Can someone give me a solution? Will Shiva come to Wai?'

'That is unlikely,' declares Krishnaji.

'Shiva has twenty-five of our hill forts. He has repaired and equipped them with garrisons, explosives, food and water. Those military strongholds were once manned by our men who had adorned them with wine jars and nautch girls. Shiva may have removed our imprudent fort keepers by sweet talk, bribes and threats. It is not easy to face a man in the hills who has some magnificent hill forts, and is unwilling to meet us on a plateau. Ten years ago, we had tried fighting him at Purandar fort when our warrior Musekhan was killed.'

The men around Afzal Khan are at a loss.

He waves his hand and continues. 'Months may pass before we seize just one of our own hill forts. We will need massive preparations for laying siege. We have an option to destroy Shiva's terrain and lay bare the villages. But what will we achieve? People will hate our new king. Shiva will still have his hill forts. His garrisons will launch fresh attacks on us. And even if we win, the Emperor will be displeased when he receives a ransacked terrain. Now, Shiva has said that he is ready to surrender all he owns at our feet. Tell me what we must do next. How do we deal with such a man without meeting him?'

'We can, once again try forcing Shiva to come to Wai. There must be some way we can do it,' says Sayed, sounding enthusiastic.

Krishnaji fidgets, his face turns red. Sayed's words imply that he has not tried earnestly. But Afzal Khan thinks of something else. The face of the blind Sufi saint floats in his vision and his words ring in his ears. 'Son, do not go,' he had said, 'I see you without your head in my vision.'

'Shiva will not surface, he will drag on. He is not in a hurry, we are,' grunts Afzal Khan, barely suppressing his anger. He has managed to steer his thoughts away from the Sufi saint and towards the court politics of Bijapur. He has heard that the new *wazir*, Khawas Khan hovers around the king. Afzal Khan is sure that the *wazir* wants him to fail. If he dies, Khawas Khan will rule unhindered from behind the throne. If he wins, he will be the *wazir*, the most powerful amongst the Bijapur noblemen. As his people may assume, Afzal Khan is not blind. He knows that entering Javali is a big risk. He does not respect Pratap Moray and does not value his opinion. He knows the valley is a death trap.

Afzal Khan once again searches his mind to check if he has has he missed anything. He is going with an army which will not be raided during the difficult journey. Shiva's Brahmin has taken an oath. He will be safe till he reaches Pratapgad. A slight smile appears on his grave face. His councillors watch him, tense, and anxious. Shiva will come and visit him in his camp. That is the moment for which he will be prepared. Afzal shuts his eyes, *'Inshalla*, everything will go well.' He opens his eyes and speaks tersely, 'As decided, we leave for Javali within a week.' The old memories and ancient hate have started bubbling in him. He was successful in bringing a shackled Shahji to Bijapur. He was also successful in killing Shahji Bhosale's first son.

'What if we wait for some more time?' Fazal throws a suggestion.

Afzal Khan smiles, a hint of pity in his eyes. What does his son know about court politics? He has promised the king to bring Shiva to Bijapur court, dead or alive. The king already knows that Shiva has agreed to surrender. If he delays further and avoids going to Javali it will look like he is being bribed. Questions will be asked, and rumours will start flying in the court corridors.

'There are ample opportunities to ambush us,' persists Fazal.

'You are scared like a woman. Wear bangles,' is what Afzal Khan wants to say to his son but he resists. 'We will do as decided,' says he and dismisses the meeting. There is no further talk on this subject. The General has decided to take half his army with him and the rest will stay at Wai. Camels will be left behind but some war elephants will enter the valley.

The day of departure does not bring the usual excitement as many of Afzal Khan's officers remain glum. Their long march through the steady climb to reach the wooded highland of Mahabaleshawar plateau takes a full day. Afzal Khan sits on a silver howdah on the back of an elephant, but soon takes to a horse. From east to west, they have to travel through ghats in the mountains, some suspended half a mile above the surrounding valley. One small mistake, a slip of a foot, or dislodging of a stone is enough for men and animals to disappear into the abyss. It is a steep, upward climb. The elephants struggle ahead in order to clear the way for the rest of the army. As the animals stagger through the dense woods, their bodies scrap against tree trunks, their thick hides are lacerated and they bleed. When they step on softer soil, they dislodge massive boulders. The rocks tumble down the slopes and crash onto the slaves plod along with the luggage. After a day's travel they come to a mountain plateau little less than a mile above the valley. They camp at the highest point. The night is windy but clear and the camp shimmers in silvery moonlight. As Afzal Khan sits smoking his hookah in his tent he feels peaceful. He has done the right thing!

The journey resumes as the sun rises above the mountains. The descend starts and it is a terrifying experience.

'It is too dangerous,' Fazal opens his mouth while riding behind his father's horse, his skin red with mosquito bites.

Afzal Khan keeps his cool. He knows that worrying is more dangerous than what lies ahead. He is sure that his army will not be attacked by Shiva during this journey. The Brahmin *vakeel* of Shiva is bound by oath, and a Brahmin's oath is a powerful assurance. But he, Afzal Khan, the General of Bijapur is not bound by any such oath. It is also imperative to take risks, it is an integral part of being a soldier, an occupation hazard. He is not afraid, he never was.

Afzal Khan's mind goes back twenty years ago when Kasturiranga, the king of Shirepattanam, had come to meet him. The *kafir* was strong, wise and famous for his sword fights. There was an element of peril in meeting him, face to face. It had taken Afzal Khan just a few moments to first crush him in his grip and then kill him with a Jambia knife. This incident had helped him win the heart of the then military general of Bijapur.

'Krishnaji, you should have told us clearly about this hazardous route,' says Fazal to the *vakeel* who rides behind him.

'Now that's enough,' Afzal Khan quietens his son. But he understands their fears when they start descending to reach the valley. The ghats of 'crying face', as the name suggests, makes some of Afzal Khan's men weep with fear. The mountains rise around them as the valleys disappear in the abyss. Many swoon when they cross very narrow trails. One elephant falls suddenly and is quickly followed by another. The enormous animals slip over the miry edge of the slender path. Villagers from the nearby hamlets hear the heartbreaking echoes as elephant's rain and the other tuskers trumpet in fear. Their screams make the mountains shudder. The shocked birds fly in fear, sparrows, ravens and parrots, create a blustering orchestra over the hills. Their frantic calls panic the horses who then bound aimlessly. Men who try to help their confused mounts are dragged along and fall into the abyss.

Afzal Khan remains in control. It is only about a hundred men, fifty horses and two elephants that he has lost. It is his war and his decisions. As his horse canters carefully through the greenish brown waters of Koyana, he glances at the enormous hill of Pratapgad. 'Nothing intimidates me,' he assures his mind. The surrounding forest is dark and discouraging. The path that leads them from the river to the camp is riddled with rocks and chasms. His fifteen thousand men and animals move towards the campsite not far from the river. It is an open space and the tents are large and comfortable. The locals have gathered and seem eager to cater to their needs. Most of them fall prostrate when they see him. 'Poor folks from the hills,' he thinks. 'They are lucky to get a glimpse of me in their lifetime.'

The relatively flat region near the banks of Koyna has been cleared, dense thickets uprooted and the uneven earth flattened. Pile of freshly sawed wooden logs and sacks of grains have started arriving from all parts of the valley. Hundreds of helpers have been called from the nearby villages before his military cavalcade starts its final expedition. Huge funds have been invested by Shiva Bhosale to pitch palatial tents befitting the status of the Bijapur General. A market with rows of shops has suddenly made its appearance along the banks of Koyana. The butchers, barbers, merchants, jewellers and even the swordsmiths have come from Pune to cater to the armies of Afzal Khan.

He scans the camp where shops have been built on wooden platforms and stuffed with grain sacks, oil drums and jars filled of salt and spices. Some butchers have skinned animals and let the carcasses hang on the hooks. He has been told that each of the thousands of tents has a pile of firewood, a large earthen pot filled with drinking water and sacks of grain, and even some jars of wine. His soldiers are scrambling to grab the tents. Thousands of local men scurry to remove their sandals, start boiling water for their bath or stand behind to fan them with bunched peacock feathers. Some carry large copper containers to water the animals. Shiva Bhosale is indeed trying hard to impress him. In his long military career, Afzal Khan has seen many infidels like Shiva, who have done whatever in their capacity to please him just to get pardoned and gain access to the king of Bijapur. But this is not the time to speculate, he orders his men to start their work at once. The camp needs to be organised. Artillery must be arranged, special infantry group readied for emergency, out-posts created to keep watch and hundreds of such other details to be taken care of.

The valley had not seen anything like this before. Unwieldy long-range guns are dragged along its virgin soil. The blacksmiths get busy sharpening and polishing swords. The chefs scurry around the earthen stoves to cook large quantities of food in huge iron vats. Birds hop from one tree to another, angry with the noise. As the camp gets busy, Afzal Khan settles down into his special tent, its floors covered with carpets and its corners furnished with divans and charpoys.

It has been a couple of weeks since our arrival, thinks Afzal Khan, unwinding himself on a huge bed in his palatial tent. Two masseurs knead his calf muscles with all their might. He can hear the laughter of women from the adjacent tent, most likely playing dice or cards and the soulful tunes emanating form the flute of some slave girl. He waves his hand signalling the masseur to stop kneading and rolls over his bed to get out. His muscles gleam under the veneer of sesame oil. Clapping his hands to call his slave, he picks up his tunic from the bed and throws it over his head. With the silken cloth is still slipping down his body he rushes towards the bath. 'My clothes,' he shouts. He needs to be ready for the short Brahmin.

Shiva Bhosale has not spared any cost. He has a huge bath tent and the stone bathtub seems to have been specially ordered for him. Even though the monsoons are over, it still drizzles in the valley now and then. The tents are covered with palm leaves to prevent the rain water from trickling in. The launderers in the camp wash his clothes and press them with coal iron boxes. The arrangements are to Afzal Khan's liking.

After a thorough scrub by his favourite slave, he gets dressed and is ready for the meeting. Krishnaji and Sayed wait at the entrance along with a number of armed men. He stands with them for a while gazing at the fort. The hill looms almost half a mile above him. While the upper portion looks steep, the lower slopes descend relatively gently towards the camp. Krishnaji has told him that the fort has been splendidly built. Its outer walls, bastions, ramparts, terraces, citadels, assembly chambers, and private palaces are stone structures. He has an urge to see the fort with his own eyes, see what a mere *jagirdar* has done. It is then that it strikes him that something is amiss. A man capable of building such fort cannot be so scared. Afzal Khan does not want to think too much as they simply perplex him. He decides to go in and wait. It is a bit warm inside the tent. He sits relaxed against the propped up pillows on his divan and signals a slave to bring his hookah.

Three men eventually walk into his tent: Krishnaji, Sayed and Bokil. Holding a thin brass cylinder in his hands while exhaling smoke through his mouth, he regards the short *vakeel* of Shiva. It is the third time that Bokil has come to meet him in the camp. Afzal Khan remembers the first visit. The clever Brahmin had been very sweet, acting as a perfect host. Making a round trip of the camp, he had ensured that everything was in proper order. He had also handed over a cloth bag made of satin to Krishnaji. It had had a thousand Ashrafi *mohurs*, a gift from Shiva to him. Before departing, Bokil had asked for an audience.

He had asked about Shiva in a rasping voice, purposely towering over the puny vakeel. To his surprise, unlike before, Bokil had looked at him in defiance and shot back in a loud voice, 'The meeting will be arranged on a neutral ground. This is the message from Raja Shivaji.' The cunning fellow had then asked for permission to depart before anyone could utter anything.

'Does that mean he will not come to the camp?' an astonished Krishnaji had asked.

'General,' Bokil had ignored Krishnaji and had fixed his eyes on him, 'you are a rich man, used to the splendour of Bijapur. We are poor and yet, Raja Shivaji wants to receive you with protocol that befits you. He has never met anyone of your status in his life.'

Afzal Khan had known at that instant that he had no choice but to accept this condition. He could not go back to Wai safely after rejecting this offer. Further negotiations on this point would mean extending his stay in Javali, a dangerous proposition.

'This neutral ground,' Afzal Khan had insisted loudly, 'will be approved by my people and that is final.'

Bokil had readily agreed to that. 'I was about to suggest the same. We would not ask you to come to a place unless it is inspected and approved by your trusted advisors.'

Afzal Khan had appointed Sayed Banda, Pratap Moray and Krishnaji as his team for approving the meeting place.

During his second visit, Bokil had said in a low tone, 'We have finally found an appropriate place for the meeting. It is a flat glade on the slopes of the Pratapgad hill, a golden middle between the fort and the camp. Our people will pitch a palatial *shamiana* in your honour, my General.'

Afzal Khan had looked at his men and they had nodded in silent agreement. Now for the third time the old fox was standing in front of him with a bowed head.

'Is the meeting place ready or are your men still at it? Are they building a Taj Mahal?' Afzal Khan has long finished his part of the bargain. He has come to Javali as decided.

'Today, we shall finalize everything, the date, time and other terms and conditions for this meeting,' says Bokil calmly.

After hours of negotiations the terms are finally agreed upon. The meeting will take place in the afternoon of the seventh new moon day, which is a Thursday. The General and Raja Shivaji will come fully armed. Each will be accompanied by his *vakeel*. Additional ten armed guards from each side will be posted at a distance of an arrow shot from the *shamiana*. These terms will be written on paper and presented to Afzal Khan for his final approval.

A worried looking Krishnaji wants to say something. Afzal Khan waves his hand to quieten his *vakeel*. He thinks for a long time making Bokil go fidgety with unease. If he declines now the whole matter may drag on. He assures himself that he is the General of Adilshahi and Shiva will not dare to do anything foolish at this point of time. And unless he meets Shiva in flesh and blood he cannot do anything at all.

Finally he shrugs and asks, 'I hope that you have not forgotten your oath.'

'Shiv, Shiv,' Bokil mutters in a quivering voice as if to ward off the evil that waits to pounce on him for even brooding over the possibility of breaching his oath. 'How can you even doubt the oath of a Brahmin? If I do so, my forty-two forefathers and I will be confined to infinite imprisonment in *Naraka*, the hell of the Hindus. We will undergo hellish tortures, they will blind us, flog us with whips, fling us in boiling water, they will make us drink molten iron, and throw us in the dungeons filled with hooded serpents.'

Afzal Khan gives Bokil his most charming smile, his beady eyes glinting smugly.

He says, 'Tell my nephew that I will see him personally as agreed. I will forgive him his past and take him to our king. At Bijapur, he will receive riches beyond his dreams.'

'By God Shiva, I must go and give our Raja this excellent news,' announces Bokil joyously.

Afzal Khan watches till Shiva's *vakeel* disappears from his sight and then asks Krishnaji,

'How tall is this Shiva?'

'His head may barely reach your chest.'

The answer brings a strange smile to Afzal Khan's face while he tries to calm his mind.

'Sayed, choose one thousand five hundred of our best infantry-men, armoured and armed with swords, bows and arrows. They will come with us to the meeting place. But keep this a secret.'

***

Two days before the meeting, Shivaji has called all his captains for one last meeting. Kanhoji has come with Mavali deshmukhs like Haibat Rao Pasalkar and Balaji Silimkar. Sonoji Dabir, Trimbak Dabir, Yesaji Kank, Tanaji Malusare, Sambhaji Kavji, Jiva Mahalya, Raghunath, Babaji Bhosale, Hiroji Farzad, Kondaji Wadkhale, Ibrahim Khan and many more have gathered at the appointed place. The air in the assembly chamber is heavy with palpable anxiety. It is a time of uncertain destinies. Men of might may fail; meticulous planning may turn into chaos, hopes may turn into despair and death. Shivaji and his men must go through their plans for the last time. His warriors and advisors stand in the sadar, with solemn, almost grim faces. This is the fourth and perhaps the last time they are meeting to discuss the plans for what they now call 'the day'. If they lose this battle, it will be death-by-blade for all of them. Their families, living on the hill forts around Pune, their mothers, fathers, sons, daughters and wives would be slaughtered, or taken as slaves.

Shivaji stands in their midst, wearing his usual saffron turban and white chintz *agirkha*. His knows that the morale of his men is not very high. They have seen Afzal Khan's camp. They have realised that they lack in numbers, equipment, and war animals. The Bijapur army has surrounded the fort, it has spread itself along the banks of Koyana. From above, one is bound to feel trapped in the fort.

He stares at his nervous men and says, 'It surprises me that the General has not objected to the campsite. His entire army is spread out on the banks of Koyana. As you can see from this hill, it is not us who are locked in by them, it is them who are trapped in the lowest part of the valley. If I were the General, I would have first thought of the possibility of the enemy squadrons pouncing down from the surrounding hills. I would have demanded strategic hill-tops to camp in, places from where I could watch the terrain.'

'He may know his strengths better than we do,' retorts Dabir.

'Or, he is oblivious of our strengths,' opines Pingle.

'He is convinced about his strength and our weakness,' announces Shivaji, 'and this conviction is our strength. All we need to do is to keep his belief intact.'

'Let us again go over our battle positions,' the *sar-e-naubat* takes over. 'Only a few hundred men are and will remain on this fort. Our squadrons will arrive tomorrow, some from Maval, and some from Konkan. They will enter the valley stealthily. At any cost, they must conceal themselves from the eyes of the General's scouts who have started roaming the nearby forest.'

'We have secured the fort. Of the two approaches to it, we have blocked the one from the north-east, from Kumbroshi village by felling trees. One can enter the fort only from the south, through Sonpar village. The upward trail that leads to the fort is circuitous. A large army cannot use it to charge,' says Shivaji.

'We must block and slay them if they move towards us or intercept and kill them when they run away from us. Our infantrymen will hide at the foothills. They will stop the enemy squadrons from entering the fort. Our cavalrymen will hide in the faraway forests. They will chase and slaughter the enemy running away from the *ranangan!*' announces the *sar-e-naubat* Palkar.

The men nod silently. Palkar gets into specifics.

'The north-west side of this fort needs no security. The rock precipice takes a straight plunge, a mile deep into the abyss. But the foothills ought to be protected from the other sides. Kanhoji Jedhe, Bandal Deshmukh and Yesaji Kank have called their chosen infantry men, five thousand in number from Maval. They will wait in ambush at the southern foothills, in the forest surrounding Sonpar. Peshwe Moroji's infantry will arrive from Rairi. One half will wait near Kineshwar village, at the western foothills of the fort, and the other half will be stationed at the ghats of Ambenali, beyond the north-east foothills.'

The tall Palkar bows slightly. Raja Shivaji must take over from where he has left.

'The *shamiana* is at the south-east, not exactly at the foothills. The General's palanquin will have to climb a part of this hill to reach the meeting place. They will enter through Sonpar village. If you see from above, you will know that the place is surrounded by natural knolls that run along the slopes. Between the knolls, there are ravines. It is as if someone has made trenches for people to hide. Raghunathpunt, Annaji Datto, Hirozi Farzad, and their infantrymen will hide in the ravines that surround the *shamiana*. They will wait in ambush.'

Palkar must go into minute details. His face is hidden in massive greying whiskers; his bushy brows peppered with more greys. But his eyes are sharp, almost lancing his men's souls with stringency.

'Now it is time to talk about the cavalry. I, along with my five thousand horsemen, shall wait a few miles east of the camp. Babaji Bhosale will block the mountain ghats of radatondi with another two thousand to block the path to Wai.'

'Any questions, any doubts?' asks Shivaji. There is silence. He goes on. 'Now, for the communication protocol, on 'the day' two trumpeters will sit near the *shamiana*. Once I go in for the meeting, anything can happen. The General will try to capture or kill me and I will have to defend myself. If either of us is killed, the trumpetteers will blow their trumpets to alert our cannoniers on the upper fort. The alerted guards will fire the cannon mounted on the eastern ramparts three times.'

He stops and looks at his grim faced men, trying to gauge their comprehension, looks at his *sar-e-naubat* and nods. Palkar takes over.

'Let us go through the remaining plan of action. As soon as the blasts echo in the valley, men hiding in the ravines surrounding the *shamiana* will rush to the meeting place. Remember, this is very vital, and all ten guards of Afzal Khan must die. They must not live to alert the camp.'

Shivaji says, 'The camp must remain unsuspecting. Once the cannon blasts are heard, Kanhoji, Yesaji and their infantrymen will descend on the camp from the southern foothills. Our *peshwa's* infantry will launch an attack from the west and the north-east. Remember we certainly want victory but we also want their horses, weapons and treasure.'

There is a long silence before the leader of the Maratha speaks again.

'In the last meeting Tanaji had asked, what we intend to do if we win. I shall answer that now. When the camp is attacked from all three sides, a huge number of enemy troopers will perish. Many of them will try to run away in the direction of Wai. Babaji Bhosle and his men will intercept them in the ghats, while our sar-e-naubat leads his cavalry to Wai. He must destroy the remaining of the General's army at Wai before the news reaches Bijapur. We have planned to infiltrate the Bijapur territory to its core. Their posts must remain unguarded, their men must rest in the secure feeling that their General is taking care of things.'

'Do you plan to attack their capital?' asks Dabir incredulously.

Shivaji just smiles and says, 'Let's first go back to the *shamiana*. Tanaji Malusare, Kavji Kondalkar, Jiva Mahalya, Ibrahim Khan and a few others will accompany me as my personal guards. The meeting will take place at noon with just four of us in the *shamiana*: Afzal Khan, his *vakeel* Krishnaji, our Puntaji Bokil and me.'

In that assembly room, the men marvel at the confidence that Shivaji exudes. With an assuring smile on his lips he says softly, as if he is sharing a secret, 'Remember, the entire operation commences at noon and the battle begins in the afternoon. It is early winter and the sun sets early. The valley becomes dark an hour before the actual sunset. That night the moon will rise late. For a couple of hours, our *ranangan* will be pitch dark. You are used to the darkness and the place while they will be blind as bats. Take advantage and act accordingly.'

'Follow the communication protocol. Do not stir unless needed, do not defy unless absolutely crucial, and do not execute until the time is right. Follow what's been told to you,' says Palkar. 'Raja's personal cavalry will wait for him at the foothills of Mahabaleshwar hill. After the battle at the foothills, we have planned to meet at Wai, early next day, just as the morning star appears in the eastern sky, at the time when the General's camp will turn in their early morning dreams. This is our war against Bijapur. The end of Afzal Khan may just be the beginning. It is not me but Raja who is the *sar-e-naubat* of this campaign.'

For a few moments men stare in astonishment. Some shake their heads with dismay.

'We are worried,' says Dabir earnestly, his eyes shining with tears. 'Have you heard of Sayed Banda, the General's personal guard who is an expert *pata* swordsman?'

'We have Mahalya. He is trained to tackle a swordsman with *pata* sword, and he will watch Sayed. If we keep worrying, Goddess Bhavani will not be pleased. It would mean that we do not trust Her. She has brought the General to our valley, to our *ranangan* as we had hoped. Now She seeks to devour this goat,' chuckles Palkar, and the chamber is suddenly filled with chortles.

'Remember Kasturiranga. He was killed by Afzal Khan during a meeting,' warns Dabir, his voice quivering.

His eyes brimming with tears, Yesaji says, 'Raja, do not forget that the General is a skilled wrestler. Afzal Khan has enquired about your height. Your head will only reach his chest. It will be easy for him to grab your neck under his left armpit and to crush your neck-bones. His right hand will remain free to strike you with a dagger perhaps, while yours will be left dangling and useless. In such a situation you will have only a few moments to defend yourself with your left hand.'

Shivaji nods. It is a pain to see one's own in tears. It may perhaps be the last time, he may not see them again.

There is one last and most important thing that he needs to share with them. He shifts his gaze from one face to another, slowly and deliberately. Then he says, 'Whatever happens, even if I am captured or killed, Afzal Khan and his men must not reach the fort. It is imperative that we win this battle. Even if I die, please continue to fight for Swaraj with my son as your King.'

The men's faces darken in their gloom, their eyes shy away the shadows of anxiety, and their jaws tighten with anticipation. Then they hear something that makes them shiver with optimism. Their leader's words fall like sparks of hope on them. 'I had a celestial vision, She showed Her divine self to me.'

'Who was She?' they ask in chorus,

'Tulja Bhavani,' says Shivaji as he trembles, as his eyes stare into nothing. 'It was an experience, outstanding and mesmerising. It was like witnessing a million lamps floating in the sky, or listening to a million bells tolling at once. I felt as if my mind was empty of desires and my soul full of yearnings. Bhavani, the giver of life, the source of primal energy had come with a message. She had shed the tears of red embers. The self-manifested Shiva linga in Her crown had sparkled like a diamond. Her lion had roared angrily. She, the ferocious avatar of Parvati had fire of rage but I could also see shades of compassion in Her eyes. Each of Her eight hands had held a weapon. A quiver full of arrows was tied to Her back, a large bow thrown on Her shoulders. *'Swaraj is His wish'*, I had heard Her whisper.'

His words have infused valour in their minds and stung their souls.

'She had continued to speak, *'I want to live on this very fort.'* She has even showed me the place for the temple, at the southern end of the lower fort. She said she can watch the main entrance from there,' says Shivaji as his voice breaks with deep spiritual passion. The men around him feel the potential energy, very tangible, very real.

'She wants Her deity to be the replica of the one in the temple of Tuljapur. And, in my dream She had insisted that the deity be made from shaligram, the holy stone found near the confluence of Saraswati, Trishool-gandagi and Shwetgandagi rivers in the Himalayas.'

The potential energy has transformed itself into a kinetic power that pounds everyone's hearts.

'You have not given me any duty in this battle. My sword is still not rusted,' declares Dabir in a trembling voice.

Shivaji quickly touches the elderly man's feet. 'Your blessings are enough,' says he.

***

The fort shimmers in clear sunlight, while the gigantic cliffs and their vertical drops of the western and northern side of the fort seem nonchalant, the eastern and southern slopes, defended by towers and bastions look vulnerable. Shivaji is in his private quarters at the upper fort, dressing up for the event. The General has come to Javali, making his intensions clear. Afzal Khan wants to either take him as a captive to the Bijapur court or present his head as proof and trophy. The very nature of the mission calls for treachery, cunning, slyness and fraudulence.

Shivaji puts on a jacket made of steel mesh and then his usual, long-sleeved silk robe, long enough to reach his knees over a pair of tight breeches. A servant rushes in with a metal helmet and places it on his head; a saffron turban with pearl strings hides the head armour. The servant ties a sash over his robe. He turns towards a small wooden desk and picks up a metal instrument. It is a concealable weapon called the *baghnach*. This 'tiger's claw' is an iron bar with two rings at the edges, two rings studded with diamonds and rubies. He slips his index and the last, small finger of his left hand into them, and opens his palm to look. Four curved, pointed blades affixed to the crossbar unfold before him like an extension of his body. He feels like a tiger with claws or a bird with talons. He smiles to himself. There is another object on the wooden desk. It is a *bichwa*, a scorpion dagger with a blade that looks like a large stinger of a scorpion. He gently picks it up and tucks it under his left sleeve. Before leaving his quarters, Shivaji glides the blade of his dhop sword into the scabbard and grits it on his waistband.

'Now everything is in God Shiva's hands. His celestial dance that shook the heaven and the earth the rudra tandava is about to begin.'

At the foothills, Bokil, nervous and irritable has reached the camp along with several local men. It is a bright and clear day and the recent monsoons have turned the surrounding valley lush green. Several carts carrying fruits, vegetables and meat roll down the tracks from the west. A group of tribal women carrying firewood bundles on their heads scamper towards the north end of the camp. Afzal Khan's men look relaxed, some are even busy playing dice. For them the battle is over now that they have reached Javali. They have won, their General is already a victor. Bokil glances at the stables, the horses are not saddled, and the elephants wander around near the edge of the camp, stuffing themselves with bamboos.

The *vakeel's* eyes search for the main guest who is attired in a light green silk *zama* with gold brocade and a glittering *zari* sash. The General's *kimoush* turban is white in colour, embellished with tiny diamonds and a single topaz. Even his leather sandals sparkle with precious stones. Ten armed guards wait behind him. Bokil recognises only two of them, one is Sayed Banda, and the other is Rahim Khan, Afzal Khan's nephew who he had seen in Wai. Krishnaji stands to the General's right, a large scabbard gritted to his belt. Before Bokil can bow, the General slinks into his palanquin. Nobody speaks a word as they move towards Sonpar village. But Bokil, who walks along with Krishnaji behind the General's palanquin, feels edgy. Something is amiss and it makes him glance behind. A squadron of armed men, with swords, shields, quivers and bows follow them, soft footed and silent.

This was not to be.

Bokil feels cheated but lets it pass. As they move silently, he contemplates that such a number of armed men around the meeting place would breed trouble for them. He looks at the hill where the gold pinnacle on the top of the *shamiana* dazzles in the morning sunlight. Gentle mountain breeze flutters the textile panels, lending a magical quality to it all. He glances ahead: they are at the edge of Sonpar village. They cross the village and enter into a ditch. The *shamiana* is not visible from this place. The hill blocks the view. He glances back, the camp too is out of sight. He is aware that Kanhoji's men hide somewhere nearby and keep a watch. They can tackle these infantrymen in an emergency. Soon they will climb the hill to reach the *shamiana*. It will not be safe to allow these soldiers to go ahead. He looks at Krishnaji and says, 'By God Shiva, how many armed men are following us, is it more than a thousand? They will have to wait here. If you insist, Raja Shivaji will vanish in the labyrinth of this valley. And that is a promise.'

Krishnaji is startled, but instead of being apologetic he sniggers.

Bokil points at a few men in loincloths hovering at the foothills and says, 'Look at those men. They may wear just a grubby loincloth, but they are the famous rock climbers of the area. They will take very little time to reach the fort to warn Shivaji.' His eyes are cold, his jaw tight.

Krishnaji jerks his head to spits the betel pulp as a mark of his anger and disregard and rushes towards Afzal Khan's palanquin. Bokil waits as an excited Krishnaji says something to his master and returns with a grim face, nodding his head in utter disbelief. 'The armed squadron will wait here.'

***

On his way out, Shivaji looks at the main entrance of the fort flanked by the majestic bastions. The thought that it might be the last time that he sees the gates cuts through his mind. He quickly dismisses it. *The goddess Bhavani had given me a kaul, and She is the power of God Shiva. My mind must not dictate my soul,* he thinks to himself. His mother's face floats before him and then there is his son. The fragile face of Sayee he sees in his inner vision gives him assurance. Pitaji Sahib, his face a blur as so many years it has been since he has last seen his father. But today he feels his father's presence, like the wind beneath wings. He travels on his palanquin, his ten guards following him on foot. As they near the *shamiana*, he notices Bokil walking briskly towards him. He knows that there is something serious on Bokil's mind in the way that he moves. Shivaji waits inside his palanquin till his *vakeel* comes near. Bokil rattles, 'The bad news is that Afzal Khan's contingent of a thousand armed men waits near Sonpar village. The good news is that the General has reached and seems pleased.' He takes a few deep breaths and announces, 'Sayed Banda is still inside.'

Shivaji looks at the *shamiana* again, it looks like destiny's indifferent hand, stern and uncaring. Beyond the *shamiana* is the impassive valley, deep and deadly. Behind him stands the fort, helpless and mute. To enter the *shamiana*, one has to cross a natural but narrow mud bridge with a steep drop on either side. There are no escape routes, for anyone, for the victor or for the defeated. The mountain stands chill and aloof, the atmosphere, silent and unmoved.

'Tell him if he wants this meeting to take place, Sayed should leave,' says Shivaji in a low voice without coming out of his palanquin.

'As per the agreement, only Krishnaji and I stay,' Bokil, on returning to the venue, declares. 'If Sayed remains inside, the meeting stays cancelled.'

The General waves his hand signalling the *pata* man to leave. It is after several months, miles long journeys, loss of men and animals in the mountains, and millions of moments of anguish and anticipation that he has finally managed to make it to his destination. He will not let it go.

Shivaji watches Sayed leave, his steps heavy and reluctant. The muscular man with a strong jaw line wears a metal helmet and a vest armour. His eyes bore into Shivaji who watches till the famous *pata* man is outside the tent. Shivaji glances at his two guards: Mahalya's eyes are fixed on Sayed, Sambhaji Kavaji stares blankly at the sky, Ibrahim Khan seems alert and others have kept their eyes on the *shamiana*. It is time to go inside. He alights from his palanquin and moves towards the venue. Bokil is back at the entrance. Shivaji removes his sword gritted to his belt and hands it over to his *vakeel*. Then he climbs the steps into the tent.

Afzal Khan sits on the divan, his back resting on the soft silk cushions, his roving eyes full of admiration and envy, the silk panels embellished with pearls, the large silver urns, and the Persian carpets. A dais with steps has been built to honour him. When Shivaji reaches the edge of the dais, he notices the General's sword lying next to him. Krishnaji stands at his master's right with a large scabbard gritted to his belt.

Moments slip by stealthily. Then, like a prowling tiger coming out in the open, the General rises to his feet. Only when the Bijapur warrior stands does Shivaji realise how immense and huge his guest is. He has to throw his head back to look at the General's face. A bulkily coiled *kimoush* turban makes him look taller. He has a rugged face with beady eyes and an enormous beard that crawls to his chest.

Afzal Khan stares down at the rebel, an impeccably attired young man. His face instantly reminds him of Shahji Bhosale, the same brown eyes, the aquiline nose, the moustache and the trimmed beard. Shiva stands there, with folded hands, an impish, charming smile playing on his lips.

As his temper rises, Afzal Khan thinks, *Shackle them, humiliate them, crush them with cannonballs, but the men of the Bhosale family keep bouncing back. Like stubborn weeds, growing at all places, multiplying, invading anything, not allowing the precious to thrive. First there was Shahji who has taken away the rich* jagir *of Bangalore and now his brazen traitor son who wants to swallow the western regions.* A stab of jealousy pierces Afzal Khan's heart, like a hawk dismembering its prey with its talons. He closely scrutinises Shivaji, his saffron turban laden with pearls, his neat sideburns, the large earrings embellished with rubies, the tear shaped pearls, his expensive, embroidered clothes and the cashmere shawl. It is Shivaji's lotus-shaped confident eyes that he hates the most. The fear, the guilt, the humility, the apology, the regret, the remorse that he had to see in them is clearly missing. He is overwhelmed with a revelation he does not anticipate at all. He had been looking forward to meeting a coward, immature Shiva, eager to fall prostrate at his feet, begging and pleading, but he now realises that his assumptions had been wrong.

Afzal Khan suddenly feels an impulse to humiliate his enemy. The emotion overtakes his planned civility. His mind spins with heat of rage and words pop out like kernels, 'You seem to have looted the Sultanate and the Mughal, you and your criminal banditry. I can see it all over the place.'

'The Almighty alone knows who the bandit is, General. Earlier, the hill forts were occupied by criminals and the land had turned barren. I have brought order to the region. The hill forts are well made up and the land generates revenue,' says Shivaji softly without taking his eyes off Afzal Khan. He is surprised by his guest's effeminate voice. He thinks, *This is the man who calls himself the slayer of the* kafirs*, this is the man who is responsible for Father's arrest and humiliation in the court of Bijapur, this is the man who had let Brother die in the trenches, this is the man who had invited Kasturiranga, the King of Shirepattan for a truce and killed him by deceit.*

'Let bygones be bygones,' the General says, 'surrender the region and the forts to me, and come with me to Bijapur.'

'Have you got the King's farman for me?' Shivaji asks with scorn. 'If so, I shall place it on my head and obey you, my General.'

Krishnaji breaks in, 'You have come under the protection of Afzal Khan Sahib, get your offences pardoned by the General and then expect a king's farman.'

Shivaji regards the General with intrepid eyes and says, 'The General and me, we both are the servants of the Bijapur king. Who is he to grant me a pardon? It should come from the King!'

The words seem to sting the General. But he needs to keep his calm. The enemy is not an ordinary coward as he was made to believe. He needs to be careful, and decides to be his gracious self. He fixes his gaze on his host. His upper lip curves for a moment but he says patronisingly, in a soft voice, 'The king trusts me, and if I pardon you he too will. I agree with you that we are equal, so we must meet like the equals do. You do not have to be scared.'

'I feel humbled but not scared,' says Shivaji, bowing to show respect. Not showing any surprise at his enemy's sudden change of attitude, he continues, 'I just cannot believe that I am standing here, face to face with the Bijapur General.'

'You seemed eager to wage war with us, my boy, you little stubborn lad. You are still young and there is enough time for you to redeem yourself. In your youthful arrogance, you have shown disrespect to our King as well as the Emperor of Hindustan. I have come to reprimand you as a senior servant of Ali Adil Shah. And you have agreed to surrender your region.'

'I shall certainly surrender all my worldly possessions as agreed before. But do you have the king's farman for me?'

The *vakeels* freeze. The General's face changes rapidly, from rage to disbelief to a smile.

'This element of courage is so rare. The King will be so blessed to meet you. And you can directly surrender to the King. Come, my boy, son of my dear friend Shahji, we are equals and must meet so.' Saying this, Afzal Khan spreads his enormous arms and starts walking towards Shivaji.

Bokil stares at the General's agility and notes something sinister in his swagger. Krishnaji, too, has not expected his master's quick actions. For a moment, time freezes, as if it is seized by a quick bout of stupor. Shivaji remains rooted but soon finds himself in the firm grip of his guest, his face buried in Afzal Khan's chest. He suffocates by the strong musk perfume the General wears. Within a fraction of time, he finds his neck under his guest's left armpit. He feels trapped as his right hand dangles aimlessly. The grip is so strong that it is difficult to breathe. Shivaji is sure that if the hold becomes any tighter, he will hear his bones crack. He decides to act with his left hand that is free. He opens his palm wide and pushes the iron claws inside his enemy's waist with full force. All four steel edges, pointed and jagged, tear through the layers of Afzal Khan's skin and muscles, just below the rib cage. It all happens a lot more easily than Shivaji had imagined. Surprisingly, the General wears no armour. With the blades still stuck in the flesh, he twists his palm, moving the blades in a circular motion. He looks uo to see the General raise his right hand that holds a *jambia* dagger and its shining L shaped blade comes down on his shoulder. His body shudders with impact, his neck twists, and he sees his headgear fly to the other end of the *shamiana*. The *jambia* tears through his *jama* and slides over his metal armour with a screeching sound.

The excruciating pain in the right abdomen makes Afzal Khan let go off his enemy. With his free right hand, Shivaji takes out the bichwa tucked in his left sleeve, grits his teeth, and impales Afzal Khan's stomach. Repeatedly, once twice, thrice, with full force, as his body jerks forward and then backward. Afzal Khan looks at his host, his kohl-lined eyes cold and vacant. He lets out a horrendous shriek as a part of his innards hang out from the gaping wound. Unbalanced and swaying, the General staggers towards the entrance, leaving behind a huge trail of blood.

'*Haramzada*, bloody murderer,' Shivaji hears someone shouting. The trumpets have started calling as planned. It is a sound rising above the screams of the bodyguards. From the corner of his eyes, he sees Sayed bolting into the *shamiana*, the blade of his *pata* sword savagely cutting through the air. Shivaji prepares for a lethal blow but notices Mahalya leaping in. Mahalya's hand holding a *dhop* sword moves like a whip and chops Sayed's hand in midair. Bokil moves forward like a hood of a striking snake and hands over the sword to Shivaji. Krishnaji too pulls out his sword.

'You have broken your oath, the oath of a Brahmin,' screams the General's *vakeel*.

'By God Shiva, my oath did not include self defence,' shouts back Bokil, looking at the raised blade that is about to attack him.

Shivaji is swift. He strikes at Krishnaji's throat, before Krishnaji's sword can harm Bokil. Afzal Khan's *vakeel* crumples in a heap, his sword falls alongside, blocking the entrance of the *shamiana*. Shivaji looks around to find Sayed lying dead, his head rolling on the carpets like a round boulder and Mahalya hovering over his slaughtered enemy. The meeting place has turned into a gruesome battlefield in a matter of a few moments. Shivaji dashes out. Afzal Khan still shouts something guttural. The enormous man from Bijapur manages to cram his body into the palanquin. His bearers are quick, they start racing away. Outside, seventeen men are engaged in a violent battle. Shivaji notes that Kavji has slaughtered his opponent and has leapt towards the palanquin. His sword moves faster than a bird of prey, chopping off the legs of the bearers. They fall one after another, wailing with pain and agony. The palanquin crashes down. As Shivaji looks on, Kavji ruthlessly pulls the bleeding Afzal Khan out. His sword moves in forward motion as the Bijapur General's head falls on the ground and body drops on the crashed palanquin, like an uprooted tree.

Kavji holds Afzal Khan's head as a trophy and dances like an insane man. The fort cannon to signal Shivaji's men who are scattered around have started blasting, its sound infusing an excitement in their blood. Shivaji looks up at the sky and says, 'Swaraj is His wish!'

EPILOGUE

Circa 1660

Divan-e-khas of the *quila-e-mubarak* at Delhi is charged with unseen yet tangible energy. The drums beat to announce the arrival of the new emperor. A hundred eyes are fixed on him, and they are filled with reverence, worship and fear. Aurangzeb does not bother to look at anyone, he fumes when he enters *divan-e-khas*. He looks at the throne before he climbs the platform stairs, he always does that. It feels good, makes him feel powerful. The *takht-e-taus*, the seat, the peacock throne stands on legs made of solid gold, and is covered with an enamelled canopy. The canopy is supported by twelve emerald pillars, each of which bears two peacocks encrusted with gems. Between those dazzling, arrogant birds stands a tree so laden with diamonds, emeralds and rubies as if the stones are ready to drop like ripe fruit. The pillars are high, almost about three men in height. The entire structure has twelve sides made with geometrical precision. Parapets enclose the seat from all sides but from the front for the Emperor to enter. As he makes himself comfortable on the velvety softness of the seat, people perform *kurnish*, by placing the palm of their right hand on their forehead and then bending the head forward, expressing their obedience, as if they to say that they are ready for any service required by him.

Shaista Khan, Mirza Raja Jai Singh, Mir Jumla, Bahadur Khan, Danishmand Khan, Hakim Daud, Diler Khan, Maharaja Jaswant Singh Rathod, Jaffar Khan and many others stand before him. But the new Emperor is seething with rage. The grand clergy of Mecca has refused to recognise him as the Emperor of Hindustan. A letter has arrived. It says:

Law of the Prophet, (let the Peace be upon Him), and the law of the nature prevent you from proclaiming yourself as the Emperor during the lifetime of your father. Also, you have murdered your brother to whom the Empire rightfully belonged after the death of Emperor Shah Jahan.

There is one more letter, far more humiliating than the one from Mecca.

His envoy Tarbiyat Khan has returned from Persia after meeting the Emperor of Iran, Shah Abbas, who has openly condemned him as the murderer of Dara Shikoh and cursed him for imprisoning his own father. Shah Abbas is a man of power, and if he so wishes, he can invade Delhi with his large army. Aurangzeb had sent valuable presents like diamonds, daggers and swords with gold hilts, all worth seven hundred thousand rupees, or five hundred ser of pure gold. But the Shah has disregarded the gifts by distributing them among his servants. The Persian Emperor has offended his messenger, Tarbiyat Khan, by burning his beard in an open court. He has been sent back with a letter, the words of which are embers that burn the new Emperor's heart.

We feel that all the landlords of Hindustan have turned insurgents because their new Emperor is weak, unskilled and lacking in intelligence. How can such an Emperor face Shiva Bhosale? Till now nobody had even known of the existence of the kafir *Shiva. Now, people cannot stop talking about him. From what we hear he has taken over hill forts, cities and ports that had belonged to the southern Shia kingdoms. He has even invaded and plundered the imperial terrain. He is about to set an example to other* kafirs. *You call yourself Alamgir, the conqueror of the world! Your bravery remains limited to imprisoning your father and killing your brothers by deceit. But you cannot tackle Shiva Bhosale, and we know it is beyond your strength. We have been your refuge in the past. Do not forget that we have helped Humayun, your ancestor to get back the imperial throne of Hindustan. It seems like, you, the descendant of Humayun, too, are in dire need of our help. We will rescue you, by paying you a visit with our vast army. Only we can dowse the fires of kafir rebels in Hindustan.*

Aurangzeb's head hurts with wrath. He can no longer control his temper. He direly needs an antidote. He claps his hands.

Someone brings the sobbing emissary but Aurangzeb does not want to look at his face even though he must hear what the man says. 'Shah Abbas had laughed openly and called my Majesty a hypocrite, a disgrace to Islam.'

There is total silence in the court. The new Emperor's face turns red. He surveys the people in his court as they stand mutely, as if they have gone deaf, their eyes focussed on the ground, their gaze fallen at their feet.

'Bring in the case,' he orders, startling everyone.

A few slaves gingerly walk in holding a wicker basket. They are followed by a man wearing a long black kaftan. He holds a large, flat brass container in his hand. He places it in front of the throne. One of the guards empties the deadly contents of the case into the brass container. A green alert reptile makes a thudding sound as it hits the brass metal. It first moves like a whiplash and then slithers aimlessly, moving its triangular flat head in different directions. The man standing near the container can clearly see its yellow eyeballs with the vertical pupils radiating horror.

He claps his hands again. A few more slaves stumble in and hold the emissary in such a way that the man is not able to move. Then one of them holds his right hand like a wooden log and pulls it near the brass container. Someone takes a stick and starts prodding the deadly reptile to excite it. They seem to know that an enraged snake spews all its venom once the fangs get hold of the flesh, flesh that invariably has very little time to live. People can now hear the irate hissing sounds of the deadliest poisonous serpent – the green Himalayan Viper. Tarbiyat Khan's hand is offered to the insanely frightened and enraged snake as a consolation prize. Allah…aah, a horrendous, never-ending shriek rattles the pillars of the court. The slaves drop the man on the ground and look on impassively. People stare at their Emperor, he is counting the beads of his *tesbih*, his pale eyes distant.

The innocent envoy is sheerly unlucky, a mere victim of the Emperor's fury. The real reason for his rage is the news from the Deccan. Something sinister has taken place in the valley. The Bijapur General has been murdered by Shiva Bhosale during a meeting. After the General had been slain, Shiva's foot soldiers had encircled the General's camp and fallen upon it with vehemence. Thousands have been slaughtered and injured, thousands have fled, leaving their war animals to fend for themselves. The defeat of Bijapur seems complete. The General has fallen, his army has ceased to exist, and Shiva Bhosale's victory, in terms of carnage and booty seems glorious. The incidence has stunned the people of Hindustan, and the Deccan is alive with wandering bards singing songs that celebrate the victory of the Marathas. The Portuguese and the English have exchanged letters in frenzy, calling November 10th, 1659 as a historical landmark, the epoch. This has enraged the new Emperor. If this continues, what happens to his vision of Hindustan? What happens to his mission?

He must not allow Shiva Bhosale's ideology to take roots in the servile minds of this country's people. His forefathers have worked so hard to create the Empire and he must destroy each and every man who has the power to shake the very foundations laid by his ancestors. He has worthy warriors to deal with the enemies of the Empire, be it his uncle Shaista Khan, Rajputs like Mirza Raja Jai Singh and Maharaja Jaswant Singh Rathod or Mir Jumla, Diler Khan, Kartalab Khan. And now he has the entire imperial military with him to eliminate Shujabhai, Suleiman Shikoh and Shiva Bhosale, and not necessarily in that order.

'*La ilah ilallah,*' Aurangzeb murmurs, stops counting his beads for a moment, closes his eyes as the words of his new verse whirl in his mind.

A wise bird in the garden of this earth
Treats even rose-petals as claws of my falcon
If a partridge flies without caring
(About my power)
Blood will drop from its wound, because of its daring
(Wounds inflicted by me).

Mutamad who stands behind his master is overwhelmed with contradicting emotions. He respects and loves the third prince, but after hearing about Shivaji, and how he had treated the beautiful captive and how he has fought and won the battle against Afzal Khan, the eunuch wishes to join Shiva's army as a soldier.

***

The large cavern is cold, with only one corner illuminated by a torch hung on the wall made of natural rock face. Dinkar can see two men with a small writing desk between them. Both wear saffron robes, their long black hair falling on their shoulders, their beards covering their chests. One dictates while the other writes.

Dinkar's life has been inspired by this man, Samarth Ramdas swami, who has walked across Hindustan and trekked the Himalayas to meet the natives, has kindled the fire in the hearts of people with his scathing poetry, has started a thousand monasteries with gymnasiums in the forests insisting that only a powerful body can defend a powerful mind. He has been working on a manuscript of the book called *Dasbodh*, Das for Ramdas and bodh for learning. Dinkar has heard that the book will finally have more than seven thousand verses. *Dasbodh* also covers subjects that are more practical and less spiritual. A few years ago Dinkar would have thought differently. Why a book must dedicate countless pages leadership and its explanations? This soil had failed to sire leaders. People had lived with their minds numb with fear, and their eyes watching the horizons. Raiding parties from the north had come like waves, hunting them like animals.

Kalyan, the man behind the desk is scribbling furiously. It is tough to keep pace with Samarth's words. From somewhere a draught of chill air comes slithering and hits Dinkar. He shivers but the two men seem unmindful of the elements around them.

'What makes a leader a man of people's destinies?' Dinkar hears Samarth ask this question, its intangible energy creating fine vibrations in the air around him. 'By becoming one of them, not by being like them but making all of them a bit like him. Leadership does not stop at leading people, it also means creating people who can lead. A leader is first a creator.'

When Samarth talks, Dinkar thinks that even the earth stops to listen to him.

'Creators are not bound by destinies, destinies are bound by them.'

There is a sudden silence. Samarth looks at Dinkar, his face devoid of any surprise. 'You are here to tell me that the new Emperor is fuming. He has vowed to kill Raja Shivaji.'

Dinkar nods.

'The mightiest man of our world thinks of us as the infidel creatures, born to serve and destined to die for him. The new Emperor, in his vision has already sealed the fate of this country and its men but Raja

Shivaji has broken free. What happened in the valley is a splendid example of a counterstroke. The war has begun.'

'What happens now?' asks Dinkar.

Samarth does not answer. His face is only lit by a strange smile.

Glossary

Ashrafi mohur: A gold coin issued in the Mughal Empire and made of high quality gold. It weighed around eleven grams that is a little more than a tola. One mohur was equal to fourteen or sixteen rupees depending on the price of gold and silver.

Brahmins: The Brahmins were regarded as the supreme humans and had the right to learn Sanskrit, the language, in which sacred texts like the Vedas, Shastras and Puranas are written. Very few of them are the real Pundits; most work as scribes, accountants or as vakeels for the Muslim kings or the Hindu watandars.

Coin: A coin in 17th century India was not just a symbolic representation of its value. It was worth the metal it carried. A rupee was a Mughal coin of high purity silver with a diameter of 2 centimetres and approximately weighed a tola which is a bit more than ten grams. (12 masa = 1 tola and 80 tola = 1 ser = 870 grams = 0.87 kilograms)

Dam: A copper coin (also called a Damdi) of about 20 grams. 40 Dams were approximately equal to 1 rupee. The rate would fluctuate according to the rise and fall of the metal prices.

Deshmukh: A watandar, deshmukh was a title given to the chief of a paragana that had many villages. He was primarily responsible for increasing the extent of land under cultivation and also collecting taxes from patils, the village heads. They too, like the jagirdar maintained a personal army.

Firang: Portuguese.

Guz: A measurement – it was about a yard that is equal to 3 feet.

Hon: A gold coin that was popular in the Deccan (south India) and was called 'Pagoda' by the Europeans. It was a centimetre in diameter and weighted about three to five grams in pure gold. In exchange rate it must have been equal to five to six rupees.

Jagirdar: Warriors who wielded considerable power over local populace were granted jagirs or vast estates by their king. They were given the title of a jagirdar, meaning the trustee of the estate. Outwardly it was a show of gratitude. The ulterior reason was to let the powerful men be wealthy as they would then refrain from rebellions. People called them Rajas, meaning 'the kings' in Marathi. Jagirdars lived in a perception of being kings but their power was limited to supervising the collection of land revenue for their king. A jagirdar's personal army was to maintain peace in his jagir and also help the real king in times of war.

Kulin Marathas: The Marathas could broadly be divided into two, the kulin Marathas and the kunbi Marathas. The kulins claimed that they are born warriors, the descendants of the ancient dynasties, like Jadhavs and are linked to Yadava dynasty and Morays to Mourya dynasty.

Kunbi Marathas: Kunbi Marathas were mostly peasants or the cultivators. The kunbis were further divided into sub-castes as per their line of work or vocation like the gooraves who minded the temples, the traders, carpenters, masons, shoemakers, blacksmiths, tailors, potters, and the barbers. Balutes who carried the barrels filled with human waste to empty the toilets of the upper caste are treated as the outcastes. Even their shadow falling on the upper caste humans was considered as a sin or a bad omen.

Paraganas: A jagir was usually divided into many paraganas, a revenue unit in Farsi.

Patil: A watandar who was the head of a village.

Prabhus: The Prabhus come after the Brahmins in the caste system.

They had the right to learn Hindu scriptures and consider themselves equal to the Brahmins, but the Brahmins did not share the same sentiment.

Puntoji: The Brahmins were addressed so.

Subhedar: Between the jagirdars and the king, was the subhedar or the viceroy. He was appointed by the king to look after a subha or a province that had many jagirs. He would usually be a Muslim, a king's regional confidant (viceroy or governor).

Tesbih: Prayer beads used by Muslims, an instrument for worship.

Tukaram: Tukaram lived in a village called Dehu, on the banks of Indrayani. He was a trader by birth and a poet by passion. He penned abhangs, the religious poetry in colloquial Marathi that had opened the doors of mystic and meaning of Hindu Dharma to all, smashing the Brahmin monopoly to bits, and their egos to pieces. The myth that it was only the Brahmins' privilege to learn religion and to write literature, which they had so painstakingly guarded, had shattered. The high-caste had burnt with anger and Tukaram had braved their wrath. They had punished him by flinging his manuscripts in the waters of Indrayani but the saint poet had continued to scribble and sing, sitting nonchalantly on the banks of the same river. Millions of pilgrims had arrived year after year to listen and sing his abhangs making his words immortal.

Watan: Watan is an Arabic word for homeland but it was colloquially used in the sense of a hereditary office since the right to collect revenue remained with the same family for generations.

Watandars: Watandars were mostly Hindu natives. They inherited the right to collect revenue from the peasants. Deshmukhs and patils were the watandars, the integral part of the country's tax administration and they reported to their jagirdars.

Bibliography

Abbott, J. *Keys of Power: A Study of Indian Ritual and Belief.* New Delhi: Manohar Publishers and Distributors, 2000.

Ali, Shanti Sadiq. *The African Dispersal in the Deccan: From Medieval to Modern Times.* Hyderabad: Sangam Books, 1996.

Balkrishna. *Shivaji the Great.* Kolhapur: Bal Krishna and Arya Book Depot, 1940. https://archive.org/stream/shivajithegreat035466mbp/shivajithegreat035466mbp_djvu.txt. Accessed April 30, 2012.

Bernier, Francois. *Travels in the Mughal Empire.* Revised by Vincent A. Smith. London: Oxford Military Press, 1916. https://archive.org/details/travelsinmogulem00bernuoft. Accessed January 30, 2012.

Chima, G.S. *The Forgotten Mughals.* New Delhi: Manohar Publishers and Distributors, 2002.

Duff, James Grant. *History of the Mahrattas.* Paternoster Row: Longman Rees, Orme, Brown and Green, 1826.

Godbole, Ravindra. *Aurangzeb, Shakyata and Shokantika.* Pune: Deshmukh and Company Publishers, 2003.

Godbole, Ravindra. *Samrat Akbar.* Pune: Deshmukh and Company Publishers, 2003.

Gribble, J.D.B. *History of the Deccan.* London: Luzac and Company, 1896.

Gunaji, Milind. *Offbeat Tracks in Maharashtra.* Mumbai: Popular Prakashan, 2003.

Joshi, S., Anil Gote and Rajiv Basgrekar. *Shetkarancha Raja Shivaji.* Raigad: Farmer's Publishing House, 1988.

Khan, M.A. *Islamic Jihad.* Bloomington: I Universe, 2009.

Kurundkar, Narhar. *Chhatrapati Shivaji Maharaj Jeevan Rahasya.* Pune: Indrayani Prakashan, 2003

Mahendale, Gajanan Bhaskar. *Shivaji: His Life and Times.* Thane: Param Mitra Publicattions, 2011.

Mukhia, Harbans. *The Mughal of India.* Oxford: Blackwell Publishing, 2004. http:// hiloshistorydepartment.weebly.com/ uploads/1/2/8/7/12870319/harbans_mukhia_themughalsofindia. pdf. Accessed May 20, 2014.

Naravane, M.S. and V.P. Malik. *The Rajputs of Rajputana- A Glimpse of Medieval Rajasthan.* New Delhi: APH Publishing, 1999.

Pagadi, Setu Madhavrao. *Chhatrapati Shivaji.* New Delhi: National Book Trust India, 1911.

Palsokar, Colonel R.D. *Shivaji: The Great Guerrilla.* Dehradun: Natraj Publishers, 2003.

Samant, Dr Srinivas. *Vedh Mahamanavacha.* Pune: Deshmukh and Company Publishers, 2009.

Samant, Bal. *Shivakalyan Raja.* Mumbai: Parchure Prakashan Mandir, 1998.

Sardesai, H.S. *The Great Maratha.* New Delhi: Cosmo Publications, 2002.

Sardesai, G.S. *Marathi Riyasat.* Mumbai: Popular Prakashan, 1988.

Sardesai, G.S. *Sultan Gharani,* Vol 1 of Musalmani Riyasat. Mumbai: Popular Prakashan, 1993.

Sardesai, G.S. *Mughal Badshahi,* Vol 2 of Musalmani Riyasat. Mumbai: Popular Prakashan, 1993.

Sarkar, Sir Jadunath. *The Reign of Shah Jahan,* Vol 1 of History of Aurangzeb. Kolkata: M.C.Sarkar, 1912.

Sarkar, Sir Jadunath. *War of Succession,* Vol 2 of History of Aurangzeb. London: Longman Green and Company, 1920.

Sarkar, Sir Jadunath. *Shivaji and His Times.* Mumbai: Longman Green and Company, 1920.

Sarkar, Sir Jadunath. *Anecdotes of Aurangzeb.* Calcutta: M C Sarkar, 1925. https://archive.org/details/AnecdotesOfAurangzeb. Accessed May 27, 2012.

Sarkar, Sir Jadunath. *Short History of Aurangzeb.* Translated by Dr. B.G. Kunte. Mumbai: Maharashtra Rajya Sahitya Sanskruti Mandal, 1978.

Shimmel, Annemarie. *The Empire of the Great Mughal.* London: Reaktion Books, 2004.

Stillman, Yedida K. *Arab Dress: A Short History: From the Dawn of Islam to Modern Times.* Boston: Brill Academic Publishing, 2000.